The GODS of MARS

and

The WARLORD
of MARS

Edgar Rice Burroughs

The GODS of MARS

and

The WARLORD of MARS

Illustrations by Frank Frazetta

NELSON DOUBLEDAY, INC.   Garden City, New York

The GODS of MARS

"The great apes, towering in all their fifteen feet of height, had gone down before my sword . . ."

FOREWORD

TWELVE YEARS had passed since I had laid the body of my great-uncle, Captain John Carter, of Virginia, away from the sight of men in that strange mausoleum in the old cemetery at Richmond.

Often had I pondered on the odd instructions he had left me governing the construction of his mighty tomb, and especially those parts which directed that he be laid in an *open* casket and that the ponderous mechanism which controlled the bolts of the vault's huge door be accessible *only from the inside.*

Twelve years had passed since I had read the remarkable manuscript of this remarkable man; this man who remembered no childhood and who could not even offer a vague guess as to his age; who was always young and yet who had dandled my grandfather's great-grandfather upon his knee; this man who had spent ten years upon the planet Mars; who had fought for the green men of Barsoom and fought against them; who had fought for and against the red men and who had won the ever beautiful Dejah Thoris, Princess of Helium, for his wife, and for nearly ten years had been a prince of the house of Tardos Mors, Jeddak of Helium.

Twelve years had passed since his body had been found upon the bluff before his cottage overlooking the Hudson, and oft-times during these long years I had wondered if John Carter were really dead, or if he again roamed the dead sea bottoms of that dying planet; if he had returned to Barsoom to find that he had opened the frowning portals of the mighty atmosphere plant in time to save the countless millions who were dying of asphyxiation on that far-gone day that had seen him hurtled ruthlessly through forty-eight million miles of space back to Earth once more. I had wondered if he had found his black-haired Princess and the slender son he had dreamed was with her in the royal gardens of Tardos Mors, awaiting his return.

Or, had he found that he had been too late, and thus gone back to a living death upon a dead world? Or was he really dead after all, never to return either to his mother Earth or his beloved Mars?

Thus was I lost in useless speculation one sultry August evening when old Ben, my body servant, handed me a telegram. Tearing it open I read:

'Meet me to-morrow hotel Raleigh Richmond.

'JOHN CARTER'

Early the next morning I took the first train for Richmond and within two hours was being ushered into the room occupied by John Carter.

As I entered he rose to greet me, his old-time cordial smile of welcome lighting his handsome face. Apparently he had not aged a minute, but was still the straight, clean-limbed fighting-man of thirty. His keen grey eyes were undimmed, and the only lines upon his face were the lines of iron character and determination that always had been there since first I remembered him, nearly thirty-five years before.

'Well, nephew,' he greeted me, 'do you feel as though you were seeing a ghost, or suffering from the effects of too many of Uncle Ben's juleps?'

'Juleps, I reckon,' I replied, 'for I certainly feel mighty good; but maybe it's just the sight of you again that affects me. You have been back to Mars? Tell me. And Dejah Thoris? You found her well and awaiting you?'

'Yes, I have been to Barsoom again, and—but it's a long story, too long to tell in the limited time I have before I must return. I have learned the secret, nephew, and I may traverse the trackless void at my will, coming and going between the countless planets as I list; but my heart is always in Barsoom, and while it is there in the keeping of my Martian Princess, I doubt that I shall ever again leave the dying world that is my life.

'I have come now because my affection for you prompted me to see you once more before you pass over for ever into that other life that I shall never know, and which though I have died thrice and shall die again to-night, as you know death, I am as unable to fathom as are you.

'Even the wise and mysterious therns of Barsoom, that ancient cult which for countless ages has been credited with holding the secret of life and death in their impregnable fastnesses upon the hither slopes of the Mountains of Otz, are as ignorant as we. I have proved it, though I near lost my life in the doing of it; but you shall read it all in the notes I have been making during the last three months that I have been back upon Earth.'

He patted a swelling portfolio that lay on the table at his elbow.

'I know that you are interested and that you believe, and I know that the world, too, is interested, though they will not believe for many years; yes, for many ages, since they cannot understand. Earth men have not yet progressed to a point where they can comprehend the things that I have written in those notes.

'Give them what you wish of it, what you think will not harm them, but do not feel aggrieved if they laugh at you.'

That night I walked down to the cemetery with him. At the door of his vault he turned and pressed my hand.

'Good-bye, nephew,' he said. 'I may never see you again, for I doubt that I can ever bring myself to leave my wife and boy while they live, and the span of life upon Barsoom is often more than a thousand years.'

He entered the vault. The great door swung slowly to. The ponderous bolts grated into place. The lock clicked. I have never seen Captain John Carter, of Virginia, since.

But here is the story of his return to Mars on that other occasion, as I have gleaned it from the great mass of notes which he left for me upon the table of his room in the hotel at Richmond.

There is much which I have left out; much which I have not dared to tell; but you will find the story of his second search for Dejah Thoris, Princess of Helium, even more remarkable than was his first manuscript which I gave to an unbelieving world a short time since and through which we followed the fighting Virginian across dead sea bottoms under the moons of Mars.

E. R. B.

Contents

THE PLANT MEN

As I stood upon the bluff before my cottage on that clear cold night in the early part of March, 1886, the noble Hudson flowing like the grey and silent spectre of a dead river below me, I felt again the strange, compelling influence of the mighty god of war, my beloved Mars, which for ten long and lonesome years I had implored with outstretched arms to carry me back to my lost love.

Not since that other March night in 1866, when I had stood without that Arizona cave in which my still and lifeless body lay wrapped in the similitude of earthly death had I felt the irresistible attraction of the god of my profession.

With arms outstretched toward the red eye of the great star I stood praying for a return of that strange power which twice had drawn me through the immensity of space, praying as I had prayed on a thousand nights before during the long ten years that I had waited and hoped.

Suddenly a qualm of nausea swept over me, my senses swam, my knees gave beneath me and I pitched headlong to the ground upon the very verge of the dizzy bluff.

Instantly my brain cleared and there swept back across the threshold of my memory the vivid picture of the horrors of that ghostly Arizona cave; again, as on that far-gone night, my muscles refused to respond to my will and again, as though even here upon the banks of the placid Hudson, I could hear the awful moans and rustling of the fearsome thing which had lurked and threatened me from the dark recesses of the cave, I made the same mighty and superhuman effort to break the bonds of the strange anæsthesia which held me, and again came the sharp click as of the sudden parting of a taut wire, and I stood naked and free beside the staring, lifeless thing that had so recently pulsed with the warm, red life-blood of John Carter.

With scarcely a parting glance I turned my eyes again toward Mars, lifted my hands toward his lurid rays, and waited.

Nor did I have long to wait; for scarce had I turned ere I shot with the rapidity of thought into the awful void before me. There was the same instant of unthinkable cold and utter darkness that I had experienced twenty years before, and then I opened my eyes in another world, beneath the burning rays of a hot sun, which beat through a tiny opening in the dome of the mighty forest in which I lay.

The scene that met my eyes was so un-Martian that my heart sprang to my throat as the sudden fear swept through me that I had been aimlessly tossed upon some strange planet by a cruel fate.

Why not? What guide had I through the trackless waste of interplanetary space? What assurance that I might not as well be hurtled to some far-distant star of another solar system, as to Mars?

I lay upon a close-cropped sward of red grasslike vegetation, and about me stretched a grove of strange and beautiful trees, covered with huge and gorgeous blossoms and filled with brilliant, voiceless birds. I call them birds since they were winged, but mortal eye ne'er rested on such odd, unearthly shapes.

The vegetation was similar to that which covers the lawns of the red Martians of the great waterways, but the trees and birds were unlike anything that I had ever seen upon Mars, and then through the further trees I could see that most un-Martian of all sights—an open sea, its blue waters shimmering beneath the brazen sun.

As I rose to investigate further I experienced the same ridiculous catastrophe that had met my first attempt to walk under Martian conditions. The lesser attraction of this smaller planet and the reduced air pressure of its greatly rarefied atmosphere, afforded so little resistance to my earthly muscles that the ordinary exertion of the mere act of rising sent me several feet into the air and precipitated me upon my face in the soft and brilliant grass of this strange world.

This experience, however, gave me some slightly increased assurance that, after all, I might indeed be in some, to me, unknown corner of Mars, and this was very possible since during my ten years' residence upon the planet I had explored but a comparatively tiny area of its vast expanse.

I arose again, laughing at my forgetfulness, and soon had mastered

THE GODS OF MARS 3

once more the art of attuning my earthly sinews to these changed
conditions.

As I walked slowly down the imperceptible slope toward the sea
I could not help but note the park-like appearance of the sward and
trees. The grass was as close-cropped and carpet-like as some old
English lawn and the trees themselves showed evidence of careful
pruning to a uniform height of about fifteen feet from the ground, so
that as one turned his glance in any direction the forest had the appearance at a little distance of a vast, high-ceiled chamber.

All these evidences of careful and systematic cultivation convinced
me that I had been fortunate enough to make my entry into Mars on
this second occasion through the domain of a civilized people and that
when I should find them I would be accorded the courtesy and protection that my rank as a Prince of the house of Tardos Mors entitled
me to.

The trees of the forest attracted my deep admiration as I proceeded
toward the sea. Their great stems, some of them fully a hundred feet
in diameter, attested their prodigious height, which I could only guess
at, since at no point could I penetrate their dense foliage above me
to more than sixty or eighty feet.

As far aloft as I could see the stems and branches and twigs were
as smooth and as highly polished as the newest of American-made
pianos. The wood of some of the trees was as black as ebony, while
their nearest neighbours might perhaps gleam in the subdued light
of the forest as clear and white as the finest china, or, again, they were
azure, scarlet, yellow, or deepest purple.

And in the same way was the foliage as gay and variegated as the
stems, while the blooms that clustered thick upon them may not be
described in any earthly tongue, and indeed might challenge the language of the gods.

As I neared the confines of the forest I beheld before me, and between the grove and the open sea, a broad expanse of meadow land,
and as I was about to emerge from the shadows of the trees a sight
met my eyes that banished all romantic and poetic reflection upon the
beauties of the strange landscape.

To my left the sea extended as far as the eye could reach, before
me only a vague, dim line indicated its further shore, while at my
right a mighty river, broad, placid, and majestic, flowed between
scarlet banks to empty into the quiet sea before me.

At a little distance up the river rose mighty perpendicular bluffs, from the very base of which the great river seemed to rise.

But it was not these inspiring and magnificent evidences of Nature's grandeur that took my immediate attention from the beauties of the forest. It was the sight of a score of figures moving slowly about the meadow near the bank of the mighty river.

Odd, grotesque shapes they were; unlike anything that I had ever seen upon Mars, and yet, at a distance, most manlike in appearance. The larger specimens appeared to be about ten or twelve feet in height when they stood erect, and to be proportioned as to torso and lower extremities precisely as is earthly man.

Their arms, however, were very short, and from where I stood seemed as though fashioned much after the manner of an elephant's trunk, in that they moved in sinuous and snakelike undulations, as though entirely without bony structure, or if there were bones it seemed that they must be vertebral in nature.

As I watched them from behind the stem of a huge tree, one of the creatures moved slowly in my direction, engaged in the occupation that seemed to be the principal business of each of them, and which consisted in running their oddly shaped hands over the surface of the sward, for what purpose I could not determine.

As he approached quite close to me I obtained an excellent view of him, and though I was later to become better acquainted with his kind, I may say that that single cursory examination of this awful travesty on Nature would have proved quite sufficient to my desires had I been a free agent. The fastest flier of the Heliumetic Navy could not quickly enough have carried me far from this hideous creature.

Its hairless body was a strange and ghoulish blue, except for a broad band of white which encircled its protruding, single eye: an eye that was all dead white—pupil, iris, and ball.

Its nose was a ragged, inflamed, circular hole in the centre of its blank face; a hole that resembled more closely nothing that I could think of other than a fresh bullet wound which has not yet commenced to bleed.

Below this repulsive orifice the face was quite blank to the chin, for the thing had no mouth that I could discover.

The head, with the exception of the face, was covered by a tangled mass of jet-black hair some eight or ten inches in length. Each hair was about the bigness of a large angleworm, and as the thing moved the muscles of its scalp this awful head-covering seemed to writhe and wriggle and crawl about the fearsome face as though indeed each separate hair was endowed with independent life.

The body and the legs were as symmetrically human as Nature could have fashioned them, and the feet, too, were human in shape, but of monstrous proportions. From heel to toe they were fully three feet long, and very flat and very broad.

As it came quite close to me I discovered that its strange movements, running its odd hands over the surface of the turf, were the result of its peculiar method of feeding, which consists in cropping off the tender vegetation with its razor-like talons and sucking it up from its two mouths, which lie one in the palm of each hand, through its arm-like throats.

In addition to the features which I have already described, the beast was equipped with a massive tail about six feet in length, quite round where it joined the body, but tapering to a flat, thin blade toward the end, which trailed at right angles to the ground.

By far the most remarkable feature of this most remarkable creature, however, were the two tiny replicas of it, each about six inches in length, which dangled, one on either side, from its armpits. They were suspended by a small stem which seemed to grow from the exact tops of their heads to where it connected them with the body of the adult.

Whether they were the young, or merely portions of a composite creature, I did not know.

As I had been scrutinizing this weird monstrosity the balance of the herd had fed quite close to me and I now saw that while many had the smaller specimens dangling from them, not all were thus equipped, and I further noted that the little ones varied in size from what appeared to be but tiny unopened buds an inch in diameter through various stages of development to the full-fledged and perfectly formed creature of ten to twelve inches in length.

Feeding with the herd were many of the little fellows not much larger than those which remained attached to their parents, and from the young of that size the herd graded up to the immense adults.

Fearsome-looking as they were, I did not know whether to fear them or not, for they did not seem to be particularly well equipped for fighting, and I was on the point of stepping from my hiding-place and revealing myself to them to note the effect upon them of the sight of a man when my rash resolve was, fortunately for me, nipped in the bud by a strange shrieking wail, which seemed to come from the direction of the bluffs at my right.

Naked and unarmed, as I was, my end would have been both speedy and horrible at the hands of these cruel creatures had I had time to put my resolve into execution, but at the moment of the shriek each member of the herd turned in the direction from which the sound seemed to come, and at the same instant every particular snake-like hair upon their heads rose stiffly perpendicular as if each had been a sentient organism looking or listening for the source or meaning of the wail. And indeed the latter proved to be the truth, for this strange growth upon the craniums of the plant men of Barsoom represents the thousand ears of these hideous creatures, the last remnant of the strange race which sprang from the original Tree of Life.

Instantly every eye turned toward one member of the herd, a large fellow who evidently was the leader. A strange purring sound issued from the mouth in the palm of one of his hands, and at the same time he started rapidly toward the bluff, followed by the entire herd.

Their speed and method of locomotion were both remarkable, springing as they did in great leaps of twenty or thirty feet, much after the manner of a kangaroo.

They were rapidly disappearing when it occurred to me to follow them, and so, hurling caution to the winds, I sprang across the meadow in their wake with leaps and bounds even more prodigious than their own, for the muscles of an athletic Earth man produce remarkable results when pitted against the lesser gravity and air pressure of Mars.

Their way led directly towards the apparent source of the river at the base of the cliffs, and as I neared this point I found the meadow dotted with huge boulders that the ravages of time had evidently dislodged from the towering crags above.

For this reason I came quite close to the cause of the disturbance before the scene broke upon my horrified gaze. As I topped a great boulder I saw the herd of plant men surrounding a little group of perhaps five or six green men and women of Barsoom.

That I was indeed upon Mars I now had no doubt, for here were members of the wild hordes that people the dead sea bottoms and deserted cities of that dying planet.

Here were the great males towering in all the majesty of their imposing height; here were the gleaming white tusks protruding from their massive lower jaws to a point near the centre of their foreheads, the laterally placed, protruding eyes with which they could look for-

ward or backward, or to either side without turning their heads, here
the strange antennæ-like ears rising from the tops of their foreheads;
and the additional pair of arms extending from midway between the
shoulders and the hips.

Even without the glossy green hide and the metal ornaments which
denoted the tribes to which they belonged, I would have known them
on the instant for what they were, for where else in all the universe is
their like duplicated?

There were two men and four females in the party and their ornaments denoted them as members of different hordes, a fact which
tended to puzzle me infinitely, since the various hordes of green men
of Barsoom are eternally at deadly war with one another, and never,
except on that single historic instance when the great Tars Tarkas of
Thark gathered a hundred and fifty thousand green warriors from
several hordes to march upon the doomed city of Zodanga to rescue
Dejah Thoris, Princess of Helium, from the clutches of Than Kosis,
had I seen green Martians of different hordes associated in other
than mortal combat.

But now they stood back to back, facing, in wide-eyed amazement,
the very evidently hostile demonstrations of a common enemy.

Both men and women were armed with long-swords and daggers,
but no firearms were in evidence, else it had been short shrift for the
gruesome plant men of Barsoom.

Presently the leader of the plant men charged the little party, and
his method of attack was as remarkable as it was effective, and by its
very strangeness was the more potent, since in the science of the
green warriors there was no defence for this singular manner of attack, the like of which it soon was evident to me they were as unfamiliar with as they were with the monstrosities which confronted
them.

The plant man charged to within a dozen feet of the party and
then, with a bound, rose as though to pass directly above their heads.
His powerful tail was raised high to one side, and as he passed close
above them he brought it down in one terrific sweep that crushed a
green warrior's skull as though it had been an eggshell.

The balance of the frightful herd was now circling rapidly and with
bewildering speed about the little knot of victims. Their prodigious
bounds and the shrill, screeching purr of their uncanny mouths were
well calculated to confuse and terrorize their prey, so that as two of
them leaped simultaneously from either side, the mighty sweep of

those awful tails met with no resistance and two more green Martians went down to an ignoble death.

There were now but one warrior and two females left, and it seemed that it could be but a matter of seconds ere these, also, lay dead upon the scarlet sward.

But as two more of the plant men charged, the warrior, who was now prepared by the experiences of the past few minutes, swung his mighty long-sword aloft and met the hurtling bulk with a clean cut that clove one of the plant men from chin to groin.

The other, however, dealt a single blow with his cruel tail that laid both of the females crushed corpses upon the ground.

As the green warrior saw the last of his companions go down and at the same time perceived that the entire herd was charging him in a body, he rushed boldly to meet them, swinging his long-sword in the terrific manner that I had so often seen the men of his kind wield it in their ferocious and almost continual warfare among their own race.

Cutting and hewing to right and left, he laid an open path straight through the advancing plant men, and then commenced a mad race for the forest, in the shelter of which he evidently hoped that he might find a haven of refuge.

He had turned for that portion of the forest which abutted on the cliffs, and thus the mad race was taking the entire party farther and farther from the boulder where I lay concealed.

As I had watched the noble fight which the great warrior had put up against such enormous odds my heart had swelled in admiration for him, and acting as I am wont to do, more upon impulse than after mature deliberation, I instantly sprang from my sheltering rock and bounded quickly toward the bodies of the dead green Martians, a well-defined plan of action already formed.

Half a dozen great leaps brought me to the spot, and another instant saw me again in my stride in quick pursuit of the hideous monsters that were rapidly gaining on the fleeing warrior, but this time I grasped a mighty long-sword in my hand and in my heart was the old blood lust of the fighting-man, and a red mist swam before my eyes and I felt my lips respond to my heart in the old smile that has ever marked me in the midst of the joy of battle.

Swift as I was I was none too soon, for the green warrior had been overtaken ere he had made half the distance to the forest, and now he stood with his back to a boulder, while the herd, temporarily balked, hissed and screeched about him.

With their single eyes in the centre of their heads and every eye turned upon their prey, they did not note my soundless approach, so that I was upon them with my great long-sword and four of them lay dead ere they knew that I was among them.

For an instant they recoiled before my terrific onslaught, and in that instant the green warrior rose to the occasion and, springing to my side, laid to the right and left of him as I had never seen but one other warrior do, with great circling strokes that formed a figure eight about him and that never stopped until none stood living to oppose him, his keen blade passing through flesh and bone and metal as though each had been alike thin air.

As we bent to the slaughter, far above us rose that shrill, weird cry which I had heard once before, and which had called the herd to the attack upon their victims. Again and again it rose, but we were too much engaged with the fierce and powerful creatures about us to attempt to search out even with our eyes the author of the horrid notes.

Great tails lashed in frenzied anger about us, razor-like talons cut our limbs and bodies, and a green and sticky syrup, such as oozes from a crushed caterpillar, smeared us from head to foot, for every cut and thrust of our long-swords brought spurts of this stuff upon us from the severed arteries of the plant men, through which it courses in its sluggish viscidity in lieu of blood.

Once I felt the great weight of one of the monsters upon my back and as keen talons sank into my flesh I experienced the frightful sensation of moist lips sucking the lifeblood from the wounds to which the claws still clung.

I was very much engaged with a ferocious fellow who was endeavouring to reach my throat from in front, while two more, one on either side, were lashing viciously at me with their tails.

The green warrior was much put to it to hold his own, and I felt that the unequal struggle could last but a moment longer when the huge fellow discovered my plight, and tearing himself from those that surrounded him, he raked the assailant from my back with a single sweep of his blade, and thus relieved I had little difficulty with the others.

Once together, we stood almost back to back against the great boulder, and thus the creatures were prevented from soaring above us to deliver their deadly blows, and as we were easily their match while they remained upon the ground, we were making great headway in dispatching what remained of them when our attention was again attracted by the shrill wail of the caller above our heads.

This time I glanced up, and far above us upon a little natural balcony on the face of the cliff stood a strange figure of a man shrieking out his shrill signal, the while he waved one hand in the direction of the river's mouth as though beckoning to some one there, and with the other pointed and gesticulated toward us.

A glance in the direction toward which he was looking was sufficient to apprise me of his aims and at the same time to fill me with the dread of dire apprehension, for, streaming in from all directions across the meadow, from out of the forest, and from the far distance of the flat land across the river, I could see converging upon us a hundred different lines of wildly leaping creatures such as we were now engaged with, and with them some strange new monsters which ran with great swiftness, now erect and now upon all fours.

"It will be a great death," I said to my companion. "Look!"

As he shot a quick glance in the direction I indicated he smiled.

"We may at least die fighting and as great warriors should, John Carter," he replied.

We had just finished the last of our immediate antagonists as he spoke, and I turned in surprised wonderment at the sound of my name.

And there before my astonished eyes I beheld the greatest of the green men of Barsoom; their shrewdest statesman, their mightiest general, my great and good friend, Tars Tarkas, Jeddak of Thark.

A FOREST BATTLE

TARS TARKAS and I found no time for an exchange of experiences as we stood there before the great boulder surrounded by the corpses of our grotesque assailants, for from all directions down the broad valley was streaming a perfect torrent of terrifying creatures in response to the weird call of the strange figure far above us.

"Come," cried Tars Tarkas, "we must make for the cliffs. There lies our only hope of even temporary escape; there we may find a cave or a narrow ledge which two may defend for ever against this motley, unarmed horde."

Together we raced across the scarlet sward, I timing my speed that I might not outdistance my slower companion. We had, perhaps, three hundred yards to cover between our boulder and the cliffs, and then to search out a suitable shelter for our stand against the terrifying things that were pursuing us.

They were rapidly overhauling us when Tars Tarkas cried to me to hasten ahead and discover, if possible, the sanctuary we sought. The suggestion was a good one, for thus many valuable minutes might be saved to us, and, throwing every ounce of my earthly muscles into the effort, I cleared the remaining distance between myself and the cliffs in great leaps and bounds that put me at their base in a moment.

The cliffs rose perpendicular directly from the almost level sward of the valley. There was no accumulation of fallen debris, forming a more or less rough ascent to them, as is the case with nearly all other cliffs I have ever seen. The scattered boulders that had fallen from above and lay upon or partly buried in the turf, were the only indication that any disintegration of the massive, towering pile of rocks ever had taken place.

My first cursory inspection of the face of the cliffs filled my heart with forebodings, since nowhere could I discern, except where the weird herald stood still shrieking his shrill summons, the faintest indication of even a bare foothold upon the lofty escarpment.

To my right the bottom of the cliff was lost in the dense foliage of the forest, which terminated at its very foot, rearing its gorgeous foliage fully a thousand feet against its stern and forbidding neighbour.

To the left the cliff ran, apparently unbroken, across the head of the broad valley, to be lost in the outlines of what appeared to be a range of mighty mountains that skirted and confined the valley in every direction.

Perhaps a thousand feet from me the river broke, as it seemed, directly from the base of the cliffs, and as there seemed not the remotest chance for escape in that direction I turned my attention again toward the forest.

The cliffs towered above me a good five thousand feet. The sun was not quite upon them and they loomed a dull yellow in their own shade. Here and there they were broken with streaks and patches of dusky red, green, and occasional areas of white quartz.

Altogether they were very beautiful, but I fear that I did not regard them with a particularly appreciative eye on this, my first inspection of them.

Just then I was absorbed in them only as a medium of escape, and so, as my gaze ran quickly, time and again, over their vast expanse in search of some cranny or crevice, I came suddenly to loathe them as the prisoner must loathe the cruel and impregnable walls of his dungeon.

Tars Tarkas was approaching me rapidly, and still more rapidly came the awful horde at his heels.

It seemed the forest now or nothing, and I was just on the point of motioning Tars Tarkas to follow me in that direction when the sun passed the cliff's zenith, and as the bright rays touched the dull surface it burst out into a million scintillant lights of burnished gold, of flaming red, of soft greens, and gleaming whites—a more gorgeous and inspiring spectacle human eye has never rested upon.

The face of the entire cliff was, as later inspection conclusively proved, so shot with veins and patches of solid gold as to quite present the appearance of a solid wall of that precious metal except where it was broken by outcroppings of ruby, emerald, and diamond boulders —a faint and alluring indication of the vast and unguessable riches which lay deeply buried behind the magnificent surface.

But what caught my most interested attention at the moment that the sun's rays set the cliff's face a-shimmer, was the several black spots which now appeared quite plainly in evidence high across the gorgeous wall close to the forest's top, and extending apparently below and behind the branches.

Almost immediately I recognised them for what they were, the dark openings of caves entering the solid walls—possible avenues of escape or temporary shelter, could we but reach them.

There was but a single way, and that led through the mighty, towering trees upon our right. That I could scale them I knew full well, but Tars Tarkas, with his mighty bulk and enormous weight, would find it a task possibly quite beyond his prowess or his skill, for Martians are at best but poor climbers. Upon the entire surface of that ancient planet I never before had seen a hill or mountain that exceeded four thousand feet in height above the dead sea bottoms, and as the ascent was usually gradual, nearly to their summits they presented but few opportunities for the practice of climbing. Nor would the Martians have embraced even such opportunities as might present themselves, for they could always find a circuitous route about the base of any eminence, and these roads they preferred and followed in preference to the shorter but more arduous ways.

However, there was nothing else to consider than an attempt to scale the trees contiguous to the cliff in an effort to reach the caves above.

The Thark grasped the possibilities and the difficulties of the plan at once, but there was no alternative, and so we set out rapidly for the trees nearest the cliff.

Our relentless pursuers were now close to us, so close that it seemed that it would be an utter impossibility for the Jeddak of Thark to reach the forest in advance of them, nor was there any considerable will in the efforts that Tars Tarkas made, for the green men of Barsoom do not relish flight, nor ever before had I seen one fleeing from death in whatsoever form it might have confronted him. But that Tars Tarkas was the bravest of the brave he had proven thousands of times; yes, tens of thousands in countless mortal combats with men and beasts. And so I knew that there was another reason than fear of death behind his flight, as he knew that a greater power than pride or honour spurred me to escape these fierce destroyers. In my case it was love—love of the divine Dejah Thoris; and the cause of the Thark's great and sudden love of life I could not fathom, for it is oftener that they seek death than life—these strange, cruel, loveless, unhappy people.

At length, however, we reached the shadows of the forest, while right behind us sprang the swiftest of our pursuers—a giant plant man with claws outreaching to fasten his bloodsucking mouths upon us.

He was, I should say, a hundred yards in advance of his closest companion, and so I called to Tars Tarkas to ascend a great tree that brushed the cliff's face while I dispatched the fellow, thus giving the less agile Thark an opportunity to reach the higher branches before the entire horde should be upon us and every vestige of escape cut off.

But I had reckoned without a just appreciation either of the cunning of my immediate antagonist or the swiftness with which his fellows were covering the distance which had separated them from me.

As I raised my long-sword to deal the creature its death thrust it halted in its charge and, as my sword cut harmlessly through the empty air, the great tail of the thing swept with the power of a grizzly's arm across the sward and carried me bodily from my feet to the ground. In an instant the brute was upon me, but ere it could fasten its hideous mouths into my breast and throat I grasped a writhing tentacle in either hand.

The plant man was well muscled, heavy, and powerful but my earthly sinews and greater agility, in conjunction with the deathly strangle hold I had upon him, would have given me, I think, an eventual victory had we had time to discuss the merits of our relative prowess uninterrupted. But as we strained and struggled about the tree into which Tars Tarkas was clambering with infinite difficulty, I suddenly caught a glimpse over the shoulder of my antagonist of the great swarm of pursuers that now were fairly upon me.

Now, at last, I saw the nature of the other monsters who had come with the plant men in response to the weird calling of the man upon the cliff's face. They were that most dreaded of Martian creatures— great white apes of Barsoom.

My former experiences upon Mars had familiarized me thoroughly with them and their methods, and I may say that of all the fearsome and terrible, weird and grotesque inhabitants of that strange world, it is the white apes that come nearest to familiarizing me with the sensation of fear.

I think that the cause of this feeling which these apes engender within me is due to their remarkable resemblance in form to our Earth men, which gives them a human appearance that is most uncanny when coupled with their enormous size.

They stand fifteen feet in height and walk erect upon their hind feet. Like the green Martians, they have an intermediary set of arms midway between their upper and lower limbs. Their eyes are very close set, but do not protrude as do those of the green men of Mars; their ears are high set, but more laterally located than are the green men's, while their snouts and teeth are much like those of our African gorilla. Upon their heads grows an enormous shock of bristly hair.

It was into the eyes of such as these and the terrible plant men that I gazed above the shoulder of my foe, and then, in a mighty wave of snarling, snapping, screaming, purring rage, they swept over me— and of all the sounds that assailed my ears as I went down beneath them, to me the most hideous was the horrid purring of the plant men.

Instantly a score of cruel fangs and keen talons were sunk into my flesh; cold, sucking lips fastened themselves upon my arteries. I struggled to free myself, and even though weighed down by these immense bodies, I succeeded in struggling to my feet, where, still grasping my long-sword, and shortening my grip upon it until I could use it as a dagger, I wrought such havoc among them that at one time I stood for an instant free.

What it has taken minutes to write occurred in but a few seconds, but during that time Tars Tarkas had seen my plight and had dropped from the lower branches, which he had reached with such infinite labour, and as I flung the last of my immediate antagonists from me the great Thark leaped to my side, and again we fought, back to back, as we had done a hundred times before.

Time and again the ferocious apes sprang in to close with us, and time and again we beat them back with our swords. The great tails of the plant men lashed with tremendous power about us as they charged from various directions or sprang with the agility of greyhounds above our heads; but every attack met a gleaming blade in sword hands that had been reputed for twenty years the best that Mars ever had known; for Tars Tarkas and John Carter were names that the fighting men of the world of warriors loved best to speak.

But even the two best swords in a world of fighters can avail not for ever against overwhelming numbers of fierce and savage brutes that know not what defeat means until cold steel teaches their hearts no longer to beat, and so, step by step, we were forced back. At length we stood against the giant tree that we had chosen for our ascent, and then, as charge after charge hurled its weight upon us, we gave back again and again, until we had been forced half-way around the huge base of the colossal trunk.

Tars Tarkas was in the lead, and suddenly I heard a little cry of ex-ultation from him.

"Here is shelter for one at least, John Carter," he said, and, glancing down, I saw an opening in the base of the tree about three feet in diameter.

"In with you, Tars Tarkas," I cried, but he would not go; saying that his bulk was too great for the little aperture, while I might slip in easily.

"We shall both die if we remain without, John Carter; here is a slight chance for one of us. Take it and you may live to avenge me, it is useless for me to attempt to worm my way into so small an opening with this horde of demons besetting us on all sides."

"Then we shall die together, Tars Tarkas," I replied, "for I shall not go first. Let me defend the opening while you get in, then my smaller stature will permit me to slip in with you before they can prevent."

We still were fighting furiously as we talked in broken sentences, punctured with vicious cuts and thrusts at our swarming enemy.

At length he yielded, for it seemed the only way in which either of us might be saved from the ever-increasing numbers of our assailants, who were still swarming upon us from all directions across the broad valley.

"It was ever your way, John Carter, to think last of your own life," he said; "but still more your way to command the lives and actions of others, even to the greatest of Jeddaks who rule upon Barsoom."

There was a grim smile upon his cruel, hard face, as he, the greatest Jeddak of them all, turned to obey the dictates of a creature of another world—of a man whose stature was less than half his own.

"If you fail, John Carter," he said, "know that the cruel and heartless Thark, to whom you taught the meaning of friendship, will come out to die beside you."

"As you will, my friend," I replied; "but quickly now, head first, while I cover your retreat."

He hesitated a little at that word, for never before in his whole life of continual strife had he turned his back upon aught than a dead or defeated enemy.

"Haste, Tars Tarkas," I urged, "or we shall both go down to profitless defeat; I cannot hold them for ever alone."

As he dropped to the ground to force his way into the tree, the whole howling pack of hideous devils hurled themselves upon me. To right and left flew my shimmering blade, now green with the sticky juice of a plant man, now red with the crimson blood of a great white ape; but always flying from one opponent to another, hesitating but the barest fraction of a second to drink the lifeblood in the centre of some savage heart.

And thus I fought as I never had fought before, against such frightful odds that I cannot realize even now that human muscles could have withstood that awful onslaught, that terrific weight of hurtling tons of ferocious, battling flesh.

With the fear that we would escape them, the creatures redoubled their efforts to pull me down, and though the ground about me was piled high with their dead and dying comrades, they succeeded at last in overwhelming me, and I went down beneath them for the second time that day, and once again felt those awful sucking lips against my flesh.

But scarce had I fallen ere I felt powerful hands grip my ankles, and in another second I was being drawn within the shelter of the tree's interior. For a moment it was a tug of war between Tars Tarkas and a great plant man, who clung tenaciously to my breast, but presently I got the point of my long-sword beneath him and with a mighty thrust pierced his vitals.

Torn and bleeding from many cruel wounds, I lay panting upon the ground within the hollow of the tree, while Tars Tarkas defended the opening from the furious mob without.

For an hour they howled about the tree, but after a few attempts to reach us they confined their efforts to terrorizing shrieks and screams, to horrid growling on the part of the great white apes, and the fearsome and indescribable purring by the plant men.

At length, all but a score, who had apparently been left to prevent our escape, had left us, and our adventure seemed destined to result in a siege, the only outcome of which could be our death by starvation; for even should we be able to slip out after dark, whither in this unknown and hostile valley could we hope to turn our steps toward possible escape?

As the attacks of our enemies ceased and our eyes became accustomed to the semi-darkness of the interior of our strange retreat, I took the opportunity to explore our shelter.

The tree was hollow to an extent of about fifty feet in diameter, and from its flat, hard floor I judged that it had often been used to domicile others before our occupancy. As I raised my eyes toward its roof to note the height I saw far above me a faint glow of light.

There was an opening above. If we could but reach it we might still hope to make the shelter of the cliff caves. My eyes had now become quite used to the subdued light of the interior, and as I pursued my investigation I presently came upon a rough ladder at the far side of the cave.

Quickly I mounted it, only to find that it connected at the top with the lower of a series of horizontal wooden bars that spanned the now narrow and shaft-like interior of the tree's stem. These bars were set one above another about three feet apart, and formed a perfect ladder as far above me as I could see.

Dropping to the floor once more, I detailed my discovery to Tars

Tarkas, who suggested that I explore aloft as far as I could go in safety while he guarded the entrance against a possible attack.

As I hastened above to explore the strange shaft I found that the ladder of horizontal bars mounted always as far above me as my eyes could reach, and as I ascended, the light from above grew brighter and brighter.

For fully five hundred feet I continued to climb, until at length I reached the opening in the stem which admitted the light. It was of about the same diameter as the entrance at the foot of the tree, and opened directly upon a large flat limb, the well-worn surface of which testified to its long-continued use as an avenue for some creature to and from this remarkable shaft.

I did not venture out upon the limb for fear that I might be discovered and our retreat in this direction cut off; but instead hurried to retrace my steps to Tars Tarkas.

I soon reached him and presently we were both ascending the long ladder toward the opening above.

Tars Tarkas went in advance and as I reached the first of the horizontal bars I drew the ladder up after me and, handing it to him, he carried it a hundred feet further aloft, where he wedged it safely between one of the bars and the side of the shaft. In like manner I dislodged the lower bars as I passed them, so that we soon had the interior of the tree denuded of all possible means of ascent for a distance of a hundred feet from the base; thus precluding possible pursuit and attack from the rear.

As we were to learn later, this precaution saved us from dire predicament, and was eventually the means of our salvation.

When we reached the opening at the top Tars Tarkas drew to one side that I might pass out and investigate, as, owing to my lesser weight and greater agility, I was better fitted for the perilous threading of this dizzy, hanging pathway.

The limb upon which I found myself ascended at a slight angle toward the cliff, and as I followed it I found that it terminated a few feet above a narrow ledge which protruded from the cliff's face at the entrance to a narrow cave.

As I approached the slightly more slender extremity of the branch it bent beneath my weight until, as I balanced perilously upon its outer tip, it swayed gently on a level with the ledge at a distance of a couple of feet.

Five hundred feet below me lay the vivid scarlet carpet of the valley; nearly five thousand feet above towered the mighty, gleaming face of the gorgeous cliffs.

The cave that I faced was not one of those that I had seen from the ground, and which lay much higher, possibly a thousand feet. But so far as I might know it was as good for our purpose as another, and so I returned to the tree for Tars Tarkas.

Together we wormed our way along the waving pathway, but when we reached the end of the branch we found that our combined weight so depressed the limb that the cave's mouth was now too far above us to be reached.

We finally agreed that Tars Tarkas should return along the branch, leaving his longest leather harness strap with me, and that when the limb had risen to a height that would permit me to enter the cave I was to do so, and on Tars Tarkas' return I could then lower the strap and haul him up to the safety of the ledge.

This we did without mishap and soon found ourselves together upon the verage of a dizzy little balcony, with a magnificent view of the valley spreading out below us.

As far as the eye could reach gorgeous forest and crimson sward skirted a silent sea, and about all towered the brilliant monster guardian cliffs. Once we thought we discerned a gilded minaret gleaming in the sun amidst the waving tops of far-distant trees, but we soon abandoned the idea in the belief that it was but an hallucination born of our great desire to discover the haunts of civilized men in this beautiful, yet forbidding, spot.

Below us upon the river's bank the great white apes were devouring the last remnants of Tars Tarkas' former companions, while great herds of plant men grazed in ever-widening circles about the sward which they kept as close clipped as the smoothest of lawns.

Knowing that attack from the tree was now improbable, we determined to explore the cave, which we had every reason to believe was but a continuation of the path we had already traversed, leading the gods alone knew where, but quite evidently away from this valley of grim ferocity.

As we advanced we found a well-proportioned tunnel cut from the solid cliff. Its walls rose some twenty feet above the floor, which was about five feet in width. The roof was arched. We had no means of making a light, and so groped our way slowly into the ever-increasing darkness, Tars Tarkas keeping in touch with one wall while I felt along the other, while, to prevent our wandering into diverging branches and becoming separated or lost in some intricate and labyrinthine maze, we clasped hands.

How far we traversed the tunnel in this manner I do not know, but presently we came to an obstruction which blocked our further progress. It seemed more like a partition than a sudden ending of the cave, for it was constructed not of the material of the cliff, but of something which felt like very hard wood.

Silently I groped over its surface with my hands, and presently was rewarded by the feel of the button which as commonly denotes a door on Mars as does a door knob on Earth.

Gently pressing it, I had the satisfaction of feeling the door slowly give before me, and in another instant we were looking into a dimly lighted apartment, which, so far as we could see, was unoccupied.

Without more ado I swung the door wide open and, followed by the huge Thark, stepped into the chamber. As we stood for a moment in silence gazing about the room a slight noise behind caused me to turn quickly, when, to my astonishment, I saw the door close with a sharp click as though by an unseen hand.

Instantly I sprang toward it to wrench it open again, for something in the uncanny movement of the thing and the tense and almost palpable silence of the chamber seemed to portend a lurking evil lying hidden in this rock-bound chamber within the bowels of the Golden Cliffs.

My fingers clawed futilely at the unyielding portal, while my eyes sought in vain for a duplicate of the button which had given us ingress.

And then, from unseen lips, a cruel and mocking peal of laughter rang through the desolate place.

THE CHAMBER OF MYSTERY

FOR MOMENTS after that awful laugh had ceased reverberating through the rocky room, Tars Tarkas and I stood in tense and expectant silence. But no further sound broke the stillness, nor within the range of our vision did aught move.

At length Tars Tarkas laughed softly, after the manner of his strange kind when in the presence of the horrible or terrifying. It is not an hysterical laugh, but rather the genuine expression of the pleasure they derive from the things that move Earth men to loathing or to tears.

Often and again have I seen them roll upon the ground in mad fits of uncontrollable mirth when witnessing the death agonies of women and little children beneath the torture of that hellish green Martian fête—the Great Games.

I looked up at the Thark, a smile upon my own lips, for here in truth was greater need for a smiling face than a trembling chin.

"What do you make of it all?" I asked. "Where in the deuce are we?"

He looked at me in surprise.

"Where are we?" he repeated. "Do you tell me, John Carter, that you know not where you be?"

"That I am upon Barsoom is all that I can guess, and but for you and the great white apes I should not even guess that, for the sights I have seen this day are as unlike the things of my beloved Barsoom as I knew it ten long years ago as they are unlike the world of my birth.

"No, Tars Tarkas, I know not where we be."

"Where have you been since you opened the mighty portals of the atmosphere plant years ago, after the keeper had died and the engines stopped and all Barsoom was dying, that had not already died, of asphyxiation? Your body even was never found, though the men of a whole world sought after it for years, though the Jeddak of Helium and his granddaughter, your princess, offered such fabulous rewards that even princes of royal blood joined in the search.

"There was but one conclusion to reach when all efforts to locate you had failed, and that, that you had taken the long, last pilgrimage down the mysterious River Iss, to await in the Valley Dor upon the shores of the Lost Sea of Korus the beautiful Dejah Thoris, your princess.

"Why you had gone none could guess, for your princess still lived——"

"Thank God," I interrupted him. "I did not dare to ask you, for I feared I might have been too late to save her—she was very low when I left her in the royal gardens of Tardos Mors that long-gone night; so very low that I scarcely hoped even then to reach the atmosphere plant ere her dear spirit had fled from me for ever. And she lives yet?"

"She lives, John Carter."

"You have not told me where we are," I reminded him.

"We are where I expected to find you, John Carter—and another. Many years ago you heard the story of the woman who taught me the thing that green Martians are reared to hate, the woman who taught me to love. You know the cruel tortures and the awful death her love won for her at the hands of the beast, Tal Hajus.

"She, I thought, awaited me by the Lost Sea of Korus.

"You know that it was left for a man from another world, for yourself, John Carter, to teach this cruel Thark what friendship is; and you, I thought, also roamed the care-free Valley Dor.

"Thus were the two I most longed for at the end of the long pilgrimage I must take some day, and so as the time had elapsed which Dejah Thoris had hoped might bring you once more to her side, for she has always tried to believe that you had but temporarily returned to your own planet, I at last gave way to my great yearning and a month since I started upon the journey, the end of which you have this day witnessed. Do you understand now where you be, John Carter?"

"And that was the River Iss, emptying into the Lost Sea of Korus in the Valley Dor?" I asked.

"This is the valley of love and peace and rest to which every Barsoomian since time immemorial has longed to pilgrimage at the end of a life of hate and strife and bloodshed," he replied. "This, John Carter, is Heaven."

His tone was cold and ironical; its bitterness but reflecting the terrible disappointment he had suffered. Such a fearful disillusionment, such a blasting of life-long hopes and aspirations, such an uprooting of age-old tradition might have excused a vastly greater demonstration on the part of the Thark.

I laid my hand upon his shoulder.

"I am sorry," I said, nor did there seem aught else to say.

"Think, John Carter, of the countless billions of Barsoomians who have taken the voluntary pilgrimage down this cruel river since the beginning of time, only to fall into the ferocious clutches of the terrible creatures that to-day assailed us.

"There is an ancient legend that once a red man returned from the banks of the Lost Sea of Korus, returned from the Valley Dor, back through the mysterious River Iss, and the legend has it that he narrated a fearful blasphemy of horrid brutes that inhabited a valley of wondrous loveliness, brutes that pounced upon each Barsoomian as he terminated his pilgrimage and devoured him upon the banks of the Lost Sea where he had looked to find love and peace and happiness; but the ancients killed the blasphemer, as tradition has ordained that any shall be killed who return from the bosom of the River of Mystery.

"But now we know that it was no blasphemy, that the legend is a true one, and that the man told only of what he saw; but what does it profit us, John Carter, since even should we escape, we also would be treated as blasphemers? We are between the wild thoat of certainty and the mad zitidar of fact—we can escape neither."

"As Earth men say, we are between the devil and the deep sea, Tars Tarkas," I replied, nor could I help but smile at our dilemma.

"There is naught that we can do but take things as they come, and at least have the satisfaction of knowing that whoever slays us eventually will have far greater numbers of their own dead to count than they will get in return. White ape or plant man, green Barsoomian or red man, whosoever it shall be that takes the last toll from us will know that it is costly in lives to wipe out John Carter, Prince of the House of Tardos Mors, and Tars Tarkas, Jeddak of Thark, at the same time."

I could not help but laugh at his grim humour, and he joined in with me in one of those rare laughs of real enjoyment which was one of the attributes of this fierce Tharkian chief which marked him from the others of his kind.

"But about yourself, John Carter," he cried at last. "If you have not been here all these years where indeed have you been, and how is it that I find you here to-day?"

"I have been back to Earth," I replied. "For ten long Earth years I have been praying and hoping for the day that would carry me once more to this grim old planet of yours, for which, with all its cruel and terrible customs, I feel a bond of sympathy and love even greater than for the world that gave me birth.

"For ten years have I been enduring a living death of uncertainty and doubt as to whether Dejah Thoris lived, and now that for the first time in all these years my prayers have been answered and my doubt relieved I find myself, through a cruel whim of fate, hurled into the one tiny spot of all Barsoom from which there is apparently no escape, and if there were, at a price which would put out for ever the last flickering hope which I may cling to of seeing my princess again in this life—and you have seen to-day with what pitiful futility man yearns toward a material hereafter.

"Only a bare half-hour before I saw you battling with the plant men I was standing in the moonlight upon the banks of a broad river that taps the eastern shore of Earth's most blessed land. I have answered you, my friend. Do you believe?"

"I believe," replied Tars Tarkas, "though I cannot understand."

As we talked I had been searching the interior of the chamber with my eyes. It was, perhaps, two hundred feet in length and half as broad, with what appeared to be a doorway in the centre of the wall directly opposite that through which we had entered.

The apartment was hewn from the material of the cliff, showing mostly dull gold in the dim light which a single minute radium illuminator in the centre of the roof diffused throughout its great dimensions. Here and there polished surfaces of ruby, emerald, and diamond patched the golden walls and ceiling. The floor was of another material, very hard, and worn by much use to the smoothness of glass. Aside from the two doors I could discern no sign of other aperture, and as one we knew to be locked against us I approached the other.

As I extended my hand to search for the controlling button, that cruel and mocking laugh rang out once more, so close to me this time that I involuntarily shrank back, tightening my grip upon the hilt of my great sword.

And then from the far corner of the great chamber a hollow voice chanted: "There is no hope, there is no hope; the dead return not, the dead return not; nor is there any resurrection. Hope not, for there is no hope."

Though our eyes instantly turned toward the spot from which the voice seemed to emanate, there was no one in sight, and I must admit that cold shivers played along my spine and the short hairs at the base of my head stiffened and rose up, as do those upon a hound's neck when in the night his eyes see those uncanny things which are hidden from the sight of man.

Quickly I walked toward the mournful voice, but it had ceased ere I reached the further wall, and then from the other end of the chamber came another voice, shrill and piercing:

"Fools! Fools!" it shrieked. "Thinkest thou to defeat the eternal laws of life and death? Wouldst cheat the mysterious Issus, Goddess of Death, of her just dues? Did not her mighty messenger, the ancient

Iss, bear you upon her leaden bosom at your own behest to the Valley Dor?

"Thankest thou, O fools, that Issus wilt give up her own? Thinkest thou to escape from whence in all the countless ages but a single soul has fled?

"Go back the way thou camest, to the merciful maws of the children of the Tree of Life or the gleaming fangs of the great white apes, for there lies speedy surcease from suffering; but insist in your rash purpose to thread the mazes of the Golden Cliffs of the Mountains of Otz, past the ramparts of the impregnable fortresses of the Holy Therns, and upon your way Death in its most frightful form will overtake you—a death so horrible that even the Holy Therns themselves, who conceived both Life and Death, avert their eyes from its fiendishness and close their ears against the hideous shrieks of its victims.

"Go back, O fools, the way thou camest."

And then the awful laugh broke out from another part of the chamber.

"Most uncanny," I remarked, turning to Tars Tarkas.

"What shall we do?" he asked. "We cannot fight empty air; I would almost sooner return and face foes into whose flesh I may feel my blade bite and know that I am selling my carcass dearly before I go down to that eternal oblivion which is evidently the fairest and most desirable eternity that mortal man has the right to hope for."

"If, as you say, we cannot fight empty air, Tars Tarkas," I replied, "neither, on the other hand, can empty air fight us. I, who have faced and conquered in my time thousands of sinewy warriors and tempered blades, shall not be turned back by wind; nor no more shall you, Thark."

"But unseen voices may emanate from unseen and unseeable creatures who wield invisible blades," answered the green warrior.

"Rot, Tars Tarkas," I cried, "those voices come from beings as real as you or as I. In their veins flows lifeblood that may be let as easily as ours, and the fact that they remain invisible to us is the best proof to my mind that they are mortal; nor overly courageous mortals at that. Think you, Tars Tarkas, that John Carter will fly at the first shriek of a cowardly foe who dare not come out into the open and face a good blade?"

I had spoken in a loud voice that there might be no question that our would-be terrorizers should hear me, for I was tiring of this nerve-

*"It launched its great bulk toward me, and met cold steel instead of
the tender flesh its cruel jaws gaped so widely to engulf."*

racking fiasco. It had occurred to me, too, that the whole business was but a plan to frighten us back into the valley of death from which we had escaped, that we might be quickly disposed of by the savage creatures there.

For a long period there was silence, then of a sudden a soft, stealthy sound behind me caused me to turn suddenly to behold a great, many-legged banth creeping sinuously upon me.

The banth is a fierce beast of prey that roams the low hills surrounding the dead seas of ancient Mars. Like nearly all Martian animals it is almost hairless, having only a great bristly mane about its thick neck.

Its long, lithe body is supported by ten powerful legs, its enormous jaws are equipped, like those of the calot, or Martian hound, with several rows of long needle-like fangs; its mouth reaches to a point far back of its tiny ears, while its enormous, protruding eyes of green add the last touch of terror to its awful aspect.

As it crept toward me it lashed its powerful tail against its yellow sides, and when it saw that it was discovered it emitted the terrifying roar which often freezes its prey into momentary paralysis in the instant that it makes its spring.

And so it launched its great bulk toward me, but its mighty voice had held no paralysing terrors for me, and it met cold steel instead of the tender flesh its cruel jaws gaped so widely to engulf.

An instant later I drew my blade from the still heart of this great Barsoomian lion, and turning toward Tars Tarkas was surprised to see him facing a similar monster.

No sooner had he dispatched his than I, turning, as though drawn by the instinct of my guardian subconscious mind, beheld another of the savage denizens of the Martian wilds leaping across the chamber toward me.

From then on for the better part of an hour one hideous creature after another was launched upon us, springing apparently from the empty air about us.

Tars Tarkas was satisfied; here was something tangible that he could cut and slash with his great blade, while I, for my part, may say that the diversion was a marked improvement over the uncanny voices from unseen lips.

That there was nothing supernatural about our new foes was well evidenced by their howls of rage and pain as they felt the sharp steel at their vitals, and the very real blood which flowed from their severed arteries as they died the real death.

I noticed during the period of this new persecution that the beasts appeared only when our backs were turned; we never saw one really materialize from thin air, nor did I for an instant sufficiently lose my excellent reasoning faculties to be once deluded into the belief that the beasts came into the room other than through some concealed and well-contrived doorway.

Among the ornaments of Tars Tarkas' leather harness, which is the only manner of clothing worn by Martians other than silk capes and robes of silk and fur for protection from the cold after dark, was a small mirror, about the bigness of a lady's hand glass, which hung midway between his shoulders and his waist against his broad back.

Once as he stood looking down at a newly fallen antagonist my eyes happened to fall upon this mirror and in its shiny surface I saw pictured a sight that caused me to whisper:

"Move not, Tars Tarkas! Move not a muscle!"

He did not ask why, but stood like a graven image while my eyes watched the strange thing that meant so much to us.

What I saw was the quick movement of a section of the wall behind me. It was turning upon pivots, and with it a section of the floor directly in front of it was turning. It was as though you placed a visiting-card upon end on a silver dollar that you had laid flat upon a table, so that the edge of the card perfectly bisected the surface of the coin.

The card might represent the section of the wall that turned and the silver dollar the section of the floor. Both were so nicely fitted into the adjacent portions of the floor and wall that no crack had been noticeable in the dim light of the chamber.

As the turn was half completed a great beast was revealed sitting upon its haunches upon that part of the revolving floor that had been on the opposite side before the wall commenced to move; when the section stopped, the beast was facing toward me on our side of the partition—it was very simple.

But what had interested me most was the sight that the half-turned section had presented through the opening that it had made. A great chamber, well lighted, in which were several men and women chained to the wall, and in front of them, evidently directing and operating the movement of the secret doorway, a wicked-faced man, neither red as are the red men of Mars, nor green as are the green men, but white, like myself, with a great mass of flowing yellow hair.

The prisoners behind him were red Martians. Chained with them were a number of fierce beasts, such as had been turned upon us, and others equally as ferocious.

As I turned to meet my new foe it was with a heart considerably lightened.

"Watch the wall at your end of the chamber, Tars Tarkas," I cautioned, "it is through secret doorways in the wall that the brutes are loosed upon us." I was very close to him and spoke in a low whisper that my knowledge of their secret might not be disclosed to our tormentors.

As long as we remained each facing an opposite end of the apartment no further attacks were made upon us, so it was quite clear to me that the partitions were in some way pierced that our actions might be observed from without.

At length a plan of action occurred to me, and backing quite close to Tars Tarkas I unfolded my scheme in a low whisper, keeping my eyes still glued upon my end of the room.

The great Thark grunted his assent to my proposition when I had done, and in accordance with my plan commenced backing toward the wall which I faced while I advanced slowly ahead of him.

When we had reached a point some ten feet from the secret doorway I halted my companion, and cautioning him to remain absolutely motionless until I gave the prearranged signal I quickly turned my back to the door through which I could almost feel the burning and baleful eyes of our would-be executioner.

Instantly my own eyes sought the mirror upon Tars Tarkas' back and in another second I was closely watching the section of the wall which had been disgorging its savage terrors upon us.

I had not long to wait, for presently the golden surface commenced to move rapidly. Scarcely had it started than I gave the signal to Tars Tarkas, simultaneously springing for the receding half of the pivoting door. In like manner the Thark wheeled and leaped for the opening being made by the inswinging section.

A single bound carried me completely through into the adjoining room and brought me face to face with the fellow whose cruel face I had seen before. He was about my own height and well muscled and in every outward detail moulded precisely as are Earth men.

At his side hung a long-sword, a short-sword, a dagger, and one of the destructive radium revolvers that are common upon Mars.

The fact that I was armed only with a long-sword, and so according to the laws and ethics of battle everywhere upon Barsoom should only have been met with a similar or lesser weapon, seemed to have no effect upon the moral sense of my enemy, for he whipped out his revolver ere I scarce had touched the floor by his side, but an upper-cut from my long-sword sent it flying from his grasp before he could discharge it.

Instantly he drew his long-sword, and thus evenly armed we set to in earnest for one of the closest battles I ever have fought.

The fellow was a marvellous swordsman and evidently in practice, while I had not gripped the hilt of a sword for ten long years before that morning.

But it did not take me long to fall easily into my fighting stride, so that in a few minutes the man began to realize that he had at last met his match.

His face became livid with rage as he found my guard impregnable, while blood flowed from a dozen minor wounds upon his face and body.

"Who are you, white man?" he hissed. "That you are no Bar-soomian from the outer world is evident from your colour. And you are not of us."

His last statement was almost a question.

"What if I were from the Temple of Issus?" I hazarded on a wild guess.

"Fate forfend!" he exclaimed, his face going white under the blood that now nearly covered it.

I did not know how to follow up my lead, but I carefully laid the idea away for future use should circumstances require it. His answer indicated that for all he *knew* I might be from the Temple of Issus and in it were men like unto myself, and either this man feared the inmates of the temple or else he held their persons or their power in such reverence that he trembled to think of the harm and indignities he had heaped upon one of them.

But my present business with him was of a different nature than that which requires any considerable abstract reasoning; it was to get my sword between his ribs, and this I succeeded in doing within the next few seconds, nor was I an instant too soon.

The chained prisoners had been watching the combat in tense silence; not a sound had fallen in the room other than the clashing of our contending blades, the soft shuffling of our naked feet and the few whispered words we had hissed at each other through clenched teeth the while we continued our mortal duel.

But as the body of my antagonist sank an inert mass to the floor a cry of warning broke from one of the female prisoners.

"Turn! Turn! Behind you!" she shrieked, and as I wheeled at the first note of her shrill cry I found myself facing a second man of the same race as he who lay at my feet.

The fellow had crept stealthily from a dark corridor and was almost upon me with raised sword ere I saw him. Tars Tarkas was nowhere in sight and the secret panel in the wall, through which I had come, was closed.

How I wished that he were by my side now! I had fought almost continuously for many hours; I had passed through such experiences and adventures as must sap the vitality of man, and with all this I had not eaten for nearly twenty-four hours, nor slept.

I was fagged out, and for the first time in years felt a question as to my ability to cope with an antagonist; but there was naught else for it than to engage my man, and that as quickly and ferociously as lay in me, for my only salvation was to rush him off his feet by the impetuosity of my attack—I could not hope to win a long-drawn-out battle.

But the fellow was evidently of another mind, for he backed and parried and parried and sidestepped until I was almost completely fagged from the exertion of attempting to finish him.

He was a more adroit swordsman, if possible, than my previous foe, and I must admit that he led me a pretty chase and in the end came near to making a sorry fool of me—and a dead one into the bargain.

I could feel myself growing weaker and weaker, until at length objects commenced to blur before my eyes and I staggered and blundered about more asleep than awake, and then it was that he worked his pretty little coup that came near to losing me my life.

He had backed me around so that I stood in front of the corpse of his fellow, and then he rushed me suddenly so that I was forced back upon it, and as my heel struck it the impetus of my body flung me backward across the dead man.

My head struck the hard pavement with a resounding whack, and to that alone I owe my life, for it cleared my brain and the pain roused my temper, so that I was equal for the moment to tearing my enemy to pieces with my bare hands, and I verily believe that I should have attempted it had not my right hand, in the act of raising my body from the ground, come in contact with a bit of cold metal.

As the eyes of the layman so is the hand of the fighting-man when it comes in contact with an implement of his vocation, and thus I did not need to look or reason to know that the dead man's revolver, lying where it had fallen when I struck it from his grasp, was at my disposal.

The fellow whose ruse had put me down was springing toward me, the point of his gleaming blade directed straight at my heart, and as he came there rang from his lips the cruel and mocking peal of laughter that I had heard within the Chamber of Mystery.

And so he died, his thin lips curled in the snarl of his hateful laugh, and a bullet from the revolver of his dead companion bursting in his heart.

His body, borne by the impetus of his headlong rush, plunged upon me. The hilt of his sword must have struck my head, for with the impact of the corpse I lost consciousness.

THUVIA

IT WAS THE sound of conflict that aroused me once more to the realities of life. For a moment I could neither place my surroundings nor locate the sounds which had aroused me. And then from beyond the blank wall beside which I lay I heard the shuffling of feet, the snarling of grim beasts, the clank of metal accoutrements, and the heavy breathing of a man.

As I rose to my feet I glanced hurriedly about the chamber in which I had just encountered such a warm reception. The prisoners and the savage brutes rested in their chains by the opposite wall eyeing me with varying expressions of curiosity, sullen rage, surprise, and hope.

The latter emotion seemed plainly evident upon the handsome and intelligent face of the young red Martian woman whose cry of warning had been instrumental in saving my life.

She was the perfect type of that remarkably beautiful race whose

outward appearance is identical wtih the more god-like races of Earth
men, except that this higher race of Martians is of a light reddish
copper colour. As she was entirely unadorned I could not even guess
her station in life, though it was evident that she was either a prisoner
or slave in her present environment.

It was several seconds before the sounds upon the opposite side
of the partition jolted my slowly returning faculties into a realization
of their probable import, and then of a sudden I grasped the fact
that they were caused by Tars Tarkas in what was evidently a desperate struggle with wild beasts or savage men.

With a cry of encouragement I threw my weight against the secret
door, but as well have assayed the down-hurling of the cliffs themselves. Then I sought feverishly for the secret of the revolving panel,
but my search was fruitless, and I was about to raise my longsword
against the sullen gold when the young woman prisoner called out to
me.

"Save thy sword, O Mighty Warrior, for thou shalt need it more
where it will avail to some purpose—shatter it not against senseless
metal which yields better to the lightest finger touch of one who
knows its secret."

"Know you the secret of it then?" I asked.

"Yes; release me and I will give you entrance to the other horror
chamber, if you wish. The keys to my fetters are upon the first dead
of thy foemen. But why would you return to face again the fierce
banth, or whatever other form of destruction they have loosed within
that awful trap?"

"Because my friend fights there alone," I answered, as I hastily
sought and found the keys upon the carcass of the dead custodian
of this grim chamber of horrors.

There were many keys upon the oval ring, but the fair Martian
maid quickly selected that which sprung the great lock at her waist,
and freed she hurried toward the secret panel.

Again she sought out a key upon the ring. This time a slender,
needle-like affair which she inserted in an almost invisible hole in
the wall. Instantly the door swung upon its pivot, and the contiguous
section of the floor upon which I was standing carried me with it
into the chamber where Tars Tarkas fought.

The great Thark stood with his back against an angle of the walls,
while facing him in a semi-circle a half-dozen huge monsters crouched
waiting for an opening. Their blood-streaked heads and shoulders

testified to the cause of their wariness as well as to the swordsman-ship of the green warrior whose glossy hide bore the same mute but eloquent witness to the ferocity of the attacks that he had so far with-stood.

Sharp talons and cruel fangs had torn leg, arm, and breast literally to ribbons. So weak was he from continued exertion and loss of blood that but for the supporting wall I doubt that he even could have stood erect. But with a tenacity and indomitable courage of his kind he still faced his cruel and relentless foes—the personification of that ancient proverb of his tribe: "Leave to a Thark his head and one hand and he may yet conquer."

As he saw me enter, a grim smile touched those grim lips of his, but whether the smile signified relief or merely amusement at the sight of my own bloody and dishevelled condition I do not know.

As I was about to spring into the conflict with my sharp long-sword I felt a gentle hand upon my shoulder and turning found, to my sur-prise, that the young woman had followed me into the chamber.

"Wait," she whispered, "leave them to me," and pushing me ad-vanced, all defenceless and unarmed, upon the snarling banths.

When quite close to them she spoke a single Martian word in low but peremptory tones. Like lightning the great beasts wheeled upon her, and I looked to see her torn to pieces before I could reach her side, but instead the creatures slunk to her feet like puppies that ex-pect a merited whipping.

Again she spoke to them, but in tones so low I could not catch the words, and then she started toward the opposite side of the chamber with the six mighty monsters trailing at heel. One by one she sent them through the secret panel into the room beyond, and when the last had passed from the chamber where we stood in wide-eyed amazement she turned and smiled at us and then herself passed through, leaving us alone.

For a moment neither of us spoke. Then Tars Tarkas said:

"I heard the fighting beyond the partition through which you passed, but I did not fear for you, John Carter, until I heard the report of a revolver shot. I knew that there lived no man upon all Barsoom who could face you with naked steel and live, but the shot stripped the last vestige of hope from me, since you I knew to be without fire-arms. Tell me of it."

I did as he bade, and then together we sought the secret panel through which I had just entered the apartment—the one at the opposite end of the room from that through which the girl had led her savage companions.

To our disappointment the panel eluded our every effort to negotiate its secret lock. We felt that once beyond it we might look with some little hope of success for a passage to the outside world.

The fact that the prisoners within were securely chained led us to believe that surely there must be an avenue of escape from the terrible creatures which inhabited this unspeakable place.

Again and again we turned from one door to another, from the baffling golden panel at one end of the chamber to its mate at the other—equally baffling.

When we had about given up all hope one of the panels turned silently toward us, and the young woman who had led away the banths stood once more beside us.

"Who are you?" she asked, "and what your mission, that you have the temerity to attempt to escape from the Valley Dor and the death you have chosen?"

"I have chosen no death, maiden," I replied. "I am not a Barsoom, nor have I taken yet the voluntary pilgrimage upon the River Iss. My friend here is Jeddak of all the Tharks, and though he has not yet expressed a desire to return to the living world, I am taking him with me from the living lie that hath lured him to this frightful place.

"I am of another world. I am John Carter, Prince of the House of Tardos Mors, Jeddak of Helium. Perchance some faint rumour of me may have leaked within the confines of your hellish abode."

She smiled.

"Yes," she replied, "naught that passes in the world we have left is unknown here. I have heard of you, many years ago. The therns have ofttimes wondered whither you had flown, since you had neither taken the pilgrimage, nor could be found upon the face of Barsoom."

"Tell me," I said, "and who be you, and why a prisoner, yet with power over the ferocious beasts of the place that denotes familiarity and authority far beyond that which might be expected of a prisoner or a slave?"

"Slave I am," she answered. "For fifteen years a slave in this terrible place, and now that they have tired of me and become fearful of the power which my knowledge of their ways has given me I am but recently condemned to die the death."

She shuddered.

"What death?" I asked.

"The Holy Therns eat human flesh," she answered me; "but only that which has died beneath the sucking lips of a plant man—flesh from which the defiling blood of life has been drawn. And to this cruel end I have been condemned. It was to be within a few hours, had your advent not caused an interruption of their plans."

"Was it then Holy Therns who felt the weight of John Carter's hand?" I asked.

"Oh, no; those whom you laid low are lesser therns; but of the same cruel and hateful race. The Holy Therns abide upon the outer slopes of these grim hills, facing the broad world from which they harvest their victims and their spoils.

"Labyrinthine passages connect these caves with the luxurious palaces of the Holy Therns, and through them pass upon their many duties the lesser therns, and hordes of slaves, and prisoners, and fierce beasts; the grim inhabitants of this sunless world.

"There be within this vast network of winding passages and countless chambers men, women, and beasts who, born within its dim and gruesome underworld, have never seen the light of day—nor ever shall.

"They are kept to do the bidding of the race of therns; to furnish at once their sport and their sustenance.

"Now and again some hapless pilgrim, drifting out upon the silent sea from the cold Iss, escapes the plant men and the great white apes that guard the Temple of Issus and falls into the remorseless clutches of the therns; or, as was my misfortune, is coveted by the Holy Thern who chances to be upon watch in the balcony above the river where it issues from the bowels of the mountains through the cliffs of gold to empty into the Lost Sea of Korus.

"All who reach the Valley Dor are, by custom, the rightful prey of the plant men and the apes, while their arms and ornaments become the portion of the therns; but if one escapes the terrible denizens of the valley for even a few hours the therns may claim such a one as their own. And again the Holy Thern on watch, should he see a victim he covets, often tramples upon the rights of the unreasoning brutes of the valley and takes his prize by foul means if he cannot gain it by fair.

"It is said that occasionally some deluded victim of Barsoomian superstitition will so far escape the clutches of the countless enemies

that beset his path from the moment that he emerges from the subterranean passage through which the Iss flows for a thousand miles
before it enters the Valley Dor as to reach the very walls of the
Temple of Issus; but what fate awaits one there not even the Holy
Therns may guess, for who has passed within those gilded walls never
has returned to unfold the mysteries they have held since the beginning of time.

"The Temple of Issus is to the therns what the Valley Dor is
imagined by the peoples of the outer world to be to them; it is the
ultimate haven of peace, refuge, and happiness to which they pass
after this life and wherein an eternity of eternities is spent amidst the
delights of the flesh which appeal most strongly to this race of mental
giants and moral pygmies."

"The Temple of Issus is, I take it, a heaven within a heaven,"
I said. "Let us hope that there it will be meted to the therns as they
have meted it here unto others."

"Who knows?" the girl murmured.

"The therns, I judge from what you have said, are no less mortal
than we; and yet have I always heard them spoken of with the utmost awe and reverence by the people of Barsoom, as one might
speak of the gods themselves."

"The therns are mortal," she replied. "They die from the same
causes as you or I might: those who do not live their allotted span
of life, one thousand years, when by the authority of custom they
may take their way in happiness through the long tunnel that leads to
Issus.

"Those who die before are supposed to spend the balance of their
allotted time in the image of a plant man, and it is for this reason that
the plant men are held sacred by the therns, since they believe that
each of these hideous creatures was formerly a thern."

"And should a plant man die?" I asked.

"Should he die before the expiration of the thousand years from
the birth of the thern whose immortality abides within him then the
soul passes into a great white ape; but should the ape die short of the
exact hour that terminates the thousand years the soul is for ever lost
and passes for all eternity into the carcass of the slimy and fearsome
silian whose wriggling thousands seethe the silent sea beneath the
hurtling moons when the sun has gone and strange shapes walk
through the Valley Dor."

"We sent several Holy Therns to the silians to-day, then," said Tars Tarkas, laughing.

"And so will your death be the more terrible when it comes," said the maiden. "And come it will—you cannot escape."

"One has escaped, centuries ago," I reminded her, "and what has been done may be done again."

"It is useless even to try," she answered hopelessly.

"But try we shall," I cried, "and you shall go with us, if you wish."

"To be put to death by mine own people, and render my memory a disgrace to my family and my nation? A Prince of the House of Tardos Mors should know better than to suggest such a thing."

Tars Tarkas listened in silence, but I could feel his eyes riveted upon me and I knew that he awaited my answer as one might listen to the reading of his sentence by the foreman of a jury.

What I advised the girl to do would seal our fate as well, since if I bowed to the inevitable decree of age-old superstition we must all remain and meet our fate in some horrible form within this awful abode of horror and cruelty.

"We have the right to escape if we can," I answered. "Our own moral senses will not be offended if we succeed, for we know that the fabled life of love and peace in the blessed Valley of Dor is a rank and wicked deception. We know that the valley is not sacred; we know that the Holy Therns are not holy; that they are a race of cruel and heartless mortals, knowing no more of the real life to come than we do.

"Not only is it our right to bend every effort to escape—it is a solemn duty from which we should not shrink even though we know that we should be reviled and tortured by our own peoples when we returned to them.

"Only thus may we carry the truth to those without, and though the likelihood of our narrative being given credence is, I grant you, remote, so wedded are mortals to their stupid infatuation for impossible superstitions, we should be craven cowards indeed were we to shirk the plain duty which confronts us.

"Again there is a chance that with the weight of the testimony of several of us the truth of our statements may be accepted, and at least a compromise effected which will result in the dispatching of an expedition of investigation to this hideous mockery of heaven."

Both the girl and the green warrior stood silent in thought for some moments. The former it was who eventually broke the silence.

"Never had I considered the matter in that light before," she said. "Indeed would I give my life a thousand times if I could but save a single soul from the awful life that I have led in this cruel place. Yes, you are right, and I will go with you as far as we can go; but I doubt that we ever shall escape."

I turned an inquiring glance toward the Thark.

"To the gates of Issus, or to the bottom of Korus," spoke the green warrior; "to the snows to the north or to the snows to the south, Tars Tarkas follows where John Carter leads. I have spoken."

"Come, then," I cried, "we must make the start, for we could not be further from escape than we now are in the heart of this mountain and within the four walls of this chamber of death."

"Come, then," said the girl, "but do not flatter yourself that you can find no worse place than this within the territory of the therns."

So saying she swung the secret panel that separated us from the apartment in which I had found her, and we stepped through once more into the presence of the other prisoners.

There were in all ten red Martians, men and women, and when we had briefly explained our plan they decided to join forces with us, though it was evident that it was with some considerable misgivings that they thus tempted fate by opposing an ancient superstition, even though each knew through cruel experience the fallacy of its entire fabric.

Thuvia, the girl whom I had first freed, soon had the others at liberty. Tars Tarkas and I stripped the bodies of the two therns of their weapons, which included swords, daggers, and two revolvers of the curious and deadly type manufactured by the red Martians.

We distributed the weapons as far as they would go among our followers, giving the firearms to two of the women; Thuvia being one so armed.

With the latter as our guide we set off rapidly but cautiously through a maze of passages, crossing great chambers hewn from the solid metal of the cliff, following winding corridors, ascending steep inclines, and now and again concealing ourselves in dark recesses at the sound of approaching footsteps.

Our destination, Thuvia said, was a distant storeroom where arms and ammunition in plenty might be found. From there she was to lead us to the summit of the cliffs, from where it would require both wondrous wit and mighty fighting to win our way through the very heart of the stronghold of the Holy Therns to the world without.

"And even then, O Prince," she cried, "the arm of the Holy Thern is long. It reaches to every nation of Barsoom. His secret temples are hidden in the heart of every community. Wherever we go should we escape we shall find that word of our coming has preceded us, and death awaits us before we may pollute the air with our blasphemies."

We had proceeded for possibly an hour without serious interruption, and Thuvia had just whispered to me that we were approaching our first destination, when on entering a great chamber we came upon a man, evidently a thern.

He wore in addition to his leathern trappings and jewelled ornaments a great circlet of gold about his brow in the exact centre of which was set an immense stone, the exact counterpart of that which I had seen upon the breast of the little old man at the atmosphere plant nearly twenty years before.

It is the one priceless jewel of Barsoom. Only two are known to exist, and these were worn as the insignia of their rank and position by the two old men in whose charge was placed the operation of the great engines which pump the artificial atmosphere to all parts of Mars from the huge atmosphere plant, the secret to whose mighty portals placed in my possession the ability to save from immediate extinction the life of a whole world.

The stone worn by the thern who confronted us was of about the same size as that which I had seen before; an inch in diameter I should say. It scintillated nine different and distinct rays; the seven primary colours of our earthly prism and the two rays which are unknown upon Earth, but whose wondrous beauty is indescribable.

As the thern saw us his eyes narrowed to two nasty slits.

"Stop!" he cried. "What means this, Thuvia?"

For answer the girl raised her revolver and fired point-blank at him. Without a sound he sank to the earth, dead.

"Beast!" she hissed. "After all these years I am at last revenged."

Then as she turned toward me, evidently with a word of explanation on her lips, her eyes suddenly widened as they rested upon me, and with a little exclamation she started toward me.

"O Prince," she cried, "Fate is indeed kind to us. The way is still difficult, but through this vile thing upon the floor we may yet win to the outer world. Notest thou not the remarkable resemblance between this Holy Thern and thyself?"

The man was indeed of my precise stature, nor were his eyes and features unlike mine; but his hair was a mass of flowing yellow locks, like those of the two I had killed, while mine is black and close cropped.

"What of the resemblance?" I asked the girl Thuvia. "Do you wish me with my black, short hair to pose as a yellow-haired priest of this infernal cult?"

She smiled, and for answer approached the body of the man she had slain, and kneeling beside it removed the circlet of gold from the forehead, and then to my utter amazement lifted the entire scalp bodily from the corpse's head.

Rising, she advanced to my side and placing the yellow wig over my black hair, crowned me with the golden circlet set with the magnificent gem.

"Now don his harness, Prince," she said, "and you may pass where you will in the realms of the therns, for Sator Throg was a Holy Thern of the Tenth Cycle, and mighty among his kind."

As I stooped to the dead man to do her bidding I noted that not a hair grew upon his head, which was quite as bald as an egg.

"They are all thus from birth," explained Thuvia noting my surprise. "The race from which they sprang were crowned with a luxuriant growth of golden hair, but for many ages the present race has been entirely bald. The wig, however, has come to be a part of their apparel, and so important a part do they consider it that it is cause for the deepest disgrace were a thern to appear in public without it."

In another moment I stood barbed in the habiliments of a Holy Thern.

At Thuvia's suggestion two of the released prisoners bore the body of the dead thern upon their shoulders with us as we continued our journey toward the storeroom, which we reached without further mishap.

Here the keys which Thuvia bore from the dead thern of the prison vault were the means of giving us immediate entrance to the chamber, and very quickly we were thoroughly outfitted with arms and ammunition.

By this time I was so thoroughly fagged out that I could go no further, so I threw myself upon the floor, bidding Tars Tarkas to do likewise, and cautioning two of the released prisoners to keep careful watch.

In an instant I was asleep.

CORRIDORS OF PERIL

How LONG I slept upon the floor of the storeroom I do not know, but it must have been many hours.

I was awakened with a start by cries of alarm, and scarce were my eyes opened, nor had I yet sufficiently collected my wits to quite realize where I was, when a fusillade of shots rang out, reverberating through the subterranean corridors in a series of deafening echoes.

In an instant I was upon my feet. A dozen lesser therns confronted us from a large doorway at the opposite end of the storeroom from which we had entered. About me lay the bodies of my companions, with the exception of Thuvia and Tars Tarkas, who, like myself, had been asleep upon the floor and thus escaped the first raking fire.

As I gained my fet the therns lowered their wicked rifles, their faces distorted in mingled chagrin, consternation, and alarm.

Instantly I rose to the occasion.

"What means this?" I cried in tones of fierce anger. "Is Sator Throg to be murdered by his own vassals?"

"Have mercy, O Master of the Tenth Cycle!" cried one of the fellows, while the others edged toward the doorway as though to attempt a surreptitious escape from the presence of the mighty one.

"Ask them their mission here," whispered Thuvia at my elbow.

"What do you here, fellows?" I cried.

"Two from the outer world are at large within the dominions of the therns. We sought them at the command of the Father of Therns. One was white with black hair, the other a huge green warrior," and here the fellow cast a suspicious glance toward Tars Tarkas.

"Here, then, is one of them," spoke Thuvia, indicating the Thark, "and if you will look upon this dead man by the door perhaps you will recognize the other. It was left for Sator Throg and his poor slaves to accomplish what the lesser therns of the guard were unable to do—we have killed one and captured the other; for this had Sator Throg given us our liberty. And now in your stupidity have you come and killed all but myself, and like to have killed the mighty Sator Throg himself."

The men looked very sheepish and very scared.

"Had they not better throw these bodies to the plant men and then return to their quarters, O Mighty One?" asked Thuvia of me.

"Yes; do as Thuvia bids you," I said.

As the men picked up the bodies I noticed that the one who stooped to gather up the late Sator Throg started as his closer scrutiny fell upon the upturned face, and then the fellow stole a furtive, sneaking glance in my direction from the corner of his eye.

That he suspicioned something of the truth I could have sworn; but that it was only a suspicion which he did not dare voice was evidence by his silence.

Again, as he bore the body from the room, he shot a quick but searching glance toward me, and then his eyes fell once more upon the bald and shiny dome of the dead man in his arms. The last fleeting glimpse that I obtained of his profile as he passed from my sight without the chamber revealed a cunning smile of triumph upon his lips.

Only Tars Tarkas, Thuvia, and I were left. The fatal marksmanship of the therns had snatched from our companions whatever slender chance they had of gaining the perilous freedom of the world without.

So soon as the last of the gruesome procession had disappeared the girl urged us to take up our flight once more.

She, too, had noted the questioning attitude of the thern who had borne Sator Throg away.

"It bodes no good for us, O Prince," she said. "For even though this fellow dared not chance accusing you in error, there be those above with power sufficient to demand a closer scrutiny, and that, Prince, would indeed prove fatal."

I shrugged my shoulders. It seemed that in any event the outcome of our plight must end in death. I was refreshed from my sleep, but still weak from loss of blood. My wounds were painful. No medicinal aid seemed possible. How I longed for the almost miraculous healing power of the strange salves and lotions of the green Martian women. In an hour they would have had me as new.

I was discouraged. Never had a feeling of such utter hopelessness come over me in the face of danger. Then the long flowing, yellow locks of the Holy Thern, caught by some vagrant draught, blew about my face.

Might they not still open the way of freedom? If we acted in time, might we not even yet escape before the general alarm was sounded? We could at least try.

"What will the fellow do first, Thuvia?" I asked. "How long will it be before they may return for us?"

"He will go directly to the Father of Therns, old Matai Shang. He may have to wait for an audience, but since he is very high among the lesser therns, in fact as a thorian among them, it will not be long that Matai Shang will keep him waiting.

"Then if the Father of Therns puts credence in his story, another hour will see the galleries and chambers, the courts and gardens, filled with searchers."

"What we do then must be done within an hour. What is the best way, Thuvia, the shortest way out of this celestial Hades?"

"Straight to the top of the cliffs, Prince," she replied, "and then through the gardens to the inner courts. From there our way will lie within the temples of the therns and across them to the outer court. Then the ramparts—O Prince, it is hopeless. Ten thousand warriors could not hew a way to liberty from out this awful place.

"Since the beginning of time, little by little, stone by stone, have the therns been ever adding to the defences of their stronghold. A continuous line of impregnable fortifications circles the outer slopes of the Mountains of Otz.

"Within the temples that lie behind the ramparts a million fighting-men are ever ready. The courts and gardens are filled with slaves, with women and with children.

"None could go a stone's throw without detection."

"If there is no other way, Thuvia, why dwell upon the difficulties of this. We must face them."

"Can we not better make the attempt after dark?" asked Tars Tarkas. "There would seem to be no chance by day."

"There would be a little better chance by night, but even then the ramparts are well guarded; possibly better than by day. There are fewer abroad in the courts and gardens, though," said Thuvia.

"What is the hour?" I asked.

"It was midnight when you released me from my chains," said Thuvia. "Two hours later we reached the storeroom. There you slept for fourteen hours. It must now be nearly sundown again. Come, we will go to some nearby window in the cliff and make sure."

So saying, she led the way through winding corridors until at a sudden turn we came upon an opening which overlooked the Valley Dor.

At our right the sun was setting, a huge red orb, below the western range of Otz. A little below us stood the Holy Thern on watch upon his balcony. His scarlet robe of office was pulled tightly about him in anticipation of the cold that comes so suddenly with darkness as the sun sets. So rare is the atmosphere of Mars that it absorbs very little heat from the sun. During the daylight hours it is always extremely hot; at night it is intensely cold. Nor does the thin atmosphere refract the sun's rays or diffuse its light as upon Earth. There is no twilight on Mars. When the great orb of day disappears beneath the horizon the effect is precisely as that of the extinguishing of a single lamp within a chamber. From brilliant light you are plunged without warning into utter darkness. Then the moons come; the mysterious, magic moons of Mars, hurtling like monster meteors low across the face of the planet.

The declining sun lighted brilliantly the eastern banks of Korus, the crimson sward, the gorgeous forest. Beneath the trees we saw feeding many herds of plant men. The adults stood aloft upon their toes and their mighty tails, their talons pruning every available leaf and twig. It was then that I understood the careful trimming of the trees which had led me to form the mistaken idea when first I opened my eyes upon the grove that it was the playground of a civilized people.

As we watched, our eyes wandered to the rolling Iss, which issued from the base of the cliffs beneath us. Presently there emerged from the mountain a canoe laden with lost souls from the outer world. There were a dozen of them. All were of the highly civilized and cultured race of red men who are dominant on Mars.

The eyes of the herald upon the balcony beneath us fell upon the doomed party as soon as did ours. He raised his head and, leaning far out over the low rail that rimmed his dizzy perch, voiced the shrill, weird wail that called the demons of this hellish place to the attack.

For an instant the brutes stood with stiffly erected ears, then they poured from the grove toward the river's bank, covering the distance with great, ungainly leaps.

The party had landed and was standing on the sward as the awful horde came in sight. There was a brief and futile effort of defence. Then silence as the huge, repulsive shapes covered the bodies of their victims and scores of sucking mouths fastened themselves to the flesh of their prey.

I turned away in disgust.

"Their part is soon over," said Thuvia. "The great white apes get the flesh when the plant men have drained the arteries. Look, they are coming now."

As I turned my eyes in the direction the girl indicated, I saw a dozen of the great white monsters running across the valley toward the river bank. Then the sun went down and darkness that could almost be felt engulfed us.

Thuvia lost no time in leading us toward the corridor which winds back and forth up through the cliffs toward the surface thousands of feet above the level on which we had been.

Twice great banths, wandering loose through the galleries, blocked our progress, but in each instance Thuvia spoke a low word of command and the snarling beasts slunk sullenly away.

"If you can dissolve all our obstacles as easily as you master these fierce brutes I can see no difficulties in our way," I said to the girl, smiling. "How do you do it?"

She laughed, and then shuddered.

"I do not quite know," she said. "When first I came here I angered Sator Throg, because I repulsed him. He ordered me to be thrown into one of the great pits in the inner gardens. It was filled with banths. In my own country I had been accustomed to command. Something in my voice, I do not know what, cowed the beasts as they sprang to attack me.

"Instead of tearing me to pieces, as Sator Throg had desired, they fawned at my feet. So greatly were Sator Throg and his friends amused by the sight that they kept me to train and handle the terrible creatures. I know them all by name. There are many of them wandering through these lower regions. They are the scavengers. Many prisoners die here in their chains. The banths solve the problem of sanitation, at least in this respect.

"In the gardens and temples above they are kept in pits. The therns fear them. It is because of the banths that they seldom venture below ground except as their duties call them."

An idea occurred to me, suggested by what Thuvia had just said.

"Why not take a number of banths and set them loose before us above ground?" I asked.

Thuvia laughed.

"It would distract attention from us, I am sure," she said.

She commenced calling in a low singsong voice that was half purr. She continued this as we wound our tedious way through the maze of subterranean passages and chambers.

Presently soft, padded feet sounded close behind us, and as I turned I saw a pair of great, green eyes shining in the dark shadows at our rear. From a diverging tunnel a sinuous, tawny form crept stealthily toward us.

Low growls and angry snarls assailed our ears on every side as we hastened on and one by one the ferocious creatures answered the call of their mistress.

She spoke a word to each as it joined us. Like well-schooled terriers, they paced the corridors with us, but I could not help but note the lathering jowls, nor the hungry expressions with which they eyed Tars Tarkas and myself.

Soon we were entirely surrounded by some fifty of the brutes. Two walked close on either side of Thuvia, as guards might walk. The sleek sides of others now and then touched my own naked limbs. It was a strange experience; the almost noiseless passage of naked human feet and padded paws; the golden walls splashed with precious stones; the dim light cast by the tiny radium bulbs set at considerable distances along the roof; the huge, maned beasts of prey crowding with low growls about us; the mighty green warrior towering high above us all; myself crowned with the priceless diadem of a Holy Thern; and leading the procession the beautiful girl, Thuvia.

I shall not soon forget it.

Presently we approached a great chamber more brightly lighted than the corridors. Thuvia halted us. Quietly she stole toward the entrance and glanced within. Then she motioned us to follow her.

The room was filled with specimens of the strange beings that inhabit this underworld; a heterogeneous collection of hybrids—the offspring of the prisoners from the outside world; red and green Martians and the white race of therns.

Constant confinement below ground had wrought odd freaks upon their skins. They more resemble corpses than living beings. Many are deformed, others maimed, while the majority, Thuvia explained, are sightless.

As they lay sprawled about the floor, sometimes overlapping one another, again in heaps of several bodies, they suggested instantly to me the grotesque illustrations that I had seen in copies of Dante's

Inferno, and what more fitting comparison? Was this not indeed a veritable hell, peopled by lost souls, dead and damned beyond all hope?

Picking our way carefully we threaded a winding path across the chamber, the great banths sniffing hungrily at the tempting prey spread before them in such tantalizing and defenceless profusion.

Several times we passed the entrances to other chambers similarly peopled, and twice again we were compelled to cross directly through them. In others were chained prisoners and beasts.

"Why is it that we see no therns?" I asked of Thuvia.

"They seldom traverse the underworld at night, for then it is that the great banths prowl the dim corridors seeking their prey. The therns fear the awful denizens of this cruel and hopeless world that they have fostered and allowed to grow beneath their feet. The prisoners even sometimes turn upon them and rend them. The thern can never tell from what dark shadow an assassin may spring upon his back.

"By day it is different. Then the corridors and chambers are filled with guards passing to and fro; slaves from the temples above come by hundreds to the granaries and storerooms. All is life then. You did not see it because I led you not in the beaten tracks, but through roundabout passages seldom used. Yet it is possible that we may meet a thern even yet. They do occasionally find it necessary to come here after the sun has set. Because of this I have moved with such great caution."

But we reached the upper galleries without detection and presently Thuvia halted us at the foot of a short, steep ascent.

"Above us," she said, "is a doorway which opens on to the inner gardens. I have brought you thus far. From here on for four miles to the outer ramparts our way will be beset by countless dangers. Guards patrol the courts, the temples, the gardens. Every inch of the ramparts themselves is beneath the eye of a sentry."

I could not understand the necessity for such an enormous force of armed men about a spot so surrounded by mystery and superstition that not a soul upon Barsoom would have dared to approach it even had they known its exact location. I questioned Thuvia, asking her what enemies the therns could fear in their impregnable fortress.

We had reached the doorway now and Thuvia was opening it.

"They fear the black pirates of Barsoom, O Prince," she said, "from whom may our first ancestors preserve us."

The door swung open; the smell of growing things greeted my nostrils; the cool night air blew against my cheek. The great banths sniffed the unfamiliar odours, and then with a rush they broke past us with low growls, swarming across the gardens beneath the lurid light of the nearer moon.

Suddenly a great cry arose from the roofs of the temples; a cry of alarm and warning that, taken up from the point to point, ran off to the east and to the west, from temple, court, and rampart, until it sounded as a dim echo in the distance.

The great Thark's long-sword leaped from its scabbard; Thuvia shrank shuddering to my side.

THE BLACK PIRATES OF BARSOOM

"WHAT IS IT?" I asked of the girl.

For answer she pointed to the sky.

I looked, and there, above us, I saw shadowy bodies flitting hither and thither high over temple, court, and garden.

Almost immediately flashes of light broke from these strange objects. There was a roar of musketry, and then answering flashes and roars from temple and rampart.

"The black pirates of Barsoom, O Prince," said Thuvia.

In great circles the air craft of the marauders swept lower and lower toward the defending forces of the therns.

Volley after volley they vomited upon the temple guards; volley on volley crashed through the thin air toward the fleeting and illusive fliers.

As the pirates swooped closer toward the ground, thern soldiery poured from the temples into the gardens and courts. The sight of them in the open brought a score of fliers darting toward us from all directions.

The therns fired upon them through shields affixed to their rifles, but on, steadily on, came the grim, black craft. They were small fliers for the most part, built for two to three men. A few larger ones there were, but these kept high aloft dropping bombs upon the temples from their keel batteries.

At length, with a concerted rush, evidently in response to a signal of command, the pirates in our immediate vicinity dashed recklessly to the ground in the very midst of the thern soldiery.

Scarcely waiting for their craft to touch, the creatures manning them leaped among the therns with the fury of demons. Such fighting! Never had I witnessed its like before. I had thought the green Martians the most ferocious warriors in the universe, but the awful abandon with which the black pirates threw themselves upon their foes transcended everything I ever before had seen.

Beneath the brilliant light of Mars' two glorious moons the whole scene presented itself in vivid distinctness. The golden-haired, white-skinned therns battling with desperate courage in hand-to-hand conflict with their ebony-skinned foemen.

Here a little knot of struggling warriors trampled a bed of gorgeous pimalia; there the curved sword of a black man found the heart of a thern and left its dead foeman at the foot of a wondrous statue carved from a living ruby; yonder a dozen therns pressed a single pirate back upon a bench of emerald, upon whose iridescent surface a strangely beautiful Barsoomian design was traced out in inlaid diamonds.

A little to one side stood Thuvia, the Thark, and I. The tide of battle had not reached us, but the fighters from time to time swung close enough that we might distinctly note them.

The black pirates interested me immensely. I had heard vague rumours, little more than legends they were, during my former life on Mars; but never had I seen them, nor talked with one who had.

They were popularly supposed to inhabit the lesser moon, from which they descended upon Barsoom at long intervals. Where they visited they wrought the most horrible atrocities, and when they left carried away with them firearms and ammunition, and young girls as prisoners. These latter, the rumour had it, they sacrificed to some terrible god in an orgy which ended in the eating of their victims.

I had an excellent opportunity to examine them, as the strife occasionally brought now one and now another close to where I stood. They were large men, possibly six feet and over in height. Their features were clear cut and handsome in the extreme; their eyes were well set and large, though a slight narrowness lent them a crafty appearance; the iris, as well as I could determine by moonlight, was of extreme blackness, while the eyeball itself was quite white and clear. The physical structure of their bodies seemed identical with those of the therns, the red men, and my own. Only in the colour of their skin did they differ materially from us; that is of the appearance of polished ebony, and odd as it may seem for a Southerner to say it, adds to rather than detracts from their marvellous beauty.

But if their bodies are divine, their hearts, apparently, are quite the reverse. Never did I witness such a malign lust for blood as these demons of the outer air evinced in their mad battle with the therns.

All about us in the garden lay their sinister craft, which the therns for some reason, then unaccountable to me, made no effort to injure. Now and again a black warrior would rush from a near by temple bearing a young woman in his arms. Straight for his flier he would leap while those of his comrades who fought near by would rush to cover his escape.

The therns on their side would hasten to rescue the girl, and in an instant the two would be swallowed in the vortex of a maelstrom of yelling devils, hacking and hewing at one another, like fiends incarnate.

But always, it seemed, were the black pirates of Barsoom victorious, and the girl, brought miraculously unharmed through the conflict, borne away into the outer darkness upon the deck of a swift flier.

Fighting similar to that which surrounded us could be heard in both directions as far as sound carried, and Thuvia told me that the attacks of the black pirates were usually made simultaneously along the entire ribbon-like domain of the therns, which circles the Valley Dor on the outer slopes of the Mountains of Otz.

As the fighting receded from our position for a moment, Thuvia turned toward me with a question.

"Do you understand now, O Prince," she said, "why a million warriors guard the domains of the Holy Therns by day and by night?

"The scene you are witnessing now is but a repetition of what I have seen enacted a score of times during the fifteen years I have been a prisoner here. From time immemorial the black pirates of Barsoom have preyed upon the Holy Therns.

"Yet they never carry their expeditions to a point, as one might readily believe it was in their power to do, where the extermination of the race of therns is threatened. It is as though they but utilized the race as playthings, with which they satisfy their ferocious lust for fighting; and from whom they collect toll in arms and ammunition and in prisoners."

"Why don't they jump in and destroy these fliers?" I asked. "That would soon put a stop to the attacks, or at least the blacks would scarce be so bold. Why, see how perfectly unguarded they leave their craft, as though they were lying safe in their own hangars at home."

"The therns do not dare. They tried it once, ages ago, but the next night and for a whole moon thereafter a thousand great black battleships circled the Mountains of Otz, pouring tons of projectiles upon the temples, the gardens, and the courts, until every thern who was not killed was driven for safety into the subterranean galleries.

"The therns know that they live at all only by the sufferance of the black men. They were near to extermination that once and they will not venture risking it again."

As she ceased talking a new element was instilled into the conflict. It came from a source equally unlooked for by either thern or pirate. The great banths which we had liberated in the garden had evidently been awed at first by the sound of the battle, the yelling of the warriors and the loud report of rifle and bomb.

But now they must have become angered by the continuous noise and excited by the smell of new blood, for all of a sudden a great form shot from a clump of low shrubbery into the midst of a struggling mass of humanity. A horrid scream of bestial rage broke from the banth as he felt warm flesh beneath his powerful talons.

As though his cry was but a signal to the others, the entire great pack hurled themselves among the fighters. Panic reigned in an instant. Thern and black man turned alike against the common enemy, for the banths showed no partiality toward either.

The awful beasts bore down a hundred men by the mere weight of their great bodies as they hurled themselves into the thick of the fight. Leaping and clawing, they mowed down the warriors with their powerful paws, turning for an instant to rend their victims with frightful fangs.

The scene was fascinating in its terribleness, but suddenly it came to me that we were wasting valuable time watching this conflict, which in itself might prove a means of our escape.

The therns were so engaged with their terrible assailants that

now, if ever, escape should be comparatively easy. I turned to search
for an opening through the contending hordes. If we could but reach
the ramparts we might find that the pirates somewhere had thinned
the guarding forces and left a way open to us to the world without.

As my eyes wandered about the garden, the sight of the hundreds
of air craft lying unguarded around us suggested the simplest avenue
to freedom. Why had it not occurred to me before! I was thoroughly
familiar with the mechanism of every known make of flier on Barsoom.
For nine years I had sailed and fought with the navy of Helium. I
had raced through space on the tiny one-man air scout and I had commanded the greatest battleship that ever had floated in the thin air of
dying Mars.

To think, with me, is to act. Grasping Thuvia by the arm, I whispered to Tars Tarkas to follow me. Quickly we glided toward a small
flier which lay furthest from the battling warriors. Another instant
found us huddled on the tiny deck. My hand was on the starting
lever. I pressed my thumb upon the button which controls the ray of
repulsion, that splendid discovery of the Martians which permits
them to navigate the thin atmosphere of their planet in huge ships
that dwarf the dreadnoughts of our earthly navies into pitiful insignificance.

The craft swayed slightly but she did not move. Then a new cry
of warning broke upon our ears. Turning, I saw a dozen black pirates
dashing toward us from the mélée. We had been discovered. With
shrieks of rage the demons sprang for us. With frenzied insistence
I continued to press the little button which should have sent us racing
out into space, but still the vessel refused to budge. Then it came
to me—the reason that she would not rise.

We had stumbled upon a two-man flier. Its ray tanks were charged
only with sufficient repulsive energy to lift two ordinary men. The
Thark's great weight was anchoring us to our doom.

The blacks were nearly upon us. There was not an instant to be
lost in hesitation or doubt.

I pressed the button far in and locked it. Then I set the lever at
high speed and as the blacks came yelling upon us I slipped from the
craft's deck and with drawn long-sword met the attack.

At the same moment a girl's shriek rang out behind me and an
instant later, as the blacks fell upon me, I heard far above my head,
and faintly, in Thuvia's voice: "My Prince, O my Prince; I would

rather remain and die with—" But the rest was lost in the noise of my assailants.

I knew though that my ruse had worked and that temporarily at least Thuvia and Tars Tarkas were safe, and the means of escape was theirs.

For a moment it seemed that I could not withstand the weight of numbers that confronted me, but again, as on so many other occasions when I had been called upon to face fearful odds upon this planet of warriors and fierce beasts, I found that my earthly strength so far transcended that of my opponents that the odds were not so greatly against me as they appeared.

My seething blade wove a net of death about me. For an instant the blacks pressed close to reach me with their shorter swords, but presently they gave back, and the esteem in which they suddenly had learned to hold my sword arm was writ large upon each countenance.

I knew though that it was but a question of minutes before their greater numbers would wear me down, or get around my guard. I must go down eventually to certain death before them. I shuddered at the thought of it, dying thus in this terrible place where no word of my end ever could reach my Dejah Thoris. Dying at the hands of nameless black men in the gardens of the cruel therns.

Then my old-time spirit reasserted itself. The fighting blood of my Virginian sires coursed hot through my veins. The fierce blood lust and the joy of battle surged over me. The fighting smile that has brought consternation to a thousand foemen touched my lips. I put the thought of death out of my mind, and fell upon my antagonists with fury that those who escaped will remember to their dying day.

That others would press to the support of those who faced me I knew, so even as I fought I kept my wits at work, searching for an avenue of escape.

It came from an unexpected quarter out of the black night behind me. I had just disarmed a huge fellow who had given me a desperate struggle, and for a moment the blacks stood back for a breathing spell.

They eyed me with malignant fury, yet withal there was a touch of respect in their demeanour.

"Thern," said one, "you fight like a Dator. But for your detestable yellow hair and your white skin you would be an honour to the First Born of Barsoom."

"I am no thern," I said, and was about to explain that I was from another world, thinking that by patching a truce with these fellows and fighting with them against the therns I might enlist their aid in regaining my liberty. But just at that moment a heavy object smote me a resounding whack between my shoulders that nearly felled me to the ground.

As I turned to meet this new enemy an object passed over my shoulder, striking one of my assailants squarely in the face and knocking him senseless to the sward. At the same instant I saw that the thing that had struck us was the trailing anchor of a rather fair-sized air vessel; possibly a ten-man cruiser.

The ship was floating slowly above us, not more than fifty feet over our heads. Instantly the one chance for escape that it offered presented itself to me. The vessel was slowly rising and now the anchor was beyond the blacks who faced me and several feet above their heads.

With a bound that left them gaping in wide-eyed astonishment I sprang completely over them. A second leap carried me just high enough to grasp the now rapidly receding anchor.

But I was successful, and there I hung by one hand, dragging through the branches of the higher vegetation of the gardens, while my late foemen shrieked and howled beneath me.

Presently the vessel veered toward the west and then swung gracefully to the south. In another instant I was carried beyond the crest of the Golden Cliffs, out over the Valley Dor, where, six thousand feet below me, the Lost Sea of Korus lay shimmering in the moonlight.

Carefully I climbed to a sitting posture across the anchor's arms. I wondered if by chance the vessel might be deserted. I hoped so. Or possibly it might belong to a friendly people, and have wandered by accident almost within the clutches of the pirates and the therns. The fact that it was retreating from the scene of battle lent colour to this hypothesis.

But I decided to know positively, and at once, so, with the greatest caution, I commenced to climb slowly up the anchor chain toward the deck above me.

One hand had just reached for the vessel's rail and found it when a fierce black face was thrust over the side and eyes filled with triumphant hate looked into mine.

A FAIR GODDESS

FOR AN INSTANT the black pirate and I remained motionless, glaring into each other's eyes. Then a grim smile curled the handsome lips above me, as an ebony hand came slowly in sight from above the edge of the deck and the cold, hollow eye of a revolver sought the centre of my forehead.

Simultaneously my free hand shot out for the black throat, just within reach, and the ebony finger tightened on the trigger. The pirate's hissing, "Die, cursed thern," was half choked in his windpipe by my clutching fingers. The hammer fell with a futile click upon an empty chamber.

Before he could fire again I had pulled him so far over the edge of the deck that he was forced to drop his firearm and clutch the rail with both hands.

My grasp upon his throat effectually prevented any outcry, and so we struggled in grim silence; he to tear away from my hold, I to drag him over to his death.

His face was taking on a livid hue, his eyes were bulging from their sockets. It was evident to him that he soon must die unless he tore loose from the steel fingers that were choking the life from him. With a final effort he threw himself further back upon the deck, at the same instant releasing his hold upon the rail to tear frantically with both hands at my fingers in an effort to drag them from his throat.

That little second was all that I awaited. With one mighty downward surge I swept him clear of the deck. His falling body came near to tearing me from the frail hold that my single free hand had upon the anchor chain and plunging me with him to the waters of the sea below.

I did not relinquish my grasp upon him, however, for I knew that a single shriek from those lips as he hurtled to his death in the silent waters of the sea would bring his comrades from above to avenge him.

Instead I held grimly to him, choking, ever choking, while his frantic struggles dragged me lower and lower toward the end of the chain.

Gradually his contortions became spasmodic, lessening by degrees until they ceased entirely. Then I released my hold upon him and in an instant he was swallowed by the black shadows far below.

Again I climbed to the ship's rail. This time I succeeded in raising my eyes to the level of the deck, where I could take a careful survey of the conditions immediately confronting me.

The nearer moon had passed below the horizon, but the clear effulgence of the further satellite bathed the deck of the cruiser, bringing into sharp relief the bodies of six or eight black men sprawled about in sleep.

Huddled close to the base of a rapid fire gun was a young white girl, securely bound. Her eyes were widespread in an expression of horrified anticipation and fixed directly upon me as I came in sight above the edge of the deck.

Unutterable relief instantly filled them as they fell upon the mystic jewel which sparkled in the centre of my stolen headpiece. She did not speak. Instead her eyes warned me to beware the sleeping figures that surrounded her.

Noiselessly I gained the deck. The girl nodded to me to approach her. As I bent low she whispered to me to release her.

"I can aid you," she said, "and you will need all the aid available when they awaken."

"Some of them will awake in Korus," I replied smiling.

She caught the meaning of my words, and the cruelty of her answering smile horrified me. One is not astonished by cruelty in a hideous face, but when it touches the features of a goddess whose fine-chiselled lineaments might more fittingly portray love and beauty, the contrast is appalling.

Quickly I released her.

"Give me a revolver," she whispered. "I can use that upon those your sword does not silence in time."

I did as she bid. Then I turned toward the distasteful work that lay before me. This was no time for fine compunctions, nor for a chivalry that these cruel demons would neither appreciate nor reciprocate.

Stealthily I approached the nearest sleeper. When he awoke he was well on his journey to the bosom of Korus. His piercing shriek as consciousness returned to him came faintly up to us from the black depths beneath.

The second awoke as I touched him, and, though I succeeded in hurling him from the cruiser's deck, his wild cry of alarm brought the remaining pirates to their feet. There were five of them.

As they arose the girl's revolver spoke in sharp staccato and one sank back to the deck again to rise no more.

The others rushed madly upon me with drawn swords. The girl evidently dared not fire for fear of wounding me, but I saw her sneak stealthily and cat-like toward the flank of the attackers. Then they were on me.

For a few minutes I experienced some of the hottest fighting I had ever passed through. The quarters were too small for foot work. It was stand your ground and give and take. At first I took considerably more than I gave, but presently I got beneath one fellow's guard and had the satisfaction of seeing him collapse upon the deck.

The others redoubled their efforts. The crashing of their blades upon mine raised a terrific din that might have been heard for miles through the silent night. Sparks flew as steel smote steel, and then there was the dull and sickening sound of a shoulder bone parting beneath the keen edge of my Martian sword.

Three now faced me, but the girl was working her way to a point that would soon permit her to reduce the number by one at least. Then things happened with such amazing rapidity that I can scarce comprehend even now all that took place in that brief instant.

The three rushed me with the evident purpose of forcing me back the few steps that would carry my body over the rail into the void below. At the same instant the girl fired and my sword arm made two moves. One man dropped with a bullet in his brain; a sword flew clattering across the deck and dropped over the edge beyond as I disarmed one of my opponents and the third went down with my blade buried to the hilt in his breast and three feet of it protruding from his back, and falling wrenched the sword from my grasp.

Disarmed myself, I now faced my remaining foeman, whose own sword lay somewhere thousands of feet below us, lost in the Lost Sea.

The new conditions seemed to please my adversary, for a smile of satisfaction bared his gleaming teeth as he rushed at me bare-handed. The great muscles which rolled beneath his glossy black hide evidently assured him that here was easy prey, not worth the trouble of drawing the dagger from his harness.

I let him come almost upon me. Then I ducked beneath his outstretched arms, at the same time sidestepping to the right. Pivoting on my left toe, I swung a terrific right to his jaw, and, like a felled ox, he dropped in his tracks.

A low, silvery laugh rang out behind me.

"You are no thern," said the sweet voice of my companion, "for all your golden locks or the harness of Sator Throg. Never lived there upon all Barsoom before one who could fight as you have fought this night. Who are you?"

"I am John Carter, Prince of the House of Tardos Mors, Jeddak of Helium," I replied. "And whom," I added, "has the honour of serving been accorded me?"

She hesitated a moment before speaking. Then she asked:

"You are no thern. Are you an enemy of the therns?"

"I have been in the territory of the therns for a day and a half. During that entire time my life has been in constant danger. I have been harassed and persecuted. Armed men and fierce beasts have been set upon me. I had no quarrel with the therns before, but can you wonder that I feel no great love for them now? I have spoken."

She looked at me intently for several minutes before she replied. It was as though she were attempting to read my inmost soul, to judge my character and my standards of chivalry in that long-drawn, searching gaze.

Apparently the inventory satisfied her.

"I am Phaidor, daughter of Matai Shang, Holy Hekkador of the Holy Therns, Father of Therns, Master of Life and Death upon Barsoom, Brother of Issus, Princess of Life Eternal."

At that moment I noticed that the black I had dropped with my fist was commencing to show signs of returning consciousness. I sprang to his side. Stripping his harness from him I securely bound his hands behind his back, and after similarly fastening his feet tied him to a heavy gun carriage.

"Why not the simpler way?" asked Phaidor.

"I do not understand. What 'simpler way'?" I replied.

With a slight shrug of her lovely shoulders she made a gesture with her hands personating the casting of something over the craft's side.

"I am no murderer," I said. "I kill in self-defence only."

She looked at me narrowly. Then she puckered those divine brows of hers, and shook her head. She could not comprehend.

Well, neither had my own Dejah Thoris been able to understand what to her had seemed a foolish and dangerous policy toward enemies. Upon Barsoom, quarter is neither asked nor given, and each dead man means so much more of the waning resources of this dying planet to be divided amongst those who survive.

But there seemed a subtle difference here between the manner in which this girl contemplated the dispatching of an emeny and the tender-hearted regret of my own princess for the stern necessity which demanded it.

I think that Phaidor regretted the thrill that the spectacle would have afforded her rather than the fact that my decision left another enemy alive to threaten us.

The man had now regained full possession of his faculties, and was regarding us intently from where he lay bound upon the deck. He was a handsome fellow, clean limbed and powerful, with an intelligent face and features of such exquisite chiselling that Adonis himself might have envied him.

The vessel, unguided, had been moving slowly across the valley; but now I thought it time to take the helm and direct her course. Only in a very general way could I guess the location of the Valley Dor. That it was far south of the equator was evident from the constellations, but I was not sufficiently a Martian astronomer to come much closer than a rough guess without the splendid charts and delicate instruments with which, as an officer of the Heliumite Navy, I had formerly reckoned the positions of the vessels on which I sailed.

That a northerly course would quickest lead me toward the more settled portions of the planet immediately decided the direction that I should steer. Beneath my hand the cruiser swung gracefully about. Then the button which controlled the repulsive rays sent us soaring far out into space. With speed lever pulled to the last notch, we raced toward the north as we rose ever farther and farther above that terrible valley of death.

As we passed at a dizzy height over the narrow domains of the therns the flash of powder far below bore mute witness to the ferocity of the battle that still raged along that cruel frontier. No sound of conflict reached our ears, for in the rarefied atmosphere of our great altitude no sound wave could penetrate; they were dissipated in thin air far below us.

It became intensely cold. Breathing was difficult. The girl, Phaidor, and the black pirate kept their eyes glued upon me. At length the girl spoke.

"Unconsciousness comes quickly at this altitude," she said quietly. "Unless you are inviting death for us all you had best drop, and that quickly."

There was no fear in her voice. It was as one might say: "You had better carry an umbrella. It is going to rain."

I dropped the vessel quickly to a lower level. Nor was I a moment too soon. The girl had swooned.

The black, too, was unconscious, while I, myself, retained my senses, I think, only by sheer will. The one on whom all responsibility rests is apt to endure the most.

We were swinging along low above the foothills of the Otz. It was comparatively warm and there was plenty of air for our starved lungs, so I was not surprised to see the black open his eyes, and a moment later the girl also.

"It was a close call," she said.

"It has taught me two things though," I replied.

"What?"

"That even Phaidor, daughter of the Master of Life and Death, is mortal," I said smiling.

"There is immortality only in Issus," she replied. "And Issus is for the race of therns alone. Thus am I immortal."

I caught a fleeting grin passing across the features of the black as he heard her words. I did not then understand why he smiled. Later I was to learn, and she, too, in a most horrible manner.

"If the other thing you have just learned," she continued, "has led to as erroneous deductions as the first you are little richer in knowledge than you were before."

"The other," I replied, "is that our dusky friend here does not hail from the nearer moon—he was like to have died at a few thousand feet above Barsoom. Had we continued the five thousand miles that lie between Thuria and the planet he would have been but the frozen memory of a man."

Phaidor looked at the black in evident astonishment.

"If you are not of Thuria, then where?" she asked.

He shrugged his shoulders and turned his eyes elsewhere, but did not reply.

The girl stamped her little foot in a peremptory manner.

"The daughter of Matai Shang is not accustomed to having her queries remain unanswered," she said. "One of the lesser breed should feel honoured that a member of the holy race that was born to inherit life eternal should deign even to notice him."

Again the black smiled that wicked, knowing smile.

"Xodar, Dator of the First Born of Barsoom, is accustomed to give commands, not to receive them," replied the black pirate. Then, turning to me, "What are your intentions concerning me?"

"I intend taking you both back to Helium," I said. "No harm will come to you. You will find the red men of Helium a kindly and magnanimous race, but if they listen to me there will be no more voluntary pilgrimages down the river Iss, and the impossible belief that they have cherished for ages will be shattered into a thousand pieces."

"Are you of Helium?" he asked.

"I am a Prince of the House of Tardos Mors, Jeddak of Helium," I replied, "but I am not of Barsoom. I am of another world."

Xodar looked at me intently for a few moments.

"I can well believe that you are not of Barsoom," he said at length. "None of this world could have bested eight of the First Born single-handed. But how is it that you wear the golden hair and the jewelled circlet of a Holy Thern?" He emphasized the word holy with a touch of irony.

"I had forgotten them," I said. "They are the spoils of conquest," and with a sweep of my hand I removed the disguise from my head.

When the black's eyes fell on my close-cropped black hair they opened in astonishment. Evidently he had looked for the bald pate of a thern.

"You are indeed of another world," he said, a touch of awe in his voice. "With the skin of a thern, the black hair of a First Born and the muscles of a dozen Dators it was no disgrace even for Xodar to acknowledge your supremacy. A thing he could never do were you a Barsoomian," he added.

"You are travelling several laps ahead of me, my friend," I interrupted. "I glean that your name is Xodar, but whom, pray, are the First Born, and what a Dator, and why, if you were conquered by a Barsoomian, could you not acknowledge it?"

"The First Born of Barsoom," he explained, "are the race of black men of which I am a Dator, or, as the lesser Barsoomians would say, Prince. My race is the oldest on the planet. We trace our lineage, unbroken, direct to the Tree of Life which flourished in the centre of the Valley Dor twenty-three million years ago.

"For countless ages the fruit of this tree underwent the gradual changes of evolution, passing by degrees from true plant life to a combination of plant and animal. In the first stages the fruit of the tree possessed only the power of independent muscular action, while the stem remained attached to the parent plant; later a brain developed in the fruit, so that hanging there by their long stems they thought and moved as individuals.

"Then, with the development of perceptions came a comparison of them; judgments were reached and compared, and thus reason and the power to reason were born upon Barsoom.

"Ages passed. Many forms of life came and went upon the Tree of Life, but still all were attached to the parent plant by stems of varying lengths. At length the fruit tree consisted in tiny plant men, such as we now see reproduced in such huge dimensions in the Valley Dor, but still hanging to the limbs and branches of the tree by the stems which grew from the tops of their heads.

"The buds from which the plant men blossomed resembled large nuts about a foot in diameter, divided by double partition walls into four sections. In one section grew the plant man, in another a sixteen-legged worm, in the third the progenitor of the white ape and in the fourth the primæval black man of Barsoom.

"When the bud burst the plant man remained dangling at the end of his stem, but the three other sections fell to the ground, where the efforts of their imprisoned occupants to escape sent them hopping about in all directions.

"Thus as time went on, all Barsoom was covered with these imprisoned creatures. For countless ages they lived their long lives within their hard shells, hopping and skipping about the broad planet; falling into rivers, lakes, and seas, to be still further spread about the surface of the new world.

"Countless billions died before the first black man broke through his prison walls into the light of day. Prompted by curiosity, he broke open other shells and the peopling of Barsoom commenced.

"The pure strain of the blood of this first black man has remained untainted by admixture with other creatures in the race of which I am a member; but from the sixteen-legged worm, the first ape and renegade black man has sprung every other form of animal life upon Barsoom.

"The therns," and he smiled maliciously as he spoke, "are but the result of ages of evolution from the pure white ape of antiquity. They are a lower order still. There is but one race of true and immortal humans on Barsoom. It is the race of black men.

"The Tree of Life is dead, but before it died the plant men learned to detach themselves from it and roam the face of Barsoom with the other children of the First Parent.

"Now their bisexuality permits them to reproduce themselves after the manner of true plants, but otherwise they have progressed but little in all the ages of their existence. Their actions and movements are largely matters of instinct and not guided to any great extent by reason, since the brain of a plant man is but a trifle larger than the end of your smallest finger. They live upon vegetation and the blood of animals, and their brain is just large enough to direct their movements in the direction of food, and to translate the food sensations which are carried to it from their eyes and ears. They have no sense of self-preservation and so are entirely without fear in the face of danger. That is why they are such terrible antagonists in combat."

I wondered why the black man took such pains to discourse thus at length to enemies upon the genesis of life Barsoomian. It seemed a strangely inopportune moment for a proud member of a proud race to unbend in casual conversation with a captor. Especially in view of the fact that the black still lay securely bound upon the deck.

It was the faintest straying of his eye beyond me for the barest fraction of a second that explained his motive for thus dragging out my interest in his truly absorbing story.

He lay a little forward of where I stood at the levers, and thus he faced the stern of the vessel as he addressed me. It was at the end of his description of the plant men that I caught his eye fixed momentarily upon something behind me.

Nor could I be mistaken in the swift gleam of triumph that brightened those dark orbs for an instant.

Some time before I had reduced our speed, for we had left the Valley Dor many miles astern, and I felt comparatively safe.

I turned an apprehensive glance behind me, and the sight that I saw froze the new-born hope of freedom that had been springing up within me.

A great battleship, forging silent and unlighted through the dark night, loomed close astern.

Now I REALIZED why the black pirate had kept me engrossed with his strange tale. For miles he had sensed the approach of succour, and but for that single tell-tale glance the battleship would have been directly above us in another moment, and the boarding party which was doubtless even now swinging in their harness from the ship's keel, would have swarmed our deck, placing my rising hope of escape in sudden and total eclipse.

I was too old a hand in aerial warfare to be at a loss now for the right manœuvre. Simultaneously I reversed the engines and dropped the little vessel a sheer hundred feet.

Above my head I could see the dangling forms of the boarding party as the battleship raced over us. Then I rose at a sharp angle, throwing my speed lever to its last notch.

Like a bolt from a crossbow my splendid craft shot its steel prow straight at the whirring propellers of the giant above us. If I could but touch them the huge bulk would be disabled for hours and escape once more possible.

At the same instant the sun shot above the horizon, disclosing a hundred grim, black faces peering over the stem of the battleship upon us.

At sight of us a shout of rage went up from a hundred throats. Orders were shouted, but it was too late to save the giant propellers, and with a crash we rammed them.

Instantly with the shock of impact I reversed my engine, but my prow was wedged in the hole it had made in the battleship's stern. Only a second I hung there before tearing away, but that second was amply long to swarm my deck with black devils.

There was no fight. In the first place there was no room to fight. We were simply submerged by numbers. Then as swords menaced me a command from Xodar stayed the hands of his fellows.

"Secure them," he said, "but do not injure them."

Several of the pirates already had released Xodar. He now personally attended to my disarming and saw that I was properly bound. At least he thought that the binding was secure. It would have been had I been

a Martian, but I had to smile at the puny strands that confined my
wrists. When the time came I could snap them as they had been cotton
string.

The girl they bound also, and then they fastened us together. In
the meantime they had brought our craft alongside the disabled battleship, and soon we were transported to the latter's deck.

Fully a thousand black men manned the great engine of destruction.
Her decks were crowded with them as they pressed forward as far as
discipline would permit to get a glimpse of their captives.

The girl's beauty elicited many brutal comments and vulgar jests.
It was evident that these self-thought supermen were far inferior to
the red men of Barsoom in refinement and in chivalry.

My close-cropped black hair and thern complexion were the sub-
jects of much comment. When Xodar told his fellow-nobles of my
fighting ability and strange origin they crowded about me with numerous questions.

The fact that I wore the harness and metal of a thern who had been
killed by a member of my party convinced them that I was an enemy
of their hereditary foes, and placed me on a better footing in their
estimation.

Without exception the blacks were handsome men, and well built.
The officers were conspicuous through the wondrous magnificence of
their resplendent trappings. Many harnesses were so encrusted with
gold, platinum, silver and precious stones as to entirely hide the
leather beneath.

The harness of the commanding officer was a solid mass of diamonds. Against the ebony background of his skin they blazed out
with a peculiarly accentuated effulgence. The whole scene was en-
chanting. The handsome men; the barbaric splendour of the accoutrements; the polished skeel wood of the deck; the gloriously
grained sorapus of the cabins, inlaid with priceless jewels and precious
metals in intricate and beautiful design; the burnished gold of hand
rails; the shining metal of the guns.

Phaidor and I were taken below decks, where, still fast bound, we
were thrown into a small compartment which contained a single port-
hole. As our escort left us they barred the door behind them.

We could hear the men working on the broken propellers, and
from the port-hole we could see that the vessel was drifting lazily toward the south.

For some time neither of us spoke. Each was occupied with his own thoughts. For my part I was wondering as to the fate of Tars Tarkas and the girl, Thuvia.

Even if they succeeded in eluding pursuit they must eventually fall into the hands of either red men or green, and as fugitives from the Valley Dor they could look for but little else than a swift and terrible death.

How I wished that I might have accompanied them. It seemed to me that I could not fail to impress upon the intelligent red men of Barsoom the wicked deception that a cruel and senseless superstition had foisted upon them.

Tardos Mors would believe me. Of that I was positive. And that he would have the courage of his convictions my knowledge of his character assured me. Dejah Thoris would believe me. Not a doubt as to that entered my head. Then there were a thousand of my red and green warrior friends whom I knew would face eternal damnation gladly for my sake. Like Tars Tarkas, where I led they would follow.

My only danger lay in that should I ever escape the black pirates it might be to fall into the hands of unfriendly red or green men. Then it would mean short shrift for me.

Well, there seemed little to worry about on that score, for the likelihood of my ever escaping the blacks was extremely remote.

The girl and I were linked together by a rope which permitted us to move only about three or four feet from each other. When we had entered the compartment we had seated ourselves upon a low bench beneath the porthole. The bench was the only furniture of the room. It was of sorapus wood. The floor, ceiling and walls were of carborundum aluminum, a light, impenetrable composition extensively utilized in the construction of Martian fighting ships.

As I had sat meditating upon the future my eyes had been riveted upon the port-hole which was just level with them as I sat. Suddenly I looked toward Phaidor. She was regarding me with a strange expression I had not before seen upon her face. She was very beautiful then.

Instantly her white lids veiled her eyes, and I thought I discovered a delicate flush tinging her cheek. Evidently she was embarrassed at having been detected in the act of staring at a lesser creature, I thought.

"Do you find the study of the lower orders interesting?" I asked, laughing.

She looked up again with a nervous but relieved little laugh.

"Oh very," she said, "especially when they have such excellent profiles."

It was my turn to flush, but I did not. I felt that she was poking fun at me, and I admired a brave heart that could look for humour on the road to death, and so I laughed with her.

"Do you know where we are going?" she said.

"To solve the mystery of the eternal hereafter, I imagine," I replied.

"I am going to a worse fate than that," she said, with a little shudder.

"What do you mean?"

"I can only guess," she replied, "since no thern damsel of all the millions that have been stolen away by black pirates during the ages they have raided our domains has ever returned to narrate her experiences among them. That they never take a man prisoner lends strength to the belief that the fate of the girls they steal is worse than death."

"Is it not a just retribution?" I could not help but ask.

"What do you mean?"

"Do not the therns themselves do likewise with the poor creatures who take the voluntary pilgrimage down the River of Mystery? Was not Thuvia for fifteen years a plaything and a slave? Is it less than just that you should suffer as you have caused others to suffer?"

"You do not understand," she replied. "We therns are a holy race. It is an honour to a lesser creature to be a slave among us. Did we not occasionally save a few of the lower orders that stupidly float down an unknown river to an unknown end all would become the prey of the plant men and the apes."

"But do you not by every means encourage the superstition among those of the outside world?" I argued. "That is the wickedest of your deeds. Can you tell me why you foster the cruel deception?"

"All life on Barsoom," she said, "is created solely for the support of the race of therns. How else could we live did the outer world not furnish our labour and our food? Think you that a thern would demean himself by labour?"

"It is true then that you eat human flesh?" I asked in horror.

She looked at me in pitying commiseration for my ignorance.

"Truly we eat the flesh of the lower orders. Do not you also?"

"The flesh of beasts, yes," I replied, "but not the flesh of man."

"As man may eat of the flesh of beasts, so may gods eat of the flesh of man. The Holy Therns are the gods of Barsoom."

I was disgusted and I imagine that I showed it.

"You are an unbeliever now," she continued gently, "but should we be fortunate enough to escape the clutches of the black pirates and come again to the court of Matai Shang I think that we shall find an argument to convince you of the error of your ways. And—," she hesitated, "perhaps we shall find a way to keep you as—as—one of us."

Again her eyes dropped to the floor, and a faint colour suffused her cheek. I could not understand her meaning; nor did I for a long time. Dejah Thoris was wont to say that in some things I was a veritable simpleton, and I guess that she was right.

"I fear that I would ill requite your father's hospitality," I answered, "since the first thing that I should do were I a thern would be to set an armed guard at the mouth of the River Iss to escort the poor deluded voyagers back to the outer world. Also should I devote my life to the extermination of the hideous plant men and their horrible companions, the great white apes."

She looked at me really horror struck.

"No, no," she cried, "you must not say such terribly sacrilegious things—you must not even think them. Should they ever guess that you entertained such frightful thoughts, should we chance to regain the temples of the therns, they would mete out a frightful death to you. Not even my— my——" Again she flushed, and started over. "Not even I could save you."

I said no more. Evidently it was useless. She was even more steeped in superstition than the Martians of the outer world. They only worshipped a beautiful hope for a life of love and peace and happiness in the hereafter. The therns worshipped the hideous plant men and the apes, or at least they reverenced them as the abodes of the departed spirits of their own dead.

At this point the door of our prison opened to admit Xodar.

He smiled pleasantly at me, and when he smiled his expression was kindly—anything but cruel or vindictive.

"Since you cannot escape under any circumstances," he said, "I cannot see the necessity for keeping you confined below. I will cut your bonds and you may come on deck. You will witness something very interesting, and as you never shall return to the outer world it will do no harm to permit you to see it. You will see what no other than the First Born and their slaves know the existence of—the subterranean entrance to the Holy Land, to the real heaven of Barsoom.

"It will be an excellent lesson for this daughter of the therns," he added, "for she shall see the Temple of Issus, and Issus, perchance, shall embrace her."

Phaidor's head went high.

"What blasphemy is this, dog of a pirate?" she cried. "Issus would wipe out your entire breed an' you ever came within sight of her temple."

"You have much to learn, thern," replied Xodar, with an ugly smile, "nor do I envy you the manner in which you will learn it."

As we came on deck I saw to my surprise that the vessel was passing over a great field of snow and ice. As far as the eye could reach in any direction naught else was visible.

There could be but one solution to the mystery. We were above the south polar ice cap. Only at the poles of Mars is there ice or snow upon the planet. No sign of life appeared below us. Evidently we were too far south even for the great fur-bearing animals which the Martians so delight in hunting.

Xodar was at my side as I stood looking out over the ship's rail.

"What course?" I asked him.

"A little west of south," he replied. "You will see the Otz Valley directly. We shall skirt it for a few hundred miles."

"The Otz Valley!" I exclaimed; "but, man, is not there where lie the domains of the therns from which I but just escaped?"

"Yes," answered Xodar. "You crossed this ice field last night in the long chase that you led us. The Otz Valley lies in a mighty depression at the south pole. It is sunk thousands of feet below the level of the surrounding country, like a great round bowl. A hundred miles from its northern boundary rise the Otz Mountains which circle the inner Valley of Dor, in the exact centre of which lies the Lost Sea of Korus. On the shore of this sea stands the Golden Temple of Issus in the Land of the First Born. It is there that we are bound."

As I looked I commenced to realize why it was that in all the ages only one had escaped from the Valley Dor. My only wonder was that even the one had been successful. To cross this frozen, wind-swept waste of bleak ice alone and on foot would be impossible.

"Only by air boat could the journey be made," I finished aloud.

"It was thus that one did escape the therns in bygone times; but none has ever escaped the First Born," said Xodar, with a touch of pride in his voice.

We had now reached the southernmost extremity of the great ice barrier. It ended abruptly in a sheer wall thousands of feet high at the base of which stretched a level valley, broken here and there by low rolling hills and little clumps of forest, and with tiny rivers formed by the melting of the ice barrier at its base.

Once we passed far above what seemed to be a deep canyon-like rift stretching from the ice wall on the north across the valley as far as the eye could reach. "That is the bed of the River Iss," said Xodar. "It runs far beneath the ice field, and below the level of the Valley Otz, but its canyon is open here."

Presently I descried what I took to be a village, and pointing it out to Xodar asked him what it might be.

"It is a village of lost souls," he answered, laughing. "This strip between the ice barrier and the mountains is considered neutral ground. Some turn off from their voluntary pilgrimage down the Iss, and, scaling the awful walls of its canyon below us, stop in the valley. Also a slave now and then escapes from the therns and makes his way hither.

"They do not attempt to recapture such, since there is no escape from this outer valley, and as a matter of fact they fear the patrolling cruisers of the First Born too much to venture from their own domains.

"The poor creatures of this outer valley are not molested by us since they have nothing that we desire, nor are they numerically strong enough to give us an interesting fight—so we too leave them alone.

"There are several villages of them, but they have increased in numbers but little in many years since they are always warring among themselves."

Now we swung a little north of west, leaving the valley of lost souls, and shortly I discerned over our starboard bow what appeared to be a black mountain rising from the desolate waste of ice. It was not high and seemed to have a flat top.

Xodar had left us to attend to some duty on the vessel, and Phaidor and I stood alone beside the rail. The girl had not once spoken since we had been brought to the deck.

"Is what he has been telling me true?" I asked her.

"In part, yes," she answered. "That about the outer valley is true, but what he says of the location of the Temple of Issus in the centre of his country is false. If it is not false—" she hesitated. "Oh, it cannot be true, it cannot be true. For if it were true then for countless ages have my people gone to torture and ignominious death at the hands of their cruel enemies, instead of to the beautiful Life Eternal that we have been taught to believe Issus holds for us."

"As the lesser Barsoomians of the outer world have been lured by you to the terrible Valley Dor, so may it be that the therns themselves have been lured by the First Born to an equally horrid fate," I suggested. "It would be a stern and awful retribution, Phaidor; but a just one."

"I cannot believe it," she said.

"We shall see," I answered, and then we fell silent again for we were rapidly approaching the black mountain, which in some indefinable way seemed linked with the answer to our problem.

As we neared the dark, truncated cone the vessel's speed was diminished until we barely moved. Then we topped the crest of the mountain and below us I saw yawning the mouth of a huge circular well, the bottom of which was lost in inky blackness.

The diameter of this enormous pit was fully a thousand feet. The walls were smooth and appeared to be composed of a black, basaltic rock.

For a moment the vessel hovered motionless directly above the centre of the gaping void, then slowly she began to settle into the black chasm. Lower and lower she sank until as darkness enveloped us her lights were thrown on and in the dim halo of her own radiance the monster battleship dropped on and on down into what seemed to me must be the very bowels of Barsoom.

For quite half an hour we descended and then the shaft terminated abruptly in the dome of a mighty subterranean world. Below us rose and fell the billows of a buried sea. A phosphorescent radiance illuminated the scene. Thousands of ships dotted the bosom of the ocean. Little islands rose here and there to support the strange and colourless vegetation of this strange world.

Slowly and with majestic grace the battleship dropped until she rested on the water. Her great propellers had been drawn and housed during our descent of the shaft and in their place had been run out the smaller but more powerful water propellers. As these commenced to revolve the ship took up its journey once more, riding the new element as buoyantly and as safely as she had the air.

Phaidor and I were dumbfounded. Neither had either heard or dreamed that such a world existed beneath the surface of Barsoom.

Nearly all the vessels we saw were war craft. There were a few lighters and barges, but none of the great merchantmen such as ply the upper air between the cities of the outer world.

"Here is the harbour of the navy of the First Born," said a voice behind us, and turning we saw Xodar watching us with an amused smile on his lips.

"This sea," he continued, "is larger than Korus. It receives the waters of the lesser sea above it. To keep it from filling above a certain level we have four great pumping stations that force the over-supply back into the reservoirs far north from which the red men draw the water which irrigates their farm lands."

A new light burst on me with this explanation. The red men had always considered it a miracle that caused great columns of water to spurt from the solid rock of their reservoir sides to increase the supply of the precious liquid which is so scarce in the outer world of Mars.

Never had their learned men been able to fathom the secret of the source of this enormous volume of water. As ages passed they had simply come to accept it as a matter of course and ceased to question its origin.

We passed several islands on which were strangely shaped circular buildings, apparently roofless, and pierced midway between the ground and their tops with small, heavily barred windows. They bore the earmarks of prisons, which were further accentuated by the armed guards who squatted on low benches without, or patrolled the short beach lines.

Few of these islets contained over an acre of ground, but presently we sighted a much larger one directly ahead. This proved to be our destination, and the great ship was soon made fast against the steep shore.

Xodar signalled us to follow him and with a half-dozen officers and men we left the battleship and approached a large oval structure a couple of hundred yards from the shore.

"You shall soon see Issus," said Xodar to Phaidor. "The few prisoners we take are presented to her. Occasionally she selects slaves from among them to replenish the ranks of her handmaidens. None serves Issus above a single year," and there was a grim smile on the black's lips that lent a cruel and sinister meaning to his simple statement.

Phaidor, though loath to believe that Issus was allied to such as these, had commenced to entertain doubts and fears. She clung very closely to me, no longer the proud daughter of the Master of Life and Death upon Barsoom, but a young and frightened girl in the power of relentless enemies.

The building which we now entered was entirely roofless. In its centre was a long tank of water, set below the level of the floor like the swimming pool of a natatorium. Near one side of the pool floated an odd-looking black object. Whether it were some strange monster of these buried waters, or a queer raft, I could not at once perceive.

We were soon to know, however, for as we reached the edge of the pool directly above the thing, Xodar cried out a few words in a strange tongue. Immediately a hatch cover was raised from the surface of the object, and a black seaman sprang from the bowels of the strange craft.

Xodar addressed the seaman.

"Transmit to your officer," he said, "the commands of Dator Xodar. Say to him that Dator Xodar, with officers and men, escorting two prisoners, would be transported to the gardens of Issus beside the Golden Temple."

"Blessed be the shell of thy first ancestor, most noble Dator," replied the man. "It shall be done even as thou sayest," and raising both hands, palms backward, above his head after the manner of salute which is common to all races of Barsoom, he disappeared once more into the entrails of his ship.

A moment later an officer resplendent in the gorgeous trappings of his rank appeared on deck and welcomed Xodar to the vessel, and in the latter's wake we filed aboard and below.

The cabin in which we found ourselves extended entirely across the ship, having port-holes on either side below the water line. No sooner were all below than a number of commands were given, in accordance with which the hatch was closed and secured, and the vessel commenced to vibrate to the rhythmic purr of its machinery.

"Where can we be going in such a tiny pool of water?" asked Phaidor.

"Not up," I replied, "for I noticed particularly that while the building is roofless it is covered with a strong metal grating."

"Then where?" she asked again.

"From the appearance of the craft I judge we are going down," I replied.

Phaidor shuddered. For such long ages have the waters of Barsoom's seas been a thing of tradition only that even this daughter of the therns, born as she had been within sight of Mars' only remaining sea, had the same terror of deep water as is a common attribute of all Martians.

Presently the sensation of sinking became very apparent. We were going down swiftly. Now we could hear the water rushing past the port-holes, and in the dim light that filtered through them to the water beyond the swirling eddies were plainly visible.

Phaidor grasped my arm.

"Save me!" she whispered. "Save me and your every wish shall be granted. Anything within the power of the Holy Therns to give will be yours. Phaidor—" she stumbled a little here, and then in a very low voice, "Phaidor already is yours."

I felt very sorry for the poor child, and placed my hand over hers where it rested on my arm. I presume my motive was misunderstood, for with a swift glance about the apartment to assure herself that we were alone, she threw both her arms about my neck and dragged my face down to hers.

ISSUS, GODDESS OF LIFE ETERNAL

THE CONFESSION of love which the girl's fright had wrung from her touched me deeply; but it humiliated me as well, since I felt that in some thoughtless word or act I had given her reason to believe that I reciprocated her affection.

Never have I been much of a ladies' man, being more concerned with fighting and kindred arts which have ever seemed to me more befitting a man than mooning over a scented glove four sizes too small for him, or kissing a dead flower that has begun to smell like a cabbage. So I was quite at a loss as to what to do or say. A thousand times rather face the wild hordes of the dead sea bottoms than meet the eyes of this beautiful young girl and tell her the thing that I must tell her.

But there was nothing else to be done, and so I did it. Very clumsily too, I fear.

Gently I unclasped her hands from about my neck, and still holding them in mine I told her the story of my love for Dejah Thoris.

That of all the women of two worlds that I had known and admired during my long life she alone had I loved.

The tale did not seem to please her. Like a tigress she sprang, panting, to her feet. Her beautiful face was distorted in an expression of horrible malevolence. Her eyes fairly blazed into mine.

"Dog," she hissed. "Dog of a blasphemer! Think you that Phaidor, daughter of Matai Shang, supplicates? She commands. What to her is your puny outer world passion for the vile creature you chose in your other life?

"Phaidor has glorified you with her love, and you have spurned her. Ten thousand unthinkably atrocious deaths could not atone for the affront that you have put upon me. The thing that you call Dejah Thoris shall die the most horrible of them all. You have sealed the warrant for her doom.

"And you! You shall be the meanest slave in the service of the goddess you have attempted to humiliate. Tortures and ignominies shall be heaped upon you until you grovel at my feet asking the boon of death.

"In my gracious generosity I shall at length grant your prayer, and from the high balcony of the Golden Cliffs I shall watch the great white apes tear you asunder."

She had it all fixed up. The whole lovely programme from start to finish. It amazed me to think that one so divinely beautiful could at the same time be so fiendishly vindictive. It occurred to me, however, that she had overlooked one little factor in her revenge, and so, without any intent to add to her discomfiture, but rather to permit her to rearrange her plans along more practical lines, I pointed to the nearest port-hole.

Evidently she had entirely forgotten her surroundings and her present circumstances, for a single glance at the dark, swirling waters without sent her crumpled upon a low bench, where with her face buried in her arms she sobbed more like a very unhappy little girl than a proud and all-powerful goddess.

Down, down we continued to sink until the heavy glass of the port-holes became noticeably warm from the heat of the water without. Evidently we were very far beneath the surface crust of Mars.

Presently our downward motion ceased, and I could hear the propellers swirling through the water at our stern and forcing us ahead at high speed. It was very dark down there, but the light from our port-holes, and the reflection from what must have been a powerful searchlight on the submarine's nose showed that we were forging through a narrow passage, rock-lined, and tube-like.

After a few minutes the propellers ceased their whirring. We came to a full stop, and then commenced to rise swiftly toward the surface. Soon the light from without increased and we came to a stop.

Xodar entered the cabin with his men.

"Come," he said, and we followed him through the hatchway which had been opened by one of the seamen.

We found ourselves in a small subterranean vault, in the centre of which was the pool in which lay our submarine, floating as we had first seen her with only her black back showing.

Around the edge of the pool was a level platform, and then the walls of the cave rose perpendicularly for a few feet to arch toward the centre of the low roof. The walls about the ledge were pierced with a number of entrances to dimly lighted passageways.

Toward one of these our captors led us, and after a short walk halted before a steel cage which lay at the bottom of a shaft rising above us as far as one could see.

The cage proved to be one of the common types of elevator cars that I had seen in other parts of Barsoom. They are operated by means of enormous magnets which are suspended at the top of the shaft. By an electrical device the volume of magnetism generated is regulated and the speed of the car varied.

In long stretches they move at a sickening speed, especially on the upward trip, since the small force of gravity inherent to Mars results in very little opposition to the powerful force above.

Scarcely had the door of the car closed behind us than we were slowing up to stop at the landing above, so rapid was our ascent of the long shaft.

When we emerged from the little building which houses the upper terminus of the elevator, we found ourselves in the midst of a veritable fairyland of beauty. The combined languages of Earth men hold no words to convey to the mind the gorgeous beauties of the scene.

One may speak of scarlet sward and ivory-stemmed trees decked with brilliant purple blooms; of winding walks paved with crushed rubies, with emerald, with turquoise, even with diamonds themselves; of a magnificent temple of burnished gold, hand-wrought with marvellous designs; but where are the words to describe the glorious colours that are unknown to earthly eyes? where the mind or the imagination that can grasp the gorgeous scintillations of unheard-of rays as they emanate from the thousand nameless jewels of Barsoom?

Even my eyes, for long years accustomed to the barbaric splendours of a Martian Jeddak's court, were amazed at the glory of the scene.

Phaidor's eyes were wide in amazement.

"The Temple of Issus," she whispered, half to herself.

Xodar watched us with his grim smile, partly of amusement and partly malicious gloating.

The gardens swarmed with brilliantly trapped black men and women. Among them moved red and white females serving their every want. The places of the outer world and the temples of the therns had been robbed of their princesses and goddesses that the blacks might have their slaves.

Through this scene we moved toward the temple. At the main entrance we were halted by a cordon of armed guards. Xodar spoke a few words to an officer who came forward to question us. Together they entered the temple, where they remained for some time.

When they returned it was to announce that Issus desired to look upon the daughter of Matai Shang, and the strange creature from another world who had been a Prince of Helium.

Slowly we moved through endless corridors of unthinkable beauty; through magnificent apartments, and noble halls. At length we were halted in a spacious chamber in the centre of the temple. One of the officers who had accompanied us advanced to a large door in the further end of the chamber. Here he must have made some sort of signal for immediately the door opened and another richly trapped courtier emerged.

We were then led up to the door, where we were directed to get down on our hands and knees with our backs toward the room we were to enter. The doors were swung open and after being cautioned not to turn our heads under penalty of instant death we were commanded to back into the presence of Issus.

Never have I been in so humiliating a position in my life, and only my love for Dejah Thoris and the hope which still clung to me that I might again see her kept me from rising to face the goddess of the First Born and go down to my death like a gentleman, facing my foes and with their blood mingling with mine.

After we had crawled in this disgusting fashion for a matter of a couple of hundred feet we were halted by our escort.

"Let them rise," said a voice behind us; a thin, wavering voice, yet one that had evidently been accustomed to command for many years.

"Rise," said our escort, "but do not face toward Issus."

"The woman pleases me," said the thin, wavering voice again after a few moments of silence. "She shall serve me the allotted time. The man you may return to the Isle of Shador which lies against the northern shore of the Sea of Omean. Let the woman turn and look upon Issus, knowing that those of the lower orders who gaze upon the holy vision of her radiant face survive the blinding glory but a single year."

I watched Phaidor from the corner of my eye. She paled to a ghastly hue. Slowly, very slowly she turned, as though drawn by some invisible yet irresistible force. She was standing quite close to me, so close that her bare arm touched mine as she finally faced Issus, Goddess of Life Eternal.

I could not see the girl's face as her eyes rested for the first time on the Supreme Deity of Mars, but felt the shudder that ran through her in the trembling flesh of the arm that touched mine.

"It must be dazzling loveliness indeed," thought I, "to cause such emotion in the breast of so radiant a beauty as Phaidor, daughter of Matai Shang."

"Let the woman remain. Remove the man. Go." Thus spoke Issus, and the heavy hand of the officer fell upon my shoulder. In accordance with his instructions I dropped to my hands and knees once more and crawled from the Presence. It had been my first audience with deity, but I am free to confess that I was not greatly impressed—other than with the ridiculous figure I cut scrambling about on my marrow bones.

Once without the chamber the doors closed behind us and I was bid to rise. Xodar joined me and together we slowly retraced our steps toward the gardens.

"You spared my life when you easily might have taken it," he said after we had proceeded some little way in silence, "and I would aid you if I might. I can help to make your life here more bearable, but your fate is inevitable. You may never hope to return to the outer world."

"What will be my fate?" I asked.

"That will depend largely upon Issus. So long as she does not send for you and reveal her face to you, you may live on for years in as mild a form of bondage as I can arrange for you."

"Why should she send for me?" I asked.

"The men of the lower orders she often uses for various purposes of amusement. Such a fighter as you, for example, would render fine sport in the monthly rites of the temple. There are men pitted against men, and against beasts for the edification of Issus and the replenishment of her larder."

"She eats human flesh?" I asked. Not in horror, however, for since my recently acquired knowledge of the Holy Therns I was prepared for anything in this still less accessible heaven, where all was evidently dictated by a single omnipotence; where ages of narrow fanaticism and self-worship had eradicated all the broader humanitarian instincts that the race might once have possessed.

They were a people drunk with power and success, looking upon the other inhabitants of Mars as we look upon the beasts of the field and the forest. Why then should they not eat of the flesh of the lower orders whose lives and characters they no more understood than do we the inmost thoughts and sensibilities of the cattle we slaughter for our earthly tables.

"She eats only the flesh of the best bred of the Holy Therns and the red Barsoomians. The flesh of the others goes to our boards. The animals are eaten by the slaves. She also eats other dainties."

I did not understand then that there lay any special significance in his reference to other dainties. I thought the limit of ghoulishness already had been reached in the recitation of Issus' menu. I still had much to learn as to the depths of cruelty and bestiality to which omnipotence may drag its possessor.

We had about reached the last of the many chambers and corridors which led to the gardens when an officer overtook us.

"Issus would look again upon this man," he said. "The girl has told her that he is of wondrous beauty and of such prowess that alone he slew seven of the First Born, and with his bare hands took Xodar captive, binding him with his own harness."

Xodar looked uncomfortable. Evidently he did not relish the thought that Issus had learned of his inglorious defeat.

Without a word he turned and we followed the officer once again to the closed doors before the audience chamber of Issus, Goddess of Life Eternal.

Here the ceremony of entrance was repeated. Again Issus bid me rise. For several minutes all was silent as the tomb. The eyes of deity were appraising me.

Presently the thin wavering voice broke the stillness, repeating in a singsong drone the words which for countless ages had sealed the doom of numberless victims.

"Let the man turn and look upon Issus, knowing that those of the lower orders who gaze upon the holy vision of her radiant face survive the blinding glory but a single year."

I turned as I had been bid, expecting such a treat as only the revealment of divine glory to mortal eyes might produce. What I saw was a solid phalanx of armed men between myself and a dais supporting a great bench of carved sorapus wood. On this bench, or throne, squatted a female black. She was evidently very old. Not a hair remained upon her wrinked skull. With the exception of two yellow fangs she was entirely toothless. On either side of her thin, hawk-like nose her eyes burned from the depths of horribly sunken sockets. The skin of her face was seamed and creased with a million deepcut furrows. Her body was as wrinkled as her face, and as repulsive.

Emaciated arms and legs attached to a torso which seemed to be mostly distorted abdomen completed the "holy vision of her radiant beauty."

Surrounding her were a number of female slaves, among them Phaidor, white and trembling.

"This is the man who slew seven of the First Born and, barehanded, bound Dator Xodar with his own harness?" asked Issus.

"Most glorious vision of divine loveliness, it is," replied the officer who stood at my side.

"Produce Dator Xodar," she commanded.

Xodar was brought from the adjoining room.

Issus glared at him, a baleful light in her hideous eyes.

"And such as you are a Dator of the First Born?" she squealed. "For the disgrace you have brought upon the Immortal Race you shall be degraded to a rank below the lowest. No longer be you a Dator, but for evermore a slave of slaves, to fetch and carry for the lower orders that serve in the gardens of Issus. Remove his harness. Cowards and slaves wear no trappings."

Xodar stood stiffly erect. Not a muscle twitched, nor a tremor shook his giant frame as a soldier of the guard roughly stripped his gorgeous trappings from him.

"Begone," screamed the infuriated little old woman. "Begone, but instead of the light of the gardens of Issus let you serve as a slave of this slave who conquered you in the prison on the Isle of Shador in the Sea of Omean. Take him away out of the sight of my divine eyes."

Slowly and with high held head the proud Xodar turned and stalked from the chamber. Issus rose and turned to leave the room by another exit.

Turning to me, she said: "You shall be returned to Shador for the present. Later Issus will see the manner of your fighting. Go." Then she disappeared, followed by her retinue. Only Phaidor lagged behind, and as I started to follow my guard toward the gardens, the girl came running after me.

"Oh, do not leave me in this terrible place," she begged. "Forgive the things I said to you, my Prince. I did not mean them. Only take me away with you. Let me share your imprisonment on Shador." Her words were an almost incoherent volley of thoughts, so rapidly she spoke. "You did not understand the honour that I did you. Among the therns there is no marriage or giving in marriage, as among the lower orders of the outer world. We might have lived together for ever in love and happiness. We have both looked upon Issus and in a year we die. Let us live that year at least together in what measure of joy remains for the doomed."

"If it was difficult for me to understand you, Phaidor," I replied, "can you not understand that possibly it is equally difficult for you to understand the motives, the customs and the social laws that guide me? I do not wish to hurt you, nor to seem to undervalue the honour which you have done me, but the thing you desire may not be. Regardless of the foolish belief of the peoples of the outer world, or of Holy Thern, or ebon First Born, I am not dead. While I live my heart beats for but one woman—the incomparable Dejah Thoris, Princess of Helium. When death overtakes me my heart shall have ceased to beat; but what comes after that I know not. And in that I am as wise as Matai Shang, Master of Life and Death upon Barsoom; or Issus, Goddess of Life Eternal."

Phaidor stood looking at me intently for a moment. No anger showed in her eyes this time, only a pathetic expression of hopeless sorrow.

"I do not understand," she said, and turning walked slowly in the direction of the door through which Issus and her retinue had passed. A moment later she had passed from my sight.

THE PRISON ISLE OF SHADOR

IN THE OUTER GARDENS to which the guard now escorted me, I found Xodar surrounded by a crowd of noble blacks. They were reviling and cursing him. The men slapped his face. The women spat upon him.

When I appeared they turned their attentions toward me.

"Ah," cried one, "so this is the creature who overcame the great Xodar bare-handed. Let us see how it was done."

"Let him bind Thurid," suggested a beautiful woman, laughing. "Thurid is a noble Dator. Let Thurid show the dog what it means to face a real man."

"Yes, Thurid! Thurid!" cried a dozen voices.

"Here he is now," exclaimed another, and turning in the direction indicated I saw a huge black weighed down with resplendent ornaments and arms advancing with noble and gallant bearing toward us.

"What now?" he cried. "What would you of Thurid?"

Quickly a dozen voices explained.

Thurid turned toward Xodar, his eyes narrowing to two nasty slits.

"Calot!" he hissed. "Ever did I think you carried the heart of a sorak in your putrid breast. Often have you bested me in the secret councils of Issus, but now in the field of war where men are truly gauged your scabby heart hath revealed its sores to all the world. Calot, I spurn you with my foot," and with the words he turned to kick Xodar.

My blood was up. For minutes it had been boiling at the cowardly treatment they had been according this once powerful comrade because he had fallen from the favour of Issus. I had no love for Xodar, but I cannot stand the sight of cowardly injustice and persecution without seeing red as through a haze of bloody mist, and doing things on the impulse of the moment that I presume I never should do after mature deliberation.

I was standing close beside Xodar as Thurid swung his foot for the cowardly kick. The degraded Dator stood erect and motionless as a carven image. He was prepared to take whatever his former comrades had to offer in the way of insults and reproaches, and take them in manly silence and stoicism.

But as Thurid's foot swung so did mine, and I caught him a painful blow upon the shin bone that saved Xodar from this added ignominy.

For a moment there was tense silence, then Thurid, with a roar of rage sprang for my throat; just as Xodar had upon the deck of the cruiser. The results were identical. I ducked beneath his outstretched arms, and as he lunged past me planted a terrific right on the side of his jaw.

The big fellow spun around like a top, his knees gave beneath him and he crumpled to the ground at my feet.

The blacks gazed in astonishment, first at the still form of the proud Dator lying there in the ruby dust of the pathway, then at me as though they could not believe that such a thing could be.

"You asked me to bind Thurid," I cried; "behold!" And then I stooped beside the prostrate form, tore the harness from it, and bound the fellow's arms and legs securely.

"As you have done to Xodar, now do you likewise to Thurid. Take him before Issus, bound in his own harness, that she may see with her own eyes that there be one among you now who is greater than the First Born."

"Who are you?" whispered the woman who had first suggested that I attempt to bind Thurid.

"I am a citizen of two worlds; Captain John Carter of Virginia, Prince of the House of Tardos Mors, Jeddak of Helium. Take this man to your goddess, as I have said, and tell her, too, that as I have done to Xodar and Thurid, so also can I do to the mightiest of her Dators. With naked hands, with long-sword or with short-sword, I challenge the flower of her fighting-men to combat."

"Come," said the officer who was guarding me back to Shador; "my orders are imperative; there is to be no delay. Xodar, come you also."

There was little of disrespect in the tone that the man used in addressing either Xodar or myself. It was evident that he felt less contempt for the former Dator since he had witnessed the ease with which I disposed of the powerful Thurid.

That his respect for me was greater than it should have been for a slave was quite apparent from the fact that during the balance of the return journey he walked or stood always behind me, a drawn short-sword in his hand.

The return to the Sea of Omean was uneventful. We dropped down the awful shaft in the same car that had brought us to the surface. There we entered the submarine, taking the long dive to the tunnel far beneath the upper world. Then through the tunnel and up again to the pool from which we had had our first introduction to the wonderful passageway from Omean to the Temple of Issus.

From the island of the submarine we were transported on a small cruiser to the distant Isle of Shador. Here we found a small stone prison and a guard of half a dozen blacks. There was no ceremony wasted in completing our incarceration. One of the blacks opened the door of the prison with a huge key, we walked in, the door closed behind us, the lock grated, and with the sound there swept over me again that terrible feeling of hopelessness that I had felt in the Chamber of Mystery in the Golden Cliffs beneath the gardens of the Holy Therns.

Then Tars Tarkas had been with me, but now I was utterly alone in so far as friendly companionship was concerned. I fell to wondering about the fate of the great Thark, and of his beautiful companion, the girl, Thuvia. Even should they by some miracle have escaped and been received and spared by a friendly nation, what hope had I of the succour which I knew they would gladly extend if it lay in their power.

They could not guess my whereabouts or my fate, for none on all Barsoom even dream of such a place as this. Nor would it have advantaged me any had they known the exact location of my prison, for who could hope to penetrate to this buried sea in the face of the mighty navy of the First Born? No: my case was hopeless.

Well, I would make the best of it, and, rising, I swept aside the brooding despair that had been endeavouring to claim me. With the idea of exploring my prison, I started to look around.

Xodar sat, with bowed head, upon a low stone bench near the centre of the room in which we were. He had not spoken since Issus had degraded him.

The building was roofless, the walls rising to a height of about thirty feet. Half-way up were a couple of small, heavily barred windows. The prison was divided into several rooms by partitions twenty feet high. There was no one in the room which we occupied, but two doors which led to other rooms were opened. I entered one of these rooms, but found it vacant. Thus I continued through several of the chambers until in the last one I found a young red Martian boy

sleeping upon the stone bench which constituted the only furniture
of any of the prison cells.

Evidently he was the only other prisoner. As he slept I leaned
over and looked at him. There was something strangely familiar
about his face, and yet I could not place him. His features were very
regular and, like the proportions of his graceful limbs and body, beautiful in the extreme. He was very light in colour for a red man, but in
other respects he seemed a typical specimen of this handsome race.

I did not awaken him, for sleep in prison is such a priceless boon
that I have seen men transformed into raging brutes when robbed by
one of their fellow-prisoners of a few precious moments of it.

Returning to my own cell, I found Xodar still sitting in the same
position in which I had left him.

"Man," I cried, "it will profit you nothing to mope thus. It were
no disgrace to be bested by John Carter. You have seen that in the
ease with which I accounted for Thurid. You knew it before when on
the cruiser's deck you saw me slay three of your comrades."

"I would that you had dispatched me at the same time," he said.

"Come, come!" I cried. "There is hope yet. Neither of us is dead.
We are great fighters. Why not win to freedom?"

He looked at me in amazement.

"You know not of what you speak," he replied. "Issus is omnipotent. Issus is omniscient. She hears now the words you speak. She
knows the thoughts you think. It is sacrilege even to dream of breaking her commands."

"Rot, Xodar," I ejaculated impatiently.

He sprang to his feet in horror.

"The curse of Issus will fall upon you," he cried. "In another instant
you will be smitten down, writhing to your death in horrible agony."

"Do you believe that, Xodar?" I asked.

"Of course; who would dare doubt?"

"I doubt; yes, and further, I deny," I said. "Why, Xodar, you tell
me that she even knows my thoughts. The red men have all had that
power for ages. And another wonderful power. They can shut their
minds so that none may read their thoughts. I learned the first secret
years ago; the other I never had to learn, since upon all Barsoom
is none who can read what passes in the secret chambers of my brain.

"Your goddess cannot read my thoughts; nor can she read yours
when you are out of sight, unless you will it. Had she been able to
read mine, I am afraid that her pride would have suffered a rather

severe shock when I turned at her command to 'gaze upon the holy vision of her radiant face.'"

"What do you mean?" he whispered in an affrighted voice, so low that I could scarcely hear him.

"I mean that I thought her the most repulsive and vilely hideous creature my eyes ever had rested upon."

For a moment he eyed me in horror-stricken amazement, and then with a cry of "Blasphemer" he sprang upon me.

I did not wish to strike him again, nor was it necessary, since he was unarmed and therefore quite harmless to me.

As he came I grasped his left wrist with my left hand, and, swinging my right arm about his left shoulder, caught him beneath the chin with my elbow and bore him backward across my thigh.

There he hung helpless for a moment, glaring up at me in impotent rage.

"Xodar," I said, "let us be friends. For a year, possibly, we may be forced to live together in the narrow confines of this tiny room. I am sorry to have offended you, but I could not dream that one who had suffered from the cruel injustice of Issus still could believe her divine.

"I will say a few more words, Xodar, with no intent to wound your feelings further, but rather that you may give thought to the fact that while we live we are still more the arbiters of our own fate than is any god.

"Issus, you see, has not struck me dead, nor is she rescuing her faithful Xodar from the clutches of the unbeliever who defamed her fair beauty. No, Xodar, your Issus is a mortal old woman. Once out of her clutches and she cannot harm you.

"With your knowledge of this strange land, and my knowledge of the outer world, two such fighting-men as you and I should be able to win our way to freedom. Even though we died in the attempt, would not our memories be fairer than as though we remained in servile fear to be butchered by a cruel and unjust tyrant—call her goddess or mortal, as you will."

As I finished I raised Xodar to his feet and released him. He did not renew the attack upon me, nor did he speak. Instead, he walked toward the bench, and, sinking down upon it, remained lost in deep thought for hours.

A long time afterward I heard a soft sound at the doorway leading to one of the other apartments, and, looking up, beheld the red Martian youth gazing intently at us.

"Kaor," I cried, after the red Martian manner of greeting.

"Kaor," he replied. "What do you here?"

"I await my death, I presume," I replied with a wry smile.

He too smiled, a brave and winning smile.

"I also," he said. "Mine will come soon. I looked upon the radiant beauty of Issus nearly a year since. It has always been a source of keen wonder to me that I did not drop dead at the first sight of that hideous countenance. And her belly! By my first ancestor, but never was there so grotesque a figure in all the universe. That they should call such a one Goddess of Life Eternal, Goddess of Death, Mother of the Nearer Moon, and fifty other equally impossible titles, is quite beyond me."

"How came you here?" I asked.

"It is very simple. I was flying a one-man air scout far to the south when the brilliant idea occurred to me that I should like to search for the Lost Sea of Korus which tradition places near to the south pole. I must have inherited from my father a wild lust for adventure, as well as a hollow where my bump of reverence should be.

"I had reached the area of eternal ice when my port propeller jammed, and I dropped to the ground to make repairs. Before I knew it the air was black with fliers, and a hundred of these First Born devils were leaping to the ground all about me.

"With drawn swords they made for me, but before I went down beneath them they had tasted of the steel of my father's sword, and I had given such an account of myself as I know would have pleased my sire had he lived to witness it."

"Your father is dead?" I asked.

"He died before the shell broke to let me step out into a world that has been very good to me. But for the sorrow that I had never the honour to know my father, I have been very happy. My only sorrow now is that my mother must mourn me as she has for ten long years mourned my father."

"Who was your father?" I asked.

He was about to reply when the outer door of our prison opened and a burly guard entered and ordered him to his own quarters for the night, locking the door after him as he passed through into the further chamber.

"It is Issus' wish that you two be confined in the same room," said the guard when he had returned to our cell. "This cowardly slave of a slave is to serve you well," he said to me, indicating Xodar with a wave of his hand. "If he does not, you are to beat him into submission. It is Issus' wish that you heap upon him every indignity and degradation of which you can conceive."

With these words he left us.

Xodar still sat with his face buried in his hands. I walked to his side and placed my hand upon his shoulder.

"Xodar," I said, "you have heard the commands of Issus, but you need not fear that I shall attempt to put them into execution. You are a brave man, Xodar. It is your own affair if you wish to be persecuted and humiliated; but were I you I should assert my manhood and defy my enemies."

"I have been thinking very hard, John Carter," he said, "of all the new ideas you gave me a few hours since. Little by little I have been piecing together the things that you said which sounded blasphemous to me then with the things that I have seen in my past life and dared not even think about for fear of bringing down upon me the wrath of Issus.

"I believe now that she is a fraud; no more divine than you or I. More I am willing to concede—that the First Born are no holier than the Holy Therns, nor the Holy Therns more holy than the red men.

"The whole fabric of our religion is based on superstitious belief in lies that have been foisted upon us for ages by those directly above us, to whose personal profit and aggrandizement it was to have us continue to believe as they wished us to believe.

"I am ready to cast off the ties that have bound me. I am ready to defy Issus herself; but what will it avail us? Be the First Born gods or mortals, they are a powerful race, and we are as fast in their clutches as though we were already dead. There is no escape."

"I have escaped from bad plights in the past, my friend," I replied; "nor while life is in me shall I despair of escaping from the Isle of Shador and the Sea of Omean."

"But we cannot escape even from the four walls of our prison," urged Xodar. "Test this flint-like surface," he cried, smiting the solid rock that confined us. "And look upon this polished surface; none could cling to it to reach the top."

I smiled.

"That is the least of our troubles, Xodar," I replied. "I will guarantee to scale the wall and take you with me, if you will help with your knowledge of the customs here to appoint the best time for the attempt, and guide me to the shaft that lets from the dome of this abysmal sea to the light of God's pure air above."

"Night time is the best and offers the only slender chance we have, for then men sleep, and only a dozing watch nods in the tops of the battleships. No watch is kept upon the cruisers and smaller craft. The watchers upon the larger vessels see to all about them. It is night now."

"But," I exclaimed, "it is not dark! How can it be night, then?" He smiled.

"You forget," he said, "that we are far below ground. The light of the sun never penetrates here. There are no moons and no stars reflected in the bosom of Omean. The phosphorescent light you now see pervading this great subterranean vault emanates from the rocks that form its dome; it is always thus upon Omean, just as the billows are always as you see them—rolling, ever rolling over a windless sea.

"At the appointed hour of night upon the world above, the men whose duties hold them here sleep, but the light is ever the same."

"It will make escape more difficult," I said, and then I shrugged my shoulders; for what, pray, is the pleasure of doing an easy thing?

"Let us sleep on it to-night," said Xodar. "A plan may come with our awakening."

So we threw ourselves upon the hard stone floor of our prison and slept the sleep of tired men.

WHEN HELL BROKE LOOSE

EARLY THE NEXT MORNING Xodar and I commenced work upon our plans for escape. First I had him sketch upon the stone floor of our cell as accurate a map of the south polar regions as was possible with the crude instruments at our disposal—a buckle from my harness, and the sharp edge of the wondrous gem I had taken from Sator Throg.

From this I computed the general direction of Helium and the distance at which it lay from the opening which led to Omean.

Then I had him draw a map of Omean, indicating plainly the position of Shador and of the opening in the dome which led to the outer world.

These I studied until they were indelibly imprinted in my memory. From Xodar I learned the duties and customs of the guards who patrolled Shador. It seemed that during the hours set aside for sleep only one man was on duty at a time. He paced a beat that passed around the prison, at a distance of about a hundred feet from the building.

The pace of the sentries, Xodar said, was very slow, requiring nearly ten minutes to make a single round. This meant that for practically five minutes at a time each side of the prison was unguarded as the sentry pursued his snail-like pace upon the opposite side.

"This information you ask," said Xodar, "will be all very valuable *after* we get out, but nothing that you have asked has any bearing on that first and most important consideration."

"We will get out all right," I replied, laughing. "Leave that to me."

"When shall we make the attempt?" he asked.

"The first night that finds a small craft moored near the shore of Shador," I replied.

"But how will you know that any craft is moored near Shador? The windows are far beyond our reach."

"Not so, friend Xodar; look!"

With a bound I sprang to the bars of the window opposite us, and took a quick survey of the scene without.

Several small craft and two large battleships lay within a hundred yards of Shador.

"To-night," I thought, and was just about to voice my decision to Xodar, when, without warning, the door of our prison opened and a guard stepped in.

If the fellow saw me there our chances of escape might quickly go glimmering, for I knew that they would put me in irons if they had the slightest conception of the wonderful agility which my earthly muscles gave me upon Mars.

The man had entered and was standing facing the centre of the room, so that his back was toward me. Five feet above me was the top of a partition wall separating our cell from the next.

There was my only chance to escape detection. If the fellow turned, I was lost; nor could I have dropped to the floor undetected, since he was so nearly below me that I would have struck him had I done so.

"Where is the white man?" cried the guard of Xodar. "Issus commands his presence." He started to turn to see if I were in another part of the cell.

I scrambled up the iron grating of the window until I could catch a good footing on the sill with one foot; then I let go my hold and sprang for the partition top.

"What was that?" I heard the deep voice of the black bellow as my metal grated against the stone wall as I slipped over. Then I dropped lightly to the floor of the cell beyond.

"Where is the white slave?" again cried the guard.

"I know not," replied Xodar. "He was here even as you entered. I am not his keeper—go find him."

The black grumbled something that I could not understand, and then I heard him unlocking the door into one of the other cells on the further side. Listening intently, I caught the sound as the door closed behind him. Then I sprang once more to the top of the partition and dropped into my own cell beside the astonished Xodar.

"Do you see now how we will escape?" I asked him in a whisper.

"I see how you may," he replied, "but I am no wiser than before as to how I am to pass these walls. Certain it is that I cannot bounce over them as you do."

We heard the guard moving about from cell to cell, and finally, his rounds completed, he again entered ours. When his eyes fell upon me they fairly bulged from his head.

"By the shell of my first ancestor!" he roared. "Where have you been?"

"I have been in prison since you put me here yesterday," I answered. "I was in this room when you entered. You had better look to your eyesight."

He glared at me in mingled rage and relief.

"Come," he said. "Issus commands your presence."

He conducted me outside the prison, leaving Xodar behind. There we found several other guards, and with them the red Martian youth who occupied another cell upon Shador.

The journey I had taken to the Temple of Issus on the preceding day was repeated. The guards kept the red boy and myself separated, so that we had no opportunity to continue the conversation that had been interrupted the previous night.

The youth's face had haunted me. Where had I seen him before. There was something strangely familiar in every line of him; in his carriage, his manner of speaking, his gestures. I could have sworn that I knew him, and yet I knew too that I had never seen him before.

When we reached the gardens of Issus we were led away from the temple instead of toward it. The way wound through enchanted parks to a mighty wall that towered a hundred feet in air.

Massive gates gave egress upon a small plain, surrounded by the same gorgeous forests that I had seen at the foot of the Golden Cliffs.

Crowds of blacks were strolling in the same direction that our guards were leading us, and with them mingled my old friends the plant men and great white apes.

The brutal beasts moved among the crowd as pet dogs might. If they were in the way the blacks pushed them roughly to one side, or whacked them with the flat of a sword, and the animals slunk away as in great fear.

Presently we came upon our destination, a great amphitheatre situated at the further edge of the plain, and about half a mile beyond the garden walls.

Through a massive arched gateway the blacks poured in to take their seats, while our guards led us to a smaller entrance near one end of the structure.

Through this we passed into an enclosure beneath the seats, where we found a number of other prisoners herded together under guard. Some of them were in irons, but for the most part they seemed sufficiently awed by the presence of their guards to preclude any possibility of attempted escape.

During the trip from Sador I had had no opportunity to talk with my fellow-prisoner, but now that we were safely within the barred paddock our guards abated their watchfulness, with the result that I found myself able to approach the red Martian youth for whom I felt such a strange attraction.

"What is the object of this assembly?" I asked him. "Are we to fight for the edification of the First Born, or is it something worse than that?"

"It is a part of the monthly rites of Issus," he replied, "in which black men wash the sins from their souls in the blood of men from the outer world. If, perchance, the black is killed, it is evidence of his disloyalty to Issus—the unpardonable sin. If he lives through the contest he is held acquitted of the charge that forced the sentence of the rites, as it is called, upon him.

"The forms of combat vary. A number of us may be pitted together against an equal number, or twice the number of blacks; or

singly we may be sent forth to face wild beasts, or some famous
black warrior."

"And if we are victorious," I asked, "what then—freedom?"

He laughed.

"Freedom, forsooth. The only freedom for us is death. None who
enters the domains of the First Born ever leave. If we prove able
fighters we are permitted to fight often. If we are not mighty
fighters——" He shrugged his shoulders. "Sooner or later we die in
the arena."

"And you have fought often?" I asked.

"Very often," he replied. "It is my only pleasure. Some hundred
black devils have I accounted for during nearly a year of the rites
of Issus. My mother would be very proud could she only know how
well I have maintained the traditions of my father's prowess."

"Your father must have been a mighty warrior!" I said. "I have
known most of the warriors of Barsoom in my time; doubtless I knew
him. Who was he?"

"My father was——"

"Come, calots!" cried the rough voice of a guard. "To the slaughter
with you," and roughly we were hustled to the steep incline that led
to the chambers far below which let out upon the arena.

The amphitheatre, like all I had ever seen upon Barsoom, was
built in a large excavation. Only the highest seats, which formed the
low wall surrounding the pit, were above the level of the ground.
The arena itself was far below the surface.

Just beneath the lowest tier of seats was a series of barred cages
on a level with the surface of the arena. Into these we were herded.
But, unfortunately, my youthful friend was not of those who occupied
a cage with me.

Directly opposite my cage was the throne of Issus. Here the horrid
creature squatted, surrounded by a hundred slave maidens sparkling
in jewelled trappings. Brilliant cloths of many hues and strange patterns
formed the soft cushion covering of the dais upon which they re-
clined about her.

On four sides of the throne and several feet below it stood three
solid ranks of heavily armed soldiery, elbow to elbow. In front of
these were the high dignitaries of this mock heaven—gleaming blacks
bedecked with precious stones, upon their foreheads the insignia of
their rank set in circles of gold.

On both sides of the throne stretched a solid mass of humanity from top to bottom of the amphitheatre. There were as many women as men, and each was clothed in the wondrously wrought harness of his station and his house. With each black was from one to three slaves, drawn from the domains of the therns and from the outer world. The blacks are all "noble." There is no peasantry among the First Born. Even the lowest soldier is a god, and has his slaves to wait upon him.

The First Born do no work. The men fight—that is a sacred privilege and duty; to fight and die for Issus. The women do nothing, absolutely nothing. Slaves wash them, slaves dress them, slaves feed them. There are some, even, who have slaves that talk for them, and I saw one who sat during the rites with closed eyes while a slave narrated to her the events that were transpiring within the arena.

The first event of the day was the Tribute to Issus. It marked the end of those poor unfortunates who had looked upon the divine glory of the goddess a full year before. There were ten of them—splendid beauties from the proud courts of mighty Jeddaks and from the temples of the Holy Therns. For a year they had served in the retinue of Issus; to-day they were to pay the price of this divine preferment with their lives; tomorrow they would grace the tables of the court functionaries.

A huge black entered the arena with the young women. Carefully he inspected them, felt of their limbs and poked them in the ribs. Presently he selected one of their number whom he led before the throne of Issus. He addressed some words to the goddess which I could not hear. Issus nodded her head. The black raised his hands above his head in token of salute, grasped the girl by the wrist, and dragged her from the arena through a small doorway below the throne.

"Issus will dine well to-night," said a prisoner beside me.

"What do you mean?" I asked.

"That was her dinner that old Thabis is taking to the kitchens. Didst not note how carefully he selected the plumpest and tenderest of the lot?"

I growled out my curses on the monster sitting opposite us on the gorgeous throne.

"Fume not," admonished my companion; "you will see far worse than that if you live even a month among the First Born."

I turned again in time to see the gate of a nearby cage thrown open and three monstrous white apes spring into the arena. The girls shrank in a frightened group in the centre of the enclosure.

"I sprang into the arena, my long-sword whirring through the air . . ."

One was on her knees with imploring hands outstreched toward Issus; but the hideous deity only leaned further forward in keener anticipation of the entertainment to come. At length the apes spied the huddled knot of terror-stricken maidens and with demoniacal shrieks of bestial frenzy, charged upon them.

A wave of mad fury surged over me. The cruel cowardliness of the power-drunk creature whose malignant mind conceived such frightful forms of torture stirred to their uttermost depths my resentment and my manhood. The blood-red haze that presaged death to my foes swam before my eyes.

The guard lolled before the unbarred gate of the cage which confined me. What need of bars, indeed, to keep those poor victims from rushing into the arena which the edict of the gods had appointed as their death place!

A single blow sent the black unconscious to the ground. Snatching up his long-sword, I sprang into the arena. The apes were almost upon the maidens, but a couple of mighty bounds were all my earthly muscles required to carry me to the centre of the sand-strewn floor.

For an instant silence reigned in the great amphitheatre, then a wild shout arose from the cages of the doomed. My long-sword circled whirring through the air, and a great ape sprawled, headless, at the feet of the fainting girls.

The other apes turned now upon me, and as I stood facing them a sullen roar from the audience answered the wild cheers from the cages. From the tail of my eye I saw a score of guards rushing across the glistening sand toward me. Then a figure broke from one of the cages behind them. It was the youth whose personality so fascinated me.

He paused a moment before the cages, with upraised sword.

"Come, men of the outer world!" he shouted. "Let us make our deaths worth while, and at the back of this unknown warrior turn this day's Tribute to Issus into an orgy of revenge that will echo through the ages and cause black skins to blanch at each repetition of the rites of Issus. Come! The racks without your cages are filled with blades."

Without waiting to note the outcome of his plea, he turned and bounded toward me. From every cage that harboured red men a thunderous shout went up in answer to his exhortation. The inner guards went down beneath howling mobs, and the cages vomited forth their inmates hot with the lust to kill.

The racks that stood without were stripped of the swords with which the prisoners were to have been armed to enter their allotted combats, and a swarm of determined warriors sped to our support.

The great apes, towering in all their fifteen feet of height, had gone down before my sword while the charging guards were still some distance away. Close behind them pursued the youth. At my back were the young girls, and as it was in their service that I fought, I remained standing there to meet my inevitable death, but with the determination to give such an account of myself as would long be remembered in the land of the First Born.

I noted the marvellous speed of the young red man as he raced after the guards. Never had I seen such speed in any Martian. His leaps and bounds were little short of those which my earthly muscles had produced to create such awe and respect on the part of the green Martians into whose hands I had fallen on that long-gone day that had seen my first advent upon Mars.

The guards had not reached me when he fell upon them from the rear, and as they turned, thinking from the fierceness of his onslaught that a dozen were attacking them, I rushed them from my side.

In the rapid fighting that followed I had little chance to note aught else than the movements of my immediate adversaries, but now and again I caught a fleeting glimpse of a purring sword and a lightly springing figure of sinewy steel that filled my heart with a strange yearning and a mighty but unaccountable pride.

On the handsome face of the boy a grim smile played, and ever and anon he threw a taunting challenge to the foes that faced him. In this and other ways his manner of fighting was similar to that which had always marked me on the field of combat.

Perhaps it was this vague likeness which made me love the boy, while the awful havoc that his sword played amongst the blacks filled my soul with a tremendous respect for him.

For my part, I was fighting as I had fought a thousand times before —now sidestepping a wicked thrust, now stepping quickly in to let my sword's point drink deep in a foeman's heart, before it buried itself in the throat of his companion.

We were having a merry time of it, we two, when a great body of Issus' own guards were ordered into the arena. On they came with fierce cries, while from every side the armed prisoners swarmed upon them.

For half an hour it was as though all hell had broken loose. In the walled confines of the arena we fought in an inextricable mass—howling, cursing, blood-streaked demons; and ever the sword of the young red man flashed beside me.

Slowly and by repeated commands I had succeeded in drawing the prisoners into a rough formation about us, so that at last we fought formed into a rude circle in the centre of which were the doomed maids.

Many had gone down on both sides, but by far the greater havoc had been wrought in the ranks of the guards of Issus. I could see messengers running swiftly through the audience, and as they passed the nobles there unsheathed their swords and sprang into the arena. They were going to annihilate us by force of numbers—that was quite evidently their plan.

I caught a glimpse of Issus leaning far forward upon her throne, her hideous countenance distorted in a horrid grimace of hate and rage, in which I thought I could distinguish an expression of fear. It was that face that inspired me to the thing that followed.

Quickly I ordered fifty of the prisoners to drop back behind us and form a new circle about the maidens.

"Remain and protect them until I return," I commanded.

Then, turning to those who formed the outer line, I cried, "Down with Issus! Follow me to the throne; we will reap vengeance where vengeance is deserved."

The youth at my side was the first to take up the cry of "Down with Issus!" and then at my back and from all sides rose a hoarse shout, "To the throne! To the throne!"

As one man we moved, an irresistible fighting mass, over the bodies of dead and dying foes toward the gorgeous throne of the Martian deity. Hordes of the doughtiest fighting-men of the First Born poured from the audience to check our progress. We mowed them down before us as they had been paper men.

"To the seats, some of you!" I cried as we approached the arena's barrier wall. "Ten of us can take the throne," for I had seen that Issus' guards had for the most part entered the fray within the arena.

On both sides of me the prisoners broke to left and right for the seats, vaulting the low wall with dripping swords lusting for the crowded victims who awaited them.

In another moment the entire amphitheatre was filled with the shrieks of the dying and the wounded, mingled with the clash of arms and triumphant shouts of the victors.

Side by side the young red man and I, with perhaps a dozen others, fought our way to the foot of the throne. The remaining guards, reinforced by the high dignitaries and nobles of the First Born, closed in between us and Issus, who sat leaning far forward upon her carved sorapus bench, now screaming high-pitched commands to her following, now hurling blighting curses upon those who sought to desecrate her godhood.

The frightened slaves about her trembled in wide-eyed expectancy, knowing not whether to pray for our victory or our defeat. Several among them, proud daughters no doubt of some of Barsoom's noblest warriors, snatched swords from the hands of the fallen and fell upon the guards of Issus, but they were soon cut down; glorious martyrs to a hopeless cause.

The men with us fought well, but never since Tars Tarkas and I fought out that long, hot afternoon shoulder to shoulder against the hordes of Warhoon in the dead sea bottom before Thark, had I seen two men fight to such good purpose and with such unconquerable ferocity as the young red man and I fought that day before the throne of Issus, Goddess of Death, and of Life Eternal.

Man by man those who stood between us and the carven sorapus wood bench went down before our blades. Others swarmed in to fill the breach, but inch by inch, foot by foot we won nearer and nearer to our goal.

Presently a cry went up from a section of the stands near by—"Rise slaves!" "Rise slaves!" it rose and fell until it swelled to a mighty volume of sound that swept in great billows around the entire amphitheatre.

For an instant, as though by common assent, we ceased our fighting to look for the meaning of this new note nor did it take but a moment to translate its significance. In all parts of the structure the female slaves were falling upon their masters with whatever weapon came first to hand. A dagger snatched from the harness of her mistress was waved aloft by some fair slave, its shimmering blade crimson with the lifeblood of its owner; swords plucked from the bodies of the dead about them; heavy ornaments which could be turned into bludgeons—such were the implements with which these fair women wreaked the long-pent vengeance which at best could but partially recompense them for the unspeakable cruelties and indignities which their black masters had heaped upon them. And those who could find no other weapons used their strong fingers and their gleaming teeth.

It was at once a sight to make one shudder and to cheer; but in a brief second we were engaged once more in our own battle with only the unquenchable battlecry of the women to remind us that they still fought—"Rise slaves!" "Rise slaves!"

Only a single thin rank of men now stood between us and Issus. Her face was blue with terror. Foam flecked her lips. She seemed too paralysed with fear to move. Only the youth and I fought now. The others all had fallen, and I was like to have gone down too from a nasty long-sword cut had not a hand reached out from behind my adversary and clutched his elbow as the blade was falling upon me. The youth sprang to my side and ran his sword through the fellow before he could recover to deliver another blow.

I should have died even then but for that as my sword was tight wedged in the breastbone of a Dator of the First Born. As the fellow went down I snatched his sword from him and over his prostrate body looked into the eyes of the one whose quick hand had saved me from the first cut of his sword—it was Phaidor, daughter of Matai Shang.

"Fly, my Prince!" she cried. "It is useless to fight them longer. All within the arena are dead. All who charged the throne are dead but you and this youth. Only among the seats are there left any of your fighting-men, and they and the slave women are fast being cut down. Listen! You can scarce hear the battle-cry of the women now for nearly all are dead. For each one of you there are ten thousand blacks within the domains of the First Born. Break for the open and the sea of Korus. With your mighty sword arm you may yet win to the Golden Cliffs and the templed gardens of the Holy Therns. There tell your story to Matai Shang, my father. He will keep you, and together you may find a way to rescue me. Fly while there is yet a bare chance for flight."

But that was not my mission, nor could I see much to be preferred in the cruel hospitality of the Holy Therns to that of the First Born.

"Down with Issus!" I shouted, and together the boy and I took up the fight once more. Two blacks went down with our swords in their vitals, and we stood face to face with Issus. As my sword went up to end her horrid career her paralysis left her, and with an ear-piercing shriek she turned to flee. Directly behind her a black gulf suddenly yawned in the flooring of the dais. She sprang for the opening with the youth and I close at her heels. Her scattered guard rallied at her cry and rushed for us. A blow fell upon the head of the youth. He staggered and would have fallen, but I caught him in my left arm and turned to face an infuriated mob of religious fanatics crazed by the affront I had put upon their goddess, just as Issus disappeared into the black depths beneath me.

DOOMED TO DIE

FOR AN INSTANT I stood there before they fell upon me, but the first rush of them forced me back a step or two. My foot felt for the floor but found only empty space. I had backed into the pit which had received Issus. For a second I toppled there upon the brink. Then I too with the boy still tightly clutched in my arms pitched backward into the black abyss.

We struck a polished chute, the opening above us closed as magically as it had opened, and we shot down, unharmed, into a dimly lighted apartment far below the arena.

As I rose to my feet the first thing I saw was the malignant countenance of Issus glaring at me through the heavy bars of a grated door at one side of the chamber.

"Rash mortal!" she shrilled. "You shall pay the awful penalty for your blasphemy in this secret cell. Here you shall lie alone and in darkness with the carcass of your accomplice festering in its rottenness by your side, until crazed by loneliness and hunger you feed upon the crawling maggots that were once a man."

That was all. In another instant she was gone, and the dim light which had filled the cell faded into Cimmerian blackness.

"Pleasant old lady," said a voice at my side.

"Who speaks?" I asked.

" 'Tis I, your companion, who has had the honour this day of fighting shoulder to shoulder with the greatest warrior that ever wore metal upon Barsoom."

"I thank God that you are not dead," I said. "I feared for that nasty cut upon your head."

"It but stunned me," he replied. "A mere scratch."

"Maybe it were as well had it been final," I said. "We seem to be in a pretty fix here with a splendid chance of dying of starvation and thirst."

"Where are we?"

"Beneath the arena," I replied. "We tumbled down the shaft that swallowed Issus as she was almost at our mercy."

He laughed a low laugh of pleasure and relief, and then reaching out through the inky blackness he sought my shoulder and pulled my ear close to his mouth.

"Nothing could be better," he whispered. "There are secrets within the secrets of Issus of which Issus herself does not dream."

"What do you mean?"

"I laboured with the other slaves a year since in the remodelling of these subterranean galleries, and at that time we found below these an ancient system of corridors and chambers that had been sealed up for ages. The blacks in charge of the work explored them, taking several of us along to do whatever work there might be occasion for. I know the entire system perfectly.

"There are miles of corridors honeycombing the ground beneath the gardens and the temple itself, and there is one passage that leads down to and connects with the lower regions that open on the water shaft that gives passage to Omean.

"If we can reach the submarine undetected we may yet make the sea in which there are many islands where the blacks never go. There we may live for a time, and who knows what may transpire to aid us to escape?"

He had spoken all in a low whisper, evidently fearing spying ears even here, and so I answered him in the same subdued tone.

"Lead back to Shador, my friend," I whispered. "Xodar, the black, is there. We were to attempt our escape together, so I cannot desert him."

"No," said the boy, "one cannot desert a friend. It were better to be recaptured ourselves than that."

Then he commenced groping his way about the floor of the dark chamber searching for the trap that led to the corridors beneath. At length he summoned me by a low, "S-s-t," and I crept toward the sound of his voice to find him kneeling on the brink of an opening in the floor.

"There is a drop here of about ten feet," he whispered. "Hang by your hands and you will alight safely on a level floor of soft sand."

Very quietly I lowered myself from the inky cell above into the inky pit below. So utterly dark was it that we could not see our hands at an inch from our noses. Never, I think, have I known such complete absence of light as existed in the pits of Issus.

For an instant I hung in mid air. There is a strange sensation connected with an experience of that nature which is quite difficult to describe. When the feet tread empty air and the distance below is shrouded in darkness there is a feeling akin to panic at the thought of releasing the hold and taking the plunge into unknown depths.

Although the boy had told me that it was but ten feet to the floor below I experienced the same thrills as though I were hanging above a bottomless pit. Then I released my hold and dropped—four feet to a soft cushion of sand.

The boy followed me.

"Raise me to your shoulders," he said, "and I will replace the trap."

This done he took me by the hand, leading me very slowly, with much feeling about and frequent halts to assure himself that he did not stray into wrong passageways.

Presently we commenced the descent of a very steep incline.

"It will not be long," he said, "before we shall have light. At the lower levels we meet the same strata of phosphorescent rock that illuminates Omean."

Never shall I forget that trip through the pits of Issus. While it was devoid of important incidents yet it was filled for me with a strange charm of excitement and adventure which I think I must have hinged principally on the unguessable antiquity of these long-forgotten corridors. The things which the Stygian darkness hid from my objective eye could not have been half so wonderful as the pictures which my imagination wrought as it conjured to life again the ancient peoples of this dying world and set them once more to the labours, the intrigues, the mysteries and the cruelties which they had practised to make their last stand against the swarming hordes of the dead sea bottoms that had driven them step by step to the uttermost pinnacle of the world where they were now intrenched behind an impenetrable barrier of superstition.

In addition to the green men there had been three principal races upon Barsoom. The blacks, the whites, and a race of yellow men. As the waters of the planet dried and the seas receded, all other resources dwindled until life upon the planet became a constant battle for survival.

The various races had made war upon one another for ages, and the three higher types had easily bested the green savages of the water places of the world, but now that the receding seas necessitated constant abandonment of their fortified cities and forced upon them a more or less nomadic life in which they became separated into smaller communities they soon fell prey to the fierce hordes of green men. The result was a partial amalgamation of the blacks, whites and yellows, the result of which is shown in the present splendid race of red men.

I had always supposed that all traces of the original races had disappeared from the face of Mars, yet within the past four days I had found both whites and blacks in great multitudes. Could it be possible that in some far-off corner of the planet there still existed a remnant of the ancient race of yellow men?

My reveries were broken in upon by a low exclamation from the boy.

"At last, the lighted way," he cried, and looking up I beheld at a long distance before us a dim radiance.

As we advanced the light increased until presently we emerged into well-lighted passageways. From then on our progress was rapid until we came suddenly to the end of a corridor that let directly upon the ledge surrounding the pool of the submarine.

The craft lay at her moorings with uncovered hatch. Raising his finger to his lips and then tapping his sword in a significant manner, the youth crept noiselessly toward the vessel. I was close at his heels.

Silently we dropped to the deserted deck, and on hands and knees crawled toward the hatchway. A stealthy glance below revealed no guard in sight, and so with the quickness and the soundlessness of cats we dropped together into the main cabin of the submarine. Even here was no sign of life. Quickly we covered and secured the hatch.

Then the boy stepped into the pilot house, touched a button and the boat sank amid swirling waters toward the bottom of the shaft. Even then there was no scurrying of feet as we had expected, and while the boy remained to direct the boat I slid from cabin to cabin in futile search for some member of the crew. The craft was entirely deserted. Such good fortune seemed almost unbelievable.

When I returned to the pilot house to report the good news to my companion he handed me a paper.

"This may explain the absence of the crew," he said.

It was a radio-aerial message to the commander of the submarine:

"The slaves have risen. Come with what men you have and those that you can gather on the way. Too late to get aid from Omean. They are massacring all within the amphitheatre. Issus is threatened. Haste.

"ZITHAD"

"Zithad is Dator of the guards of Issus," explained the youth. "We gave them a bad scare—one that they will not soon forget."

"Let us hope that it is but the beginning of the end of Issus," I said.

"Only our first ancestor knows," he replied.

We reached the submarine pool in Omean without incident. Here we debated the wisdom of sinking the craft before leaving her, but finally decided that it would add nothing to our chances for escape. There were plenty of blacks on Omean to thwart us were we apprehended; however many more might come from the temples and gardens of Issus would not in any way decrease our chances.

We were now in a quandary as to how to pass the guards who patrolled the island about the pool. At last I hit upon a plan.

"What is the name or title of the officer in charge of these guards?" I asked the boy.

"A fellow named Torith was on duty when we entered this morning," he replied.

"Good. And what is the name of the commander of the submarine?"

"Yersted."

I found a dispatch blank in the cabin and wrote the following order:

"Dator Torith: Return these two slaves at once to Shador.

YERSTED"

"That will be the simpler way to return," I said, smiling, as I handed the forged order to the boy. "Come, we shall see now how well it works."

"But our swords!" he exclaimed. "What shall we say to explain them?"

"Since we cannot explain them we shall have to leave them behind us," I replied.

"Is it not the extreme of rashness to thus put ourselves again, unarmed, in the power of the First Born?"

"It is the only way," I answered. "You may trust me to find a way out of the prison of Shador, and I think, once out, that we shall find no great difficulty in arming ourselves once more in a country which abounds so plentifully in armed men."

"As you say," he replied with a smile and shrug. "I could not follow another leader who inspired greater confidence than you. Come, let us put your ruse to the test."

Boldly we emerged from the hatchway of the craft, leaving our swords behind us, and strode to the main exit which led to the sentry's post and the office of the Dator of the guard.

At sight of us the members of the guard sprang forward in surprise, and with levelled rifles halted us. I held out the message to one of them. He took it and seeing to whom it was addressed turned and handed it to Torith who was emerging from his office to learn the cause of the commotion.

The black read the order, and for a moment eyed us with evident suspicion.

"Where is Dator Yersted?" he asked, and my heart sank within me, as I cursed myself for a stupid fool in not having sunk the submarine to make good the lie that I must tell.

"His orders were to return immediately to the temple landing," I replied.

Torith took a half step toward the entrance to the pool as though to corroborate my story. For that instant everything hung in the balance, for had he done so and found the empty submarine still lying at her wharf the whole weak fabric of my concoction would have tumbled about our heads; but evidently he decided that the message must be genuine, nor indeed was there any good reason to doubt it since it would scarce have seemed credible to him that two slaves would voluntarily have given themselves into custody in any such manner as this. It was the very boldness of the plan which rendered it successful.

"Were you connected with the rising of the slaves?" asked Torith. "We have just had meagre reports of some such event."

"All were involved," I replied. "But it amounted to little. The guards quickly overcame and killed the majority of us."

He seemed satisfied with this reply. "Take them to Shador," he ordered, turning to one of his subordinates. We entered a small boat lying beside the island, and in a few minutes were disembarking upon Shador. Here we were returned to our respective cells; I with Xodar, the boy by himself; and behind locked doors we were again prisoners of the First Born.

A BREAK FOR LIBERTY

Xodar listened in incredulous astonishment to my narration of the events which had transpired within the arena at the rites of Issus. He could scarce conceive, even though he had already professed his doubt as to the deity of Issus, that one could threaten her with sword in hand and not be blasted into a thousand fragments by the mere fury of her divine wrath.

"It is the final proof," he said, at last. "No more is needed to completely shatter the last remnant of my superstitious belief in the divinity of Issus. She is only a wicked old woman, wielding a mighty power for evil through machinations that have kept her own people and all Barsoom in religious ignorance for ages."

"She is still all-powerful here, however," I replied. "So it behooves us to leave at the first moment that appears at all propitious."

"I hope that you may find a propitious moment," he said, with a laugh, "for it is certain that in all my life I have never seen one in which a prisoner of the First Born might escape."

"To-night will do as well as any," I replied.

"It will soon be night," said Xodar. "How may I aid in the adventure?"

"Can you swim?" I asked him.

"No slimy silian that haunts the depths of Korus is more at home in water than is Xodar," he replied.

"Good. The red one in all probability cannot swim," I said, "since there is scarce enough water in all their domains to float the tiniest craft. One of us therefore will have to support him through the sea to the craft we select. I had hoped that we might make the entire distance below the surface, but I fear that the red youth could not thus perform the trip. Even the bravest of the brave among them are terrorized at the mere thought of deep water, for it has been ages since their forebears saw a lake, a river or a sea.

"The red one is to accompany us?" asked Xodar.

"Yes."

"It is well. Three swords are better than two. Especially when the third is as mighty as this fellow's. I have seen him battle in the arena at the rites of Issus many times. Never, until I saw you fight, had I seen one who seemed unconquerable even in the face of great odds. One might think you two master and pupil, or father and son. Come to recall his face there is a resemblance between you. It is very marked when you fight—there is the same grim smile, the same maddening contempt for your adversary apparent in every movement of your bodies and in every changing expression of your faces."

"Be that as it may, Xodar, he is a great fighter. I think that we will make a trio difficult to overcome, and if my friend Tars Tarkas, Jeddak of Thark, were but one of us we could fight our way from one end of Barsoom to the other even though the whole world were pitted against us."

"It will be," said Xodar, "when they find from whence you have come. That is but one of the superstitions which Issus has foisted upon a credulous humanity. She works through the Holy Therns who are as ignorant of her real self as are the Barsoomians of the outer world. Her decrees are borne to the therns written in blood upon a strange parchment. The poor deluded fools think that they are receiving the revelations of a goddess through some supernatural agency, since they find these messages upon their guarded altars to which none could have access without detection. I myself have borne these messages for Issus for many years. There is a long tunnel from the temple of Issus to the principal temple of Matai Shang. It was dug ages ago by the slaves of the First Born in such utter secrecy that no thern ever guessed its existence.

"The therns for their part have temples dotted about the entire civilized world. Here priests whom the people never see communicate the doctine of the Mysterious River Iss, the Valley Dor, and the Lost Sea of Korus to persuade the poor deluded creatures to take the voluntary pilgrimage that swells the wealth of the Holy Therns and adds to the numbers of their slaves.

"Thus the therns are used as the principal means for collecting the wealth and labour that the First Born wrest from them as they need it. Occasionally the First Born themselves make raids upon the outer world. It is then that they capture many females of the royal houses of the red men, and take the newest in battleships and the trained artisans who build them, that they may copy what they cannot create.

"We are a non-productive race, priding ourselves upon our non-productiveness. It is criminal for a First Born to labour or invent. That is the work of the lower orders, who live merely that the First

Born may enjoy long lives of luxury and idleness. With us fighting is all that counts; were it not for that there would be more of the First Born than all the creatures of Barsoom could support, for in so far as I know none of us ever dies a natural death. Our females would live for ever but for the fact that we tire of them and remove them to make place for others. Issus alone of all is protected against death. She has lived for countless ages."

"Would not the other Barsoomians live for ever but for the doctrine of the voluntary pilgrimage which drags them to the bosom of Iss at or before their thousandth year?" I asked him.

"I feel now that there is no doubt but that they are precisely the same species of creature as the First Born, and I hope that I shall live to fight for them in atonement of the sins I have committed against them through the ignorance born of generations of false teaching."

As he ceased speaking a weird call rang out across the waters of Omean. I had heard it at the same time the previous evening and knew that it marked the ending of the day, when the men of Omean spread their silks upon the deck of battleship and cruiser and fall into the dreamless sleep of Mars.

Our guard entered to inspect us for the last time before the new day broke upon the world above. His duty was soon performed and the heavy door of our prison closed behind him—we were alone for the night.

I gave him time to return to his quarters, as Xodar said he probably would do, then I sprang to the grated window and surveyed the nearby waters. At a little distance from the island, a quarter of a mile perhaps, lay a monster battleship, while between her and the shore were a number of smaller cruisers and one-man scouts. Upon the battleship alone was there a watch. I could see him plainly in the upper works of the ship, and as I watched I saw him spread his sleeping silks upon the tiny platform in which he was stationed. Soon he threw himself at full length upon his couch. The discipline on Omean was lax indeed. But it is not to be wondered at since no enemy guessed the existence upon Barsoom of such a fleet, or even of the First Born, or the Sea of Omean. Why indeed should they maintain a watch?

Presently I dropped to the floor again and talked with Xodar, describing the various craft I had seen.

"There is one there," he said, "my personal property, built to carry five men, that is the swiftest of the swift. If we can board her we can at least make a memorable run for liberty," and then he went on to describe to me the equipment of the boat; her engines, and all that went to make her the flier that she was.

In his explanation I recognized a trick of gearing that Kantos Kan had taught me that time we sailed under false names in the navy of Zodanga beneath Sab Than, the Prince. And I knew then that the First Born had stolen it from the ships of Helium, for only they are thus geared. And I knew too that Xodar spoke the truth when he lauded the speed of his little craft, for nothing that cleaves the thin air of Mars can approximate the speed of the ships of Helium.

We decided to wait for an hour at least until all the stragglers had sought their silks. In the meantime I was to fetch the red youth to our cell so that we would be in readiness to make our rash break for freedom together.

I sprang to the top of our partition wall and pulled myself up on to it. There I found a flat surface about a foot in width and along this I walked until I came to the cell in which I saw the boy sitting upon his bench. He had been leaning back against the wall looking up at the glowing dome above Omean, and when he spied me balancing upon the partition wall above him his eyes opened wide in astonishment. Then a wide grin of appreciative understanding spread across his countenance.

As I stooped to drop to the floor beside him he motioned me to wait, and coming close below me whispered: "Catch my hand; I can almost leap to the top of that wall myself. I have tried it many times, and each day I come a little closer. Some day I should have been able to make it."

I lay upon my belly across the wall and reached my hand far down toward him. With a little run from the centre of the cell he sprang up until I grasped his outstretched hand, and thus I pulled him to the wall's top beside me.

"You are the first jumper I ever saw among the red men of Barsoom," I said.

He smiled. "It is not strange. I will tell you why when we have more time."

Together we returned to the cell in which Xodar sat; descending to talk with him until the hour had passed.

There we made our plans for the immediate future, binding ourselves by a solemn oath to fight to the death for one another against whatsoever enemies should confront us, for we knew that even should we succeed in escaping the First Born we might still have a whole world against us—the power of religious superstition is mighty.

It was agreed that I should navigate the craft after we had reached her, and that if we made the outer world in safety we should attempt to reach Helium without a stop.

"Why Helium?" asked the red youth.

"I am a prince of Helium," I replied.

He gave me a peculiar look, but said nothing further on the subject. I wondered at the time what the significance of his expression might be, but in the press of other matters it soon left my mind, nor did I have occasion to think of it again until later.

"Come," I said at length, "now is as good a time as any. Let us go."

Another moment found me at the top of the partition wall again with the boy beside me. Unbuckling my harness I snapped it together with a single long strap which I lowered to the waiting Xodar below. He grasped the end and was soon sitting beside us.

"How simple," he laughed.

"The balance should be even simpler," I replied. Then I raised myself to the top of the outer wall of the prison, just so that I could peer over and locate the passing sentry. For a matter of five minutes I waited and then he came in sight on his slow and snail-like beat about the structure.

I watched him until he had made the turn at the end of the building which carried him out of sight of the side of the prison that was to witness our dash for freedom. The moment his form disappeared I grasped Xodar and drew him to the top of the wall. Placing one end of my harness strap in his hands I lowered him quickly to the ground below. Then the boy grasped the strap and slid down to Xodar's side.

In accordance with our arrangement they did not wait for me, but walked slowly toward the water, a matter of a hundred yards, directly past the guard-house filled with sleeping soldiers.

They had taken scarce a dozen steps when I too dropped to the ground and followed them leisurely toward the shore. As I passed the guard-house the thought of all the good blades lying there gave me pause, for if ever men were to have need of swords it was my companions and I on the perilous trip upon which we were about to embark.

I glanced toward Xodar and the youth and saw that they had slipped over the edge of the dock into the water. In accordance with our plan they were to remain there clinging to the metal rings which studded the concrete-like substance of the dock at the water's level, with only their mouths and noses above the surface of the sea, until I should join them.

The lure of the swords within the guard-house was strong upon me, and I hesitated a moment, half inclined to risk the attempt to take the few we needed. That he who hesitates is lost proved itself a true aphorism in this instance, for another moment saw me creeping stealthily toward the door of the guard-house.

Gently I pressed it open a crack; enough to discover a dozen blacks stretched upon their silks in profound slumber. At the far side of the room a rack held the swords and firearms of the men. Warily I pushed the door a trifle wider to admit my body. A hinge gave out a resentful groan. One of the men stirred, and my heart stood still. I cursed myself for a fool to have thus jeopardized our chances for escape; but there was nothing for it now but to see the adventure through.

With a spring as swift and as noiseless as a tiger's I lit beside the guardsman who had moved. My hands hovered about his throat awaiting the moment that his eyes should open. For what seemed an eternity to my overwrought nerves I remained poised thus. Then the fellow turned again upon his side and resumed the even respiration of deep slumber.

Carefully I picked my way between and over the soldiers until I had gained the rack at the far side of the room. Here I turned to survey the sleeping men. All were quiet. Their regular breathing rose and fell in a soothing rhythm that seemed to me the sweetest music I ever had heard.

Gingerly I drew a long-sword from the rack. The scraping of the scabbard against its holder as I withdrew it sounded like the filing of cast iron with a great rasp, and I looked to see the room immediately filled with alarmed and attacking guardsmen. But none stirred.

The second sword I withdrew noiselessly, but the third clanked in its scabbard with a frightful din. I knew that it must awaken some of the men at least, and was on the point of forestalling their attack by a rapid charge for the doorway, when again, to my intense surprise, not a black moved. Either they were wondrous heavy sleepers or else the noises that I made were really much less than they seemed to me.

I was about to leave the rack when my attention was attracted by the revolvers. I knew that I could not carry more than one away with me, for I was already too heavily laden to move quietly with any degree of safety or speed. As I took one of them from its pin my eye fell for the first time on an open window beside the rack. Ah, here was a splendid means of escape, for it let directly upon the dock, not twenty feet from the water's edge.

And as I congratulated myself, I heard the door opposite me open, and there looking me full in the face stood the officer of the guard. He evidently took in the situation at a glance and appreciated the gravity of it as quickly as I, for our revolvers came up simultaneously and the sounds of the two reports were as one as we touched the buttons on the grips that exploded the cartridges.

I felt the wind of his bullet as it whizzed past my ear, and at the same instant I saw him crumple to the ground. Where I hit him I do not know, nor if I killed him, for scarce had he started to collapse when I was through the window at my rear. In another second the waters of Omean closed above my head, and the three of us were making for the little flier a hundred yards away.

Xodar was burdened with the boy, and I with the three long-swords. The revolver I had dropped, so that while we were both strong swimmers it seemed to me that we moved at a snail's pace through the water. I was swimming entirely beneath the surface, but Xodar was compelled to rise often to let the youth breathe, so it was a wonder that we were not discovered long before we were.

In fact we reached the boat's side and were all aboard before the watch upon the battleship, aroused by the shots, detected us. Then an alarm gun bellowed from the ship's bow, its deep boom reverberating in deafening tones beneath the rocky dome of Omean.

Instantly the sleeping thousands were awake. The decks of a thousand monster craft teemed with fighting-men, for an alarm on Omean was a thing of rare occurrence.

We cast away before the sound of the first gun had died, and another second saw us rising swiftly from the surface of the sea. I lay at full length along the deck with the levers and buttons of control before me. Xodar and the boy were stretched directly behind me, prone also that we might offer as little resistance to the air as possible.

"Rise high," whispered Xodar. "They dare not fire their heavy guns toward the dome—the fragments of the shells would drop back among their own craft. If we are high enough our keel plates will protect us from rifle fire."

I did as he bade. Below us we could see the men leaping into the water by hundreds, and striking out for the small cruisers and one-man fliers that lay moored about the big ships. The larger craft were getting under way, following us rapidly, but not rising from the water.

"A little to your right," cried Xodar, for there are no points of compass upon Omean where every direction is due north.

The pandemonium that had broken out below us was deafening. Rifles cracked, officers shouted orders, men yelled directions to one another from the water and from the decks of myriad boats, while through all ran the purr of countless propellers cutting water and air.

I had not dared pull my speed lever to the highest for fear of over-running the mouth of the shaft that passed from Omean's dome to the world above, but even so we were hitting a clip that I doubt has ever been equalled on the windless sea.

The smaller fliers were commencing to rise toward us when Xodar shouted: "The shaft! The shaft! Dead ahead," and I saw the opening, black and yawning in the glowing dome of this underworld.

A ten-man cruiser was rising directly in front to cut off our escape. It was the only vessel that stood in our way, but at the rate that it was travelling it would come between us and the shaft in plenty of time to thwart our plans.

It was rising at an angle of about forty-five degrees dead ahead of us, with the evident intention of combing us with grappling hooks from above as it skimmed low over our deck.

There was but one forlorn hope for us, and I took it. It was useless to try to pass over her, for that would have allowed her to force us against the rocky dome above, and we were already too near that as it was. To have attempted to dive below her would have put us entirely at her mercy, and precisely where she wanted us. On either side a hundred other menacing craft were hastening toward us. The alternative was filled with risk—in fact it was all risk, with but a slender chance of success.

As we neared the cruiser I rose as though to pass above her, so that she would do just what she did do, rise at a steeper angle to force me still higher. Then as we were almost upon her I yelled to my companions to hold tight, and throwing the little vessel into her highest speed I deflected her bows at the same instant until we were running horizontally and at terrific velocity straight for the cruiser's keel.

Her commander may have seen my intentions then, but it was too late. Almost at the instant of impact I turned my bows upward, and then with a shattering jolt we were in collision. What I had hoped for happened. The cruiser, already tilted at a perilous angle, was carried completely over backward by the impact of my smaller vessel. Her crew fell twisting and screaming through the air to the water far below, while the cruiser, her propellers still madly churning, dived swiftly headforemost after them to the bottom of the Sea of Omean.

The collision crushed our steel bows, and notwithstanding every effort on our part came near to hurling us from the deck. As it was we landed in a wildly clutching heap at the very extremity of the flier, where Xodar and I succeeded in grasping the hand-rail, but the boy would have plunged overboard had I not fortunately grasped his ankle as he was already partially over.

Unguided, our vessel careened wildly in its mad flight, rising ever nearer the rocks above. It took but an instant, however, for me to regain the levers, and with the roof barely fifty feet above I turned her nose once more into the horizontal plane and headed her again for the black mouth of the shaft.

The collision had retarded our progress and now a hundred swift scouts were close upon us. Xodar had told me that ascending the shaft by virtue of our repulsive rays alone would give our enemies their best chance to overtake us, since our propellers would be idle and in rising we would be outclassed by many of our pursuers. The swifter craft are seldom equipped with large buoyancy tanks, since the added bulk of them tends to reduce a vessel's speed.

As many boats were now quite close to us it was inevitable that we would be quickly overhauled in the shaft, and captured or killed in short order.

To me there always seems a way to gain the opposite side of an obstacle. If one cannot pass over it, or below it, or around it, why then there is but a single alternative left, and that is to pass through it. I could not get around the fact that many of these other boats could rise faster than ours by the fact of their greater buoyancy, but I was none the less determined to reach the outer world far in advance of them or die a death of my own choosing in event of failure.

"Reverse!" screamed Xodar, behind me. "For the love of your first ancestor, reverse. We are at the shaft."

"Hold tight!" I screamed in reply. "Grasp the boy and hold tight— we are going straight up the shaft."

The words were scarce out of my mouth as we swept beneath the pitch-black opening. I threw the bow hard up, dragged the speed lever to its last notch, and clutching a stanchion with one hand and the steering-wheel with the other hung on like grim death and consigned my soul to its author.

I heard a little exclamation of surprise from Xodar, followed by a grim laugh. The boy laughed too and said something which I could not catch for the whistling of the wind of our awful speed.

I looked above my head, hoping to catch the gleam of stars by which I could direct our course and hold the hurtling thing that bore us true to the centre of the shaft. To have touched the side at the speed we were making would doubtless have resulted in instant death for us all. But not a star showed above—only utter and impenetrable darkness.

Then I glanced below me, and there I saw a rapidly diminishing circle of light—the mouth of the opening above the phosphorescent radiance of Omean. By this I steered, endeavouring to keep the circle of light below me ever perfect. At best it was but a slender cord that held us from destruction, and I think that I steered that night more by intuition and blind faith than by skill or reason.

We were not long in the shaft, and possibly the very fact of our enormous speed saved us, for evidently we started in the right direction and so quickly were we out again that we had no time to alter our course. Omean lies perhaps two miles below the surface crust of Mars. Our speed must have approximated two hundred miles an hour, for Martian fliers are swift, so that at most we were in the shaft not over forty seconds.

We must have been out of it for some seconds before I realised that we had accomplished the impossible. Black darkness enshrouded all about us. There were neither moons nor stars. Never before had I seen such a thing upon Mars, and for the moment I was nonplussed. Then the explanation came to me. It was summer at the south pole. The ice cap was melting and those meteoric phenomena, clouds, unknown upon the greater part of Barsoom, were shutting out the light of heaven from this portion of the planet.

Fortunate indeed it was for us, nor did it take me long to grasp the opportunity for escape which this happy condition offered us. Keeping the boat's nose at a stiff angle I raced her for the impenetrable curtain which Nature had hung above this dying world to shut us out from the sight of our pursuing enemies.

We plunged through the cold damp fog without diminishing our speed, and in a moment emerged into the glorious light of the two moons and the million stars. I dropped into a horizontal course and headed due north. Our enemies were a good half-hour behind us with no conception of our direction. We had performed the miraculous and come through a thousand dangers unscathed—we had escaped from the land of the First Born. No other prisoners in all the ages of Barsoom had done this thing, and now as I looked back upon it it did not seem to have been so difficult after all.

I said as much to Xodar, over my shoulder.

"It is very wonderful, nevertheless," he replied. "No one else could have accomplished it but John Carter."

At the sound of that name the boy jumped to his feet.

"John Carter!" he cried. "John Carter! Why, man, John Carter, Prince of Helium, has been dead for years. I am his son."

THE EYES IN THE DARK

MY SON! I could not believe my ears. Slowly I rose and faced the handsome youth. Now that I looked at him closely I commenced to see why his face and personality had attracted me so strongly. There was much of his mother's incomparable beauty in his clear-cut features, but it was strongly masculine beauty, and his grey eyes and the expression of them were mine.

The boy stood facing me, half hope and half uncertainty in his look.

"Tell me of your mother," I said. "Tell me all you can of the years that I have been robbed by a relentless fate of her dear companionship."

With a cry of pleasure he sprang toward me and threw his arms about my neck, and for a brief moment as I held my boy close to me the tears welled to my eyes and I was like to have choked after the manner of some maudlin fool—but I do not regret it, nor am I ashamed. A long life has taught me that a man may seem weak where women and children are concerned and yet be anything but a weakling in the sterner avenues of life.

"Your stature, your manner, the terrible ferocity of your swordsmanship," said the boy, "are as my mother has described them to me a thousand times—but even with such evidence I could scarce credit the truth of what seemed so improbable to me, however much I desired it to be true. Do you know what thing it was that convinced me more than all the others?"

"What, my boy?" I asked.

"Your first words to me—they were of my mother. None else but the man who loved her as she has told me my father did would have thought first of her."

"For long years, my son, I can scarce recall a moment that the radiant vision of your mother's face has not been ever before me. Tell me of her."

"Those who have known her longest say that she has not changed, unless it be to grow more beautiful—were that possible. Only, when she thinks I am not about to see her, her face grows very sad, and, oh, so wistful. She thinks ever of you, my father, and all Helium mourns with her and for her. Her grandfather's people love her. They loved you also, and fairly worship your memory as the saviour of Barsoom.

"Each year that brings its anniversary of the day that saw you racing across a near dead world to unlock the secret of that awful portal behind which lay the mighty power of life for countless millions a great festival is held in your honour; but there are tears mingled with the thanksgiving—tears of real regret that the author of the happiness is not with them to share the joy of living he died to give them. Upon all Barsoom there is no greater name than John Carter."

"And by what name has your mother called you, my boy?" I asked.

"The people of Helium asked that I be named with my father's name, but my mother said no, that you and she had chosen a name for me together, and that your wish must be honoured before all others, so the name that she called me is the one that you desired, a combination of hers and yours—Carthoris."

Xodar had been at the wheel as I talked with my son, and now he called me.

"She is dropping badly by the head, John Carter," he said. "So long as we were rising at a stiff angle it was not noticeable, but now that I am trying to keep a horizontal course it is different. The wound in her bow has opened one of her forward ray tanks."

It was true, and after I had examined the damage I found it a much graver matter than I had anticipated. Not only was the forced angle at which we were compelled to maintain the bow in order to keep a horizontal course greatly impeding our speed, but at the rate that we were losing our repulsive rays from the forward tanks it was but a question of an hour or more when we would be floating stern up and helpless.

We had slightly reduced our speed with the dawning of a sense of security, but now I took the helm once more and pulled the noble little engine wide open, so that again we raced north at terrific velocity. In the meantime Carthoris and Xodar with tools in hand were puttering with the great rent in the bow in a hopeless endeavour to stem the tide of escaping rays.

It was still dark when we passed the northern boundary of the ice cap and the area of clouds. Below us lay a typical Martian landscape. Rolling ochre sea bottom of long dead seas, low surrounding hills, with here and there the grim and silent cities of the dead past; great piles of mighty architecture tenanted only by age-old memories of a once powerful race, and by the great white apes of Barsoom.

It was becoming more and more difficult to maintain our little vessel in a horizontal position. Lower and lower sagged the bow until it became necessary to stop the engine to prevent our flight terminating in a swift dive to the ground.

As the sun rose and the light of a new day swept away the darkness of night our craft gave a final spasmodic plunge, turned half upon her side, and then with deck tilting at a sickening angle swung in a slow circle, her bow dropping further below her stern each moment.

To hand-rail and stanchion we clung, and finally as we saw the end approaching, snapped the buckles of our harness to the rings at her sides. In another moment the deck reared at an angle of ninety degrees and we hung in our leather with feet dangling a thousand yards above the ground.

I was swinging quite close to the controlling devices, so I reached out to the lever that directed the rays of repulsion. The boat responded to the touch, and very gently we began to sink toward the ground.

It was fully half an hour before we touched. Directly north of us rose a rather lofty range of hills, toward which we decided to make our way, since they afforded greater opportunity for concealment from the pursuers we were confident might stumble in this direction.

An hour later found us in the time-rounded gullies of the hills, amid the beautiful flowering plants that abound in the arid waste places of Barsoom. There we found numbers of huge milk-giving shrubs—that strange plant which serves in great part as food and drink for the wild hordes of green men. It was indeed a boon to us, for we all were nearly famished.

Beneath a cluster of these which afforded perfect concealment from wandering air scouts, we lay down to sleep—for me the first time in many hours. This was the beginning of my fifth day upon Barsoom since I had found myself suddenly translated from my cottage on the Hudson to Dor, the valley beautiful, the valley hideous. In all this time I had slept but twice, though once the clock around within the storehouse of the therns.

It was mid-afternoon when I was awakened by some one seizing my hand and covering it with kisses. With a start I opened my eyes to look into the beautiful face of Thuvia.

"My Prince! My Prince!" she cried, in an ecstasy of happiness. "'Tis you whom I had mourned as dead. My ancestors have been good to me; I have not lived in vain."

The girl's voice awoke Xodar and Carthoris. The boy gazed upon the woman in surprise, but she did not seem to realize the presence of another than I. She would have thrown her arms about my neck and smothered me with caresses, had I not gently but firmly disengaged myself.

"Come, come, Thuvia," I said soothingly; "you are overwrought by the danger and hardships you have passed through. You forget yourself, as you forget that I am the husband of the Princess of Helium."

"I forget nothing, my Prince," she replied. "You have spoken no word of love to me, nor do I expect that you ever shall; but nothing can prevent me loving you. I would not take the place of Dejah Thoris. My greatest ambition is to serve you, my Prince, for ever as your slave. No greater boon could I ask, no greater honour could I crave, no greater happiness could I hope."

As I have before said, I am no ladies' man, and I must admit that I seldom have felt so uncomfortable and embarrassed as I did that moment. While I was quite familiar with the Martian custom which allows female slaves to Martian men, whose high and chivalrous honour is always ample protection for every woman in his household, yet I had never myself chosen other than men as my body servants.

"And I ever return to Helium, Thuvia," I said, "you shall go with me, but as an honoured equal, and not as a slave. There you shall find plenty of handsome young nobles who would face Issus herself to win a smile from you, and we shall have you married in short order to one of the best of them. Forget your foolish gratitude-begotten infatuation, which your innocence has mistaken for love. I like your friendship better, Thuvia."

"You are my master; it shall be as you say," she replied simply, but there was a note of sadness in her voice.

"How came you here, Thuvia?" I asked. "And where is Tars Tarkas?"

"The great Thark, I fear, is dead," she replied sadly. "He was a mighty fighter, but a multitude of green warriors of another horde than his overwhelmed him. The last that I saw of him they were bearing him, wounded and bleeding, to the deserted city from which they had sallied to attack us."

"You are not sure that he is dead, then?" I asked. "And where is this city of which you speak?"

"It is just beyond this range of hills. The vessel in which you so nobly resigned a place that we might escape defied our small skill in navigation, with the result that we drifted aimlessly about for two days. Then we decided to abandon the craft and attempt to make our way on foot to the nearest waterway. Yesterday we crossed these hills and came upon the dead city beyond. We had passed within its streets and were walking toward the central portion, when at an intersecting avenue we saw a body of green warriors approaching.

"Tars Tarkas was in advance, and they saw him, but me they did not see. The Thark sprang back to my side and forced me into an adjacent doorway, where he told me to remain in hiding until I could escape, making my way to Helium if possible.

"'There will be no escape for me now,' he said, 'for these be the Warhoons of the South. When they have seen my metal it will be to the death.'

"Then he stepped out to meet them. Ah, my Prince, such fighting! For an hour they swarmed about him, until the Warhoon dead formed a hill where he had stood; but at last they overwhelmed him, those behind pushing the foremost upon him until there remained no space to swing his great sword. Then he stumbled and went down and they rolled over him like a huge wave. When they carried him away toward the heart of the city, he was dead, I think, for I did not see him move."

"Before we go farther we must be sure," I said. "I cannot leave Tars Tarkas alive among the Warhoons. To-night I shall enter the city and make sure."

"And I shall go with you," spoke Carthoris.

"And I," said Xodar.

"Neither one of you shall go," I replied. "It is work that requires stealth and strategy, not force. One man alone may succeed where more would invite disaster. I shall go alone. If I need your help, I will return for you."

They did not like it, but both were good soldiers, and it had been agreed that I should command. The sun already was low, so that I did not have long to wait before the sudden darkness of Barsoom engulfed us.

With a parting word of instructions to Carthoris and Xodar, in case I should not return, I bade them all farewell and set forth at a rapid dogtrot toward the city.

As I emerged from the hills the nearer moon was winging its wild flight through the heavens, its bright beams turning to burnished silver the barbaric splendour of the ancient metropolis. The city had been built upon the gently rolling foothills that in the dim and distant past had sloped down to meet the sea. It was due to this fact that I had no difficulty in entering the streets unobserved.

The green hordes that use these deserted cities seldom occupy more than a few squares about the central plaza, and as they come and go always across the dead sea bottoms that the cities face, it is usually a matter of comparative ease to enter from the hillside.

Once within the streets, I kept close in the dense shadows of the walls. At intersections I halted a moment to make sure that none was in sight before I sprang quickly to the shadows of the opposite side. Thus I made the journey to the vicinity of the plaza without detection. As I approached the purlieus of the inhabited portion of the city I was made aware of the proximity of the warriors' quarters by the squealing and grunting of the thoats and zitidars corralled within the hollow courtyards formed by the buildings surrounding each square.

These old familiar sounds that are so distinctive of green Martian life sent a thrill of pleasure surging through me. It was as one might feel on coming home after a long absence. It was amid such sounds that I had first courted the incomparable Dejah Thoris in the age-old marble halls of the dead city of Korad.

As I stood in the shadows at the far corner of the first square which housed members of the horde, I saw warriors emerging from several of the buildings. They all went in the same direction, toward a great building which stood in the centre of the plaza. My knowledge of green Martian customs convinced me that this was either the quarters of the principal chieftain or contained the audience chamber wherein the Jeddak met his jeds and lesser chieftains. In either event, it was evident that something was afoot which might have a bearing on the recent capture of Tars Tarkas.

To reach this building, which I now felt it imperative that I do, I must needs traverse the entire length of one square and cross a broad avenue and a portion of the plaza. From the noises of the animals which came from every courtyard about me, I knew that there were many people in the surrounding buildings—probably several communities of the great horde of the Warhoons of the South.

To pass undetected among all these people was in itself a difficult task, but if I was to find and rescue the great Thark I must expect even more formidable obstacles before success could be mine. I had entered the city from the south and now stood on the corner of the avenue through which I had passed and the first intersecting avenue south of the plaza. The buildings upon the south side of this square did not appear to be inhabited, as I could see no lights, and so I decided to gain the inner courtyard through one of them.

Nothing occurred to interrupt my progress through the deserted pile I chose, and I came into the inner court close to the rear walls of the east buildings without detection. Within the court a great herd of thoats and zitidars moved restlessly about, cropping the moss-like ochre vegetation which overgrows practically the entire uncultivated area of Mars. What breeze there was came from the north-west, so there was little danger that the beasts would scent me. Had they, their squealing and grunting would have grown to such a volume as to attract the attention of the warriors within the buildings.

Close to the east wall, beneath the overhanging balconies of the second floors, I crept in dense shadows the full length of the courtyard, until I came to the buildings at the north end. These were lighted for about three floors up, but above the third floor all was dark.

To pass through the lighted rooms was, of course, out of the question, since they swarmed with green Martian men and women. My only path lay through the upper floors, and to gain these it was necessary to scale the face of the wall. The reaching of the balcony of the second floor was a matter of easy accomplishment—an agile leap gave my hands a grasp upon the stone hand-rail above. In another instant I had drawn myself upon the balcony.

Here through the open windows I saw the green folk squatting upon their sleeping silks and furs, grunting an occasional monosyllable, which, in connection with their wondrous telepathic powers, is ample for their conversational requirements. As I drew closer to listen to their words a warrior entered the room from the hall beyond.

"Come, Tan Gama," he cried, "we are to take the Thark before Kab Kadja. Bring another with you."

The warrior addressed arose and, beckoning to a fellow squatting near, the three turned and left the apartment.

If I could but follow them the chance might come to free Tars Tarkas at once. At least I would learn the location of his prison.

At my right was a door leading from the balcony into the building. It was at the end of an unlighted hall, and on the impulse of the moment I stepped within. The hall was broad and led straight through to the front of the building. On either side were the doorways of the various apartments which lined it.

I had no more than entered the corridor than I saw the three warriors at the other end—those whom I had just seen leaving the apartment. Then a turn to the right took them from my sight again. Quickly I hastened along the hallway in pursuit. My gait was reckless, but I felt that Fate had been kind indeed to throw such an opportunity within my grasp, and I could not afford to allow it to elude me now.

At the far end of the corridor I found a spiral stairway leading to the floors above and below. The three had evidently left the floor by this avenue. That they had gone down and not up I was sure from my knowledge of these ancient buildings and the methods of the Warhoons.

I myself had once been a prisoner of the cruel hordes of northern Warhoon, and the memory of the underground dungeon in which I lay still is vivid in my memory. And so I felt certain that Tars Tarkas lay in the dark pits beneath some nearby building, and that in that direction I should find the trail of the three warriors leading to his cell.

Nor was I wrong. At the bottom of the runway, or rather at the landing on the floor below, I saw that the shaft descended into the pits beneath, and as I glanced down the flickering light of a torch revealed the presence of the three I was trailing.

Down they went toward the pits beneath the structure, and at a safe distance behind I followed the flicker of their torch. The way led through a maze of tortuous corridors, unlighted save for the wavering light they carried. We had gone perhaps a hundred yards when the party turned abruptly through a doorway at their right. I hastened on as rapidly as I dared through the darkness until I reached the point at which they had left the corridor. There, through an open door, I saw them removing the chains that secured the great Thark, Tars Tarkas, to the wall.

Hustling him roughly between them, they came immediately from the chamber, so quickly in fact that I was near to being apprehended. But I managed to run along the corridor in the direction I had been going in my pursuit of them far enough to be without the radius of their meagre light as they emerged from the cell.

I had naturally assumed that they would return with Tars Tarkas the same way that they had come, which would have carried them away from me; but, to my chagrin, they wheeled directly in my direction as they left the room. There was nothing for me but to hasten on in advance and keep out of the light of their torch. I dared not attempt to halt in the darkness of any of the many intersecting corridors, for I knew nothing of the direction they might take. Chance was as likely as not to carry me into the very corridor they might choose to enter.

The sensation of moving rapidly through these dark passages was far from reassuring. I knew not at what moment I might plunge head-long into some terrible pit or meet with some of the ghoulish creatures that inhabit these lower worlds beneath the dead cities of dying Mars. There filtered to me a faint radiance from the torch of the men behind—just enough to permit me to trace the direction of the winding passageways directly before me, and so keep me from dashing myself against the walls at the turns.

Presently I came to a place where five corridors diverged from a common point. I had hastened along one of them for some little distance when suddenly the faint light of the torch disappeared from about me. I paused to listen for sounds of the party behind me, but the silence was as utter as the silence of the tomb.

Quickly I realized that the warriors had taken one of the other corridors with their prisoner, and so I hastened back with a feeling of considerable relief to take up a much safer and more desirable position behind them. It was much slower work returning, however, than it had been coming, for now the darkness was as utter as the silence.

It was necessary to feel every foot of the way back with my hand against the side wall, that I might not pass the spot where the five roads radiated. After what seemed an eternity to me, I reached the place and recognized it by groping across the entrances to the several corridors until I had counted five of them. In not one, however, showed the faintest sign of light.

I listened intently, but the naked feet of the green men sent back no guiding echoes, though presently I thought I detected the clank of side arms in the far distance of the middle corridor. Up this, then, I hastened, searching for the light, and stopping to listen occasionally for a repetition of the sound; but soon I was forced to admit that I must have been following a blind lead, as only darkness and silence rewarded my efforts.

Again I retraced my steps toward the parting of the ways, when to my surprise I came upon the entrance to three diverging corridors, any one of which I might have traversed in my hasty dash after the false clue I had been following. Here was a pretty fix, indeed! Once back at the point where the five passageways met, I might wait with some assurance for the return of the warriors with Tars Tarkas. My knowledge of their customs lent colour to the belief that he was but being escorted to the audience chamber to have sentence passed upon him. I had not the slightest doubt but that they would preserve so doughty a warrior as the great Thark for the rare sport he would furnish at the Great Games.

But unless I could find my way back to that point the chances were most excellent that I would wander for days through the awful blackness, until, overcome by thirst and hunger, I lay down to die, or—— What was that!

A faint shuffling sounded behind me, and as I cast a hasty glance over my shoulder my blood froze in my veins for the thing I saw there. It was not so much fear of the present danger as it was the horrifying memories it recalled of that time I near went mad over the corpse of the man I had killed in the dungeons of the Warhoons, when blazing eyes came out of the dark recesses and dragged the thing that had been a man from my clutches and I heard it scraping over the stone of my prison as they bore it away to their terrible feast.

And now in these black pits of the other Warhoons I looked into those same fiery eyes, blazing at me through the terrible darkness, revealing no sign of the beast behind them. I think that the most fearsome attribute of these awesome creatures is their silence and the fact that one never sees them—nothing but those baleful eyes glaring unblinkingly out of the dark void behind.

Grasping my long-sword tightly in my hand, I backed slowly along the corridor away from the thing that watched me, but ever as I retreated the eyes advanced, nor was there any sound, not even the sound of breathing, except the occasional shuffling sound as of the dragging of a dead limb, that had first attracted my attention.

On and on I went, but I could not escape my sinister pursuer. Suddenly I heard the shuffling noise at my right, and, looking, saw another pair of eyes, evidently approaching from an intersecting corridor. As I started to renew my slow retreat I heard the noise repeated behind me, and then before I could turn I heard it again at my left.

The things were all about me. They had me surrounded at the intersection of two corridors. Retreat was cut off in all directions, unless I chose to charge one of the beasts. Even then I had no doubt but that the others would hurl themselves upon my back. I could not even guess the size or nature of the weird creatures. That they were of goodly proportions I guessed from the fact that the eyes were on a level with my own.

Why is it that darkness so magnifies our dangers? By day I would have charged the great banth itself, had I thought it necessary, but hemmed in by the darkness of these silent pits I hesitated before a pair of eyes.

Soon I saw that the matter shortly would be taken entirely from my hands, for the eyes at my right were moving slowly nearer me, as were those at my left and those behind and before me. Gradually they were closing in upon me—but still that awful stealthy silence!

For what seemed hours the eyes approached gradually closer and closer, until I felt that I should go mad for the horror of it. I had been constantly turning this way and that to prevent any sudden rush from behind, until I was fairly worn out. At length I could endure it no longer, and, taking a fresh grasp upon my long-sword, I turned suddenly and charged down upon one of my tormentors.

As I was almost upon it the thing retreated before me, but a sound from behind caused me to wheel in time to see three pairs of eyes rushing at me from the rear. With a cry of rage I turned to meet the cowardly beasts, but as I advanced they retreated as had their fellow. Another glance over my shoulder discovered the first eyes sneaking on me again. And again I charged, only to see the eyes retreat before me and hear the muffled rush of the three at my back.

Thus we continued, the eyes always a little closer in the end than they had been before, until I thought that I should go mad with the terrible strain of the ordeal. That they were waiting to spring upon my back seemed evident, and that it would not be long before they succeeded was equally apparent, for I could not endure the wear of this repeated charge and countercharge indefinitely. In fact, I could feel myself weakening from the mental and physical strain I had been undergoing.

At that moment I caught another glimpse from the corner of my eye of the single pair of eyes at my back making a sudden rush upon me. I turned to meet the charge; there was a quick rush of the three from the other direction; but I determined to pursue the single pair until I should have at least settled my account with one of the beasts and thus be relieved of the strain of meeting attacks from both directions.

There was no sound in the corridor, only that of my own breathing, yet I knew that those three uncanny creatures were almost upon me. The eyes in front were not retreating so rapidly now; I was almost within sword reach of them. I raised my sword arm to deal the blow that should free me, and then I felt a heavy body upon my back. A cold, moist, slimy something fastened itself upon my throat. I stumbled and went down.

FLIGHT AND PURSUIT

I COULD NOT have been unconscious more than a few seconds, and yet I know that I was unconscious, for the next thing I realized was that a growing radiance was illuminating the corridor about me and the eyes were gone.

I was unharmed except for a slight bruise upon my forehead where it had struck the stone flagging as I fell.

I sprang to my feet to ascertain the cause of the light. It came from a torch in the hand of one of a party of four green warriors, who were coming rapidly down the corridor toward me. They had not yet seen me, and so I lost no time in slipping into the first intersecting corridor that I could find. This time, however, I did not advance so far away from the main corridor as on the other occasion that had resulted in my losing Tars Tarkas and his guards.

The party came rapidly toward the opening of the passageway in which I crouched against the wall. As they passed by I breathed a sigh of relief. I had not been discovered, and, best of all, the party was the same that I had followed into the pits. It consisted of Tars Tarkas and his three guards.

I fell in behind them and soon we were at the cell in which the great Thark had been chained. Two of the warriors remained without while the man with the keys entered with the Thark to fasten his irons upon him once more. The two outside started to stroll slowly in the direction of the spiral runway which led to the floors above, and in a moment were lost to view beyond a turn in the corridor.

The torch had been stuck in a socket beside the door, so that its rays illuminated both the corridor and the cell at the same time. As I saw the two warriors disappear I approached the entrance to the cell, with a well-defined plan already formulated.

While I disliked the thought of carrying out the thing that I had decided upon, there seemed no alternative if Tars Tarkas and I were to go back together to my little camp in the hills.

Keeping near the wall, I came quite close to the door to Tars Tarkas' cell, and there I stood with my longsword above my head, grasped with both hands, that I might bring it down in one quick cut upon the skull of the jailer as he emerged.

I dislike to dwell upon what followed after I heard the footsteps of the man as he approached the doorway. It is enough that within another minute or two, Tars Tarkas, wearing the metal of a Warhoon chief, was hurrying down the corridor toward the spiral runway, bearing the Warhoon's torch to light his way. A dozen paces behind him followed John Carter, Prince of Helium.

The two companions of the man who lay now beside the door of the cell that had been Tars Tarkas' had just started to ascend the runway as the Thark came in view.

"Why so long, Tan Gama?" cried one of the men.

"I had trouble with a lock," replied Tars Tarkas. "And now I find that I have left my short-sword in the Thark's cell. Go you on, I'll return and fetch it."

"As you will, Tan Gama," replied he who had before spoken. "We shall see you above directly."

"Yes," replied Tars Tarkas, and turned as though to retrace his steps to the cell, but he only waited until the two had disappeared at the floor above. Then I joined him, we extinguished the torch, and together we crept toward the spiral incline that led to the upper floors of the building.

At the first floor we found that the hallway ran but halfway through, necessitating the crossing of a rear room full of green folk, ere we could reach the inner courtyard, so there was but one thing left for us to do, and that was to gain the second floor and the hallway through which I had traversed the length of the building.

Cautiously we ascended. We could hear the sounds of conversation coming from the room above, but the hall still was unlighted, nor was any one in sight as we gained the top of the runway. Together we threaded the long hall and reached the balcony overlooking the courtyard, without being detected.

At our right was the window letting into the room in which I had seen Tan Gama and the other warriors as they started to Tars Tarkas' cell earlier in the evening. His companions had returned here, and we now overheard a portion of their conversation.

"What can be detaining Tan Gama?" asked one.

"He certainly could not be all this time fetching his short-sword from the Thark's cell," spoke another.

"His short-sword?" asked a woman. "What mean you?"

"Tan Gama left his short-sword in the Thark's cell," explained the first speaker, "and left us at the runway, to return and get it."

"Tan Gama wore no short-sword this night," said the woman. "It was broken in to-day's battle with the Thark, and Tan Gama gave it to me to repair. See, I have it here," and as she spoke she drew Tan Gama's short-sword from beneath her sleeping silks and furs.

The warriors sprang to their feet.

"There is something amiss here," cried one.

"'Tis even what I myself thought when Tan Gama left us at the runway," said another. "Methought then that his voice sounded strangely."

"Come! let us hasten to the pits."

We waited to hear no more. Slinging my harness into a long single strap, I lowered Tars Tarkas to the courtyard beneath, and an instant later dropped to his side.

We had spoken scarcely a dozen words since I had felled Tan Gama at the cell door and seen in the torch's light the expression of utter bewilderment upon the great Thark's face.

"By this time," he had said, "I should have learned to wonder at nothing which John Carter accomplishes." That was all. He did not need to tell me that he appreciated the friendship which had prompted me to risk my life to rescue him, nor did he need to say that he was glad to see me.

This fierce green warrior had been the first to greet me that day, now twenty years gone, which had witnessed my first advent upon Mars. He had met me with levelled spear and cruel hatred in his heart as he charged down upon me, bending low at the side of his mighty thoat as I stood beside the incubator of his horde upon the dead sea bottom beyond Korad. And now among the inhabitants of two worlds I counted none a better friend than Tars Tarkas, Jeddak of the Tharks.

As we reached the courtyard we stood in the shadows beneath the balcony for a moment to discuss our plans.

"There be five now in the party, Tars Tarkas," I said; "Thuvia, Xodar, Carthoris, and ourselves. We shall need five thoats to bear us."

"Carthoris!" he cried. "Your son?"

"Yes. I found him in the prison of Shador, on the Sea of Omean, in the land of the First Born."

"I know not any of these places, John Carter. Be they upon Barsoom?"

"Upon and below, my friend; but wait until we shall have made good our escape, and you shall hear the strangest narrative that ever a Barsoomian of the outer world gave ear to. Now we must steal our thoats and be well away to the north before these fellows discover how we have tricked them."

In safety we reached the great gates at the far end of the courtyard, through which it was necessary to take our thoats to the avenue beyond. It is no easy matter to handle five of these great, fierce beasts, which by nature are as wild and ferocious as their masters and held in subjection by cruelty and brute force alone.

As we approached them they sniffed our unfamiliar scent and with squeals of rage circled about us. Their long, massive necks upreared raised their great, gaping mouths high above our heads. They are fearsome appearing brutes at best, but when they are aroused they are fully as dangerous as they look. The thoat stands a good ten feet at the shoulder. His hide is sleek and hairless, and of a dark slate colour on back and sides, shading down his eight legs to a vivid yellow at the huge, padded, nailless feet; the belly is pure white. A broad, flat tail, larger at the tip than at the root, completes the picture of this ferocious green Martian mount—a fit war steed for these warlike people.

As the thoats are guided by telepathic means alone, there is no need for rein or bridle, and so our object now was to find two that would obey our unspoken commands. As they charged about us we succeeded in mastering them sufficiently to prevent any concerted attack upon us, but the din of their squealing was certain to bring investigating warriors into the courtyard were it to continue much longer.

At length I was successful in reaching the side of one great brute, and ere he knew what I was about I was firmly seated astride his glossy back. A moment later Tars Tarkas had caught and mounted another, and then between us we herded three or four more toward the great gates.

Tars Tarkas rode ahead and, leaning down to the latch, threw the barriers open, while I held the loose thoats from breaking back to the herd. Then together we rode through into the avenue with our stolen mounts and, without waiting to close the gates, hurried off toward the southern boundary of the city.

Thus far our escape had been little short of marvellous, nor did our good fortune desert us, for we passed the outer purlieus of the dead city and came to our camp without hearing even the faintest sound of pursuit.

Here a low whistle, the prearranged signal, apprised the balance of our party that I was returning, and we were met by the three with every manifestation of enthusiastic rejoicing.

But little time was wasted in narration of our adventure. Tars Tarkas and Carthoris exchanged the dignified and formal greetings common upon Barsoom, but I could tell intuitively that the Thark loved my boy and that Carthoris reciprocated his affection.

Xodar and the green Jeddak were formally presented to each other. Then Thuvia was lifted to the least fractious thoat, Xodar and Carthoris mounted two others, and we set out at a rapid pace toward the east. At the far extremity of the city we circled toward the north, and under the glorious rays of the two moons we sped noiselessly across the dead sea bottom, away from the Warhoons and the First Born, but to what new dangers and adventures we knew not.

Toward noon of the following day we halted to rest our mounts and ourselves. The beasts we hobbled, that they might move slowly about cropping the ochre moss-like vegetation which constitutes both food and drink for them on the march. Thuvia volunteered to remain on watch while the balance of the party slept for an hour.

It seemed to me that I had but closed my eyes when I felt her hand upon my shoulder and heard her soft voice warning me of a new danger.

"Arise, O Prince," she whispered. "There be that behind us which has the appearance of a great body of pursuers."

The girl stood pointing in the direction from whence we had come, and as I arose and looked, I, too, thought that I could detect a thin dark line on the far horizon. I awoke the others. Tars Tarkas, whose giant stature towered high above the rest of us, could see the farthest.

"It is a great body of mounted men," he said, "and they are travelling at high speed."

There was no time to be lost. We sprang to our hobbled thoats, freed them, and mounted. Then we turned our faces once more toward the north and took our flight again at the highest speed of our slowest beast.

For the balance of the day and all the following night we raced across that ochre wilderness with the pursuers at our back ever gaining upon us. Slowly but surely they were lessening the distance between us. Just before dark they had been close enough for us to plainly distinguish that they were green Martians, and all during the long night we distinctly heard the clanking of their accoutrements behind us.

As the sun rose on the second day of our flight it disclosed the pursuing horde not a half-mile in our rear. As they saw us a fiendish shout of triumph rose from their ranks.

Several miles in advance lay a range of hills—the farther shore of the dead sea we had been crossing. Could we but reach these hills our chances of escape would be greatly enhanced, but Thuvia's mount, although carrying the lightest burden, already was showing signs of exhaustion. I was riding beside her when suddenly her animal staggered and lurched against mine. I saw that he was going down, but ere he fell I snatched the girl from his back and swung her to a place upon my own thoat, behind me, where she clung with her arms about me.

This double burden soon proved too much for my already overtaxed beast, and thus our speed was terribly diminished, for the others would proceed no faster than the slowest of us could go. In that little party there was not one who would desert another; yet we were of different countries, different colours, different races, different religions—and one of us was of a different world.

We were quite close to the hills, but the Warhoons were gaining so rapidly that we had given up all hope of reaching them in time. Thuvia and I were in the rear, for our beast was lagging more and more. Suddenly I felt the girl's warm lips press a kiss upon my shoulder. "For thy sake, O my Prince," she murmured. Then her arms slipped from about my waist and she was gone.

I turned and saw that she had deliberately slipped to the ground in the very path of the cruel demons who pursued us, thinking that by lightening the burden of my mount it might thus be enabled to bear me to the safety of the hills. Poor child! She should have known John Carter better than that.

Turning my thoat, I urged him after her, hoping to reach her side and bear her on again in our hopeless flight. Carthoris must have glanced behind him at about the same time and taken in the situation, for by the time I had reached Thuvia's side he was there also, and, springing from his mount, he threw her upon its back and, turning the animal's head toward the hills, gave the beast a sharp crack across the rump with the flat of his sword. Then he attempted to do the same with mine.

The brave boy's act of chivalrous self-sacrifice filled me with pride, nor did I care that it had wrested from us our last frail chance for escape. The Warhoons were now close upon us. Tars Tarkas and Xodar had discovered our absence and were charging rapidly to our support. Everything pointed toward a splendid ending of my second journey to Barsoom. I hated to go out without having seen my divine Princess, and held her in my arms once again; but if it were not writ upon the book of Fate that such was to be, then would I take the most that was coming to me, and in these last few moments that were to be vouchsafed me before I passed over into that unguessed future I could at least give such an account of myself in my chosen vocation as would leave the Warhoons of the South food for discourse for the next twenty generations.

As Carthoris was not mounted, I slipped from the back of my own mount and took my place at his side to meet the charge of the howling devils bearing down upon us. A moment later Tars Tarkas and Xodar ranged themselves on either hand, turning their thoats loose that we might all be on an equal footing.

The Warhoons were perhaps a hundred yards from us when a

loud explosion sounded from above and behind us, and almost at the same instant a shell burst in their advancing ranks. At once all was confusion. A hundred warriors toppled to the ground. Riderless thoats plunged hither and thither among the dead and dying. Dismounted warriors were trampled underfoot in the stampede which followed. All semblance of order had left the ranks of the green men, and as they looked far above our heads to trace the origin of this unexpected attack, disorder turned to retreat and retreat to a wild panic. In another moment they were racing as madly away from us as they had before been charging down upon us.

We turned to look in the direction from whence the first report had come, and there we saw, just clearing the tops of the nearer hills, a great battleship swinging majestically through the air. Her bow gun spoke again even as we looked, and another shell burst among the fleeing Warhoons.

As she drew nearer I could not repress a wild cry of elation, for upon her bows I saw the device of Helium.

UNDER ARREST

As CARTHORIS, Xodar, Tars Tarkas, and I stood gazing at the magnificent vessel which meant so much to all of us, we saw a second and then a third top the summit of the hills and glide gracefully after their sister.

Now a score of one-man air scouts were launching from the upper decks of the nearer vessel, and in a moment more were speeding in long, swift dives to the ground about us.

In another instant we were surrounded by armed sailors, and an officer had stepped forward to address us, when his eyes fell upon Carthoris. With an exclamation of surprised pleasure he sprang forward, and, placing his hands upon the boy's shoulder, called him by name.

"Carthoris, my Prince," he cried, "Kaor! Kaor! Hor Vastus greets the son of Dejah Thoris, Princess of Helium, and of her husband, John Carter. Where have you been, O my Prince? All Helium has been plunged in sorrow. Terrible have been the calamities that have befallen your great-grandsire's mighty nation since the fatal day that saw you leave our midst."

"Grieve not, my good Hor Vastus," cried Carthoris, "since I bring not back myself alone to cheer my mother's heart and the hearts of my beloved people, but also one whom all Barsoom loved best—her greatest warrior and her saviour—John Carter, Prince of Helium!"

Hor Vastus turned in the direction indicated by Carthoris, and as his eyes fell upon me he was like to have collapsed from sheer surprise.

"John Carter!" he exclaimed, and then a sudden troubled look came into his eyes. "My Prince," he started, "where hast thou——" and then he stopped, but I knew the question that his lips dared not frame. The loyal fellow would not be the one to force from mine a confession of the terrible truth that I had returned from the bosom of the Iss, the River of Mystery, back from the shore of the Lost Sea of Korus, and the Valley Dor.

"Ah, my Prince," he continued, as though no thought had interrupted his greeting, "that you are back is sufficient, and let Hor Vastus' sword have the high honour of being first at thy feet." With these words the noble fellow unbuckled his scabbard and flung his sword upon the ground before me.

Could you know the customs and the character of red Martians you would appreciate the depth of meaning that that simple act conveyed to me and to all about us who witnessed it. The thing was equivalent to saying, "My sword, my body, my life, my soul are yours to do with as you wish. Until death and after death I look to you alone for authority for my every act. Be you right or wrong, your word shall be my only truth. Whoso raises his hand against you must answer to my sword."

It is the oath of fealty that men occasionally pay to a Jeddak whose high character and chivalrous acts have inspired the enthusiastic love of his followers. Never had I known this high tribute paid to a lesser mortal. There was but one response possible. I stooped and lifted the sword from the ground, raised the hilt to my lips, and then, stepping to Hor Vastus, I buckled the weapon upon him with my own hands.

"Hor Vastus," I said, placing my hand upon his shoulder, "you know best the promptings of your own heart. That I shall need your sword I have little doubt, but accept from John Carter upon his sacred honour the assurance that he will never call upon you to draw this sword other than in the cause of truth, justice, and righteousness."

"That I knew, my Prince," he replied, "ere ever I threw my beloved blade at thy feet."

As we spoke other fliers came and went between the ground and the battleship, and presently a larger boat was launched from above, one capable of carrying a dozen persons, perhaps, and dropped lightly near us. As she touched, an officer sprang from her deck to the ground, and, advancing to Hor Vastus, saluted.

"Kantos Kan desires that this party whom we have rescued be brought immediately to the deck of the *Xavarian*," he said.

As we approached the little craft I looked about for the members of my party and for the first time noticed that Thuvia was not among them. Questioning elicited the fact that none had seen her since Carthoris had sent her thoat galloping madly toward the hills, in the hope of carrying her out of harm's way.

Immediately Hor Vastus dispatched a dozen air scouts in as many directions to search for her. It could not be possible that she had gone far since we had last seen her. We others stepped to the deck of the craft that had been sent to fetch us, and a moment later were upon the *Xavarian*.

The first man to greet me was Kantos Kan himself. My old friend had won to the highest place in the navy of Helium, but he was still to me the same brave comrade who had shared with me the privations of a Warhoon dungeon, the terrible atrocities of the Great Games, and later the dangers of our search for Dejah Thoris within the hostile city of Zodanga.

Then I had been an unknown wanderer upon a strange planet, and he a simple padwar in the navy of Helium. To-day he commanded all Helium's great terrors of the skies, and I was a Prince of the House of Tardos Mors, Jeddak of Helium.

He did not ask me where I had been. Like Hor Vastus, he too dreaded the truth and would not be the one to wrest a statement from me. That it must come some time he well knew, but until it came he seemed satisfied to but know that I was with him once more. He greeted Carthoris and Tars Tarkas with the keenest delight, but he asked neither where he had been. He could scarcely keep his hands off the boy.

"You do not know, John Carter," he said to me, "how we of

Helium love this son of yours. It is as though all the great love we bore his noble father and his poor mother had been centred in him. When it became known that he was lost, ten million people wept."

"What mean you, Kantos Kan," I whispered, "by 'his poor mother'?" for the words had seemed to carry a sinister meaning which I could not fathom.

He drew me to one side.

"For a year," he said. "Ever since Carthoris disappeared, Dejah Thoris has grieved and mourned for her lost boy. The blow of years ago, when you did not return from the atmosphere plant, was lessened to some extent by the duties of motherhood, for your son broke his white shell that very night.

"That she suffered terribly then, all Helium knew, for did not all Helium suffer with her the loss of her lord! But with the boy gone there was nothing left, and after expedition upon expedition returned with the same hopeless tale of no clue as to his whereabouts, our beloved Princess drooped lower and lower, until all who saw her felt that it could be but a matter of days ere she went to join her loved ones within the precincts of the Valley Dor.

"As a last resort, Mors Kajak, her father, and Tardos Mors, her grandfather, took command of two mighty expeditions, and a month ago sailed away to explore every inch of ground in the northern hemisphere of Barsoom. For two weeks no word has come back from them, but rumours were rife that they had met with a terrible disaster and that all were dead.

"About this time Zat Arrras renewed his importunities for her hand in marriage. He has been for ever after her since you disappeared. She hated him and feared him, but with both her father and grandfather gone, Zat Arrras was very powerful, for he is still Jed of Zodanga, to which position, you will remember, Tardos Mors appointed him after you had refused the honour.

"He had a secret audience with her six days ago. What took place none knows, but the next day Dejah Thoris had disappeared, and with her had gone a dozen of her household guard and body servants, including Sola the green woman—Tars Tarkas' daughter, you recall. No word left they of their intentions, but it is always thus with those who go upon the voluntary pilgrimage from which none returns. We cannot think aught than that Dejah Thoris has sought the icy bosom of Iss, and that her devoted servants have chosen to accompany her.

"Zat Arrras was at Helium when she disappeared. He commands this fleet which has been searching for her since. No trace of her have we found, and I fear that it be a futile quest."

While we talked, Hor Vastus' fliers were returning to the *Xavarian*. Not one, however, had discovered a trace of Thuvia. I was much depressed over the news of Dejah Thoris' disappearance, and now there was added the further burden of apprehension concerning the fate of Thuvia. I felt keen responsibility for the welfare of this girl whom I believed to be the daughter of some proud Barsoomian house, and it had been my intention to make every effort to return her to her people.

I was about to ask Kantos Kan to prosecute a further search for her when a flier from the flagship of the fleet arrived at the *Xavarian* with an officer bearing a message to Kantos Kan from Arrras.

My friend read the dispatch and then turned to me.

"Zat Arrras commands me to bring our 'prisoners' before him. There is naught else to do. He is supreme in Helium, yet it would be far more in keeping with chivalry and good taste were he to come hither and greet the saviour of Barsoom with the honours that are his due."

"You know full well, my friend," I said, smiling, "that Zat Arrras has good cause to hate me. Nothing would please him better than to humiliate me and then to kill me. Now that he has so excellent an excuse, let us go and see if he has the courage to take advantage of it."

Summoning Carthoris, Tars Tarkas, and Xodar, we entered the small flier with Kantos Kan and Zat Arrras' officer, and in a moment were stepping to the deck of Zat Arrras' flagship.

As we approached the Jed of Zodanga no sign of greeting or recognition crossed his face; not even to Carthoris did he vouchsafe a friendly word. His attitude was cold, haughty, and uncompromising.

"Kaor, Zat Arrras," I said in greeting, but he did not respond.

"Why were these prisoners not disarmed?" he asked to Kantos Kan.

"They are not prisoners, Zat Arrras," replied the officer. "Two of them are of Helium's noblest family. Tars Tarkas, Jeddak of Thark, is Tardos Mors' best beloved ally. The other is a friend and companion of the Prince of Helium—that is enough for me to know."

"It is not enough for me, however," retorted Zat Arrras. "More must I hear from those who have taken the pilgrimage than their names. Where have you been, John Carter?"

"I have just come from the Valley Dor and the Land of the First Born, Zat Arrras," I replied.

"Ah!" he exclaimed in evident pleasure, "you do not deny it, then? You have returned from the bosom of Iss?"

"I have come back from a land of false hope, from a valley of torture and death; with my companions I have escaped from the hideous clutches of lying fiends. I have come back to the Barsoom that I saved from a painless death to again save her, but this time from death in its most frightful form."

"Cease, blasphemer!" cried Zat Arrras. "Hope not to save thy cowardly carcass by inventing horrid lies to——" But he got no further. One does not call John Carter "coward" and "liar" thus lightly, and Zat Arrras should have known it. Before a hand could be raised to stop me, I was at his side and one hand grasped his throat.

"Come I from heaven or hell, Zat Arrras, you will find me still the same John Carter that I have always been; nor did ever man call me such names and live—without apologizing." And with that I commenced to bend him back across my knee and tighten my grip upon his throat.

"Seize him!" cried Zat Arrras, and a dozen officers sprang forward to assist him.

Kantos Kan came close and whispered to me.

"Desist, I beg of you. It will but involve us all, for I cannot see these men lay hands upon you without aiding you. My officers and men will join me and we shall have a mutiny then that may lead to revolution. For the sake of Tardos Mors and Helium, desist."

At his words I released Zat Arrras and, turning my back upon him, walked toward the ship's rail.

"Come, Kantos Kan," I said, "the Prince of Helium would return to the *Xavarian*."

None interfered. Zat Arrras stood white and trembling amidst his officers. Some there were who looked upon him with scorn and drew toward me, while one, a man long in the service and confidence of Tardos Mors, spoke to me in a low tone as I passed him.

"You may count my metal among your fighting-men, John Carter," he said.

I thanked him and passed on. In silence we embarked, and shortly after stepped once more upon the deck of the *Xavarian*. Fifteen minutes later we received orders from the flagship to proceed toward Helium.

Our journey thither was uneventful. Carthoris and I were wrapped in the gloomiest of thoughts. Kantos Kan was sombre in contemplation of the further calamity that might fall upon Helium should Zat Arrras attempt to follow the age-old precedent that allotted a terrible death to fugitives from the Valley Dor. Tars Tarkas grieved for the loss of his daughter. Xodar alone was care-free—a fugitive and outlaw, he could be no worse off in Helium than elsewhere.

"Let us hope that we may at least go out with good red blood upon our blades," he said. It was a simple wish and one most likely to be gratified.

Among the officers of the *Xavarian* I thought I could discern division into factions ere we had reached Helium. There were those who gathered about Carthoris and myself whenever the opportunity presented, while about an equal number held aloof from us. They offered us only the most courteous treatment, but were evidently bound by their superstitious belief in the doctrine of Dor and Iss and Korus. I could not blame them, for I knew how strong a hold a creed, however ridiculous it may be, may gain upon an otherwise intelligent people.

By returning from Dor we had committed a sacrilege; by recounting our adventures there, and stating the facts as they existed we had outraged the religion of their fathers. We were blasphemers—lying heretics. Even those who still clung to us from personal love and loyalty I think did so in the face of the fact that at heart they questioned our veracity—it is very hard to accept a new religion for an old, no matter how alluring the promises of the new may be; but to reject the old as a tissue of falsehoods without being offered anything in its stead is indeed a most difficult thing to ask of any people.

Kantos Kan would not talk of our experiences among the therns and the First Born.

"It is enough," he said, "that I jeopardize my life here and hereafter by countenancing you at all—do not ask me to add still further to my sins by listening to what I have always been taught was the rankest heresy."

I knew that sooner or later the time must come when our friends and enemies would be forced to declare themselves openly. When we reached Helium there must be an accounting, and if Tardos Mors had not returned I feared that the enmity of Zat Arrras might weigh heavily against us, for he represented the government of Helium. To take sides against him were equivalent to treason. The majority of the troops would doubtless follow the lead of their officers, and I knew that many of the highest and most powerful men of both land and air forces would cleave to John Carter in the face of god, man, or devil.

On the other hand, the majority of the populace unquestionably would demand that we pay the penalty of our sacrilege. The outlook seemed dark from whatever angle I viewed it, but my mind was so torn with anguish at the thought of Dejah Thoris that I realize now that I gave the terrible question of Helium's plight but scant attention at that time.

There was always before me, day and night, a horrible nightmare of the frightful scenes through which I knew my Princess might even then be passing—the horrid plant men—the ferocious white apes. At times I would cover my face with my hands in a vain effort to shut out the fearful thing from my mind.

It was in the forenoon that we arrived above the mile-high scarlet tower which marks greater Helium from her twin city. As we descended in great circles toward the navy docks a mighty multitude could be seen surging in the streets beneath. Helium had been notified by radio-aerogram of our approach.

From the deck of the *Xavarian* we four, Carthoris, Tars Tarkas, Xodar, and I, were transferred to a lesser flier to be transported to quarters within the Temple of Reward. It is here that Martian justice is meted to benefactor and malefactor. Here the hero is decorated. Here the felon is condemned. We were taken into the temple from the landing stage upon the roof, so that we did not pass among the people at all, as is customary. Always before I had seen prisoners of note, or returned wanderers of eminence, paraded from the Gate of Jeddaks to the Temple of Reward up the broad Avenue of Ancestors through dense crowds of jeering or cheering citizens.

I knew that Zat Arrras dared not trust the people near to us, for he feared that their love for Carthoris and myself might break into a demonstration which would wipe out their superstitious horror of the crime we were to be charged with. What his plans were I could only guess, but that they were sinister was evidenced by the fact that only his most trusted servitors accompanied us upon the flier to the Temple of Reward.

We were lodged in a room upon the south side of the temple, overlooking the Avenue of Ancestors down which we could see the full length to the Gate of Jeddaks, five miles away. The people in the temple plaza and in the streets for a distance of a full mile were standing as close packed as it was possible for them to get. They were very orderly—there were neither scoffs nor plaudits, and when they saw us at the window above them there were many who buried their faces in their arms and wept.

Late in the afternoon a messenger arrived from Zat Arrras to inform us that we would be tried by an impartial body of nobles in the great hall of the temple at the 1st zode[1] on the following day, or about 8:40 A.M. Earth time.

THE DEATH SENTENCE

A FEW MOMENTS before the appointed time on the following morning a strong guard of Zat Arrras' officers appeared at our quarters to conduct us to the great hall of the temple.

In twos we entered the chamber and marched down the broad Aisle of Hope, as it is called, to the platform in the centre of the hall.

[1] Wherever Captain Carter has used Martian measurements of time, distance, weight, and the like I have translated them into as nearly their equivalent in earthly values as is possible. His notes contain many Martian tables, and a great volume of scientific data, but since the International Astronomic Society is at present engaged in classifying, investigating, and verifying this vast fund of remarkable and valuable information, I have felt that it will add nothing to the interest of Captain Carter's story or to the sum total of human knowledge to maintain a strict adherence to the original manuscript in these matters, while it might readily confuse the reader and detract from the interest of the history. For those who may be interested, however, I will explain that the Martian day is a trifle over 24 hours 37 minutes duration (Earth time). This the Martians divide into ten equal parts, commencing the day at about 6 A.M. Earth time. The zodes are divided into fifty shorter periods, each of which in turn is composed of 200 brief periods of time, about equivalent to the earthly second. The Barsoomian Table of Time as here given is but a part of the full table appearing in Captain Carter's notes.

TABLE

200 tals	. . . .	1 xat
50 xats	. . . .	1 zode
10 zodes	. . . .	1 revolution of Mars upon its axis.

Before and behind us marched armed guards, while three solid ranks of Zodangan soldiery lined either side of the aisle from the entrance to the rostrum.

As we reached the raised enclosure I saw our judges. As is the custom upon Barsoom there were thirty-one, supposedly selected by lot from men of the noble class, for nobles were on trial. But to my amazement I saw no single friendly face among them. Practically all were Zodangans, and it was I to whom Zodanga owed her defeat at the hands of the green hordes and her subsequent vassalage to Helium. There could be little justice here for John Carter, or his son, or for the great Thark who had commanded the savage tribesmen who overran Zodanga's broad avenues, looting, burning, and murdering.

About us the vast circular coliseum was packed to its full capacity. All classes were represented—all ages, and both sexes. As we entered the hall the hum of subdued conversation ceased until as we halted upon the platform, or Throne of Righteousness, the silence of death enveloped the ten thousand spectators.

The judges were seated in a great circle about the periphery of the circular platform. We were assigned seats with our backs toward a small platform in the exact centre of the larger one. This placed us facing the judges and the audience. Upon the smaller platform each would take his place while his case was being heard.

Zat Arrras himself sat in the golden chair of the presiding magistrate. As we were seated and our guards retired to the foot of the stairway leading to the platform, he arose and called my name.

"John Carter," he cried, "take your place upon the Pedestal of Truth to be judged impartially according to your acts and here to know the reward you have earned thereby." Then turning to and fro toward the audience he narrated the acts upon the value of which my reward was to be determined.

"Know you, O judges and people of Helium," he said, "that John Carter, one time Prince of Helium, has returned by his own statement from the Valley Dor and even from the Temple of Issus itself. That, in the presence of many men of Helium he has blasphemed against the Sacred Iss, and against the Valley Dor, and the Lost Sea of Korus, and the Holy Therns themselves, and even against Issus, Goddess of Death, and of Life Eternal. And know you further by witness of thine own eyes that see him here now upon the Pedestal of Truth that he has indeed returned from these sacred precincts in the face of our ancient customs, and in violation of the sanctity of our ancient religion.

"He who be once dead may not live again. He who attempts it must be made dead for ever. Judges, your duty lies plain before you —here can be no testimony in contravention of truth. What reward shall be meted to John Carter in accordance with the acts he has committed?"

"Death!" shouted one of the judges.

And then a man sprang to his feet in the audience, and raising his hand on high, cried: "Justice! Justice! Justice!" It was Kantos Kan, and as all eyes turned toward him he leaped past the Zodangan soldiery and sprang upon the platform.

"What manner of justice be this?" he cried to Zat Arrras. "The defendant has not been heard, nor has he had an opportunity to call others in his behalf. In the name of the people of Helium I demand fair and impartial treatment for the Prince of Helium."

A great cry arose from the audience then: "Justice! Justice! Justice!" and Zat Arrras dared not deny them.

"Speak, then," he snarled, turning to me; "but blaspheme not against the things that are sacred upon Barsoom."

"Men of Helium," I cried, turning to the spectators, and speaking over the heads of my judges, "how can John Carter expect justice from the men of Zodanga? He cannot nor does he ask it. It is to the men of Helium that he states his case; nor does he appeal for mercy to any. It is not in his own cause that he speaks now—it is in thine. In the cause of your wives and daughters, and of wives and daughters yet unborn. It is to save them from the unthinkably atrocious indignities that I have seen heaped upon the fair women of Barsoom in the place men call the Temple of Issus. It is to save them from the sucking embrace of the plant men, from the fangs of the great white apes of Dor, from the cruel lust of the Holy Therns, from all that the cold, dead Iss carries them to from homes of love and life and happiness.

"Sits there no man here who does not know the history of John Carter. How he came among you from another world and rose from a prisoner among the green men, through torture and persecution, to a place high among the highest of Barsoom. Nor ever did you know John Carter to lie in his own behalf, or to say aught that might harm the people of Barsoom, or to speak lightly of the strange religion which he respected without understanding.

"There be no man here, or elsewhere upon Barsoom to-day who does not owe his life directly to a single act of mine, in which I sacrificed myself and the happiness of my Princess that you might live. And so, men of Helium, I think that I have the right to demand that I be heard, that I be believed, and that you let me serve you and save you from the false hereafter of Dor and Issus as I saved you from the real death that other day.

"It is to you of Helium that I speak now. When I am done let the men of Zodanga have their will with me. Zat Arrras has taken my sword from me, so the men of Zodanga no longer fear me. Will you listen?"

"Speak, John Carter, Prince of Helium," cried a great noble from the audience, and the multitude echoed his permission, until the building rocked with the noise of their demonstration.

Zat Arrras knew better than to interfere with such a sentiment as was expressed that day in the Temple of Reward, and so for two hours I talked with the people of Helium.

But when I had finished, Zat Arrras arose and, turning to the judges, said in a low tone: "My nobles, you have heard John Carter's plea; every opportunity has been given him to prove his innocence if he be not guilty; but instead he has but utilized the time in further blasphemy. What, gentlemen, is your verdict?"

"Death to the blasphemer!" cried one, springing to his feet, and in an instant the entire thirty-one judges were on their feet with up-raised swords in token of the unanimity of their verdict.

If the people did not hear Zat Arrras' charge, they certainly did hear the verdict of the tribunal. A sullen murmur rose louder and louder about the packed coliseum, and then Kantos Kan, who had not left the platform since first he had taken his place near me, raised his hand for silence. When he could be heard he spoke to the people in a cool and level voice.

"You have heard the fate that the men of Zodanga would mete to Helium's noblest hero. It may be the duty of the men of Helium to accept the verdict as final. Let each man act according to his own heart. Here is the answer of Kantos Kan, head of the navy of Helium, to Zat Arrras and his judges," and with that he unbuckled his scabbard and threw his sword at my feet.

In an instant soldiers and citizens, officers and nobles were crowding past the soldiers of Zodanga and forcing their way to the Throne of Righteousness. A hundred men surged upon the platform, and a hundred blades rattled and clanked to the floor at my feet. Zat Arrras and his officers were furious, but they were helpless. One by one I raised the swords to my lips and buckled them again upon their owners.

"Come," said Kantos Kan, "we will escort John Carter and his party to his own palace," and they formed about us and started toward the stairs leading to the Aisle of Hope.

"Stop!" cried Zat Arrras. "Soldiers of Helium, let no prisoner leave the Throne of Righteousness."

The soldiery from Zodanga were the only organized body of Heliumetic troops within the temple, so Zat Arrras was confident that his orders would be obeyed, but I do not think that he looked for the opposition that was raised the moment the soldiers advanced toward the throne.

From every quarter of the coliseum swords flashed and men rushed threateningly upon the Zodangans. Some one raised a cry: "Tardos Mors is dead—a thousand years to John Carter, Jeddak of Helium." As I heard that and saw the ugly attitude of the men of Helium toward the soldiers of Zat Arrras, I knew that only a miracle could avert a clash that would end in civil war.

"Hold!" I cried, leaping to the Pedestal of Truth once more. "Let no man move till I am done. A single sword thrust here to-day may plunge Helium into a bitter and bloody war the results of which none can foresee. It will turn brother against brother and father against son. No man's life is worth that sacrifice. Rather would I submit to the biased judgment of Zat Arrras than be the cause of civil strife in Helium.

"Let us each give in a point to the other, and let this entire matter rest until Tardos Mors returns, or Mors Kajak, his son. If neither be back at the end of the year a second trial may be held—the thing has a precedent." And then turning to Zat Arrras, I said in a low voice: "Unless you be a bigger fool than I take you to be, you will grasp the chance I am offering you ere it is too late. Once that multitude of swords below is drawn against your soldiery no man upon Barsoom—not even Tardos Mors himself—can avert the consequences. What say you? Speak quickly."

The Jed of Zodangan Helium raised his voice to the angry sea beneath us.

"Stay your hands, men of Helium," he shouted, his voice trembling with rage. "The sentence of the court is passed, but the day of retribution has not been set. I, Zat Arrras, Jed of Zodanga, appreciating the royal connections of the prisoner and his past services to Helium and Barsoom, grant a respite of one year, or until the return of Mors Kajak, or Tardos Mors to Helium. Disperse quietly to your houses. Go."

No one moved. Instead, they stood in tense silence with their eyes fastened upon me, as though waiting for a signal to attack.

"Clear the temple," commanded Zat Arrras, in a low tone to one of his officers.

Fearing the result of an attempt to carry out this order by force, I stepped to the edge of the platform and, pointing toward the main entrance, bid them pass out. As one man they turned at my request and filed, silent and threatening, past the soldiers of Zat Arrras, Jed of Zodanga, who stood scowling in impotent rage.

Kantos Kan with the others who had sworn allegiance to me still stood upon the Throne of Righteousness with me.

"Come," said Kantos Kan to me, "we will escort you to your palace, my Prince. Come, Carthoris and Xodar. Come, Tars Tarkas." And with a haughty sneer for Zat Arrras upon his handsome lips, he turned and strode to the throne steps and up the Aisle of Hope. We four and the hundred loyal ones followed behind him, nor was a hand raised to stay us, though glowering eyes followed our triumphal march through the temple.

In the avenues we found a press of people, but they opened a pathway for us, and many were the swords that were flung at my feet as I passed through the city of Helium toward my palace upon the outskirts. Here my old slaves fell upon their knees and kissed my hands as I greeted them. They cared not where I had been. It was enough that I had returned to them.

"Ah, master," cried one, "if our divine Princess were but here this would be a day indeed."

Tears came to my eyes, so that I was forced to turn away that I might hide my emotions. Carthoris wept openly as the slaves pressed about him with expressions of affection, and words of sorrow for our common loss. It was now that Tars Tarkas for the first time learned that his daughter, Sola, had accompanied Dejah Thoris upon the last long pilgrimage. I had not had the heart to tell him what Kantos Kan had told me. With the stoicism of the green Martian he showed no sign of suffering, yet I knew that his grief was as poignant as my own. In marked contrast to his kind, he had in well-developed form the kindlier human characteristics of love, friendship, and charity.

It was a sad and sombre party that sat at the feast of welcome in the great dining hall of the palace of the Prince of Helium that day. We were over a hundred strong, not counting the members of my little court, for Dejah Thoris and I had maintained a household consistent with our royal rank.

The board, according to red Martian custom, was triangular, for there were three in our family. Carthoris and I presided in the centre of our sides of the table—midway of the third side Dejah Thoris' high-backed, carven chair stood vacant except for her gorgeous wedding trappings and jewels which were draped upon it. Behind stood a slave as in the days when his mistress had occupied her place at the board, ready to do her bidding. It was the way upon Barsoom, so I endured the anguish of it, though it wrung my heart to see that silent chair where should have been my laughing and vivacious Princess keeping the great hall ringing with her merry gaiety.

At my right sat Kantos Kan, while to the right of Dejah Thoris' empty place Tars Tarkas sat in a huge chair before a raised section of the board which years ago I had had constructed to meet the requirements of his mighty bulk. The place of honour at a Martian board is always at the hostess's right, and this place was ever reserved by Dejah Thoris for the great Thark upon the occasions that he was in Helium.

Hor Vastus sat in the seat of honour upon Carthoris' side of the table. There was little general conversation. It was a quiet and saddened party. The loss of Dejah Thoris was still fresh in the minds of all, and to this was added fear for the safety of Tardos Mors and Mors Kajak, as well as doubt and uncertainty as to the fate of Helium, should it prove true that she was permanently deprived of her great Jeddak.

Suddenly our attention was attracted by the sound of distant shouting, as of many people raising their voices at once, but whether in anger or rejoicing, we could not tell. Nearer and nearer came the tumult. A slave rushed into the dining hall to cry that a great concourse of people was swarming through the palace gates. A second burst upon the heels of the first alternately laughing and shrieking as a madman.

"Dejah Thoris is found!" he cried. "A messenger from Dejah Thoris!"

I waited to hear no more. The great windows of the dining hall overlooked the avenue leading to the main gates—they were upon the opposite side of the hall from me with the table intervening. I did not waste time in circling the great board—with a single leap I cleared table and diners and sprang upon the balcony beyond. Thirty feet below lay the scarlet sward of the lawn and beyond were many people crowding about a great thoat which bore a rider headed toward the palace. I vaulted to the ground below and ran swiftly toward the advancing party.

As I came near to them I saw that the figure on the thoat was Sola.

"Where is the Princess of Helium?" I cried.

The green girl slid from her mighty mount and ran toward me.

"O my Prince! My Prince!" she cried. "She is gone for ever. Even now she may be a captive upon the lesser moon. The black pirates of Barsoom have stolen her."

SOLA'S STORY

ONCE WITHIN THE PALACE, I drew Sola to the dining hall, and, when she had greeted her father after the formal manner of the green men, she told the story of the pilgrimage and capture of Dejah Thoris.

"Seven days ago, after her audience with Zat Arrras, Dejah Thoris attempted to slip from the palace in the dead of night. Although I had not heard the outcome of her interview with Zat Arrras I knew that something had occurred then to cause her the keenest mental agony, and when I discovered her creeping from the palace I did not need to be told her destination.

"Hastily arousing a dozen of her most faithful guards, I explained my fears to them, and as one they enlisted with me to follow our beloved Princess in her wanderings, even to the Sacred Iss and the Valley Dor. We came upon her but a short distance from the palace. With her was faithful Woola the hound, but none other. When we overtook her she feigned anger, and ordered us back to the palace, but for once we disobeyed her, and when she found that we would not let her go upon the last long pilgrimage alone, she wept and embraced us, and together we went out into the night toward the south.

"The following day we came upon a herd of small thoats, and thereafter we were mounted and made good time. We travelled very fast and very far due south until the morning of the fifth day we sighted a great fleet of battleships sailing north. They saw us before we could seek shelter, and soon we were surrounded by a horde of black men. The Princess's guard fought nobly to the end, but they were soon overcome and slain. Only Dejah Thoris and I were spared.

"When she realized that she was in the clutches of the black pirates, she attempted to take her own life, but one of the blacks tore her dagger from her, and then they bound us both so that we could not use our hands.

"The fleet continued north after capturing us. There were about twenty large battleships in all, besides a number of small swift cruisers. That evening one of the smaller cruisers that had been far in advance of the fleet returned with a prisoner—a young red woman whom they had picked up in a range of hills under the very noses, they said, of a fleet of three red Martian battleships.

"From scraps of conversation which we overheard it was evident that the black pirates were searching for a party of fugitives that had escaped them several days prior. That they considered the capture of the young woman important was evident from the long and earnest interview the commander of the fleet held with her when she was brought to him. Later she was bound and placed in the compartment with Dejah Thoris and myself.

"The new captive was a very beautiful girl. She told Dejah Thoris that many years ago she had taken the voluntary pilgrimage from the court of her father, the Jeddak of Ptarth. She was Thuvia, the Princess of Ptarth. And then she asked Dejah Thoris who she might be, and when she heard she fell upon her knees and kissed Dejah Thoris' fettered hands, and told her that that very morning she had been with John Carter, Prince of Helium, and Carthoris, her son.

"Dejah Thoris could not believe her at first, but finally when the girl had narrated all the strange adventures that had befallen her since she had met John Carter, and told her of the things John Carter, and Carthoris, and Xodar had narrated of their adventures in the Land of the First Born, Dejah Thoris knew that it could be none other than the Prince of Helium; 'For who,' she said, 'upon all Barsoom other than John Carter could have done the deeds you tell of.' And when Thuvia told Dejah Thoris of her love for John Carter, and his loyalty and devotion to the Princess of his choice, Dejah Thoris broke down and wept—cursing Zat Arrras and the cruel fate that had driven her from Helium but a few brief days before the return of her beloved lord.

"'I do not blame you for loving him, Thuvia,' she said; 'and that your affection for him is pure and sincere I can well believe from the candour of your avowal of it to me.'

"The fleet continued north nearly to Helium, but last night they evidently realized that John Carter had indeed escaped them and so they turned toward the south once more. Shortly thereafter a guard entered our compartment and dragged me to the deck.

"'There is no place in the Land of the First Born for a green one,' he said, and with that he gave me a terrific shove that carried me toppling from the deck of the battleship. Evidently this seemed to him the easiest way of ridding the vessel of my presence and killing me at the same time.

"But a kind fate intervened, and by a miracle I escaped with but slight bruises. The ship was moving slowly at the time, and as I lunged overboard into the darkness beneath I shuddered at the awful plunge I thought awaited me, for all day the fleet had sailed thousands of feet above the ground; but to my utter surprise I struck upon a soft mass of vegetation not twenty feet from the deck of the ship. In fact, the keel of the vessel must have been grazing the surface of the ground at the time.

"I lay all night where I had fallen and the next morning brought an explanation of the fortunate coincidence that had saved me from a terrible death. As the sun rose I saw a vast panorama of sea bottom and distant hills lying far below me. I was upon the highest peak of a lofty range. The fleet in the darkness of the preceding night had barely grazed the crest of the hills, and in the brief span that they hovered close to the surface the black guard had pitched me, as he supposed, to my death.

"A few miles west of me was a great waterway. When I reached it I found to my delight that it belonged to Helium. Here a thoat was procured for me—the rest you know."

For many minutes none spoke. Dejah Thoris in the clutches of the First Born! I shuddered at the thought, but of a sudden the old fire of unconquerable self-confidence surged through me. I sprang to my feet, and with back-thrown shoulders and upraised sword took a solemn vow to reach, rescue, and revenge my Princess.

A hundred swords leaped from a hundred scabbards, and a hundred fighting-men sprang to the table-top and pledged me their lives and fortunes to the expedition. Already my plans were formulated. I thanked each loyal friend, and leaving Carthoris to entertain them, withdrew to my own audience chamber with Kantos Kan, Tars Tarkas, Xodar, and Hor Vastus.

Here we discussed the details of our expedition until long after dark. Xodar was positive that Issus would choose both Dejah Thoris and Thuvia to serve her for a year.

"For that length of time at least they will be comparatively safe," he said, "and we will at least know where to look for them."

In the matter of equipping a fleet to enter Omean the details were left to Kantos Kan and Xodar. The former agreed to take such vessels as we required into dock as rapidly as possible, where Xodar would direct their equipment with water propellers.

For many years the black had been in charge of the refitting of captured battleships that they might navigate Omean, and so was familiar with the construction of the propellers, housings, and the auxiliary gearing required.

It was estimated that it would require six months to complete our preparations in view of the fact that the utmost secrecy must be maintained to keep the project from the ears of Zat Arrras. Kantos Kan was confident now that the man's ambitions were fully aroused and that nothing short of the title of Jeddak of Helium would satisfy him.

"I doubt," he said, "if he would even welcome Dejah Thoris' return, for it would mean another nearer the throne than he. With you and Carthoris out of the way there would be little to prevent him from assuming the title of Jeddak, and you may rest assured that so long as he is supreme here there is no safety for either of you."

"There is a way," cried Hor Vastus, "to thwart him effectually and for ever."

"What?" I asked.

He smiled.

"I shall whisper it here, but some day I shall stand upon the dome of the Temple of Reward and shout it to cheering multitudes below."

"What do you mean?" asked Kantos Kan.

"John Carter, Jeddak of Helium," said Hor Vastus in a low voice.

The eyes of my companions lighted, and grim smiles of pleasure and anticipation overspread their faces, as each eye turned toward me questioningly. But I shook my head.

"No, my friends," I said, smiling, "I thank you, but it cannot be. Not yet, at least. When we know that Tardos Mors and Mors Kajak are gone to return no more; if I be here, then I shall join you all to see that the people of Helium are permitted to choose fairly their next Jeddak. Whom they choose may count upon the loyalty of my sword, nor shall I seek the honour for myself. Until then Tardos Mors is Jeddak of Helium, and Zat Arrras is his representative."

"As you will, John Carter," said Hor Vastus, "but——What was that?" he whispered, pointing toward the window overlooking the gardens.

The words were scarce out of his mouth ere he had sprung to the balcony without.

"There he goes!" he cried excitedly. "The guards! Below there! The guards!"

We were close behind him, and all saw the figure of a man run quickly across a little piece of sward and disappear in the shrubbery beyond.

"He was on the balcony when I first saw him," cried Hor Vastus. "Quick! Let us follow him!"

Together we ran to the gardens, but even though we scoured the grounds with the entire guard for hours, no trace could we find of the night marauder.

"What do you make of it, Kantos Kan?" asked Tars Tarkas.

"A spy sent by Zat Arrras," he replied. "It was ever his way."

"He will have something interesting to report to his master then," laughed Hor Vastus.

"I hope he heard only our references to a new Jeddak," I said. "If he overheard our plans to rescue Dejah Thoris, it will mean civil war, for he will attempt to thwart us, and in that I will not be thwarted. There would I turn against Tardos Mors himself, were it necessary. If it throws all Helium into a bloody conflict, I shall go on with these plans to save my Princess. Nothing shall stay me now short of death, and should I die, my friends, will you take oath to prosecute the search for her and bring her back in safety to her grandfather's court?"

Upon the hilt of his sword each of them swore to do as I had asked.

It was agreed that the battleships that were to be remodelled should be ordered to Hastor, another Heliumetic city, far to the south-west. Kantos Kan thought that the docks there, in addition to their regular work, would accommodate at least six battleships at a time. As he was commander-in-chief of the navy, it would be a simple matter for him to order the vessels there as they could be handled, and thereafter keep the remodelled fleet in remote parts of the empire until we should be ready to assemble it for the dash upon Omean.

It was late that night before our conference broke up, but each man there had his particular duties outlined, and the details of the entire plan had been mapped out.

Kantos Kan and Xodar were to attend to the remodelling of the ships. Tars Tarkas was to get into communication with Thark and learn the sentiments of his people toward his return from Dor. If favourable, he was to repair immediately to Thark and devote his time to the assembling of a great horde of green warriors whom it was our plan to send in transports directly to the Valley Dor and the Temple of Issus, while the fleet entered Omean and destroyed the vessels of the First Born.

Upon Hor Vastus devolved the delicate mission of organising a secret force of fighting-men sworn to follow John Carter wherever he might lead. As we estimated that it would require over a million men to man the thousand great battleships we intended to use on Omean and the transports for the green men as well as the ships that were to convoy the transports, it was no trifling job that Hor Vastus had before him.

After they had left I bid Carthoris good-night, for I was very tired, and going to my own apartments, bathed and lay down upon my sleeping silks and furs for the first good night's sleep I had had an opportunity to look forward to since I had returned to Barsoom. But even now I was to be disappointed.

How long I slept I do not know. When I awoke suddenly it was to find a half-dozen powerful men upon me, a gag already in my mouth, and a moment later my arms and legs securely bound. So quickly had they worked and to such good purpose, that I was utterly beyond the power to resist them by the time I was fully awake.

Never a word spoke they, and the gag effectually prevented me speaking. Silently they lifted me and bore me toward the door of my chamber. As they passed the window through which the farther moon was casting its brilliant beams, I saw that each of the party had his face swathed in layers of silk—I could not recognize one of them.

When they had come into the corridor with me, they turned toward a secret panel in the wall which led to the passage that terminated in the pits beneath the palace. That any knew of this panel outside my own household, I was doubtful. Yet the leader of the band did not hesitate a moment. He stepped directly to the panel, touched the concealed button, and as the door swung open he stood aside while his companions entered with me. Then he closed the panel behind him and followed us.

Down through the passageways to the pits we went. Along winding corridors that I myself had never explored. On and on until I felt confident that we were far beyond the confines of the palace grounds, and then the way led upward again toward the surface.

Presently the party halted before a blank wall. The leader rapped upon it with the hilt of his sword—three quick, sharp blows, a pause, then three more, another pause, and then two. A second later the wall swung in, and I was pushed within a brilliantly lighted chamber in which sat three richly trapped men.

One of them turned toward me with a sardonic smile upon his thin, cruel lips—it was Zat Arrras.

BLACK DESPAIR

"Ah," said Zat Arrras, "to what kindly circumstance am I indebted for the pleasure of this unexpected visit from the Prince of Helium?"

While he was speaking, one of my guards had removed the gag from my mouth, but I made no reply to Zat Arrras: simply standing there in silence with level gaze fixed upon the Jed of Zodanga. And I doubt not that my expression was coloured by the contempt I felt for the man.

The eyes of those within the chamber were fixed first upon me and then upon Zat Arrras, until finally a flush of anger crept slowly over his face.

"You may go," he said to those who had brought me, and when only his two companions and ourselves were left in the chamber, he spoke to me again in a voice of ice—very slowly and deliberately, with many pauses, as though he would choose his words cautiously.

"John Carter," he said, "by the edict of custom, by the law of our religion, and by the verdict of an impartial court, you are condemned to die. The people cannot save you—I alone may accomplish that. You are absolutely in my power to do with as I wish—I may kill you, or I may free you, and should I elect to kill you, none would be the wiser.

"Should you go free in Helium for a year, in accordance with the conditions of your reprieve, there is little fear that the people would ever insist upon the execution of the sentence imposed upon you.

"You may go free within two minutes, upon one condition. Tardos Mors will never return to Helium. Neither will Mors Kajak, nor Dejah Thoris. Helium must select a new Jeddak within the year. Zat Arrras would be Jeddak of Helium. Say that you will espouse my cause. This is the price of your freedom. I am done."

I knew it was within the scope of Zat Arrras' cruel heart to destroy me, and if I were dead I could see little reason to doubt that he might easily become Jeddak of Helium. Free, I could prosecute the search for Dejah Thoris. Were I dead, my brave comrades might not be able to carry out our plans. So, by refusing to accede to his request, it was quite probable that not only would I not prevent him from becoming Jeddak of Helium, but that I would be the means of sealing Dejah Thoris' fate—of consigning her, through my refusal, to the horrors of the arena of Issus.

For a moment I was perplexed, but for a moment only. The proud daughter of a thousand Jeddaks would choose death to a dishonourable alliance such as this, nor could John Carter do less for Helium than his Princess would do.

Then I turned to Zat Arrras.

"There can be no alliance," I said, "between a traitor to Helium and a prince of the House of Tardos Mors. I do not believe, Zat Arrras, that the great Jeddak is dead."

Zat Arrras shrugged his shoulders.

"It will not be long, John Carter," he said, "that your opinions will be of interest even to yourself, so make the best of them while you can. Zat Arrras will permit you in due time to reflect further upon the magnanimous offer he has made you. Into the silence and darkness of the pits you will enter upon your reflection this night with the knowledge that should you fail within a reasonable time to agree to the alternative which has been offered you, never shall you emerge from the darkness and the silence again. Nor shall you know at what minute the hand will reach out through the darkness and the silence with the keen dagger that shall rob you of your last chance to win again the warmth and the freedom and joyousness of the outer world."

Zat Arrras clapped his hands as he ceased speaking. The guards returned.

Zat Arrras waved his hand in my direction.

"To the pits," he said. That was all. Four men accompanied me from the chamber, and with a radium hand-light to illumine the way, escorted me through seemingly interminable tunnels, down, ever down beneath the city of Helium.

At length they halted within a fair-sized chamber. There were rings set in the rocky walls. To them chains were fastened, and at the ends of many of the chains were human skeletons. One of these they kicked aside, and, unlocking the huge padlock that had held a chain about what had once been a human ankle, they snapped the iron band about my own leg. Then they left me, taking the light with them.

Utter darkness prevailed. For a few minutes I could hear the clanking of accoutrements, but even this grew fainter and fainter, until at last the silence was as complete as the darkness. I was alone with my gruesome companions—with the bones of dead men whose fate was likely but the index of my own.

How long I stood listening in the darkness I do not know, but the silence was unbroken, and at last I sunk to the hard floor of my prison, where, leaning my head against the stony wall, I slept.

It must have been several hours later that I awakened to find a young man standing before me. In one hand he bore a light, in the other a receptacle containing a gruel-like mixture—the common prison fare of Barsoom.

"Zat Arrras sends you greetings," said the young man, "and commands me to inform you that though he is fully advised of the plot to make you Jeddak of Helium, he is, however, not inclined to withdraw the offer which he has made you. To gain your freedom you have but to request me to advise Zat Arrras that you accept the terms of his proposition.

I but shook my head. The youth said no more, and, after placing the food upon the floor at my side, returned up the corridor, taking the light with him.

Twice a day for many days this youth came to my cell with food, and ever the same greetings from Zat Arras. For a long time I tried to engage him in conversation upon other matters, but he would not talk, and so, at length, I desisted.

For months I sought to devise methods to inform Carthoris of my whereabouts. For months I scraped and scraped upon a single link of the massive chain which held me, hoping eventually to wear it through, that I might follow the youth back through the winding tunnels to a point where I could make a break for liberty.

I was beside myself with anxiety for knowledge of the progress of the expedition which was to rescue Dejah Thoris. I felt that Carthoris would not let the matter drop, were he free to act, but in so far as I knew, he also might be a prisoner in Zat Arrras' pits.

That Zat Arrras' spy had overheard our conversation relative to the selection of a new Jeddak, I knew, and scarcely a half-dozen minutes prior we had discussed the details of the plan to rescue Dejah Thoris. The chances were that that matter, too, was well known to him. Carthoris, Kantos Kan, Tars Tarkas, Hor Vastus, and Xodar might even now be the victims of Zat Arrras' assassins, or else his prisoners.

I determined to make at least one more effort to learn something, and to this end I adopted strategy when next the youth came to my cell. I had noticed that he was a handsome fellow, about the size and age of Carthoris. And I had also noticed that his shabby trappings but illy comported with his dignified and noble bearing.

It was with these observations as a basis that I opened my negotiations with him upon his next subsequent visit.

"You have been very kind to me during my imprisonment here," I said to him, "and as I feel that I have at best but a very short time to live, I wish, ere it is too late, to furnish substantial testimony of my appreciation of all that you have done to render my imprisonment bearable.

"Promptly you have brought my food each day, seeing that it was pure and of sufficient quantity. Never by word or deed have you attempted to take advantage of my defenceless condition to insult or torture me. You have been uniformly courteous and considerate—it is this more than any other thing which prompts my feeling of gratitude and my desire to give you some slight token of it.

"In the guard-room of my palace are many fine trappings. Go thou there and select the harness which most pleases you—it shall be yours. All I ask is that you wear it, that I may know that my wish has been realized. Tell me that you will do it."

The boy's eyes had lighted with pleasure as I spoke, and I saw him glance from his rusty trappings to the magnificence of my own. For a moment he stood in thought before he spoke, and for that mo-

THE GODS OF MARS

ment my heart fairly ceased beating—so much for me there was which
hung upon the substance of his answer.

"And I went to the palace of the Prince of Helium with any such
demand, they would laugh at me and, into the bargain, would more
than likely throw me headforemost into the avenue. No, it cannot
be, though I thank you for the offer. Why, if Zat Arrras even
dreamed that I contemplated such a thing he would have my heart
cut out of me."

"There can be no harm in it, my boy," I urged. "By night you may
go to my palace with a note from me to Carthoris, my son. You may
read the note before you deliver it, that you may know that it con-
tains nothing harmful to Zat Arrras. My son will be discreet, and so
none but us three need know. It is very simple, and such a harmless
act that it could be condemned by no one."

Again he stood silently in deep thought.

"And there is a jewelled short-sword which I took from the body
of a northern Jeddak. When you get the harness, see that Carthoris
gives you that also. With it and the harness which you may select
there will be no more handsomely accoutred warrior in all Zodanga.

"Bring writing materials when you come next to my cell, and within
a few hours we shall see you garbed in a style befitting your birth and
carriage."

Still in thought, and without speaking, he turned and left me. I
could not guess what his decision might be, and for hours I sat fretting
over the outcome of the matter.

If he accepted a message to Carthoris it would mean to me that
Carthoris still lived and was free. If the youth returned wearing the
harness and the sword, I would know that Carthoris had received my
note and that he knew that I still lived. That the bearer of the note
was a Zodangan would be sufficient to explain to Carthoris that I was
a prisoner of Zat Arrras.

It was with feelings of excited expectancy which I could scarce
hide that I heard the youth's approach upon the occasion of his next
regular visit. I did not speak beyond my accustomed greeting of him.
As he placed the food upon the floor by my side he also deposited
writing materials at the same time.

My heart fairly bounded for joy. I had won my point. For a moment I looked at the materials in feigned surprise, but soon I permitted an expression of dawning comprehension to come into my
face, and then, picking them up, I penned a brief order to Carthoris

to deliver to Parthak a harness of his selection and the short-sword which I described. That was all. But it meant everything to me and to Carthoris.

I laid the note open upon the floor. Parthak picked it up and, without a word, left me.

As nearly as I could estimate, I had at this time been in the pits for three hundred days. If anything was to be done to save Dejah Thoris it must be done quickly, for, were she not already dead, her end must soon come, since those whom Issus chose lived but a single year.

The next time I heard approaching footsteps I could scarce await to see if Parthak wore the harness and the sword, but judge, if you can, my chagrin and disappointment when I saw that he who bore my food was not Parthak.

"What has become of Parthak?" I asked, but the fellow would not answer, and as soon as he had deposited my food, turned and retraced his steps to the world above.

Days came and went, and still my new jailer continued his duties, nor would he ever speak a word to me, either in reply to the simplest question or of his own initiative.

I could only speculate on the cause of Parthak's removal, but that it was connected in some way directly with the note I had given him was most apparent to me. After all my rejoicing, I was no better off than before, for now I did not even know that Carthoris lived, for if Parthak had wished to raise himself in the estimation of Zat Arrras he would have permitted me to go on precisely as I did, so that he could carry my note to his master, in proof of his own loyalty and devotion.

Thirty days had passed since I had given the youth the note. Three hundred and thirty days had passed since my incarceration. As closely as I could figure, there remained a bare thirty days ere Dejah Thoris would be ordered to the arena for the rites of Issus.

As the terrible picture forced itself vividly across my imagination, I buried my face in my arms, and only with the greatest difficulty was it that I repressed the tears that welled to my eyes despite my every effort. To think of that beautiful creature torn and rended by the cruel fangs of the hideous white apes! It was unthinkable. Such a horrid fact could not be; and yet my reason told me that within thirty days my incomparable Princess would be fought over in the arena of the First Born by those very wild beasts; that her bleeding corpse would be dragged through the dirt and the dust, until at last a part of it would be rescued to be served as food upon the tables of the black nobles.

I think that I should have gone crazy but for the sound of my approaching jailer. It distracted my attention from the terrible thoughts that had been occupying my entire mind. Now a new and grim determination came to me. I would make one super-human effort to escape. Kill my jailer by a ruse, and trust to fate to lead me to the outer world in safety.

With the thought came instant action. I threw myself upon the floor of my cell close by the wall, in a strained and distorted posture, as though I were dead after a struggle or convulsions. When he should stoop over me I had but to grasp his throat with one hand and strike him a terrific blow with the slack of my chain, which I gripped firmly in my right hand for the purpose.

Nearer and nearer came the doomed man. Now I heard him halt before me. There was a muttered exclamation, and then a step as he came to my side. I felt him kneel beside me. My grip tightened upon the chain. He leaned close to me. I must open my eyes to find his throat, grasp it, and strike one mighty final blow all at the same instant.

The thing worked just as I had planned. So brief was the interval between the opening of my eyes and the fall of the chain that I could not check it, though in that minute interval I recognized the face so close to mine as that of my son, Carthoris.

God! What cruel and malign fate had worked to such a frightful end! What devious chain of circumstances had led my boy to my side at this one particular minute of our lives when I could strike him down and kill him, in ignorance of his identity! A benign though tardy Providence blurred my vision and my mind as I sank into unconsciousness across the lifeless body of my only son.

When I regained consciousness it was to feel a cool, firm hand pressed upon my forehead. For an instant I did not open my eyes. I was endeavouring to gather the loose ends of many thoughts and memories which flitted elusively through my tired and overwrought brain.

At length came the cruel recollection of the thing that I had done in my last conscious act, and then I dared not to open my eyes for fear of what I should see lying beside me. I wondered who it could be who ministered to me. Carthoris must have had a companion whom I had not seen. Well, I must face the inevitable some time, so why not now, and with a sigh I opened my eyes.

Leaning over me was Carthoris, a great bruise upon his forehead where the chain had struck, but alive, thank God, alive! There was no one with him. Reaching out my arms, I took my boy within them, and if ever there arose from any planet a fervent prayer of gratitude, it was there beneath the crust of dying Mars as I thanked the Eternal Mystery for my son's life.

The brief instant in which I had seen and recognized Carthoris before the chain fell must have been ample to check the force of the blow. He told me that he had lain unconscious for a time—how long he did not know.

"How came you here at all?" I asked, mystified that he had found me without a guide.

"It was by your wit in apprising me of your existence and imprisonment through the youth, Parthak. Until he came for his harness and his sword, we had thought you dead. When I had read your note I did as you had bid, giving Parthak his choice of the harness in the guardroom, and later bringing the jewelled short-sword to him; but the minute that I had fulfilled the promise you evidently had made him, my obligation to him ceased. Then I commenced to question him, but he would give me no information as to your whereabouts. He was intensely loyal to Zat Arrras.

"Finally I gave him a fair choice between freedom and the pits beneath the palace—the price of freedom to be full information as to where you were imprisoned and directions which would lead us to you; but still he maintained his stubborn partisanship. Despairing, I had him removed to the pits, where he still is.

"No threats of torture or death, no bribes, however fabulous, would move him. His only reply to all our importunities was that whenever Parthak died, were it to-morrow or a thousand years hence, no man could truly say, 'A traitor is gone to his deserts.'

"Finally, Xodar, who is a fiend for subtle craftiness, evolved a plan whereby we might worm the information from him. And so I caused Hor Vastus to be harnessed in the metal of a Zodangan soldier and chained in Parthak's cell beside him. For fifteen days the noble Hor Vastus has languished in the darkness of the pits, but not in vain. Little by little he won the confidence and friendship of the

Zodangan, until only to-day Parthak, thinking that he was speaking not only to a countryman, but to a dear friend, revealed to Hor Vastus the exact cell in which you lay.

"It took me but a short time to locate the plans of the pits of Helium among thy official papers. To come to you, though, was a trifle more difficult matter. As you know, while all the pits beneath the city are connected, there are but single entrances from those beneath each section and its neighbour, and that at the upper level just underneath the ground.

"Of course, these openings which lead from contiguous pits to those beneath government buildings are always guarded, and so, while I easily came to the entrance to the pits beneath the palace which Zat Arrras is occupying, I found there a Zodangan soldier on guard. There I left him when I had gone by, but his soul was no longer with him.

"And here I am, just in time to be nearly killed by you," he ended, laughing.

As he talked Carthoris had been working at the lock which held my fetters, and now, with an exclamation of pleasure, he dropped the end of the chain to the floor, and I stood up once more, freed from the galling irons I had chafed in for almost a year.

He had brought a long-sword and a dagger for me, and thus armed we set out upon the return journey to my palace.

At the point where we left the pits of Zat Arrras we found the body of the guard Carthoris had slain. It had not yet been discovered, and, in order to still further delay search and mystify the jed's people, we carried the body with us for a short distance, hiding it in a tiny cell off the main corridor of the pits beneath an adjoining estate.

Some half-hour later we came to the pits beneath our own palace, and soon thereafter emerged into the audience chamber itself, where we found Kantos Kan, Tars Tarkas, Hor Vastus, and Xodar awaiting us most impatiently.

No time was lost in fruitless recounting of my imprisonment. What I desired to know was how well the plans we had laid nearly a year ago had been carried out.

"It has taken much longer than we had expected," replied Kantos Kan. "The fact that we were compelled to maintain utter secrecy has handicapped us terribly. Zat Arrras' spies are everywhere. Yet, to the best of my knowledge, no word of our real plans has reached the villain's ear.

"To-night there lies about the great docks at Hastor a fleet of a thousand of the mightiest battleships that ever sailed above Barsoom, and each equipped to navigate the air of Omean and the waters of Omean itself. Upon each battleship there are five ten-man cruisers, and ten five-man scouts, and a hundred one-man scouts; in all, one hundred and sixteen thousand craft fitted with both air and water propellers.

"At Thark lie the transports for the green warriors of Tars Tarkas, nine hundred large troopships, and with them their convoys. Seven days ago all was in readiness, but we waited in the hope that by so doing your rescue might be encompassed in time for you to command the expedition. It is well we waited, my Prince."

"How is it, Tars Tarkas," I asked, "that the men of Thark take not the accustomed action against one who returns from the bosom of Iss?"

"They sent a council of fifty chieftains to talk with me here," replied the Thark. "We are a just people, and when I had told them the entire story they were as one man in agreeing that their action toward me would be guided by the action of Helium toward John Carter. In the meantime, at their request, I was to resume my throne as Jeddak of Thark, that I might negotiate with neighboring hordes for warriors to compose the land forces of the expedition. I have done that which I agreed. Two hundred and fifty thousand fighting-men, gathered from the ice cap at the north to the ice cap at the south, and representing a thousand different communities, from a hundred wild and warlike hordes, fill the great city of Thark to-night. They are ready to sail for the Land of the First Born when I give the word and fight there until I bid them stop. All they ask is the loot they take and transportation to their own territories when the fighting and the looting are over. I am done."

"And thou, Hor Vastus," I asked, "what has been thy success?"

"A million veteran fighting-men from Helium's thin waterways man the battleships, the transports, and the convoys," he replied. "Each is sworn to loyalty and secrecy, nor were enough recruited from a single district to cause suspicion."

"Good!" I cried. "Each has done his duty, and now, Kantos Kan, may we not repair at once to Hastor and get under way before to-morrow's sun?"

"We should lose no time, Prince," replied Kantos Kan. "Already the people of Hastor are questioning the purpose of so great a fleet fully manned with fighting-men. I wonder much that word of it has not before reached Zat Arrras. A cruiser awaits above at your own dock; let us leave at——" A fusillade of shots from the palace gardens just without cut short his further words.

Together we rushed to the balcony in time to see a dozen members of my palace guard disappear in the shadows of some distant shrubbery as in pursuit of one who fled. Directly beneath us upon the scarlet sward a handful of guardsmen were stooping above a still and prostrate form.

While we watched they lifted the figure in their arms and at my command bore it to the audience chamber where we had been in council. When they stretched the body at our feet we saw that it was that of a red man in the prime of life—his metal was plain, such as common soldiers wear, or those who wish to conceal their identity.

"Another of Zat Arrras' spies," said Hor Vastus.

"So it would seem," I replied, and then to the guard: "You may remove the body."

"Wait!" said Xodar. "If you will, Prince, ask that a cloth and a little thoat oil be brought."

I nodded to one of the soldiers, who left the chamber, returning presently with the things that Xodar had requested. The black kneeled beside the body and, dipping a corner of the cloth in the thoat oil, rubbed for a moment on the dead face before him. Then he turned to me with a smile, pointing to his work. I looked and saw that where Xodar had applied the thoat oil the face was white, as white as mine, and then Xodar seized the black hair of the corpse and with a sudden wrench tore it all away, revealing a hairless pate beneath.

Guardsmen and nobles pressed close about the silent witness upon the marble floor. Many were the exclamations of astonishment and questioning wonder as Xodar's acts confirmed the suspicion which he had held.

"A thern!" whispered Tars Tarkas.

"Worse than that, I fear," replied Xodar. "But let us see."

With that he drew his dagger and cut open a locked pouch which had dangled from the thern's harness, and from it he brought forth a circlet of gold set with a large gem—it was the mate to that which I had taken from Sator Throg.

"He was a Holy Thern," said Xodar. "Fortunate indeed it is for us that he did not escape."

The officer of the guard entered the chamber at this juncture.

"My Prince," he said, "I have to report that this fellow's companion escaped us. I think that it was with the connivance of one or more of the men at the gate. I have ordered them all under arrest."

Xodar handed him the thoat oil and cloth.

"With this you may discover the spy among you," he said.

I at once ordered a secret search within the city, for every Martian noble maintains a secret service of his own.

A half-hour later the officer of the guard came again to report. This time it was to confirm our worst fears—half the guards at the gate that night had been therns disguised as red men.

"Come!" I cried. "We must lose no time. On to Hastor at once. Should the therns attempt to check us at the southern verge of the ice cap it may result in the wrecking of all our plans and the total destruction of the expedition."

Ten minutes later we were speeding through the night toward Hastor, prepared to strike the first blow for the preservation of Dejah Thoris.

THE AIR BATTLE

TWO HOURS after leaving my palace in Helium, or about midnight, Kantos Kan, Xodar, and I arrived at Hastor. Carthoris, Tars Tarkas, and Hor Vastus had gone directly to Thark upon another cruiser.

The transports were to get under way immediately and move slowly south. The fleet of battleships would overtake them on the morning of the second day.

At Hastor we found all in readiness, and so perfectly had Kantos Kan planned every detail of the campaign that within ten minutes of our arrival the first of the fleet had soared aloft from its dock, and thereafter, at the rate of one a second, the great ships floated gracefully out into the night to form a long, thin line which stretched for miles toward the south.

It was not until after we had entered the cabin of Kantos Kan that I thought to ask the date, for up to now I was not positive how long I had lain in the pits of Zat Arrras. When Kantos Kan told me, I realized with a pang of dismay that I had misreckoned the time while

I lay in the utter darkness of my cell. Three hundred and sixty-five days had passed—it was too late to save Dejah Thoris.

The expedition was no longer one of rescue but of revenge. I did not remind Kantos Kan of the terrible fact that ere we could hope to enter the Temple of Issus, the Princess of Helium would be no more. In so far as I knew she might be already dead, for I did not know the exact date on which she first viewed Issus.

What now the value of burdening my friends with my added personal sorrows—they had shared quite enough of them with me in the past. Hereafter I would keep my grief to myself, and so I said nothing to any other of the fact that we were too late. The expedition could yet do much if it could but teach the people of Barsoom the facts of the cruel deception that had been worked upon them for countless ages, and thus save thousands each year from the horrid fate that awaited them at the conclusion of the voluntary pilgrimage.

If it could open to the red men the fair Valley Dor it would have accomplished much, and in the Land of Lost Souls between the Mountains of Otz and the ice barrier were many broad acres that needed no irrigation to bear rich harvests.

Here at the bottom of a dying world was the only naturally productive area upon its surface. Here alone were dews and rains, here alone was an open sea, here was water in plenty; and all this was but the stamping ground of fierce brutes and from its beauteous and fertile expanse the wicked remnants of two once mighty races barred all the other millions of Barsoom. Could I but succeed in once breaking down the barrier of religious superstition which had kept the red races from this El Dorado it would be a fitting memorial to the immortal virtues of my Princess—I should have again served Barsoom and Dejah Thoris' martyrdom would not have been in vain.

On the morning of the second day we raised the great fleet of transports and their consorts at the first flood of dawn, and soon were near enough to exchange signals. I may mention here that radio-aerograms are seldom if ever used in war time, or for the transmission of secret dispatches at any time, for as often as one nation discovers a new cipher, or invents a new instrument for wireless purposes its neighbours bend every effort until they are able to intercept and translate the messages. For so long a time has this gone on that practically every possibility of wireless communication has been exhausted and no nation dares transmit dispatches of importance in this way.

Tars Tarkas reported all well with the transports. The battleships passed through to take an advanced position, and the combined fleets moved slowly over the ice cap, hugging the surface closely to prevent detection by the therns whose land we were approaching.

Far in advance of all a thin line of one-man air scouts protected us from surprise, and on either side they flanked us, while a smaller number brought up the rear some twenty miles behind the transports. In this formation we had progressed toward the entrance to Omean for several hours when one of our scouts returned from the front to report that the cone-like summit of the entrance was in sight. At almost the same instant another scout from the left flank came racing toward the flagship.

His very speed bespoke the importance of his information. Kantos Kan and I awaited him upon the little forward deck which corresponds with the bridge of earthly battleships. Scarcely had his tiny flier come to rest upon the broad landing-deck of the flagship ere he was bounding up the stairway to the deck where we stood.

"A great fleet of battleships south-south-east, my Prince," he cried. "There must be several thousands and they are bearing down directly upon us."

"The thern spies were not in the palace of John Carter for nothing," said Kantos Kan to me. "Your orders, Prince."

"Dispatch ten battleships to guard the entrance to Omean, with orders to let no hostile vessel enter or leave the shaft. That will bottle up the great fleet of the First Born.

"Form the balance of the battleships into a great V with the apex pointing directly south-south-east. Order the transports, surrounded by their convoys, to follow closely in the wake of the battleships until the point of the V has entered the enemies' line, then the V must open outward at the apex, the battleships of each leg engage the enemy fiercely and drive him back to form a lane through his line into which the transports with their convoys must race at top speed that they may gain a position above the temples and gardens of the therns.

"Here let them land and teach the Holy Therns such a lesson in ferocious warfare as they will not forget for countless ages. It had not been my intention to be distracted from the main issue of the campaign, but we must settle this attack with the therns once and for all, or there will be no peace for us while our fleet remains near

Dor, and our chances of ever returning to the outer world will be greatly minimized."

Kantos Kan saluted and turned to deliver my instructions to his waiting aides. In an incredibly short space of time the formation of the battleships changed in accordance with my commands, the ten that were to guard the way to Omean were speeding toward their destination, and the troopships and convoys were closing up in preparation for the spurt through the lane.

The order of full speed ahead was given, the fleet sprang through the air like coursing greyhounds, and in another moment the ships of the enemy were in full view. They formed a ragged line as far as the eye could reach in either direction and about three ships deep. So sudden was our onslaught that they had no time to prepare for it. It was as unexpected as lightning from a clear sky.

Every phase of my plan worked splendidly. Our huge ships mowed their way entirely through the line of thern battlecraft; then the V opened up and a broad lane appeared through which the transports leaped toward the temples of the therns which could now be plainly seen glistening in the sunlight. By the time the therns had rallied from the attack a hundred thousand green warriors were already pouring through their courts and gardens, while a hundred and fifty thousand others leaned from low swinging transports to direct their almost uncanny marksmanship upon the thern soldiery that manned the ramparts, or attempted to defend the temples.

Now the two great fleets closed in a titanic struggle far above the fiendish din of battle in the gorgeous gardens of the therns. Slowly the two lines of Helium's battleships joined their ends, and then commenced the circling within the line of the enemy which is so marked a characteristic of Barsoomian naval warfare.

Around and around in each other's tracks moved the ships under Kantos Kan, until at length they formed nearly a perfect circle. By this time they were moving at high speed so that they presented a difficult target for the enemy. Broadside after broadside they delivered as each vessel came in line with the ships of the therns. The latter attempted to rush in and break up the formation, but it was like stopping a buzz saw with the bare hand.

From my position on the deck beside Kantos Kan I saw ship after ship of the enemy take the awful, sickening dive which proclaims its total destruction. Slowly we manœuvred our circle of death until we hung above the gardens where our green warriors were engaged.

The order was passed down for them to embark. Then they rose slowly to a position within the centre of the circle.

In the meantime the therns' fire had practically ceased. They had had enough of us and were only too glad to let us go on our way in peace. But our escape was not to be encompassed with such ease, for scarcely had we gotten under way once more in the direction of the entrance to Omean than we saw far to the north a great black line topping the horizon. It could be nothing other than a fleet of war.

Whose or whither bound, we could not even conjecture. When they had come close enough to make us out at all, Kantos Kan's operator received a radio-aerogram, which he immediately handed to my companion. He read the thing and handed it to me.

"Kantos Kan:" it read. "Surrender, in the name of the Jeddak of Helium, for you cannot escape," and it was signed, "Zat Arrras."

The therns must have caught and translated the message almost as soon as did we, for they immediately renewed hostilities when they realized that we were soon to be set upon by other enemies.

Before Zat Arrras had approached near enough to fire a shot we were again hotly engaged with the thern fleet, and as soon as he drew near he too commenced to pour a terrific fusillade of heavy shot into us. Ship after ship reeled and staggered into uselessness beneath the pitiless fire that we were undergoing.

The thing could not last much longer. I ordered the transports to descend again into the gardens of the therns.

"Wreak your vengeance to the utmost," was my message to the green allies, "for by night there will be none left to avenge your wrongs."

Presently I saw the ten battleships that had been ordered to hold the shaft of Omean. They were returning at full speed, firing their stern batteries almost continuously. There could be but one explanation. They were being pursued by another hostile fleet. Well, the situation could be no worse. The expedition already was doomed. No man that had embarked upon it would return across that dreary ice cap. How I wished that I might face Zat Arrras with my longsword for just an instant before I died! It was he who had caused our failure.

As I watched the oncoming ten I saw their pursuers race swiftly into sight. It was another great fleet; for a moment I could not believe my eyes, but finally I was forced to admit that the most fatal calamity had overtaken the expedition, for the fleet I saw was none other than the fleet of the First Born, that should have been safely bottled up in Omean. What a series of misfortunes and disasters! What awful fate hovered over me, that I should have been so terribly thwarted at every angle of my search for my lost love! Could it be possible that the curse of Issus was upon me! That there was, indeed, some malign divinity in that hideous carcass! I would not believe it, and, throwing back my shoulders, I ran to the deck below to join my men in repelling boarders from one of the thern craft that had grappled us broadside. In the wild lust of hand-to-hand combat my old dauntless hopefulness returned. And as thern after thern went down beneath my blade, I could almost feel that we should win success in the end, even from apparent failure.

My presence among the men so greatly inspirited them that they fell upon the luckless whites with such terrible ferocity that within a few moments we had turned the tables upon them and a second later as we swarmed their own decks I had the satisfaction of seeing their commander take the long leap from the bows of his vessel in token of surrender and defeat.

Then I joined Kantos Kan. He had been watching what had taken place on the deck below, and it seemed to have given him a new thought. Immediately he passed an order to one of his officers, and presently the colours of the Prince of Helium broke from every point of the flagship. A great cheer arose from the men of our own ship, a cheer that was taken up by every other vessel of our expedition as they in turn broke my colours from their upper works.

Then Kantos Kan sprang his coup. A signal legible to every sailor of all the fleets engaged in that fierce struggle was strung aloft upon the flagship.

"Men of Helium for the Prince of Helium against all his enemies," it read. Presently my colours broke from one of Zat Arrras' ships. Then from another and another. On some we could see fierce battles waging between the Zodangan soldiery and the Heliumetic crews, but eventually the colours of the Prince of Helium floated above every ship that had followed Zat Arrras upon our trail—only his flagship flew them not.

Zat Arrras had brought five thousand ships. The sky was back with the three enormous fleets. It was Helium against the field now, and the fight had settled to countless individual duels. There could be little or no manoeuvring of fleets in that crowded, fire-split sky.

Zat Arrras' flagship was close to my own. I could see the thin
features of the man from where I stood. His Zodangan crew was
pouring broadside after broadside into us and we were returning their
fire with equal ferocity. Closer and closer came the two vessels until
but a few yards intervened. Grapplers and boarders lined the contiguous rails of each. We were preparing for the death struggle with
our hated enemy.

There was but a yard between the two mighty ships as the first
grappling irons were hurled. I rushed to the deck to be with my men
as they boarded. Just as the vessels came together with a slight shock,
I forced my way through the lines and was the first to spring to the
deck of Zat Arrras' ship. After me poured a yelling, cheering, cursing
throng of Helium's best fighting-men. Nothing could withstand them
in the fever of battle lust which enthralled them.

Down went the Zodangans before that surging tide of war, and
as my men cleared the lower decks I sprang to the forward deck
where stood Zat Arrras.

"You are my prisoner, Zat Arrras," I cried. "Yield and you shall
have quarter."

For a moment I could not tell whether he contemplated acceding
to my demand or facing me with drawn sword. For an instant he
stood hesitating, and then throwing down his arms he turned and
rushed to the opposite side of the deck. Before I could overtake him
he had sprung to the rail and hurled himself headforemost into the
awful depths below.

And thus came Zat Arrras, Jed of Zodanga, to his end.

On and on went that strange battle. The therns and blacks had
not combined against us. Wherever thern ship met ship of the First
Born was a battle royal, and in this I thought I saw our salvation.
Wherever messages could be passed between us that could not be
intercepted by our enemies I passed the word that all our vessels
were to withdraw from the fight as rapidly as possible, taking a
position to the west and south of the combatants. I also sent an air
scout to the fighting green men in the gardens below to re-embark,
and to the transports to join us.

My commanders were further instructed that when engaged with
an enemy to draw him as rapidly as possible toward a ship of his
hereditary foeman, and by careful manœuvring to force the two to
engage, thus leaving himself free to withdraw. This stratagem worked
to perfection, and just before the sun went down I had the satisfaction

of seeing all that was left of my once mighty fleet gathered nearly twenty miles southwest of the still terrific battle between the blacks and whites.

I now transferred Xodar to another battleship and sent him with all the transports and five thousand battleships directly overhead to the Temple of Issus. Carthoris and I, with Kantos Kan, took the remaining ships and headed for the entrance to Omean.

Our plan now was to attempt to make a combined assault upon Issus at dawn of the following day. Tars Tarkas with his green warriors and Hor Vastus with the red men, guided by Xodar, were to land within the garden of Issus or the surrounding plains; while Carthoris, Kantos Kan, and I were to lead our smaller force from the sea of Omean through the pits beneath the temple, which Carthoris knew so well.

I now learned for the first time the cause of my ten ships' retreat from the mouth of the shaft. It seemed that when they had come upon the shaft the navy of the First Born were already issuing from its mouth. Fully twenty vessels had emerged, and though they gave battle immediately in an effort to stem the tide that rolled from the black pit, the odds against them were too great and they were forced to flee.

With great caution we approached the shaft, under cover of darkness. At a distance of several miles I caused the fleet to be halted, and from there Carthoris went ahead alone upon a one-man flier to reconnoitre. In perhaps half an hour he returned to report that there was no sign of a patrol boat or of the enemy in any form, and so we moved swiftly and noiselessly forward once more toward Omean.

At the mouth of the shaft we stopped again for a moment for all the vessels to reach their previously appointed stations, then with the flagship I dropped quickly into the black depths, while one by one the other vessels followed me in quick succession.

We had decided to stake all on the chance that we would be able to reach the temple by the subterranean way and so we left no guard of vessels at the shaft's mouth. Nor would it have profited us any to have done so, for we did not have sufficient force all told to have withstood the vast navy of the First Born had they returned to engage us.

For the safety of our entrance upon Omean we depended largely upon the very boldness of it, believing that it would be some little time before the First Born on guard there would realize that it was an enemy and not their own returning fleet that was entering the vault of the buried sea.

And such proved to be the case. In fact, four hundred of my fleet of five hundred rested safely upon the bosom of Omean before the first shot was fired. The battle was short and hot, but there could have been but one outcome, for the First Born in the carelessness of fancied security had left but a handful of ancient and obsolete hulks to guard their mighty harbour.

It was at Carthoris' suggestion that we landed our prisoners under guard upon a couple of the larger islands, and then towed the ships of the First Born to the shaft, where we managed to wedge a number of them securely in the interior of the great well. Then we turned on the buoyancy rays in the balance of them and let them rise by themselves to further block the passage to Omean as they came into contact with the vessels already lodged there.

We now felt that it would be some time at least before the returning First Born could reach the surface of Omean, and that we would have ample opportunity to make for the subterranean passages which lead to Issus. One of the first steps I took was to hasten personally with a good-sized force to the island of the submarine, which I took without resistance on the part of the small guard there.

I found the submarine in its pool, and at once placed a strong guard upon it and the island, where I remained to wait the coming of Carthoris and the others.

Among the prisoners was Yersted, commander of the submarine. He recognized me from the three trips that I had taken with him during my captivity among the First Born.

"How does it seem," I asked him, "to have the tables turned? To be prisoner of your erstwhile captive?"

He smiled, a very grim smile pregnant with hidden meaning.

"It will not be for long, John Carter," he replied. "We have been expecting you and we are prepared."

"So it would appear," I answered, "for you were all ready to become my prisoners with scarce a blow struck on either side."

"The fleet must have missed you," he said, "but it will return to Omean, and then that will be a very different matter—for John Carter."

"I do not know that the fleet has missed me as yet," I said, but of course he did not grasp my meaning, and only looked puzzled.

"Many prisoners travel to Issus in your grim craft, Yersted?" I asked.

"Very many," he assented.

"Might you remember one whom men called Dejah Thoris?"

"Well, indeed, for her great beauty, and then, too, for the fact that she was wife to the first mortal that ever escaped from Issus through all the countless ages of her godhood. And they say that Issus remembers her best as the wife of one and the mother of another who raised their hands against the Goddess of Life Eternal."

I shuddered for fear of the cowardly revenge that I knew Issus might have taken upon the innocent Dejah Thoris for the sacrilege of her son and her husband.

"And where is Dejah Thoris now?" I asked, knowing that he would say the words I most dreaded, but yet I loved her so that I could not refrain from hearing even the worst about her fate so that it fell from the lips of one who had seen her but recently. It was to me as though it brought her closer to me.

"Yesterday the monthly rites of Issus were held," replied Yersted, "and I saw her then sitting in her accustomed place at the foot of Issus."

"What," I cried, "she is not dead, then?"

"Why, no," replied the black, "it has been no year since she gazed upon the divine glory of the radiant face of—"

"No year?" I interrupted.

"Why, no," insisted Yersted. "It cannot have been upward of three hundred and seventy or eighty days."

A great light burst upon me. How stupid I had been! I could scarcely retain an outward exhibition of my great joy. Why had I forgotten the great difference in the length of Martian and Earthly years! The ten Earth years I had spent upon Barsoom had encompassed but five years and ninety-six days of Martian time, whose days are forty-one minutes longer than ours, and whose years number six hundred and eighty-seven days.

I am in time! I am in time! The words surged through my brain again and again, until at last I must have voiced them audibly, for Yersted shook his head.

"In time to save your Princess?" he asked, and then without waiting for my reply, "No, John Carter, Issus will not give up her own. She knows that you are coming, and ere ever a vandal foot is set within the precincts of the Temple of Issus, if such a calamity should befall, Dejah Thoris will be put away for ever from the last faint hope of rescue."

"You mean that she will be killed merely to thwart me?" I asked.

"Not that, other than as a last resort," he replied. "Hast ever heard of the Temple of the Sun? It is there that they will put her. It lies far within the inner court of the Temple of Issus, a little temple that raises a thin spire far above the spires and minarets of the great temple that surrounds it. Beneath it, in the ground, there lies the main body of the temple consisting in six hundred and eighty-seven circular chambers, one below another. To each chamber a single corridor leads through solid rock from the pits of Issus.

"As the entire Temple of the Sun revolves once with each revolution of Barsoom about the sun, but once each year does the entrance to each separate chamber come opposite the mouth of the corridor which forms its only link to the world without.

"Here Issus puts those who displease her, but whom she does not care to execute forthwith. Or to punish a noble of the First Born she may cause him to be placed within a chamber of the Temple of the Sun for a year. Ofttimes she imprisons an executioner with the condemned, that death may come in a certain horrible form upon a given day, or again but enough food is deposited in the chamber to sustain life but the number of days that Issus has allotted for mental anguish.

"Thus will Dejah Thoris die, and her fate will be sealed by the first alien foot that crosses the threshold of Issus."

So I was to be thwarted in the end, although I had performed the miraculous and come within a few short moments of my divine Princess, yet was I as far from her as when I stood upon the banks of the Hudson forty-eight million miles away.

THROUGH FLOOD AND FLAME

YERSTED'S INFORMATION convinced me that there was no time to be lost. I must reach the Temple of Issus secretly before the forces under Tars Tarkas assaulted at dawn. Once within its hated walls I was positive that I could overcome the guards of Issus and bear away my Princess, for at my back I would have a force ample for the occasion.

No sooner had Carthoris and the others joined me than we commenced the transportation of our men through the submerged passage to the mouth of the gangways which lead from the submarine pool at the temple end of the watery tunnel to the pits of Issus.

Many trips were required, but at last all stood safely together again at the beginning of the end of our quest. Five thousand strong we were, all seasoned fighting-men of the most warlike race of the red men of Barsoom.

As Carthoris alone knew the hidden ways of the tunnels we could not divide the party and attack the temple at several points at once as would have been most desirable, and so it was decided that he lead us all as quickly as possible to a point near the temple's centre.

As we were about to leave the pool and enter the corridors, an officer called my attention to the waters upon which the submarine floated. At first they seemed to be merely agitated as from the movement of some great body beneath the surface, and I at once conjectured that another submarine was rising to the surface in pursuit of us; but presently it became apparent that the level of the waters was rising, not with extreme rapidity, but very surely, and that soon they would overflow the sides of the pool and submerge the floor of the chamber.

For a moment I did not fully grasp the terrible import of the slowly rising water. It was Carthoris who realized the full meaning of the thing—its cause and the reason for it.

"Haste!" he cried. "If we delay, we all are lost. The pumps of Omean have been stopped. They would drown us like rats in a trap. We must reach the upper levels of the pits in advance of the flood or we shall never reach them. Come."

"Lead the way, Carthoris," I cried. "We will follow."

At my command, the youth leaped into one of the corridors, and in column of twos the soldiers followed him in good order, each company entering the corridor only at the command of its dwar, or captain.

Before the last company filed from the chamber the water was ankle deep, and that the men were nervous was quite evident. Entirely unaccustomed to water except in quantities sufficient for drinking and bathing purposes the red Martians instinctively shrank from it in such formidable depths and menacing activity. That they were undaunted while it swirled and eddied about their ankles, spoke well for their bravery and their discipline.

I was the last to leave the chamber of the submarine, and as I followed the rear of the column toward the corridor, I moved through water to my knees. The corridor, too, was flooded to the same depth, for its floor was on a level with the floor of the chamber from which it led, nor was there any perceptible rise for many yards.

The march of the troops through the corridor was as rapid as was consistent with the number of men that moved through so narrow a passage, but it was not ample to permit us to gain appreciably on the pursuing tide. As the level of the passage rose, so, too, did the waters rise until it soon became apparent to me, who brought up the rear, that they were gaining rapidly upon us. I could understand the reason for this, as with the narrowing expanse of Omean as the waters rose toward the apex of its dome, the rapidity of its rise would increase in inverse ratio to the ever-lessening space to be filled.

Long ere the last of the column could hope to reach the upper pits which lay above the danger point I was convinced that the waters would surge after us in overwhelming volume, and that fully half the expedition would be snuffed out.

As I cast about for some means of saving as many as possible of the doomed men, I saw a diverging corridor which seemed to rise at a steep angle at my right. The waters were now swirling about my waist. The men directly before me were quickly becoming panic-stricken. Something must be done at once or they would rush forward upon their fellows in a mad stampede that would result in trampling down hundreds beneath the flood and eventually clogging the passage beyond any hope of retreat for those in advance.

Raising my voice to its utmost, I shouted my command to the dwars ahead of me.

"Call back the last twenty-five utans," I shouted. "Here seems a way of escape. Turn back and follow me."

My orders were obeyed by nearer thirty utans, so that some three thousand men came about and hastened into the teeth of the flood to reach the corridor up which I directed them.

As the first dwar passed in with his utan I cautioned him to listen closely for my commands, and under no circumstances to venture into the open, or leave the pits for the temple proper until I should have come up with him, "or you know that I died before I could reach you."

The officer saluted and left me. The men filed rapidly past me and entered the diverging corridor which I hoped would lead to safety. The water rose breast high. Men stumbled, floundered, and went down. Many I grasped and set upon their feet again, but alone the work was greater than I could cope with. Soldiers were being swept beneath the boiling torrent, never to rise. At length the dwar of the 10th utan took a stand beside me. He was a valorous soldier, Gur Tus by name, and together we kept the now thoroughly frightened troops in the semblance of order and rescued many that would have drowned otherwise.

Djor Kantos, son of Kantos Kan, and a padwar of the fifth utan joined us when his utan reached the opening through which the men were fleeing. Thereafter not a man was lost of all the hundreds that remained to pass from the main corridor to the branch.

As the last utan was filing past us the waters had risen until they surged about our necks, but we clasped hands and stood our ground until the last man had passed to the comparative safety of the new passageway. Here we found an immediate and steep ascent, so that within a hundred yards we had reached a point above the waters.

For a few minutes we continued rapidly up the steep grade, which I hoped would soon bring us quickly to the upper pits that led into the Temple of Issus. But I was to meet with a cruel disappointment.

Suddenly I heard a cry of "fire" far ahead, followed almost at once by cries of terror and the loud commands of dwars and padwars who were evidently attempting to direct their men away from some grave danger. At last the report came back to us. "They have fired the pits ahead." "We are hemmed in by flames in front and flood behind." "Help, John Carter; we are suffocating," and then there swept back upon us at the rear a wave of dense smoke that sent us, stumbling and blinded, into a choking retreat.

There was naught to do other than seek a new avenue of escape. The fire and smoke were to be feared a thousand times over the water, and so I seized upon the first gallery which led out of and up from the suffocating smoke that was engulfing us.

Again I stood to one side while the soldiers hastened through on the new way. Some two thousand must have passed at a rapid run, when the stream ceased, but I was not sure that all had been rescued who had not passed the point of origin of the flames, and so to assure myself that no poor devil was left behind to die a horrible death, unsuccoured, I ran quickly up the gallery in the direction of the flames which I could now see burning with a dull glow far ahead.

It was hot and stifling work, but at last I reached a point where the fire lit up the corridor sufficiently for me to see that no soldier of Helium lay between me and the conflagration—what was in it or upon the far side I could not know, nor could any man have passed through that seething hell of chemicals and lived to learn.

Having satisfied my sense of duty, I turned and ran rapidly back to the corridor through which my men had passed. To my horror, however, I found that my retreat in this direction had been blocked —across the mouth of the corridor stood a massive steel grating that had evidently been lowered from its resting-place above for the purpose of effectually cutting off my escape.

That our principal movements were known to the First Born I could not have doubted, in view of the attack of the fleet upon us the day before, nor could the stopping of the pumps of Omean at the psychological moment have been due to chance, nor the starting of a chemical combustion within the one corridor through which we were advancing upon the Temple of Issus been due to aught than well-calculated design.

And now the dropping of the steel gate to pen me effectually between fire and flood seemed to indicate that invisible eyes were upon us at every moment. What chance had I, then, to rescue Dejah Thoris were I to be compelled to fight foes who never showed themselves. A thousand times I berated myself for being drawn into such a trap as I might have known these pits easily could be. Now I saw that it would have been much better to have kept our force intact and made a concerted attack upon the temple from the valley side, trusting to chance and our great fighting ability to have overwhelmed the First Born and compelled the safe delivery of Dejah Thoris to me.

The smoke from the fire was forcing me further and further back down the corridor toward the waters which I could hear surging through the darkness. With my men had gone the last torch, nor was this corridor lighted by the radiance of phosphorescent rock as were those of the lower levels. It was this fact that assured me that I was not far from the upper pits which lie directly beneath the temple.

Finally I felt the lapping waters about my feet. The smoke was thick behind me. My suffering was intense. There seemed but one thing to do, and that to choose the easier death which confronted me, and so I moved on down the corridor until the cold waters of Omean closed about me, and I swam on through utter blackness toward— what?

The instinct of self-preservation is strong even when one, unafraid and in the possession of his highest reasoning faculties, knows that death—positive and unalterable—lies just ahead. And so I swam slowly on, waiting for my head to touch the top of the corridor, which would mean that I had reached the limit of my flight and the point where I must sink for ever to an unmarked grave.

But to my surprise I ran against a blank wall before I reached a point where the waters came to the roof of the corridor. Could I be mistaken? I felt around. No, I had come to the main corridor, and still there was a breathing space between the surface of the water and the rocky ceiling above. And then I turned up the main corridor in the direction that Carthoris and the head of the column had passed a half-hour before. On and on I swam, my heart growing lighter at every stroke, for I knew that I was approaching closer and closer to the point where there would be no chance that the waters ahead could be deeper than they were about me. I was positive that I must soon feel the solid floor beneath my feet again and that once more my chance would come to reach the Temple of Issus and the side of the fair prisoner who languished there.

But even as hope was at its highest I felt the sudden shock of contact as my head struck the rocks above. The worst, then, had come to me. I had reached one of those rare places where a Martian tunnel dips suddenly to a lower level. Somewhere beyond I knew that it rose again, but of what value was that to me, since I did not know how great the distance that it maintained a level entirely beneath the surface of the water!

There was but a single forlorn hope, and I took it. Filling my lungs with air, I dived beneath the surface and swam through the inky, icy blackness on and on along the submerged gallery. Time and time again I rose with upstretched hand, only to feel the disappointing rocks close above me.

Not for much longer would my lungs withstand the strain upon them. I felt that I must soon succumb, nor was there any retreating now that I had gone this far. I knew positively that I could never endure to retrace my path now to the point from which I had felt the waters close above my head. Death stared me in the face, nor ever can I recall a time that I so distinctly felt the icy breath from his dead lips upon my brow.

One more frantic effort I made with my fast ebbing strength. Weakly

I rose for the last time—my tortured lungs gasped for the breath that would fill them with a strange and numbing element, but instead I felt the revivifying breath of life-giving air surge through my starving nostrils into my dying lungs. I was saved.

A few more strokes brought me to a point where my feet touched the floor, and soon thereafter I was above the water level entirely, and racing like mad along the corridor searching for the first doorway that would lead me to Issus. If I could not have Dejah Thoris again I was at least determined to avenge her death, nor would any life satisfy me other than that of the fiend incarnate who was the cause of such immeasurable suffering upon Barsoom.

Sooner than I had expected I came to what appeared to me to be a sudden exit into the temple above. It was at the right side of the corridor, which ran on, probably, to other entrances to the pile above.

To me one point was as good as another. What knew I where any of them led! And so without waiting to be again discovered and thwarted, I ran quickly up the short, steep incline and pushed open the doorway at its end.

The portal swung slowly in, and before it could be slammed against me I sprang into the chamber beyond. Although not yet dawn, the room was brilliantly lighted. Its sole occupant lay prone upon a low couch at the further side, apparently in sleep. From the hangings and sumptuous furniture of the room I judged it to be a living-room of some priestess, possibly of Issus herself.

At the thought the blood tingled through my veins. What, indeed, if fortune had been kind enough to place the hideous creature alone and unguarded in my hands. With her as hostage I could force acquiescence to my every demand. Cautiously I approached the recumbent figure, on noiseless feet. Closer and closer I came to it, but I had crossed but little more than half the chamber when the figure stirred, and, as I sprang, rose and faced me.

At first an expression of terror overspread the features of the woman who confronted me—then startled incredulity—hope—thanksgiving.

My heart pounded within my breast as I advanced toward her—tears came to my eyes—and the words that would have poured forth in a perfect torrent choked in my throat as I opened my arms and took into them once more the woman I loved—Dejah Thoris, Princess of Helium.

"JOHN CARTER, John Carter," she sobbed, with her dear head upon my shoulder; "even now I can scarce believe the witness of my own eyes. When the girl, Thuvia, told me that you had returned to Barsoom, I listened, but I could not understand, for it seemed that such happiness would be impossible for one who had suffered so in silent loneliness for all these long years. At last, when I realized that it was truth, and then came to know the awful place in which I was held prisoner, I learned to doubt that even you could reach me here.

"As the days passed, and moon after moon went by without bringing even the faintest rumour of you, I resigned myself to my fate. And now that you have come, scarce can I believe it. For an hour I have heard the sounds of conflict within the palace. I knew not what they meant, but I have hoped against hope that it might be the men of Helium headed by my Prince.

"And tell me, what of Carthoris, our son?"

"He was with me less than an hour since, Dejah Thoris," I replied. "It must have been he whose men you have heard battling within the precincts of the temple.

"Where is Issus?" I asked suddenly.

Dejah Thoris shrugged her shoulders.

"She sent me under guard to this room just before the fighting began within the temple halls. She said that she would send for me later. She seemed very angry and somewhat fearful. Never have I seen her act in so uncertain and almost terrified a manner. Now I know that it must have been because she had learned that John Carter, Prince of Helium, was approaching to demand an accounting of her for the imprisonment of his Princess."

The sounds of conflict, the clash of arms, the shouting and the hurrying of many feet came to us from various parts of the temple. I knew that I was needed there, but I dared not leave Dejah Thoris, nor dared I take her with me into the turmoil and danger of battle.

At last I bethought me of the pits from which I had just emerged. Why not secrete her there until I could return and fetch her away in safety and for ever from this awful place. I explained my plan to her.

For a moment she clung more closely to me.

"I cannot bear to be parted from you now, even for a moment, John Carter," she said. "I shudder at the thought of being alone again where that terrible creature might discover me. You do not know her. None can imagine her ferocious cruelty who has not witnessed her daily acts for over half a year. It has taken me nearly all this time to realize even the things that I have seen with my own eyes."

"I shall not leave you, then, my Princess," I replied.

She was silent for a moment, then she drew my face to hers and kissed me.

"Go, John Carter," she said. "Our son is there, and the soldiers of Helium, fighting for the Princess of Helium. Where they are you should be. I must not think of myself now, but of them and of my husband's duty. I may not stand in the way of that. Hide me in the pits, and go."

I led her to the door through which I had entered the chamber from below. There I pressed her dear form to me, and then, though it tore my heart to do it, and filled me only with the blackest shadows of terrible foreboding, I guided her across the threshold, kissed her once again, and closed the door upon her.

Without hesitating longer, I hurried from the chamber in the direction of the greatest tumult. Scarce half a dozen chambers had I traversed before I came upon the theatre of a fierce struggle. The blacks were massed at the entrance to a great chamber where they were attempting to block the further progress of a body of red men toward the inner sacred precincts of the temple.

Coming from within as I did, I found myself behind the blacks, and, without waiting to even calculate their numbers or the foolhardiness of my venture, I charged swiftly across the chamber and fell upon them from the rear with my keen long-sword.

As I struck the first blow I cried aloud, "For Helium!" And then I rained cut after cut upon the surprised warriors, while the reds without took heart at the sound of my voice, and with shouts of "John Carter! John Carter!" redoubled their efforts so effectually that before the blacks could recover from their temporary demoralization their ranks were broken and the red men had burst into the chamber.

The fight within that room, had it had but a competent chronicler, would go down in the annals of Barsoom as a historic memorial to the grim ferocity of her warlike people. Five hundred men fought there that day, the black men against the red. No man asked quarter or gave it. As though by common assent they fought, as though to determine once and for all their right to live, in accordance with the law of the survival of the fittest.

I think we all knew that upon the outcome of this battle would hinge for ever the relative positions of these two races upon Barsoom. It was a battle between the old and the new, but not for once did I question the outcome of it. With Carthoris at my side I fought for the red men of Barsoom and for their total emancipation from the throttling bondage of a hideous superstition.

Back and forth across the room we surged, until the floor was ankle deep in blood, and dead men lay so thickly there that half the time we stood upon their bodies as we fought. As we swung toward the great windows which overlooked the gardens of Issus a sight met my gaze which sent a wave of exultation over me.

"Look!" I cried. "Men of the First Born, look!"

For an instant the fighting ceased, and with one accord every eye turned in the direction I had indicated, and the sight they saw was one no man of the First Born had ever imagined could be.

Across the gardens, from side to side, stood a wavering line of black warriors, while beyond them and forcing them ever back was a great horde of green warriors astride their mighty thoats. And as we watched, one, fiercer and more grimly terrible than his fellows, rode forward from the rear, and as he came he shouted some fierce command to his terrible legion.

It was Tars Tarkas, Jeddak of Thark, and as he couched his great forty-foot metal-shod lance we saw his warriors do likewise. Then it was that we interpreted his command. Twenty yards now separated the green men from the black line. Another word from the great Thark, and with a wild and terrifying battle-cry the green warriors charged. For a moment the black line held, but only for a moment— then the fearsome beasts that bore equally terrible riders passed completely through it.

After them came utan upon utan of red men. The green horde broke to surround the temple. The red men charged for the interior, and then we turned to continue our interrupted battle; but our foes had vanished.

My first thought was of Dejah Thoris. Calling to Carthoris that I had found his mother, I started on a run toward the chamber where

I had left her, with my boy close beside me. After us came those of our little force who had survived the bloody conflict.

The moment I entered the room I saw that some one had been there since I had left. A silk lay upon the floor. It had not been there before. There were also a dagger and several metal ornaments strewn about as though torn from their wearer in a struggle. But worst of all, the door leading to the pits where I had hidden my Princess was ajar.

With a bound I was before it, and, thrusting it open, rushed within. Dejah Thoris had vanished. I called her name aloud again and again, but there was no response. I think in that instant I hovered upon the verge of insanity. I do not recall what I said or did, but I know that for an instant I was seized with the rage of a maniac.

"Issus!" I cried. "Issus! Where is Issus? Search the temple for her, but let no man harm her but John Carter. Carthoris, where are the apartments of Issus?"

"This way," cried the boy, and, without waiting to know that I had heard him, he dashed off at breakneck speed, further into the bowels of the temple. As fast as he went, however, I was still beside him, urging him on to greater speed.

At last we came to a great carved door, and through this Carthoris dashed, a foot ahead of me. Within, we came upon such a scene as I had witnessed within the temple once before—the throne of Issus, with the reclining slaves, and about it the ranks of soldiery.

We did not even give the men a chance to draw, so quickly were we upon them. With a single cut I struck down two in the front rank. And then by the mere weight and momentum of my body, I rushed completely through the two remaining ranks and sprang upon the dais beside the carved sorapus throne.

The repulsive creature, squatting there in terror, attempted to escape me and leap into a trap behind her. But this time I was not to be outwitted by any such petty subterfuge. Before she had half arisen I had grasped her by the arm, and then, as I saw the guard starting to make a concerted rush upon me from all sides, I whipped out my dagger and, holding it close to that vile breast, ordered them to halt.

"Back!" I cried to them. "Back! The first black foot that is planted upon this platform sends my dagger into Issus' heart."

For an instant they hesitated. Then an officer ordered them back, while from the outer corridor there swept into the throne room at the heels of my little party of survivors a full thousand red men under Kantos Kan, Hor Vastus, and Xodar.

"Where is Dejah Thoris?" I cried to the thing within my hands.

For a moment her eyes roved wildly about the scene beneath her. I think that it took a moment for the true condition to make any impression upon her—she could not at first realize that the temple had fallen before the assault of men of the outer world. When she did, there must have come, too, a terrible realization of what it meant to her—the loss of power—humiliation—the exposure of the fraud and imposture which she had for so long played upon her own people.

There was just one thing needed to complete the reality of the picture she was seeing, and that was added by the highest noble of her realm—the high priest of her religion—the prime minister of her government.

"Issus, Goddess of Death, and of Life Eternal," he cried, "arise in the might of thy righteous wrath and with one single wave of thy omnipotent hand strike dead thy blasphemers! Let not one escape. Issus, thy people depend upon thee. Daughter of the Lesser Moon, thou only art all-powerful. Thou only canst save thy people. I am done. We await thy will. Strike!"

And then it was that she went mad. A screaming, gibbering maniac writhed in my grasp. It bit and clawed and scratched in impotent fury. And then it laughed a weird and terrible laughter that froze the blood. The slave girls upon the dais shrieked and cowered away. And the thing jumped at them and gnashed its teeth and then spat upon them from frothing lips. God, but it was a horrid sight.

Finally, I shook the thing, hoping to recall it for a moment to rationality.

"Where is Dejah Thoris?" I cried again.

The awful creature in my grasp mumbled inarticulately for a moment, then a sudden gleam of cunning shot into those hideous, close-set eyes.

"Dejah Thoris? Dejah Thoris?" and then that shrill, unearthly laugh pierced our ears once more.

"Yes, Dejah Thoris—I know. And Thuvia, and Phaidor, daughter of Matai Shang. They each love John Carter. Ha-ah! but it is droll. Together for a year they will meditate within the Temple of the Sun, but ere the year is quite gone there will be no more food for them. Ho-oh! what divine entertainment," and she licked the froth from her cruel lips "There will be no more food—except each other. Ha-ah! Ha-ah!"

The horror of the suggestion nearly paralysed me. To this awful fate the creature within my power had condemned my Princess. I trembled in the ferocity of my rage. As a terrier shakes a rat I shook Issus, Goddess of Life Eternal.

"Countermand your orders!" I cried. "Recall the condemned. Haste, or you die!"

"It is too late. Ha-ah! Ha-ah!" and then she commenced her gibbering and shrieking again.

Almost of its own volition, my dagger flew up above that putrid heart. But something stayed my hand, and I am now glad that it did. It were a terrible thing to have struck down a woman with one's own hand. But a fitter fate occurred to me for this false deity.

"First Born," I cried, turning to those who stood within the chamber, "you have seen to-day the impotency of Issus—the gods are omnipotent. Issus is no god. She is a cruel and wicked old woman, who has deceived and played upon you for ages. Take her. John Carter, Prince of Helium, would not contaminate his hand with her blood," and with that I pushed the raving beast, whom a short half-hour before a whole world had worshipped as divine, from the platform of her throne into the waiting clutches of her betrayed and vengeful people.

Spying Xodar among the officers of the red men, I called him to lead me quickly to the Temple of the Sun, and, without waiting to learn what fate the First Born would wreak upon their goddess, I rushed from the chamber with Xodar, Carthoris, Hor Vastus, Kantos Kan, and a score of other red nobles.

The black led us rapidly through the inner chambers of the temple, until we stood within the central court—a great circular space paved with a transparent marble of exquisite whiteness. Before us rose a golden temple wrought in the most wondrous and fanciful designs, inlaid with diamond, ruby, sapphire, turquoise, emerald, and the thousand nameless gems of Mars, which far transcend in loveliness and purity of ray the most priceless stones of Earth.

"This way," cried Xodar, leading us toward the entrance to a tunnel which opened in the courtyard beside the temple. Just as we were on the point of descending we heard a deep-toned roar burst from the Temple of Issus, which we had but just quitted, and then a red man, Djor Kantos, padwar of the fifth utan, broke from a nearby gate, crying to us to return.

"The blacks have fired the temple," he cried. "In a thousand places it is burning now. Haste to the outer gardens, or you are lost."

As he spoke we saw smoke pouring from a dozen windows looking out upon the courtyard of the Temple of the Sun, and far above the highest minaret of Issus hung an ever-growing pall of smoke.

"Go back! Go back!" I cried to those who had accompanied me. "The way! Xodar; point the way and leave me. I shall reach my Princess yet."

"Follow me, John Carter," replied Xodar, and without waiting for my reply he dashed down into the tunnel at our feet. At his heels I ran down through a half-dozen tiers of galleries, until at last he led me along a level floor at the end of which I discerned a lighted chamber.

Massive bars blocked our further progress, but beyond I saw her—my incomparable Princess, and with her were Thuvia and Phaidor. When she saw me she rushed toward the bars that separated us. Already the chamber had turned upon its slow way so far that but a portion of the opening in the temple wall was opposite the barred end of the corridor. Slowly the interval was closing. In a short time there would be but a tiny crack, and then even that would be closed, and for a long Barsoomian year the chamber would slowly revolve until once more for a brief day the aperture in its wall would pass the corridor's end.

But in the meantime what horrible things would go on within that chamber!

"Xodar!" I cried. "Can no power stop this awful revolving thing? Is there none who holds the secret of these terrible bars?"

"None, I fear, whom we could fetch in time, though I shall go and make the attempt. Wait for me here."

After he had left I stood and talked with Dejah Thoris, and she stretched her dear hand through those cruel bars that I might hold it until the last moment.

Thuvia and Phaidor came close also, but when Thuvia saw that we would be alone she withdrew to the further side of the chamber. Not so the daughter of Matai Shang.

"John Carter," she said, "this be the last time that you shall see any of us. Tell me that you love me, that I may die happy."

"I love only the Princess of Helium," I replied quietly. "I am sorry, Phaidor, but it is as I have told you from the beginning."

She bit her lip and turned away, but not before I saw the black and ugly scowl she turned upon Dejah Thoris. Thereafter she stood a little way apart, but not so far as I should have desired, for I had many little confidences to impart to my long-lost love.

For a few minutes we stood thus talking in low tones. Ever smaller and smaller grew the opening. In a short time now it would be too small even to permit the slender form of my Princess to pass. Oh, why did not Xodar haste. Above we could hear the faint echoes of a great tumult. It was the multitude of black and red and green men fighting their way through the fire from the burning Temple of Issus.

A draught from above brought the fumes of smoke to our nostrils. As we stood waiting for Xodar the smoke became thicker and thicker. Presently we heard shouting at the far end of the corridor, and hurrying feet.

"Come back, John Carter, come back!" cried a voice, "even the pits are burning."

In a moment a dozen men broke through the now blinding smoke to my side. There was Carthoris, and Kantos Kan, and Hor Vastus, and Xodar, with a few more who had followed me to the temple court.

"There is no hope, John Carter," cried Xodar. "The keeper of the keys is dead and his keys are not upon his carcass. Our only hope is to quench this conflagration and trust to fate that a year will find your Princess alive and well. I have brought sufficient food to last them. When this crack closes no smoke can reach them, and if we hasten to extinguish the flames I believe they will be safe."

"Go, then, yourself and take these others with you," I replied. "I shall remain here beside my Princess until a merciful death releases me from my anguish. I care not to live."

As I spoke Xodar had been tossing a great number of tiny cans within the prison cell. The remaining crack was not over an inch in width a moment later. Dejah Thoris stood as close to it as she could, whispering words of hope and courage to me, and urging me to save myself.

Suddenly beyond her I saw the beautiful face of Phaidor contorted into an expression of malign hatred. As my eyes met hers she spoke.

"Think not, John Carter, that you may so lightly cast aside the love of Phaidor, daughter of Matai Shang. Nor ever hope to hold thy Dejah Thoris in thy arms again. Wait you the long, long year; but know that when the waiting is over it shall be Phaidor's arms which shall welcome you—not those of the Princess of Helium. Behold, she dies!"

And as she finished speaking I saw her raise a dagger on high, and then I saw another figure. It was Thuvia's. As the dagger fell toward the unprotected breast of my love, Thuvia was almost between them. A blinding gust of smoke blotted out the tragedy within that fearsome cell—a shriek rang out, a single shriek, as the dagger fell.

The smoke cleared away, but we stood gazing upon a blank wall. The last crevice had closed, and for a long year that hideous chamber would retain its secret from the eyes of men.

They urged me to leave.

"In a moment it will be too late," cried Xodar. "There is, in fact, but a bare chance that we can come through to the outer garden alive even now. I have ordered the pumps started, and in five minutes the pits will be flooded. If we would not drown like rats in a trap we must hasten above and make a dash for safety through the burning temple."

"Go," I urged them. "Let me die here beside my Princess—there is no hope or happiness elsewhere for me. When they carry her dear body from that terrible place a year hence let them find the body of her lord awaiting her."

Of what happened after that I have only a confused recollection. It seems as though I struggled with many men, and then that I was picked bodily from the ground and borne away. I do not know. I have never asked, nor has any other who was there that day intruded on my sorrow or recalled to my mind the occurrences which they know could but at best reopen the terrible wound within my heart.

Ah! If I could but know one thing, what a burden of suspense would be lifted from my shoulders! But whether the assassin's dagger reached one fair bosom or another, only time will divulge.

The WARLORD
of MARS

"Her right hand went high with its gleaming blade . . . and her sharp point pierced the vile heart of the great villain."

Contents

ON THE RIVER ISS

IN THE SHADOWS of the forest that flanks the crimson plain by the side of the Lost Sea of Korus in the Valley Dor, beneath the hurtling moons of Mars, speeding their meteoric way close above the bosom of the dying planet, I crept stealthily along the trail of a shadowy form that hugged the darker places with a persistency that proclaimed the sinister nature of its errand.

For six long Martian months I had haunted the vicinity of the hateful Temple of the Sun, within whose slow-revolving shaft, far beneath the surface of Mars, my princess lay entombed—but whether alive or dead I knew not. Had Phaidor's slim blade found that beloved heart? Time only would reveal the truth.

Six hundred and eighty-seven Martian days must come and go before the cell's door would again come opposite the tunnel's end where last I had seen my ever-beautiful Dejah Thoris.

Half of them had passed, or would on the morrow, yet vivid in my memory, obliterating every event that had come before or after, there remained the last scene before the gust of smoke blinded my eyes and the narrow slit that had given me sight of the interior of her cell closed between me and the Princess of Helium for a long Martian year.

As if it were yesterday, I still saw the beautiful face of Phaidor, daughter of Matai Shang, distorted with jealous rage and hatred as she sprang forward with raised dagger upon the woman I loved.

I saw the red girl, Thuvia of Ptarth, leap forward to prevent the hideous deed.

The smoke from the burning temple had come then to blot out the tragedy, but in my ears rang the single shriek as the knife fell. Then silence, and when the smoke had cleared, the revolving temple had shut off all sight or sound from the chamber in which the three beautiful women were imprisoned.

Much there had been to occupy my attention since that terrible moment; but never for an instant had the memory of the thing faded, and all the time that I could spare from the numerous duties that had devolved upon me in the reconstruction of the government of the First Born since our victorious fleet and land forces had overwhelmed them, had been spent close to the grim shaft that held the mother of my boy, Carthoris of Helium.

The race of blacks that for ages had worshiped Issus, the false deity of Mars, had been left in a state of chaos by my revealment of her as naught more than a wicked old woman. In their rage they had torn her to pieces.

From the high pinnacle of their egotism the First Born had been plunged to the depths of humiliation. Their deity was gone, and with her the whole false fabric of their religion. Their vaunted navy had fallen in defeat before the superior ships and fighting men of the red men of Helium.

Fierce green warriors from the ocher sea bottoms of outer Mars had ridden their wild thoats across the sacred gardens of the Temple of Issus, and Tars Tarkas, Jeddak of Thark, fiercest of them all, had sat upon the throne of Issus and ruled the First Born while the allies were deciding the conquered nation's fate.

Almost unanimous was the request that I ascend the ancient throne of the black men, even the First Born themselves concurring in it; but I would have none of it. My heart could never be with the race that had heaped indignities upon my princess and my son.

At my suggestion Xodar became Jeddak of the First Born. He had been a dator, or prince, until Issus had degraded him, so that his fitness for the high office bestowed was unquestioned.

The peace of the Valley Dor thus assured, the green warriors dispersed to their desolate sea bottoms, while we of Helium returned to our own country. Here again was a throne offered me, since no word had been received from the missing Jeddak of Helium, Tardos Mors, grandfather of Dejah Thoris, or his son, Mors Kajak, Jed of Helium, her father.

Over a year had elapsed since they had set out to explore the northern hemisphere in search of Carthoris, and at last their disheartened people had accepted as truth the vague rumors of their death that had filtered in from the frozen region of the pole.

Once again I refused a throne, for I would not believe that the mighty Tardos Mors, or his no less redoubtable son, was dead.

"Let one of their own blood rule you until they return," I said to the assembled nobles of Helium, as I addressed them from the Pedestal of Truth beside the Throne of Righteousness in the Temple of Reward, from the very spot where I had stood a year before when Zat Arrras pronounced the sentence of death upon me.

As I spoke I stepped forward and laid my hand upon the shoulder of Carthoris where he stood in the front rank of the circle of nobles about me.

As one, the nobles and the people lifted their voices in a long cheer of approbation. Ten thousand swords sprang on high from as many scabbards, and the glorious fighting men of ancient Helium hailed Carthoris Jeddak of Helium.

His tenure of office was to be for life or until his great-grandfather, or grandfather, should return. Having thus satisfactorily arranged this important duty for Helium, I started the following day for the Valley Dor that I might remain close to the Temple of the Sun until the fateful day that should see the opening of the prison cell where my lost love lay buried.

Hor Vastus and Kantos Kan, with my other noble lieutenants, I left with Carthoris at Helium, that he might have the benefit of their wisdom, bravery, and loyalty in the performance of the arduous duties which had devolved upon him. Only Woola, my Martian hound, accompanied me.

At my heels tonight the faithful beast moved softly in my tracks. As large as a Shetland pony, with hideous head and frightful fangs, he was indeed an awesome spectacle, as he crept after me on his ten short, muscular legs; but to me he was the embodiment of love and loyalty.

The figure ahead was that of the black dator of the First Born, Thurid, whose undying enmity I had earned that time I laid him low with my bare hands in the courtyard of the Temple of Issus, and bound him with his own harness before the noble men and women who had but a moment before been extolling his prowess.

Like many of his fellows, he had apparently accepted the new order of things with good grace, and had sworn fealty to Xodar, his new ruler; but I knew that he hated me, and I was sure that in his heart he envied and hated Xodar, so I had kept a watch upon his comings and goings, to the end that of late I had become convinced that he was occupied with some manner of intrigue.

Several times I had observed him leaving the walled city of the First Born after dark, taking his way out into the cruel and horrible Valley Dor, where no honest business could lead any man.

Tonight he moved quickly along the edge of the forest until well beyond sight or sound of the city, then he turned across the crimson sward toward the shore of the Lost Sea of Korus.

The rays of the nearer moon, swinging low across the valley, touched his jewel-incrusted harness with a thousand changing lights and glanced from the glossy ebony of his smooth hide. Twice he turned his head back toward the forest, after the manner of one who is upon an evil errand, though he must have felt quite safe from pursuit.

I did not dare follow him there beneath the moonlight, since it best suited my plans not to interrupt his—I wished him to reach his destination unsuspecting, that I might learn just where that destination lay and the business that awaited the night prowler there.

So it was that I remained hidden until after Thurid had disappeared over the edge of the steep bank beside the sea a quarter of a mile away. Then, with Woola following, I hastened across the open after the black dator.

The quiet of the tomb lay upon the mysterious valley of death, crouching deep in its warm nest within the sunken area at the south pole of the dying planet. In the far distance the Golden Cliffs raised their mighty barrier faces far into the starlit heavens, the precious metals and scintillating jewels that composed them sparkling in the brilliant light of Mars's two gorgeous moons.

At my back was the forest, pruned and trimmed like the sward to parklike symmetry by the browsing of the ghoulish plant men.

Before me lay the Lost Sea of Korus, while farther on I caught the shimmering ribbon of Iss, the River of Mystery, where it wound out from beneath the Golden Cliffs to empty into Korus, to which for countless ages had been borne the deluded and unhappy Martians of the outer world upon the voluntary pilgrimage to this false heaven.

The plant men, with their blood-sucking hands, and the monstrous white apes that make Dor hideous by day, were hidden in their lairs for the night.

There was no longer a Holy Thern upon the balcony in the Golden

Cliffs above the Iss to summon them with weird cry to the victims floating down to their maws upon the cold, broad bosom of ancient Iss.

The navies of Helium and the First Born had cleared the fortresses and the temples of the therns when they had refused to surrender and accept the new order of things that had swept their false religion from long-suffering Mars.

In a few isolated countries they still retained their age-old power; but Matai Shang, their hekkador, Father of Therns, had been driven from his temple. Strenuous had been our endeavors to capture him; but with a few of the faithful he had escaped, and was in hiding—where we knew not.

As I came cautiously to the edge of the low cliff overlooking the Lost Sea of Korus I saw Thurid pushing out upon the bosom of the shimmering water in a small skiff—one of those strangely wrought craft of unthinkable age which the Holy Therns, with their organization of priests and lesser therns, were wont to distribute along the banks of the Iss, that the long journey of their victims might be facilitated.

Drawn up on the beach below me were a score of similar boats, each with its long pole, at one end of which was a pike, at the other a paddle. Thurid was hugging the shore, and as he passed out of sight round a near-by promontory I shoved one of the boats into the water and, calling Woola into it, pushed out from shore.

The pursuit of Thurid carried me along the edge of the sea toward the mouth of the Iss. The farther moon lay close to the horizon, casting a dense shadow beneath the cliffs that fringed the water. Thuria, the nearer moon, had set, nor would it rise again for near four hours, so that I was ensured concealing darkness for that length of time at least.

On and on went the black warrior. Now he was opposite the mouth of the Iss. Without an instant's hesitation he turned up the grim river, paddling hard against the strong current.

After him came Woola and I, closer now, for the man was too intent upon forcing his craft up the river to have any eyes for what might be transpiring behind him. He hugged the shore where the current was less strong.

Presently he came to the dark cavernous portal in the face of the Golden Cliffs, through which the river poured. On into the Stygian darkness beyond he urged his craft.

It seemed hopeless to attempt to follow him here where I could not see my hand before my face, and I was almost on the point of giving up the pursuit and drifting back to the mouth of the river, there to await his return, when a sudden bend showed a faint luminosity ahead.

My quarry was plainly visible again, and in the increasing light from the phosphorescent rock that lay embedded in great patches in the roughly arched roof of the cavern I had no difficulty in following him.

It was my first trip upon the bosom of Iss, and the things I saw there will live forever in my memory.

Terrible as they were, they could not have commenced to approximate the horrible conditions which must have obtained before Tars Tarkas, the great green warrior, Xodar, the black dator, and I brought the light of truth to the outer world and stopped the mad rush of millions upon the voluntary pilgrimage to what they believed would end in a beautiful valley of peace and happiness and love.

Even now the low islands which dotted the broad stream were choked with the skeletons and half devoured carcasses of those who, through fear or a sudden awakening to the truth, had halted almost at the completion of their journey.

In the awful stench of these frightful charnel isles haggard maniacs screamed and gibbered and fought among the torn remnants of their grisly feats; while on those which contained but clean-picked bones they battled with one another, the weaker furnishing sustenance for the stronger; or with clawlike hands clutched at the bloated bodies that drifted down with the current.

Thurid paid not the slightest attention to the screaming things that either menaced or pleaded with him as the mood directed them— evidently he was familiar with the horrid sights that surrounded him. He continued up the river for perhaps a mile; and then, crossing over to the left bank, drew his craft up on a low ledge that lay almost on a level with the water.

I dared not follow across the stream, for he most surely would have seen me. Instead I stopped close to the opposite wall beneath an overhanging mass of rock that cast a dense shadow beneath it. Here I could watch Thurid without danger of discovery.

The black was standing upon the ledge beside his boat, looking up the river, as though he were awaiting one whom he expected from that direction.

As I lay there beneath the dark rocks I noticed that a strong current seemed to flow directly toward the center of the river, so that it was difficult to hold my craft in its position. I edged farther into the shadow that I might find a hold upon the bank; but, though I proceeded several yards, I touched nothing; and then, finding that I would soon reach a point from where I could no longer see the black man, I was compelled to remain where I was, holding my position as best I could by paddling strongly against the current which flowed from beneath the rocky mass behind me.

I could not imagine what might cause this strong lateral flow, for the main channel of the river was plainly visible to me from where I sat, and I could see the rippling junction of it and the mysterious current which had aroused my curiosity.

While I was still speculating upon the phenomenon, my attention was suddenly riveted upon Thurid, who had raised both palms forward above his head in the universal salute of Martians, and a moment later his "Kaor!" the Barsoomian word of greeting, came in low but distinct tones.

I turned my eyes up the river in the direction that his were bent, and presently there came within my limited range of vision a long boat, in which were six men. Five were at the paddles, while the sixth sat in the seat of honor.

The white skins, the flowing yellow wigs which covered their bald pates, and the gorgeous diadems set in circlets of gold about their heads marked them as Holy Therns.

As they drew up beside the ledge upon which Thurid awaited them, he in the bow of the boat arose to step ashore, and then I saw that it was none other than Matai Shang, Father of Therns.

The evident cordiality with which the two men exchanged greetings filled me with wonder, for the black and white men of Barsoom were hereditary enemies—nor ever before had I known of two meeting other than in battle.

Evidently the reverses that had recently overtaken both peoples had resulted in an alliance between these two individuals—at least against the common enemy—and now I saw why Thurid had come so often out into the Valley Dor by night, and that the nature of his conspiring might be such as to strike very close to me or to my friends.

I wished that I might have found a point closer to the two men from which to have heard their conversation; but it was out of the question now to attempt to cross the river, and so I lay quietly watch-

ing them, who would have given so much to have known how close I
lay to them, and how easily they might have overcome and killed me
with their superior force.

Several times Thurid pointed across the river in my direction, but
that his gestures had any reference to me I did not for a moment
believe. Presently he and Matai Shang entered the latter's boat, which
turned out into the river and, swinging round, forged steadily across
in my direction.

As they advanced I moved my boat farther and farther in beneath
the overhanging wall, but at last it became evident that their craft was
holding the same course. The five paddlers sent the larger boat ahead
at a speed that taxed my energies to equal.

Every instant I expected to feel my prow crash against solid rock.
The light from the river was no longer visible, but ahead I saw the
faint tinge of a distant radiance, and still the water before me was
open.

At last the truth dawned upon me—I was following a subterranean
river which emptied into the Iss at the very point where I had hidden.

The rowers were now quite close to me. The noise of their own
paddles drowned the sound of mine, but in another instant the growing light ahead would reveal me to them.

There was no time to be lost. Whatever action I was to take must
be taken at once. Swinging the prow of my boat toward the right, I
sought the river's rocky side, and there I lay while Matai Shang and
Thurid approached up the center of the stream, which was much
narrower than the Iss.

As they came nearer I heard the voices of Thurid and the Father
of Therns raised in argument.

"I tell you, Thern," the black dator was saying, "that I wish only
vengeance upon John Carter, Prince of Helium. I am leading you into
no trap. What could I gain by betraying you to those who have ruined
my nation and my house?"

"Let us stop here a moment that I may hear your plans," replied
the hekkador, "and then we may proceed with a better understanding
of our duties and obligations."

To the rowers he issued the command that brought their boat in
toward the bank not a dozen paces beyond the spot where I lay.

Had they pulled in below me they must surely have seen me against
the faint glow of light ahead, but from where they finally came to rest
I was as secure from detection as though miles separated us.

The few words I had already overheard whetted my curiosity, and I was anxious to learn what manner of vengeance Thurid was planning against me. Nor had I long to wait. I listened intently.

"There are no obligations, Father of Therns," continued the First Born. "Thurid, Dator of Issus, has no price. When the thing has been accomplished I shall be glad if you will see to it that I am well received, as is befitting my ancient lineage and noble rank, at some court that is yet loyal to thy ancient faith, for I cannot return to the Valley Dor or elsewhere within the power of the Prince of Helium; but even that I do not demand—it shall be as your own desire in the matter directs."

"It shall be as you wish, Dator," replied Matai Shang; "nor is that all—power and riches shall be yours if you restore my daughter, Phaidor, to me, and place within my power Dejah Thoris, Princess of Helium.

"Ah," he continued with a malicious snarl, "but the Earth man shall suffer for the indignities he has put upon the holy of holies, nor shall any vileness be too vile to inflict upon his princess. Would that it were in my power to force him to witness the humiliation and degradation of the red woman."

"You shall have your way with her before another day has passed, Matai Shang," said Thurid, "if you but say the word."

"I have heard of the Temple of the Sun, Dator," replied Matai Shang, "but never have I heard that its prisoners could be released before the allotted year of their incarceration had elapsed. How, then, may you accomplish the impossible?"

"Access may be had to any cell of the temple at any time," replied Thurid. "Only Issus knew this; nor was it ever Issus' way to divulge more of her secrets than were necessary. By chance, after her death, I came upon an ancient plan of the temple, and there I found, plainly writ, the most minute directions for reaching the cells at any time.

"And more I learned—that many men had gone thither for Issus in the past, always on errands of death and torture to the prisoners; but those who thus learned the secret way were wont to die mysteriously immediately they had returned and made their reports to cruel Issus."

"Let us proceed, then," said Matai Shang at last. "I must trust you, yet at the same time you must trust me, for we are six to your one."

"I do not fear," replied Thurid, "nor need you. Our hatred of the common enemy is sufficient bond to insure our loyalty to each other, and after we have defiled the Princess of Helium there will be still greater reason for the maintenance of our allegiance—unless I greatly mistake the temper of her lord."

Matai Shang spoke to the paddlers. The boat moved on up the tributary.

It was with difficulty that I restrained myself from rushing upon them and slaying the two vile plotters; but quickly I saw the mad rashness of such an act, which would cut down the only man who could lead the way to Dejah Thoris' prison before the long Martian year had swung its interminable circle.

If he should lead Matai Shang to that hollowed spot, then, too, should he lead John Carter, Prince of Helium.

With silent paddle I swung slowly into the wake of the larger craft.

UNDER THE MOUNTAINS

As WE ADVANCED up the river which winds beneath the Golden Cliffs out of the bowels of the Mountains of Otz to mingle its dark waters with the grim and mysterious Iss the faint glow which had appeared before us grew gradually into an all-enveloping radiance.

The river widened until it presented the aspect of a large lake whose vaulted dome, lighted by glowing phosphorescent rock, was splashed with the vivid rays of the diamond, the sapphire, the ruby, and the countless, nameless jewels of Barsoom which lay incrusted in the virgin gold which forms the major portion of these magnificent cliffs.

Beyond the lighted chamber of the lake was darkness—what lay behind the darkness I could not even guess.

To have followed the thern boat across the gleaming water would have been to invite instant detection, and so, though I was loath to permit Thurid to pass even for an instant beyond my sight, I was forced to wait in the shadows until the other boat had passed from my sight at the far extremity of the lake.

Then I paddled out upon the brilliant surface in the direction they had taken.

When, after what seemed an eternity, I reached the shadows at the upper end of the lake I found that the river issued from a low aperture, to pass beneath which it was necessary that I compel Woola to lie flat in the boat, and I, myself, must need bend double before the low roof cleared my head.

Immediately the roof rose again upon the other side, but no longer was the way brilliantly lighted. Instead only a feeble glow emanated from small and scattered patches of phosphorescent rock in wall and roof.

Directly before me the river ran into this smaller chamber through three separate arched openings.

Thurid and the therns were nowhere to be seen—into which of the dark holes had they disappeared? There was no means by which I might know, and so I chose the center opening as being as likely to lead me in the right direction as another.

Here the way was through utter darkness. The stream was narrow —so narrow that in the blackness I was constantly bumping first one rock wall and then another as the river wound hither and thither along its flinty bed.

Far ahead I presently heard a deep and sullen roar which increased in volume as I advanced, and then broke upon my ears with all the intensity of its mad fury as I swung round a sharp curve into a dimly lighted stretch of water.

Directly before me the river thundered down from above in a mighty waterfall that filled the narrow gorge from side to side, rising far above me several hundred feet—as magnificent a spectacle as I ever had seen.

But the roar—the awful, deafening roar of those tumbling waters penned in the rocky, subterranean vault! Had the fall not entirely blocked my further passage and shown me that I had followed the wrong course I believe that I should have fled anyway before the maddening tumult.

Thurid and the therns could not have come this way. By stumbling upon the wrong course I had lost the trail, and they had gained so much ahead of me that now I might not be able to find them before it was too late, if, in fact, I could find them at all.

It had taken several hours to force my way up to the falls against the strong current, and other hours would be required for the descent, although the pace would be much swifter.

With a sigh I turned the prow of my craft down stream, and with mighty strokes hastened with reckless speed through the dark and tortuous channel until once again I came to the chamber into which flowed the three branches of the river.

Two unexplored channels still remained from which to choose; nor was there any means by which I could judge which was the more likely to lead me to the plotters.

Never in my life, that I can recall, have I suffered such an agony of indecision. So much depended upon a correct choice; so much depended upon haste.

The hours that I had already lost might seal the fate of the incomparable Dejah Thoris were she not already dead—to sacrifice other hours, and maybe days in a fruitless exploration of another blind lead would unquestionably prove fatal.

Several times I essayed the right-hand entrance only to turn back as though warned by some strange intuitive sense that this was not the way. At last, convinced by the oft-recurring phenomenon, I cast my all upon the left-hand archway; yet it was with a lingering doubt that I turned a parting look at the sullen waters which rolled, dark and forbidding, from beneath the grim, low archway on the right.

And as I looked there came bobbing out upon the current from the Stygian darkness of the interior the shell of one of the great, succulent fruits of the sorapus tree.

I could scarce restrain a shout of elation as this silent, insensate messenger floated past me, on toward the Iss and Korus, for it told me that journeying Martians were above me on that very stream.

They had eaten of this marvelous fruit which nature concentrates within the hard shell of the sorapus nut, and having eaten had cast the husk overboard. It could have come from no others than the party I sought.

Quickly I abandoned all thought of the left-hand passage, and a moment later had turned into the right. The stream soon widened, and recurring areas of phosphorescent rock lighted my way.

I made good time, but was convinced that I was nearly a day behind those I was tracking. Neither Woola nor I had eaten since the previous day, but in so far as he was concerned it mattered but little, since practically all the animals of the dead sea bottoms of Mars are able to go for incredible periods without nourishment.

Nor did I suffer. The water of the river was sweet and cold, for it was unpolluted by decaying bodies—unlike the Iss—and as for food, why the mere thought that I was nearing my beloved princess raised me above every material want.

As I proceeded, the river became narrower and the current swift and turbulent—so swift in fact that it was with difficulty that I forced my craft upward at all. I could not have been making to exceed a hundred yards an hour when, at a bend, I was confronted by a series of rapids through which the river foamed and boiled at a terrific rate.

My heart sank within me. The sorapus nutshell had proved a false prophet, and, after all, my intuition had been correct—it was the left-hand channel that I should have followed.

Had I been a woman I should have wept. At my right was a great, slow-moving eddy that circled far beneath the cliff's overhanging side, and to rest my tired muscles before turning back I let my boat drift into its embrace.

I was almost prostrated by disappointment. It would mean another half-day's loss of time to retrace my way and take the only passage that yet remained unexplored. What hellish fate had led me to select from three possible avenues the two that were wrong?

As the lazy current of the eddy carried me slowly about the periphery of the watery circle my boat twice touched the rocky side of the river in the dark recess beneath the cliff. A third time it struck, gently as it had before, but the contact resulted in a different sound—the sound of wood scraping upon wood.

In an instant I was on the alert, for there could be no wood within that buried river that had not been man brought. Almost coincidentally with my first apprehension of the noise, my hand shot out across the boat's side, and a second later I felt my fingers gripping the gunwale of another craft.

As though turned to stone I sat in tense and rigid silence, straining my eyes into the utter darkness before me in an effort to discover if the boat were occupied.

It was entirely possible that there might be men on board it who were still ignorant of my presence, for the boat was scraping gently against the rocks upon one side, so that the gentle touch of my boat upon the other easily could have gone unnoticed.

Peer as I would I could not penetrate the darkness, and then I listened intently for the sound of breathing near me; but except for the noise of the rapids, the soft scraping of the boats, and the lapping of the water at their sides I could distinguish no sound. As usual, I thought rapidly.

A rope lay coiled in the bottom of my own craft. Very softly I gathered it up, and making one end fast to the bronze ring in the prow I stepped gingerly into the boat beside me. In one hand I grasped the rope, in the other my keen long-sword.

For a full minute, perhaps, I stood motionless after entering the strange craft. It had rocked a trifle beneath my weight, but it had been the scraping of its side against the side of my own boat that had seemed most likely to alarm its occupants, if there were any.

But there was no answering sound, and a moment later I had felt from stem to stern and found the boat deserted.

Groping with my hands along the face of the rocks to which the craft was moored, I discovered a narrow ledge which I knew must be the avenue taken by those who had come before me. That they could be none other than Thurid and his party I was convinced by the size and build of the boat I had found.

Calling to Woola to follow me I stepped out upon the ledge. The great, savage brute, agile as a cat, crept after me.

As he passed through the boat that had been occupied by Thurid and the therns he emitted a single low growl, and when he came beside me upon the ledge and my hand rested upon his neck I felt his short mane bristling with anger. I think he sensed telepathically the recent presence of an enemy, for I had made no effort to impart to him the nature of our quest or the status of those we tracked.

This omission I now made haste to correct, and, after the manner of green Martians with their beasts, I let him know partially by the weird and uncanny telepathy of Barsoom and partly by word of mouth that we were upon the trail of those who had recently occupied the boat through which we had just passed.

A soft purr, like that of a great cat, indicated that Woola understood, and then, with a word to him to follow, I turned to the right along the ledge, but scarcely had I done so than I felt his mighty fangs tugging at my leathern harness.

As I turned to discover the cause of his act he continued to pull me steadily in the opposite direction, nor would he desist until I had turned about and indicated that I would follow him voluntarily.

Never had I known him to be in error in a matter of tracking, so it was with a feeling of entire security that I moved cautiously in the huge beast's wake. Through Cimmerian darkness he moved along the narrow ledge beside the boiling rapids.

As we advanced, the way led from beneath the overhanging cliffs out into a dim light, and then it was that I saw that the trail had been cut from the living rock, and that it ran up along the river's side beyond the rapids.

For hours we followed the dark and gloomy river farther and farther into the bowels of Mars. From the direction and distance I knew that we must be well beneath the Valley Dor, and possibly beneath the Sea of Omean as well—it could not be much farther now to the Temple of the Sun.

Even as my mind framed the thought Woola halted suddenly before a narrow, arched doorway in the cliff by the trail's side. Quickly he crouched back away from the entrance, at the same time turning his eyes toward me.

Words could not have more plainly told me that danger of some sort lay near by, and so I pressed quietly forward to his side, and passing him looked into the aperture at our right.

Before me was a fair-sized chamber that, from its appointments, I knew must have at one time been a guardroom. There were racks for weapons, and slightly raised platforms for the sleeping silks and furs of the warriors, but now its only occupants were two of the therns who had been of the party with Thurid and Matai Shang.

The men were in earnest conversation, and from their tones it was apparent that they were entirely unaware that they had listeners.

"I tell you," one of them was saying, "I do not trust the black one. There was no necessity for leaving us here to guard the way. Against what, pray, should we guard this long-forgotten, abysmal path? It was but a ruse to divide our numbers.

"He will have Matai Shang leave others elsewhere on some pretext or other, and then at last he will fall upon us with his confederates and slay us all."

"I believe you, Lakor," replied the other, "there can never be aught else than deadly hatred between thern and First Born. And what think you of the ridiculous matter of the light? 'Let the light shine with the intensity of three radium units for fifty tals, and for one xat let it shine with the intensity of one radium unit, and then for twenty-five tals with nine units.' Those were his very words, and to think that wise old Matai Shang should listen to such foolishness."

"Indeed, it is silly," replied Lakor. "It will open nothing other than the way to a quick death for us all. He had to make some answer when Matai Shang asked him flatly what he should do when he came to the Temple of the Sun, and so he made his answer quickly from his imagination—I would wager a hekkador's diadem that he could not now repeat it himself."

"Let us not remain here longer, Lakor," spoke the other thern. "Perchance if we hasten after them we may come in time to rescue Matai Shang, and wreak our own vengeance upon the black dator. What say you?"

"Never in a long life," answered Lakor, "have I disobeyed a single command of the Father of Therns. I shall stay here until I rot if he does not return to bid me elsewhere."

Lakor's companion shook his head.

"You are my superior," he said; "I cannot do other than you sanction, though I still believe that we are foolish to remain."

I, too, thought that they were foolish to remain, for I saw from Woola's actions that the trail led through the room where the two therns held guard. I had no reason to harbor any considerable love for this race of self-deified demons, yet I would have passed them by were it possible without molesting them.

It was worth trying anyway, for a fight might delay us considerably, or even put an end entirely to my search—better men than I have gone down before fighters of meaner ability than that possessed by the fierce thern warriors.

Signaling Woola to heel I stepped suddenly into the room before the two men. At sight of me their long-swords flashed from the harness at their sides, but I raised my hand in a gesture of restraint.

"I seek Thurid, the black dator," I said. "My quarrel is with him, not with you. Let me pass then in peace, for if I mistake not he is as much your enemy as mine, and you can have no cause to protect him."

They lowered their swords and Lakor spoke.

"I know not whom you may be, with the white skin of a thern and the black hair of a red man; but were it only Thurid whose safety were at stake you might pass, and welcome, in so far as we be concerned.

"Tell us who you be, and what mission calls you to this unknown world beneath the Valley Dor, then maybe we can see our way to let you pass upon the errand which we should like to undertake would our orders permit."

I was surprised that neither of them had recognized me, for I thought that I was quite sufficiently well known either by personal experience or reputation to every thern upon Barsoom as to make my identity immediately apparent in any part of the planet. In fact, I was the only white man upon Mars whose hair was black and whose eyes were gray, with the exception of my son, Carthoris.

To reveal my identity might be to precipitate an attack, for every thern upon Barsoom knew that to me they owed the fall of their age-old spiritual supremacy. On the other hand my reputation as a fighting man might be sufficient to pass me by these two were their livers not of the right complexion to welcome a battle to the death.

To be quite candid I did not attempt to delude myself with any such sophistry, since I knew well that upon warlike Mars there are few cowards, and that every man, whether prince, priest, or peasant, glories in deadly strife. And so I gripped my long-sword the tighter as I replied to Lakor.

"I believe that you will see the wisdom of permitting me to pass unmolested," I said, "for it would avail you nothing to die uselessly in the rocky bowels of Barsoom merely to protect a hereditary enemy, such as Thurid, Dator of the First Born.

"That you shall die should you elect to oppose me is evidenced by the moldering corpses of all the many great Barsoomian warriors who have gone down beneath this blade—I am John Carter, Prince of Helium."

For a moment that name seemed to paralyze the two men; but only for a moment, and then the younger of them, with a vile name upon his lips, rushed toward me with ready sword.

He had been standing a little behind his companion, Lakor, during our parley, and now, ere he could engage me, the older man grasped his harness and drew him back.

"Hold!" commanded Lakor. "There will be plenty of time to fight if we find it wise to fight at all. There be good reasons why every thern upon Barsoom should yearn to spill the blood of the blasphemer, the sacrilegist; but let us mix wisdom with our righteous hate. The Prince of Helium is bound upon an errand which we ourselves, but a moment since, were wishing that we might undertake.

"Let him go then and slay the black. When he returns we shall still be here to bar his way to the outer world, and thus we shall have rid ourselves of two enemies, nor have incurred the displeasure of the Father of Therns."

As he spoke I could not but note the crafty glint in his evil eyes, and while I saw the apparent logic of his reasoning I felt, subconsciously perhaps, that his words did but veil some sinister intent. The other thern turned toward him in evident surprise, but when Lakor had whispered a few brief words into his ear he, too, drew back and nodded acquiescence to his superior's suggestion.

"Proceed, John Carter," said Lakor; "but know that if Thurid does not lay you low there will be those awaiting your return who will see that you never pass again into the sunlight of the upper world. Go!"

During our conversation Woola had been growling and bristling close to my side. Occasionally he would look up into my face with a low, pleading whine, as though begging for the word that would send him headlong at the bare throats before him. He, too, sensed the villainy behind the smooth words.

Beyond the therns several doorways opened off the guardroom, and toward the one upon the extreme right Lakor motioned.

"That way leads to Thurid," he said.

But when I would have called Woola to follow me there the beast whined and held back, and at last ran quickly to the first opening at the left, where he stood emitting his coughing bark, as though urging me to follow him upon the right way.

I turned a questioning look upon Lakor.

"The brute is seldom wrong," I said, "and while I do not doubt your superior knowledge, Thern, I think that I shall do well to listen to the voice of instinct that is backed by love and loyalty."

As I spoke I smiled grimly that he might know without words that I distrusted him.

"As you will," the fellow replied with a shrug. "In the end it shall be all the same."

I turned and followed Woola into the left-hand passage, and though my back was toward my enemies, my ears were on the alert; yet I heard no sound of pursuit. The passageway was dimly lighted by occasional radium bulbs, the universal lighting medium of Barsoom.

These same lamps may have been doing continuous duty in these subterranean chambers for ages, since they require no attention and are so compounded that they give off but the minutest of their substance in the generation of years of luminosity.

We had proceeded for but a short distance when we commenced to pass the mouths of diverging corridors, but not once did Woola hesitate. It was at the opening to one of these corridors upon my right that I presently heard a sound that spoke more plainly to John Carter, fighting man, than could the words of my mother tongue— it was the clank of metal—the metal of a warrior's harness—and it came from a little distance up the corridor upon my right.

Woola heard it, too, and like a flash he had wheeled and stood facing the threatened danger, his mane all abristle and all his rows of glistening fangs bared by snarling, backdrawn lips. With a gesture I silenced him, and together we drew aside into another corridor a few paces farther on.

Here we waited; nor did we have long to wait, for presently we saw the shadows of two men fall upon the floor of the main corridor athwart the doorway of our hiding place. Very cautiously they were moving now—the accidental clank that had alarmed me was not repeated.

Presently they came opposite our station; nor was I surprised to see that the two were Lakor and his companion of the guardroom.

They walked very softly, and in the right hand of each gleamed a keen long-sword. They halted quite close to the entrance of our retreat, whispering to each other.

"Can it be that we have distanced them already?" said Lakor.

"Either that or the beast has led the man upon a wrong trail," replied the other, "for the way which we took is by far the shorter to this point—for him who knows it. John Carter would have found it a short road to death had he taken it as you suggested to him."

"Yes," said Lakor, "no amount of fighting ability would have saved him from the pivoted flagstone. He surely would have stepped upon it, and by now, if the pit beneath it has a bottom, which Thurid denies, he should have been rapidly approaching it. Curses on that calot of his that warned him toward the safer avenue!"

"There be other dangers ahead of him, though," spoke Lakor's fellow, "which he may not so easily escape—should he succeed in escaping our two good swords. Consider, for example, what chance he will have, coming unexpectedly into the chamber of——"

I would have given much to have heard the balance of that conversation that I might have been warned of the perils that lay ahead, but fate intervened, and just at the very instant of all other instants that I would not have elected to do it, I sneezed.

THERE WAS NOTHING for it now other than to fight; nor did I have any advantage as I sprang, sword in hand, into the corridor before the two therns, for my untimely sneeze had warned them of my presence and they were ready for me.

There were no words, for they would have been a waste of breath. The very presence of the two proclaimed their treachery. That they were following to fall upon me unawares was all too plain, and they, of course, must have known that I understood their plan.

In an instant I was engaged with both, and though I loathe the very name of thern, I must in all fairness admit that they are mighty swordsmen; and these two were no exception, unless it were that they were even more skilled and fearless than the average among their race.

While it lasted it was indeed as joyous a conflict as I ever had experienced. Twice at least I saved my breast from the mortal thrust of piercing steel only by the wondrous agility with which my earthly muscles endow me under the conditions of lesser gravity and air pressure upon Mars.

Yet even so I came near to tasting death that day in the gloomy corridor beneath Mars's southern pole, for Lakor played a trick upon me that in all my experience of fighting upon two planets I never before had witnessed the like of.

The other thern was engaging me at the time, and I was forcing him back—touching him here and there with my point until he was bleeding from a dozen wounds, yet not being able to penetrate his marvelous guard to reach a vulnerable spot for the brief instant that would have been sufficient to send him to his ancestors.

It was then that Lakor quickly unslung a belt from his harness, and as I stepped back to parry a wicked thrust he lashed one end of it about my left ankle so that it wound there for an instant, while he jerked suddenly upon the other end, throwing me heavily upon my back.

Then, like leaping panthers, they were upon me; but they had reckoned without Woola, and before ever a blade touched me, a roaring embodiment of a thousand demons hurtled above my prostrate form and my loyal Martian calot was upon them.

Imagine, if you can, a huge grizzly with ten legs armed with mighty talons and an enormous froglike mouth splitting his head from ear to ear, exposing three rows of long, white tusks. Then endow this creature of your imagination with the agility and ferocity of a half-starved Bengal tiger and the strength of a span of bulls, and you will have some faint conception of Woola in action.

Before I could call him off he had crushed Lakor into a jelly with a single blow of one mighty paw, and had literally torn the other thern to ribbons; yet when I spoke to him sharply he cowed sheepishly as though he had done a thing to deserve censure and chastisement.

Never had I had the heart to punish Woola during the long years that had passed since that first day upon Mars when the green jed of the Tharks had placed him on guard over me, and I had won his love and loyalty from the cruel and loveless masters of his former life, yet I believe he would have submitted to any cruelty that I might have inflicted upon him, so wondrous was his affection for me.

The diadem in the center of the circlet of gold upon the brow of Lakor proclaimed him a Holy Thern, while his companion, not thus adorned, was a lesser thern, though from his harness I gleaned that he had reached the Ninth Cycle, which is but one below that of the Holy Therns.

As I stood for a moment looking at the gruesome havoc Woola had wrought, there recurred to me the memory of that other occasion upon which I had masqueraded in the wig, diadem, and harness of Sator Throg, the Holy Thern whom Thuvia of Ptarth had slain, and now it occurred to me that it might prove of worth to utilize Lakor's trappings for the same purpose.

A moment later I had torn his yellow wig from his bald pate and transferred it and the circlet, as well as all his harness, to my own person.

Woola did not approve of the metamorphosis. He sniffed at me and growled ominously, but when I spoke to him and patted his huge head he at length became reconciled to the change, and at my command trotted off along the corridor in the direction we had been going when our progress had been interrupted by the therns.

We moved cautiously now, warned by the fragment of conversation I had overheard. I kept abreast of Woola that we might have the benefit of all our eyes for what might appear suddenly ahead to menace us, and well it was that we were forewarned.

At the bottom of a flight of narrow steps the corridor turned sharply back upon itself, immediately making another turn in the original direction, so that at that point it formed a perfect letter S, the top leg of which debouched suddenly into a large chamber, illy lighted, and the floor of which was completely covered by venomous snakes and loathsome reptiles.

To have attempted to cross that floor would have been to court instant death, and for a moment I was almost completely discouraged. Then it occurred to me that Thurid and Matai Shang with their party must have crossed it, and so there was a way.

Had it not been for the fortunate accident by which I overheard even so small a portion of the therns' conversation we should have blundered at least a step or two into that wriggling mass of destruction, and a single step would have been all-sufficient to have sealed our doom.

These were the only reptiles I had ever seen upon Barsoom, but I knew from their similarity to the fossilized remains of supposedly extinct species I had seen in the museums of Helium that they comprised many of the known prehistoric reptilian genera, as well as others undiscovered.

A more hideous aggregation of monsters had never before assailed my vision. It would be futile to attempt to describe them to Earth men, since substance is the only thing which they possess in common with any creature of the past or present with which you are familiar —even their venom is of an unearthly virulence that, by comparison, would make the cobra de capello seem quite as harmless as an angleworm.

As they spied me there was a concerted rush by those nearest the entrance where we stood, but a line of radium bulbs inset along the threshold of their chamber brought them to a sudden halt—evidently they dared not cross that line of light.

I had been quite sure that they would not venture beyond the room in which I had discovered them, though I had not guessed at what deterred them. The simple fact that we had found no reptiles in the corridor through which we had just come was sufficient assurance that they did not venture there.

I drew Woola out of harm's way, and then began a careful survey of as much of the Chamber of Reptiles as I could see from where I stood. As my eyes became accustomed to the dim light of its interior I gradually made out a low gallery at the far end of the apartment from which opened several exits.

Coming as close to the threshold as I dared, I followed this gallery with my eyes, discovering that it circled the room as far as I could see. Then I glanced above me along the upper edge of the entrance to which we had come, and there, to my delight, I saw an end of the gallery not a foot above my head. In an instant I had leaped to it and called Woola after me.

Here there were no reptiles—the way was clear to the opposite side of the hideous chamber—and a moment later Woola and I dropped down to safety in the corridor beyond.

Not ten minutes later we came into a vast circular apartment of white marble, the walls of which were inlaid with gold in the strange hieroglyphics of the First Born.

From the high dome of this mighty apartment a huge circular column extended to the floor, and as I watched I saw that it slowly revolved.

I had reached the base of the Temple of the Sun!

Somewhere above me lay Dejah Thoris, and with her were Phaidor, daughter of Matai Shang, and Thuvia of Ptarth. But how to reach them, now that I had found the only vulnerable spot in their mighty prison, was still a baffling riddle.

Slowly I circled the great shaft, looking for a means of ingress. Part way around I found a tiny radium flash torch, and as I examined it in mild curiosity as to its presence there in this almost inaccessible and unknown spot, I came suddenly upon the insignia of the house of Thurid jewel-inset in its metal case.

I am upon the right trail, I thought, as I slipped the bauble into the pocket-pouch which hung from my harness. Then I continued my search for the entrance, which I knew must be somewhere about; nor had I long to search, for almost immediately thereafter I came upon a small door so cunningly inlaid in the shaft's base that it might have passed unnoticed by a less keen or careful observer.

There was the door that would lead me within the prison, but where was the means to open it? No button or lock were visible. Again and again I went carefully over every square inch of its surface, but the most that I could find was a tiny pinhole a little above and to the right of the door's center—a pinhole that seemed only an accident of manufacture or an imperfection of material.

Into this minute aperture I attempted to peer, but whether it was but a fraction of an inch deep or passed completely through the door I could not tell—at least no light showed beyond it. I put my ear to it next and listened, but again my efforts brought negligible results.

During these experiments Woola had been standing at my side gazing intently at the door, and as my glance fell upon him it occurred to me to test the correctness of my hypothesis, that this portal had been the means of ingress to the temple used by Thurid, the black dator, and Matai Shang, Father of Therns.

Turning away abruptly, I called to him to follow me. For a moment he hesitated, and then leaped after me, whining and tugging at my harness to draw me back. I walked on, however, some distance from the door before I let him have his way, that I might see precisely what he would do. Then I permitted him to lead me wherever he would.

Straight back to that baffling portal he dragged me, again taking up his position facing the blank stone, gazing straight at its shining surface. For an hour I worked to solve the mystery of the combination that would open the way before me.

Carefully I recalled every circumstance of my pursuit of Thurid, and my conclusion was identical with my original belief—that Thurid had come this way without other assistance than his own knowledge and passed through the door that barred my progress, unaided from within. But how had he accomplished it?

I recalled the incident of the Chamber of Mystery in the Golden Cliffs that time I had freed Thuvia of Ptarth from the dungeon of the therns, and she had taken a slender, needle-like key from the key-ring of her dead jailer to open the door leading back into the Chamber of Mystery where Tars Tarkas fought for his life with the great banths. Such a tiny keyhole as now defied me had opened the way to the intricate lock in that other door.

Hastily I dumped the contents of my pocket-pouch upon the ground before me. Could I but find a slender bit of steel I might yet fashion a key that would give me ingress to the temple prison.

As I examined the heterogeneous collection of odds and ends that is always to be found in the pocket-pouch of a Martian warrior my hand fell upon the emblazoned radium flash torch of the black dator.

As I was about to lay the thing aside as of no value in my present predicament my eyes chanced upon a few strange characters roughly and freshly scratched upon the soft gold of the case.

Casual curiosity prompted me to decipher them, but what I read carried no immediate meaning to my mind. There were three sets of characters, one below another:

$$3 \; |-| \; 50 \; T$$
$$1 \; |-| \;\;\; 1 \; X$$
$$9 \; |-| \; 25 \; T$$

For only an instant my curiosity was piqued, and then I replaced the torch in my pocket-pouch, but my fingers had not unclasped from it when there rushed to my memory the recollection of the conversation between Lakor and his companion when the lesser thern had quoted the words of Thurid and scoffed at them: "And what think you of the ridiculous matter of the light? Let the light shine with the intensity of three radium units for fifty tals"—ah, there was the first line of characters upon the torch's metal case—3—50 T; "and for one xat let it shine with the intensity of one radium unit"—there was the second line; "and then for twenty-five tals with nine units."

The formula was complete; but—what did it mean?

I thought I knew, and, seizing a powerful magnifying glass from the litter of my pocket-pouch, I applied myself to a careful examination of the marble immediately about the pinhole in the door. I could have cried aloud in exultation when my scrutiny disclosed the almost invisible incrustation of particles of carbonized electrons which are thrown off by these Martian torches.

It was evident that for countless ages radium torches had been applied to this pinhole, and for what purpose there could be but a single answer—the mechanism of the lock was actuated by light rays; and I, John Carter, Prince of Helium, held the combination in my hand—scratched by the hand of my enemy upon his own torch case.

In a cylindrical bracelet of gold about my wrist was my Barsoomian chronometer—a delicate instrument that records the tals and xats and zodes of Martian time, presenting them to view beneath a strong crystal much after the manner of an earthly odometer.

Timing my operations carefully, I held the torch to the small aperture in the door, regulating the intensity of the light by means of the thumb-lever upon the side of the case.

For fifty tals I let three units of light shine full in the pinhole, then one unit for one xat, and for twenty-five tals nine units. Those last twenty-five tals were the longest twenty-five seconds of my life.

Would the lock click at the end of those seemingly interminable intervals of time?

Twenty-three! Twenty-four! Twenty-five!

I shut off the light with a snap. For seven tals I waited—there had been no appreciable effect upon the lock's mechanism. Could it be that my theory was entirely wrong?

Hold! Had the nervous strain resulted in a hallucination, or did the door really move? Slowly the solid stone sank noiselessly back into the wall—there was no hallucination here.

Back and back it slid for ten feet until it had disclosed at its right a narrow doorway leading into a dark and narrow corridor that paralleled the outer wall. Scarcely was the entrance uncovered than Woola and I had leaped through—then the door slipped quietly back into place.

Down the corridor at some distance I saw the faint reflection of a light, and toward this we made our way. At the point where the light shone was a sharp turn, and a little distance beyond this a brilliantly lighted chamber.

Here we discovered a spiral stairway leading up from the center of the circular room.

Immediately I knew that we had reached the center of the base of the Temple of the Sun—the spiral runway led upward past the inner walls of the prison cells. Somewhere above me was Dejah Thoris, unless Thurid and Matai Shang had already succeeded in stealing her.

We had scarcely started up the runway when Woola suddenly displayed the wildest excitement. He leaped back and forth, snapping at my legs and harness, until I thought that he was mad, and finally when I pushed him from me and started once more to ascend he grasped my sword arm between his jaws and dragged me back.

No amount of scolding or cuffing would suffice to make him release me, and I was entirely at the mercy of his brute strength unless I cared to use my dagger upon him with my left hand; but, mad or no, I had not the heart to run the sharp blade into that faithful body.

Down into the chamber he dragged me, and across it to the side opposite that at which we had entered. Here was another doorway leading into a corridor which ran directly down a steep incline. Without a moment's hesitation Woola jerked me along this rocky passage.

Presently he stopped and released me, standing between me and the way we had come, looking up into my face as though to ask if I would now follow him voluntarily or if he must still resort to force.

Looking ruefully at the marks of his great teeth upon my bare arm I decided to do as he seemed to wish me to do. After all, his strange instinct might be more dependable than my faulty human judgment.

And well it was that I had been forced to follow him. But a short distance from the circular chamber we came suddenly into a brilliantly lighted labyrinth of crystal glass partitioned passages.

At first I thought it was one vast, unbroken chamber, so clear and transparent were the walls of the winding corridors, but after I had nearly brained myself a couple of times by attempting to pass through solid vitreous walls I went more carefully.

We had proceeded but a few yards along the corridor that had given us entrance to this strange maze when Woola gave mouth to a most frightful roar, at the same time dashing against the clear partition at our left.

The resounding echoes of that fearsome cry were still reverberating through the subterranean chambers when I saw the thing that had startled it from the faithful beast.

Far in the distance, dimly through the many thicknesses of intervening crystal, as in a haze that made them seem unreal and ghostly, I discerned the figures of eight people—three females and five men.

At the same instant, evidently startled by Woola's fierce cry, they halted and looked about. Then, of a sudden, one of them, a woman, held her arms out toward me, and even at that great distance I could see that her lips moved—it was Dejah Thoris, my ever beautiful and ever youthful Princess of Helium.

With her were Thuvia of Ptarth, Phaidor, daughter of Matai Shang, and Thurid, and the Father of Therns, and the three lesser therns that had accompanied them.

Thurid shook his fist at me, and then two of the therns grasped Dejah Thoris and Thuvia roughly by their arms and hurried them on. A moment later they had disappeared into a stone corridor beyond the labyrinth of glass.

They say that love is blind; but so great a love as that of Dejah Thoris that knew me even beneath the thern disguise I wore and across the misty vista of that crystal maze must indeed be far from blind.

THE SECRET TOWER

I HAVE no stomach to narrate the monotonous events of the tedious days that Woola and I spent ferreting our way across the labyrinth of glass, through the dark and devious ways beyond that led beneath the Valley Dor and Golden Cliffs to emerge at last upon the flank of the Otz Mountains just above the Valley of Lost Souls—that pitiful purgatory peopled by the poor unfortunates who dare not continue their abandoned pilgrimage to Dor, or return to the various lands of the outer world from whence they came.

Here the trail of Dejah Thoris' abductors led along the mountains' base, across steep and rugged ravines, by the side of appalling precipices, and sometimes out into the valley, where we found fighting aplenty with the members of the various tribes that make up the population of this vale of hopelessness.

But through it all we came at last to where the way led up a narrow gorge that grew steeper and more impracticable at every step until before us loomed a mighty fortress buried beneath the side of an overhanging cliff.

Here was the secret hiding place of Matai Shang, Father of Therns. Here, surrounded by a handful of the faithful, the hekkador of the ancient faith, who had once been served by millions of vassals and dependents, dispensed the spiritual word among the half dozen nations of Barsoom that still clung tenaciously to their false and discredited religion.

Darkness was just falling as we came in sight of the seemingly impregnable walls of this mountain stronghold, and lest we be seen I drew back with Woola behind a jutting granite promontory, into a clump of the hardy, purple scrub that thrives upon the barren sides of Otz.

Here we lay until the quick transition from daylight to darkness had passed. Then I crept out to approach the fortress walls in search of a way within.

Either through carelessness or over-confidence in the supposed inaccessibility of their hiding place, the triple-barred gate stood ajar.

Beyond were a handful of guards, laughing and talking over one of their incomprehensible Barsoomian games.

I saw that none of the guardsmen had been of the party that accompanied Thurid and Matai Shang; and so, relying entirely upon my disguise, I walked boldly through the gateway and up to the thern guard.

The men stopped their game and looked up at me, but there was no sign of suspicion. Similarly they looked at Woola, growling at my heel.

"Kaor!" I said in true Martian greeting, and the warriors arose and saluted me. "I have but just found my way hither from the Golden Cliffs," I continued, "and seek audience with the hekkador, Matai Shang, Father of Therns. Where may he be found?"

"Follow me," said one of the guard, and, turning, led me across the outer courtyard toward a second buttressed wall.

Why the apparent ease with which I seemingly deceived them did not rouse my suspicions I know not, unless it was that my mind was still so full of that fleeting glimpse of my beloved princess that there was room in it for naught else. Be that as it may, the fact is that I marched buoyantly behind my guide straight into the jaws of death.

Afterward I learned that thern spies had been aware of my coming for hours before I reached the hidden fortress.

The gate had been purposely left ajar to tempt me on. The guards had been schooled well in their part of the conspiracy; and I, more like a schoolboy than a seasoned warrior, ran headlong into the trap.

At the far side of the outer court a narrow door let into the angle made by one of the buttresses with the wall. Here my guide produced a key and opened the way within; then, stepping back, he motioned me to enter.

"Matai Shang is in the temple court beyond," he said; and as Woola and I passed through, the fellow closed the door quickly upon us.

The nasty laugh that came to my ears through the heavy planking of the door after the lock clicked was my first intimation that all was not as it should be.

I found myself in a small, circular chamber, within the buttress. Before me a door opened, presumably, upon the inner court beyond. For a moment I hesitated, all my suspicions now suddenly, though tardily, aroused; then, with a shrug of my shoulders, I opened the door and stepped out into the glare of torches that lighted the inner court.

Directly opposite me a massive tower rose to a height of three hundred feet. It was of the strangely beautiful modern Barsoomian style of architecture, its entire surface hand carved in bold relief with intricate and fanciful designs. Thirty feet above the courtyard and overlooking it was a broad balcony, and there, indeed, was Matai Shang, and with him were Thurid and Phaidor, Thuvia, and Dejah Thoris—the last two heavily ironed. A handful of thern warriors stood just behind the little party.

As I entered the enclosure the eyes of those in the balcony were full upon me.

An ugly smile distorted the cruel lips of Matai Shang. Thurid hurled a taunt at me and placed a familiar hand upon the shoulder of my princess. Like a tigress she turned upon him, striking the beast a heavy blow with the manacles upon her wrist.

He would have struck back had not Matai Shang interfered, and then I saw that the two men were not over-friendly; for the manner of the thern was arrogant and domineering as he made it plain to the First Born that the Princess of Helium was the personal property of the Father of Therns. And Thurid's bearing toward the ancient hekkador savored not at all of liking or respect.

When the altercation in the balcony had subsided Matai Shang turned again to me.

"Earth man," he cried, "you have earned a more ignoble death than now lies within our weakened power to inflict upon you; but that the death you die tonight may be doubly bitter, know you that when you have passed, your widow becomes the wife of Matai Shang, Hekkador of the Holy Therns, for a Martian year.

"At the end of that time, as you know, she shall be discarded, as is the law among us, but not, as is usual, to lead a quiet and honored life as high priestess of some hallowed shrine. Instead, Dejah Thoris, Princess of Helium, shall become the plaything of my lieutenants— perhaps of thy most hated enemy, Thurid, the black dator."

As he ceased speaking he awaited in silence evidently for some outbreak of rage upon my part—something that would have added to the spice of his revenge. But I did not give him the satisfaction that he craved.

Instead, I did the one thing of all others that might rouse his anger and increase his hatred of me; for I knew that if I died Dejah Thoris,

too, would find a way to die before they could heap further tortures
or indignities upon her.

Of all the holy of holies which the thern venerates and worships
none is more revered than the yellow wig which covers his bald pate,
and next thereto comes the circlet of gold and the great diadem,
whose scintillant rays mark the attainment of the Tenth Cycle.

And, knowing this, I removed the wig and circlet from my head,
tossing them carelessly upon the flagging of the court. Then I wiped
my feet upon the yellow tresses; and as a groan of rage arose from
the balcony I spat full upon the holy diadem.

Matai Shang went livid with anger, but upon the lips of Thurid I
could see a grim smile of amusement, for to him these things were
not holy; so, lest he should derive too much amusement from my act,
I cried: "And thus did I with the holies of Issus, Goddess of Life
Eternal, ere I threw Issus herself to the mob that once had worshiped
her, to be torn to pieces in her own temple."

That put an end to Thurid's grinning, for he had been high in
the favor of Issus.

"Let us have an end to this blaspheming!" he cried, turning to
the Father of Therns.

Matai Shang rose and, leaning over the edge of the balcony, gave
voice to the weird call that I had heard from the lips of the priests
upon the tiny balcony upon the face of the Golden Cliffs overlooking
the Valley Dor, when, in times past, they called the fearsome white
apes and the hideous plant men to the feast of victims floating down
the broad bosom of the mysterious Iss toward the silian-infested
waters of the Lost Sea of Korus.

"Let loose the death!" he cried, and immediately a dozen doors
in the base of the tower swung open, and a dozen grim and terrible
banths sprang into the arena.

This was not the first time that I had faced the ferocious Barsoomian lion, but never had I been pitted, single-handed, against a full
dozen of them. Even with the assistance of the fierce Woola, there
could be but a single outcome to so unequal a struggle.

For a moment the beasts hesitated beneath the brilliant glare of
the torches; but presently their eyes, becoming accustomed to the
light, fell upon Woola and me, and with bristling manes and deep-
throated roars they advanced, lashing their tawny sides with their
powerful tails.

In the brief interval of life that was left me I shot a last, parting

"She called the fierce banths about her and led them as a shepherdess might lead her flock of meek and harmless sheep."

glance toward my Dejah Thoris. Her beautiful face was set in an expression of horror; and as my eyes met hers she extended both arms toward me as, struggling with the guards who now held her, she endeavored to cast herself from the balcony into the pit beneath, that she might share my death with me. Then, as the banths were about to close upon me, she turned and buried her dear face in her arms.

Suddenly my attention was drawn toward Thuvia of Ptarth. The beautiful girl was leaning far over the edge of the balcony, her eyes bright with excitement.

In another instant the banths would be upon me, but I could not force my gaze from the features of the red girl, for I knew that her expression meant anything but the enjoyment of the grim tragedy that would so soon be enacted below her; there was some deeper, hidden meaning which I sought to solve.

For an instant I thought of relying on my earthly muscles and agility to escape the banths and reach the balcony, which I could easily have done, but I could not bring myself to desert the faithful Woola and leave him to die alone beneath the cruel fangs of the hungry banths; that is not the way upon Barsoom, nor was it ever the way of John Carter.

Then the secret of Thuvia's excitement became apparent as from her lips there issued the purring sound I had heard once before; that time that, within the Golden Cliffs, she called the fierce banths about her and led them as a shepherdess might lead her flock of meek and harmless sheep.

At the first note of that soothing sound the banths halted in their tracks, and every fierce head went high as the beasts sought the origin of the familiar call. Presently they discovered the red girl in the balcony above them, and, turning, roared out their recognition and their greeting.

Guards sprang to drag Thuvia away, but ere they had succeeded she had hurled a volley of commands at the listening brutes, and as one they turned and marched back into their dens.

"You need not fear them now, John Carter!" cried Thuvia, before they could silence her. "Those banths will never harm you now, nor Woola, either."

It was all I cared to know. There was naught to keep me from that balcony now, and with a long, running leap I sprang far aloft until my hands grasped its lowest sill.

In an instant all was wild confusion. Matai Shang shrank back. Thurid sprang forward with drawn sword to cut me down.

Again Dejah Thoris wielded her heavy irons and fought him back. Then Matai Shang grasped her about the waist and dragged her away through a door leading within the tower.

For an instant Thurid hesitated, and then, as though fearing that the Father of Therns would escape him with the Princess of Helium, he, too, dashed from the balcony in their wake.

Phaidor alone retained her presence of mind. Two of the guards she ordered to bear away Thuvia of Ptarth; the others she commanded to remain and prevent me from following. Then she turned toward me.

"John Carter," she cried, "for the last time I offer you the love of Phaidor, daughter of the Holy Hekkador. Accept and your princess shall be returned to the court of her grandfather, and you shall live in peace and happiness. Refuse and the fate that my father has threatened shall fall upon Dejah Thoris.

"You cannot save her now, for by this time they have reached a place where even you may not follow. Refuse and naught can save you; for, though the way to the last stronghold of the Holy Therns was made easy for you, the way hence hath been made impossible. What say you?"

"You knew my answer, Phaidor," I replied, "before ever you spoke. Make way," I cried to the guards, "for John Carter, Prince of Helium, would pass!"

With that I leaped over the low baluster that surrounded the balcony, and with drawn long-sword faced my enemies.

There were three of them; but Phaidor must have guessed what the outcome of the battle would be, for she turned and fled from the balcony the moment she saw that I would have none of her proposition.

The three guardsmen did not wait for my attack. Instead, they rushed me—the three of them simultaneously; and it was that which gave me an advantage, for they fouled one another in the narrow precincts of the balcony, so that the foremost of them stumbled full upon my blade at the first onslaught.

The red stain upon my point roused to its full the old blood-lust of the fighting man that has ever been so strong within my breast, so that my blade flew through the air with a swiftness and deadly accuracy that threw the two remaining therns into wild despair.

When at last the sharp steel found the heart of one of them the other turned to flee, and, guessing that his steps would lead him along the way taken by those I sought, I let him keep ever far enough ahead to think that he was safely escaping my sword.

Through several inner chambers he raced until he came to a spiral runway. Up this he dashed, I in close pursuit. At the upper end we came out into a small chamber, the walls of which were blank except for a single window overlooking the slopes of Otz and the Valley of Lost Souls beyond.

Here the fellow tore frantically at what appeared to be but a piece of the blank wall opposite the single window. In an instant I guessed that it was a secret exit from the room, and so I paused that he might have an opportunity to negotiate it, for I cared nothing to take the life of this poor servitor—all I craved was a clear road in pursuit of Dejah Thoris, my long-lost princess.

But, try as he would, the panel would yield neither to cunning nor force, so that eventually he gave it up and turned to face me.

"Go thy way, Thern," I said to him, pointing toward the entrance to the runway up which we had but just come. "I have no quarrel with you, nor do I crave your life. Go!"

For answer he sprang upon me with his sword, and so suddenly, at that, that I was like to have gone down before his first rush. So there was nothing for it but to give him what he sought, and that as quickly as might be, that I might not be delayed too long in this chamber while Matai Shang and Thurid made way with Dejah Thoris and Thuvia of Ptarth.

The fellow was a clever swordsman—resourceful and extremely tricky. In fact, he seemed never to have heard that there existed such a thing as a code of honor, for he repeatedly outraged a dozen Barsoomian fighting customs that an honorable man would rather die than ignore.

He even went so far as to snatch his holy wig from his head and throw it in my face, so as to blind me for a moment while he thrust at my unprotected breast.

When he thrust, however, I was not there, for I had fought with therns before; and while none had ever resorted to precisely that same expedient, I knew them to be the least honorable and most treacherous fighters upon Mars, and so was ever on the alert for some new and devilish subterfuge when I was engaged with one of their race.

But at length he overdid the thing; for, drawing his short-sword, he hurled it, javelinwise, at my body, at the same instant rushing upon me with his long-sword. A single sweeping circle of my own blade caught the flying weapon and hurled it clattering against the far wall, and then, as I sidestepped my antagonist's impetuous rush, I let him have my point full in the stomach as he hurtled by.

Clear to the hilt my weapon passed through his body, and with a frightful shriek he sank to the floor, dead.

Halting only for the brief instant that was required to wrench my sword from the carcass of my late antagonist, I sprang across the chamber to the blank wall beyond, through which the thern had attempted to pass. Here I sought for the secret of its lock, but all to no avail.

In despair I tried to force the thing, but the cold, unyielding stone might well have laughed at my futile, puny endeavors. In fact, I could have sworn that I caught the faint suggestion of taunting laughter from beyond the baffling panel.

In disgust I desisted from my useless efforts and stepped to the chamber's single window.

The slopes of Otz and the distant Valley of Lost Souls held nothing to compel my interest then; but, towering far above me, the tower's carved wall riveted my keenest attention.

Somewhere within that massive pile was Dejah Thoris. Above me I could see windows. There, possibly, lay the only way by which I could reach her. The risk was great, but not too great when the fate of a world's most wondrous woman was at stake.

I glanced below. A hundred feet beneath lay jagged granite boulders at the brink of a frightful chasm upon which the tower abutted; and if not upon the boulders, then at the chasm's bottom, lay death, should a foot slip but once, or clutching fingers loose their hold for the fraction of an instant.

But there was no other way and with a shrug, which I must admit was half shudder, I stepped to the window's outer sill and began my perilous ascent.

To my dismay I found that, unlike the ornamentation upon most Heliumetic structures, the edges of the carvings were quite generally rounded, so that at best my every hold was most precarious.

Fifty feet above me commenced a series of projecting cylindrical stones some six inches in diameter. These apparently circled the tower at six-foot intervals, in bands six feet apart; and as each stone cylinder protruded some four or five inches beyond the surface of the other ornamentation, they presented a comparatively easy mode of ascent could I but reach them.

Laboriously I climbed toward them by way of some windows which lay below them, for I hoped that I might find ingress to the tower through one of these, and thence an easier avenue along which to prosecute my search.

At times so slight was my hold upon the rounded surfaces of the carving's edges that a sneeze, a cough, or even a slight gust of wind would have dislodged me and sent me hurtling to the depths below.

But finally I reached a point where my fingers could just clutch the sill of the lowest window, and I was on the point of breathing a sigh of relief when the sound of voices came to me from above through the open window.

"He can never solve the secret of that lock." The voice was Matai Shang's. "Let us proceed to the hangar above that we may be far to the south before he finds another way—should that be possible."

"All things seem possible to that vile calot," replied another voice, which I recognized as Thurid's.

"Then let us haste," said Matai Shang. "But to be doubly sure, I will leave two who shall patrol this runway. Later they may follow us upon another flier—overtaking us at Kaol."

My upstretched fingers never reached the window's sill. At the first sound of the voices I drew back my hand and clung there to my perilous perch, flattened against the perpendicular wall, scarce daring to breathe.

What a horrible position, indeed, in which to be discovered by Thurid! He had but to lean from the window to push me with his sword's point into eternity.

Presently the sound of the voices became fainter, and once again I took up my hazardous ascent, now more difficult, since more circuitous, for I must climb so as to avoid the windows.

Matai Shang's reference to the hangar and the fliers indicated that my destination lay nothing short of the roof of the tower, and toward this seemingly distant goal I set my face.

The most difficult and dangerous part of the journey was accomplished at last, and it was with relief that I felt my fingers close about the lowest of the stone cylinders.

It is true that these projections were too far apart to make the balance of the ascent anything of a sinecure, but I at least had always within my reach a point of safety to which I might cling in case of accident.

Some ten feet below the roof, the wall inclined slightly inward possibly a foot in the last ten feet, and here the climbing was indeed immeasurably easier, so that my fingers soon clutched the eaves.

As I drew my eyes above the level of the tower's top I saw a flier all but ready to rise.

Upon her deck were Matai Shang, Phaidor, Dejah Thoris, Thuvia of Ptarth, and a few thern warriors, while near her was Thurid in the act of clambering aboard.

He was not ten paces from me, facing in the opposite direction; and what cruel freak of fate should have caused him to turn about just as my eyes topped the roof's edge I may not even guess.

But turn he did; and when his eyes met mine his wicked face lighted with a malignant smile as he leaped toward me, where I was hastening to scramble to the secure footing of the roof.

Dejah Thoris must have seen me at the same instant, for she screamed a useless warning just as Thurid's foot, swinging in a mighty kick, landed full in my face.

Like a felled ox, I reeled and tumbled backward over the tower's side.

ON THE KAOLIAN ROAD

IF THERE be a fate that is sometimes cruel to me, there surely is a kind and merciful Providence which watches over me.

As I toppled from the tower into the horrid abyss below I counted myself already dead; and Thurid must have done likewise, for he evidently did not even trouble himself to look after me, but must have turned and mounted the waiting flier at once.

Ten feet only I fell, and then a loop of my tough, leathern harness caught upon one of the cylindrical stone projections in the tower's surface—and held. Even when I had ceased to fall I could not believe the miracle that had preserved me from instant death, and for a moment I hung there, cold sweat exuding from every pore of my body.

But when at last I had worked myself back to a firm position I hesitated to ascend, since I could not then know that Thurid was not still awaiting me above.

Presently, however, there came to my ears the whirring of the propellers of a flier, and as each moment the sound grew fainter I realized that the party had proceeded toward the south without assuring themselves as to my fate.

Cautiously I retraced my way to the roof, and I must admit that it was with no pleasant sensation that I raised my eyes once more above its edge; but, to my relief, there was no one in sight, and a moment later I stood safely upon its broad surface.

To reach the hangar and drag forth the only other flier which it contained was the work of but an instant; and just as the two thern warriors whom Matai Shang had left to prevent this very contingency emerged upon the roof from the tower's interior, I rose above them with a taunting laugh.

Then I dived rapidly to the inner court where I had last seen Woola, and to my immense relief found the faithful beast still there.

The twelve great banths lay in the doorways of their lairs, eyeing him and growling ominously, but they had not disobeyed Thuvia's injunction; and I thanked the fate that had made her their keeper within the Golden Cliffs, and endowed her with the kind and sympathetic nature that had won the loyalty and affection of these fierce beasts for her.

Woola leaped in frantic joy when he discovered me; and as the flier touched the pavement of the court for a brief instant he bounded to the deck beside me, and in the bearlike manifestation of his exuberant happiness all but caused me to wreck the vessel against the courtyard's rocky wall.

Amid the angry shouting of thern guardsmen we rose high above the last fortress of the Holy Therns, and then raced straight toward the northeast and Kaol, the destination which I had heard from the lips of Matai Shang.

Far ahead, a tiny speck in the distance, I made out another flier late in the afternoon. It could be none other than that which bore my lost love and my enemies.

I had gained considerably on the craft by night; and then, knowing that they must have sighted me and would show no lights after dark, I set my destination compass upon her—that wonderful little

Martian mechanism which, once attuned to the object of destination, points away toward it, irrespective of every change in its location.

All that night we raced through the Barsoomian void, passing over low hills and dead sea bottoms; above long-deserted cities and populous centers of red Martian habitation upon the ribbon-like lines of cultivated land which border the globe-encircling waterways, which Earth men call the canals of Mars.

Dawn showed that I had gained appreciably upon the flier ahead of me. It was a larger craft than mine, and not so swift; but even so, it had covered an immense distance since the flight began.

The change in vegetation below showed me that we were rapidly nearing the equator. I was now near enough to my quarry to have used my bow gun; but, though I could see that Dejah Thoris was not on deck, I feared to fire upon the craft which bore her.

Thurid was deterred by no such scruples; and though it must have been difficult for him to believe that it was really I who followed them, he could not very well doubt the witness of his own eyes; and so he trained their stern gun upon me with his own hands, and an instant later an explosive radium projectile whizzed perilously close above my deck.

The black's next shot was more accurate, striking my flier full upon the prow and exploding with the instant of contact, ripping wide open the bow buoyancy tanks and disabling the engine.

So quickly did my bow drop after the shot that I scarce had time to lash Woola to the deck and buckle my own harness to a gunwale ring before the craft was hanging stern up and making her last long drop to ground.

Her stern buoyancy tanks prevented her dropping with great rapidity; but Thurid was firing rapidly now in an attempt to burst these also, that I might be dashed to death in the swift fall that would instantly follow a successful shot.

Shot after shot tore past or into us, but by a miracle neither Woola nor I was hit, nor were the after tanks punctured. This good fortune could not last indefinitely, and, assured that Thurid would not again leave me alive, I awaited the bursting of the next shell that hit; and then, throwing my hands above my head, I let go my hold and crumpled, limp and inert, dangling in my harness like a corpse.

The ruse worked, and Thurid fired no more at us. Presently I heard the diminishing sound of whirring propellers, and realized that again I was safe.

Slowly the stricken flier sank to the ground, and when I had freed myself and Woola from the entangling wreckage I found that we were upon the verge of a natural forest—so rare a thing upon the bosom of dying Mars that, outside of the forest in the Valley Dor beside the Lost Sea of Korus, I never before had seen its like upon the planet.

From books and travelers I had learned something of the little-known land of Kaol, which lies along the equator almost halfway round the planet to the east of Helium.

It comprises a sunken area of extreme tropical heat, and is inhabited by a nation of red men varying but little in manners, customs, and appearance from the balance of the red men of Barsoom.

I knew that they were among those of the outer world who still clung tenaciously to the discredited religion of the Holy Therns, and that Matai Shang would find a ready welcome and safe refuge among them; while John Carter could look for nothing better than an ignoble death at their hands.

The isolation of the Kaolians is rendered almost complete by the fact that no waterway connects their land with that of any other nation, nor have they any need of a waterway since the low, swampy land which comprises the entire area of their domain self-waters their abundant tropical crops.

For great distances in all directions rugged hills and arid stretches of dead sea bottom discourage intercourse with them, and since there is practically no such thing as foreign commerce upon warlike Barsoom, where each nation is sufficient to itself, really little has been known relative to the court of the Jeddak of Kaol and the numerous strange, but interesting, people over whom he rules.

Occasional hunting parties have traveled to this out-of-the-way corner of the globe, but the hostility of the natives has usually brought disaster upon them, so that even the sport of hunting the strange and savage creatures which haunt the jungle fastnesses of Kaol has of later years proved insufficient lure even to the most intrepid warriors.

It was upon the verge of the land of the Kaols that I now knew myself to be, but in what direction to search for Dejah Thoris, or how far into the heart of the great forest I might have to penetrate I had not the faintest idea.

But not so Woola.

Scarcely had I disentangled him than he raised his head high in air and commenced circling about at the edge of the forest. Presently he halted, and, turning to see if I were following, set off straight into the maze of trees in the direction we had been going before Thurid's shot had put an end to our flier.

As best I could, I stumbled after him down a steep declivity beginning at the forest's edge.

Immense trees reared their mighty heads far above us, their broad fronds completely shutting off the slightest glimpse of the sky. It was easy to see why the Kaolians needed no navy; their cities, hidden in the midst of this towering forest, must be entirely invisible from above, nor could a landing be made by any but the smallest fliers, and then only with the greatest risk of accident.

How Thurid and Matai Shang were to land I could not imagine, though later I was to learn that to the level of the forest top there rises in each city of Kaol a slender watchtower which guards the Kaolians by day and by night against the secret approach of a hostile fleet. To one of these the hekkador of the Holy Therns had no difficulty in approaching, and by its means the party was safely lowered to the ground.

As Woola and I approached the bottom of the declivity the ground became soft and mushy, so that it was with the greatest difficulty that we made any headway whatever.

Slender purple grasses topped with red and yellow fernlike fronds grew rankly all about us to the height of several feet above my head.

Myriad creepers hung festooned in graceful loops from tree to tree, and among them were several varieties of the Martian "man-flower," whose blooms have eyes and hands with which to see and seize the insects which form their diet.

The repulsive calot tree was, too, much in evidence. It is a carnivorous plant of about the bigness of a large sagebrush such as dots our western plains. Each branch ends in a set of strong jaws, which have been known to drag down and devour large and formidable beasts of prey.

Both Woola and I had several narrow escapes from these greedy, arboreous monsters.

Occasional areas of firm sod gave us intervals of rest from the arduous labor of traversing this gorgeous, twilight swamp, and it was upon one of these that I finally decided to make camp for the night which my chronometer warned me would soon be upon us.

Many varieties of fruit grew in abundance about us; and as Martian calots are omnivorous, Woola had no difficulty in making a square meal after I had brought down the viands for him. Then, having eaten, too, I lay down with my back to that of my faithful hound, and dropped into a deep and dreamless sleep.

The forest was shrouded in impenetrable darkness when a low growl from Woola awakened me. All about us I could hear the stealthy movement of great, padded feet, and now and then the wicked gleam of green eyes upon us. Arising, I drew my long-sword and waited.

Suddenly a deep-toned, horrid roar burst from some savage throat almost at my side. What a fool I had been not to have found safer lodgings for myself and Woola among the branches of one of the countless trees that surrounded us!

By daylight it would have been comparatively easy to have hoisted Woola aloft in one manner or another, but now it was too late. There was nothing for it but to stand our ground and take our medicine, though, from the hideous racket which now assailed our ears, and for which that first roar had seemed to be the signal, I judged that we must be in the midst of hundreds, perhaps thousands, of the fierce, man-eating denizens of the Kaolian jungle.

All the balance of the night they kept up their infernal din, but why they did not attack us I could not guess, nor am I sure to this day, unless it is that none of them ever venture upon the patches of scarlet sward which dot the swamp.

When morning broke they were still there, walking about as in a circle, but always just beyond the edge of the sward. A more terrifying aggregation of fierce and blood-thirsty monsters it would be difficult to imagine.

Singly and in pairs they commenced wandering off into the jungle shortly after sunrise, and when the last of them had departed Woola and I resumed our journey.

Occasionally we caught glimpses of horrid beasts all during the day; but, fortunately, we were never far from a sward island, and when they saw us their pursuit always ended at the verge of the solid sod.

Toward noon we stumbled upon a well-constructed road running in the general direction we had been pursuing. Everything about this highway marked it as the work of skilled engineers, and I was confident, from the indications of antiquity which it bore, as well as from the very evident signs of its being still in everyday use, that it must lead to one of the principal cities of Kaol.

Just as we entered it from one side a huge monster emerged from the jungle upon the other, and at sight of us charged madly in our direction.

Imagine, if you can, a bald-faced hornet of your earthly experience grown to the size of a prize Hereford bull, and you will have some faint conception of the ferocious appearance and awesome formidability of the winged monster that bore down upon me.

Frightful jaws in front and mighty, poisoned sting behind made my relatively puny long-sword seem a pitiful weapon of defense indeed. Nor could I hope to escape the lightning-like movements or hide from those myriad facet eyes which covered three-fourths of the hideous head, permitting the creature to see in all directions at one and the same time.

Even my powerful and ferocious Woola was as helpless as a kitten before that frightful thing. But to flee were useless, even had it ever been to my liking to turn my back upon a danger; so I stood my ground, Woola snarling at my side, my only hope to die as I had always lived—fighting.

The creature was upon us now, and at the instant there seemed to me a single slight chance for victory. If I could but remove the terrible menace of certain death hidden in the poison sacs that fed the sting the struggle would be less unequal.

At the thought I called to Woola to leap upon the creature's head and hang there, and as his mighty jaws closed upon that fiendish face, and glistening fangs buried themselves in the bone and cartilage and lower part of one of the huge eyes, I dived beneath the great body as the creature rose, dragging Woola from the ground, that it might bring its sting beneath and pierce the body of the thing hanging to its head.

To put myself in the path of that poison-laden lance was to court instant death, but it was the only way; and as the thing shot lightning-like toward me I swung my long-sword in a terrific cut that severed the deadly member close to the gorgeously marked body.

Then, like a battering-ram, one of the powerful hind legs caught me full in the chest and hurled me, half stunned and wholly winded, clear across the broad highway and into the underbrush of the jungle that fringes it.

Fortunately, I passed between the boles of trees; had I struck one of them I should have been badly injured, if not killed, so swiftly had I been catapulted by that enormous hind leg.

Dazed though I was, I stumbled to my feet and staggered back to Woola's assistance, to find his savage antagonist circling ten feet above the ground, beating madly at the clinging calot with all six powerful legs.

Even during my sudden flight through the air I had not once released my grip upon my long-sword, and now I ran beneath the two battling monsters, jabbing the winged terror repeatedly with its sharp point.

The thing might easily have risen out of my reach, but evidently it knew as little concerning retreat in the face of danger as either Woola or I, for it dropped quickly toward me, and before I could escape had grasped my shoulder between its powerful jaws.

Time and again the now useless stub of its giant sting struck futilely against my body, but the blows alone were almost as effective as the kick of a horse; so that when I say futilely, I refer only to the natural function of the disabled member—eventually the thing would have hammered me to a pulp.

Nor was it far from accomplishing this when an interruption occurred that put an end forever to its hostilities.

From where I hung a few feet above the road I could see along the highway a few hundred yards to where it turned toward the east, and just as I had about given up all hope of escaping the perilous position in which I now was I saw a red warrior come into view from around the bend.

He was mounted on a splendid thoat, one of the smaller species used by red men, and in his hand was a wondrous long, light lance.

His mount was walking sedately when I first perceived them, but the instant that the red man's eyes fell upon us a word to the thoat brought the animal at full charge down upon us. The long lance of the warrior dipped toward us, and as thoat and rider hurtled beneath, the point passed through the body of our antagonist.

With a convulsive shudder the thing stiffened, the jaws relaxed, dropping me to the ground, and then, careening once in mid air, the creature plunged headforemost to the road, full upon Woola, who still clung tenaciously to its gory head.

By the time I had regained my feet the red man had turned and ridden back to us. Woola, finding his enemy inert and lifeless, released his hold at my command and wriggled from beneath the body that had covered him, and together we faced the warrior looking down upon us.

I started to thank the stranger for his timely assistance, but he cut me off peremptorily.

"Who are you," he asked, "who dare enter the land of Kaol and hunt in the royal forest of the jeddak?"

Then, as he noted my white skin through the coating of grime and blood that covered me, his eyes went wide and in an altered tone he whispered: "Can it be that you are a Holy Thern?"

I might have deceived the fellow for a time, as I had deceived others, but I had cast away the yellow wig and the holy diadem in the presence of Matai Shang, and I knew that it would not be long ere my new acquaintance discovered that I was no thern at all.

"I am not a thern," I replied, and then, flinging caution to the winds, I said: "I am John Carter, Prince of Helium, whose name may not be entirely unknown to you."

If his eyes had gone wide when he thought that I was a Holy Thern, they fairly popped now that he knew that I was John Carter. I grasped my long-sword more firmly as I spoke the words which I was sure would precipitate an attack, but to my surprise they precipitated nothing of the kind.

"John Carter, Prince of Helium," he repeated slowly, as though he could not quite grasp the truth of the statement. "John Carter, the mightiest warrior of Barsoom!"

And then he dismounted and placed his hand upon my shoulder after the manner of most friendly greeting upon Mars.

"It is my duty, and it should be my pleasure, to kill you, John Carter," he said, "but always in my heart of hearts have I admired your prowess and believed in your sincerity the while I have questioned and disbelieved the therns and their religion.

"It would mean my instant death were my heresy to be suspected in the court of Kulan Tith, but if I may serve you, Prince, you have but to command Torkar Bar, Dwar of the Kaolian Road."

Truth and honesty were writ large upon the warrior's noble countenance, so that I could not but have trusted him, enemy though he should have been. His title of Captain of the Kaolian Road ex-

plained his timely presence in the heart of the savage forest, for every
highway upon Barsoom is patrolled by doughty warriors of the noble
class, nor is there any service more honorable than this lonely and
dangerous duty in the less frequented sections of the domains of the
red men of Barsoom.

"Torkar Bar has already placed a great debt of gratitude upon my
shoulders," I replied, pointing to the carcass of the creature from
whose heart he was dragging his long spear.

The red man smiled.

"It was fortunate that I came when I did," he said. "Only this
poisoned spear pricking the very heart of a sith can kill it quickly
enough to save its prey. In this section of Kaol we are all armed with
a long sith spear, whose point is smeared with the poison of the
creature it is intended to kill; no other virus acts so quickly upon the
beast as its own.

"Look," he continued, drawing his dagger and making an incision
in the carcass a foot above the root of the sting, from which he
presently drew forth two sacs, each of which held fully a gallon of
the deadly liquid.

"Thus we maintain our supply, though were it not for certain com-
mercial uses to which the virus is put it would scarcely be necessary
to add to our present store, since the sith is almost extinct.

"Only occasionally do we now run upon one. Of old, however,
Kaol was overrun with the frightful monsters that often came in
herds of twenty or thirty, darting down from above into our cities
and carrying away women, children, and even warriors."

As he spoke I had been wondering just how much I might safely
tell this man of the mission which brought me to his land, but his
next words anticipated the broaching of the subject on my part, and
rendered me thankful that I had not spoken too soon.

"And now as to yourself, John Carter," he said, "I shall not ask
your business here, nor do I wish to hear it. I have eyes and ears
and ordinary intelligence, and yesterday morning I saw the party that
came to the city of Kaol from the north in a small flier. But one thing
I ask of you, and that is: the word of John Carter that he contem-
plates no overt act against either the nation of Kaol or its jeddak."

"You have my word as to that, Torkar Bar," I replied.

"My way leads along the Kaolian road, away from the city of Kaol," he continued. "I have seen no one—John Carter least of all. Nor have you seen Torkar Bar, nor ever heard of him. You understand?"

"Perfectly," I replied.

He laid his hand upon my shoulder.

"This road leads directly into the city of Kaol," he said. "I wish you fortune," and vaulting to the back of his thoat he trotted away without even a backward glance.

It was after dark when Woola and I spied through the mighty forest the great wall which surrounds the city of Kaol.

We had traversed the entire way without mishap or adventure, and though the few we had met had eyed the great calot wonderingly, none had pierced the red pigment with which I had smoothly smeared every square inch of my body.

But to traverse the surrounding country, and to enter the guarded city of Kulan Tith, Jeddak of Kaol, were two very different things. No man enters a Martian city without giving a very detailed and satisfactory account of himself, nor did I delude myself with the belief that I could for a moment impose upon the acumen of the officers of the guard to whom I should be taken the moment I applied at any one of the gates.

My only hope seemed to lie in entering the city surreptitiously under cover of the darkness, and once in, trust to my own wits to hide myself in some crowded quarter where detection would be less liable to occur.

With this idea in view I circled the great wall, keeping within the fringe of the forest, which is cut away for a short distance from the wall all about the city, that no enemy may utilize the trees as a means of ingress.

Several times I attempted to scale the barrier at different points, but not even my earthly muscles could overcome that cleverly constructed rampart. To a height of thirty feet the face of the wall slanted outward, and then for almost an equal distance it was perpendicular, above which it slanted in again for some fifteen feet to the crest.

And smooth! Polished glass could not be more so. Finally I had to admit that at last I had discovered a Barsoomian fortification which I could not negotiate.

Discouraged, I withdrew into the forest beside a broad highway which entered the city from the east, and with Woola beside me lay down to sleep.

A HERO IN KAOL

IT WAS DAYLIGHT when I was awakened by the sound of stealthy movement near by.

As I opened my eyes Woola, too, moved and, coming up to his haunches, stared through the intervening brush toward the road, each hair upon his neck stiffly erect.

At first I could see nothing, but presently I caught a glimpse of a bit of smooth and glossy green moving among the scarlet and purple and yellow of the vegetation.

Motioning Woola to remain quietly where he was, I crept forward to investigate, and from behind the bole of a great tree I saw a long line of the hideous green warriors of the dead sea bottoms hiding in the dense jungle beside the road.

As far as I could see, the silent line of destruction and death stretched away from the city of Kaol. There could be but one explanation. The green men were expecting an exodus of a body of red troops from the nearest city gate, and they were lying there in ambush to leap upon them.

I owed no fealty to the Jeddak of Kaol, but he was of the same race of noble red men as my own princess, and I would not stand supinely by and see his warriors butchered by the cruel and heartless demons of the waste places of Barsoom.

Cautiously I retraced my steps to where I had left Woola, and warning him to silence, signaled him to follow me. Making a considerable detour to avoid the chance of falling into the hands of the green men, I came at last to the great wall.

A hundred yards to my right was the gate from which the troops were evidently expected to issue, but to reach it I must pass the flank of the green warriors within easy sight of them, and, fearing that my plan to warn the Kaolians might thus be thwarted, I decided upon hastening toward the left, where another gate a mile away would give me ingress to the city.

I knew that the word I brought would prove a splendid passport to Kaol, and I must admit that my caution was due more to my ardent desire to make my way into the city than to avoid a brush with the green men. As much as I enjoy a fight, I cannot always indulge myself, and just now I had more weighty matters to occupy my time than spilling the blood of strange warriors.

Could I but win beyond the city's wall, there might be opportunity in the confusion and excitement which were sure to follow my announcement of an invading force of green warriors to find my way within the palace of the jeddak, where I was sure Matai Shang and his party would be quartered.

But scarcely had I taken a hundred steps in the direction of the farther gate when the sound of marching troops, the clank of metal, and the squealing of thoats just within the city apprised me of the fact that the Kaolians were already moving toward the other gate.

There was no time to be lost. In another moment the gate would be opened and the head of the column pass out upon the death-bordered highway.

Turning back toward the fateful gate, I ran rapidly along the edge of the clearing, taking the ground in the mighty leaps that had first made me famous upon Barsoom. Thirty, fifty, a hundred feet at a bound are nothing for the muscles of an athletic Earth man upon Mars.

As I passed the flank of the waiting green men they saw my eyes turned upon them, and in an instant, knowing that all secrecy was at an end, those nearest me sprang to their feet in an effort to cut me off before I could reach the gate.

At the same instant the mighty portal swung wide and the head of the Kaolian column emerged. A dozen green warriors had succeeded in reaching a point between me and the gate, but they had but little idea who it was they had elected to detain.

I did not slacken my speed an iota as I dashed among them, and as they fell before my blade I could not but recall the happy memory of those other battles when Tars Tarkas, Jeddak of Thark, mightiest of Martian green men, had stood shoulder to shoulder with me through long, hot Martian days, as together we hewed down our enemies until the pile of corpses about us rose higher than a tall man's head.

When several pressed me too closely, there before the carved gateway of Kaol, I leaped above their heads, and fashioning my tactics after those of the hideous plant men of Dor, struck down upon my enemies' heads as I passed above them.

From the city the red warriors were rushing toward us, and from the jungle the savage horde of green men were coming to meet them. In a moment I was in the very center of as fierce and bloody a battle as I had ever passed through.

These Kaolians are most noble fighters, nor are the green men of the equator one whit less warlike than their cold, cruel cousins of the temperate zone. There were many times when either side might have withdrawn without dishonor and thus ended hostilities, but from the mad abandon with which each invariably renewed hostilities I soon came to believe that what need not have been more than a trifling skirmish would end only with the complete extermination of one force or the other.

With the joy of battle once roused within me, I took keen delight in the fray, and that my fighting was noted by the Kaolians was often evidenced by the shouts of applause directed at me.

If I sometimes seem to take too great pride in my fighting ability, it must be remembered that fighting is my vocation. If your vocation be shoeing horses, or painting pictures, and you can do one or the other better than your fellows, then you are a fool if you are not proud of your ability. And so I am very proud that upon two planets no greater fighter has ever lived than John Carter, Prince of Helium.

And I outdid myself that day to impress the fact upon the natives of Kaol, for I wished to win a way into their hearts—and their city. Nor was I to be disappointed in my desire.

All day we fought, until the road was red with blood and clogged with corpses. Back and forth along the slippery highway the tide of battle surged, but never once was the gateway to Kaol really in danger.

There were breathing spells when I had a chance to converse with the red men beside whom I fought, and once the jeddak, Kulan Tith himself, laid his hand upon my shoulder and asked my name.

"I am Dotar Sojat," I replied, recalling a name given me by the Tharks many years before, from the surnames of the first two of their warriors I had killed, which is the custom among them.

"You are a mighty warrior, Dotar Sojat," he replied, "and when this day is done I shall speak with you again in the great audience chamber."

And then the fight surged upon us once more and we were separated, but my heart's desire was attained, and it was with renewed vigor and a joyous soul that I laid about me with my long-sword until the last of the green men had had enough and had withdrawn toward their distant sea bottom.

Not until the battle was over did I learn why the red troops had sallied forth that day. It seemed that Kulan Tith was expecting a visit from a mighty jeddak of the north—a powerful and the only ally of the Kaolians, and it had been his wish to meet his guest a full day's journey from Kaol.

But now the march of the welcoming host was delayed until the following morning, when the troops again set out from Kaol. I had not been bidden to the presence of Kulan Tith after the battle, but he had sent an officer to find me and escort me to comfortable quarters in that part of the palace set aside for the officers of the royal guard.

There, with Woola, I had spent a comfortable night, and rose much refreshed after the arduous labors of the past few days. Woola had fought with me through the battle of the previous day, true to the instincts and training of a Martian war dog, great numbers of which are often to be found with the savage green hordes of the dead sea bottoms.

Neither of us had come through the conflict unscathed, but the marvelous, healing salves of Barsoom had sufficed, overnight, to make us as good as new.

I breakfasted with a number of the Kaolian officers, whom I found as courteous and delightful hosts as even the nobles of Helium, who are renowned for their ease of manners and excellence of breeding. The meal was scarcely concluded when a messenger arrived from Kulan Tith summoning me before him.

As I entered the royal presence the jeddak rose, and stepping from the dais which supported his magnificent throne, came forward to meet me—a mark of distinction that is seldom accorded to other than a visiting ruler.

"Kaor, Dotar Sojat!" he greeted me. "I have summoned you to receive the grateful thanks of the people of Kaol, for had it not been for your heroic bravery in daring fate to warn us of the ambuscade we must surely have fallen into the well-laid trap. Tell me more of yourself—from what country you come, and what errand brings you to the court of Kulan Tith."

"I am from Hastor," I said, for in truth I had a small palace in that southern city which lies within the far-flung dominions of the Heliumetic nation.

"My presence in the land of Kaol is partly due to accident, my flier being wrecked upon the southern fringe of your great forest.

It was while seeking entrance to the city of Kaol that I discovered the green horde lying in wait for your troops."

If Kulan Tith wondered what business brought me in a flier to the very edge of his domain he was good enough not to press me further for an explanation, which I should indeed have had difficulty in rendering.

During my audience with the jeddak another party entered the chamber from behind me, so that I did not see their faces until Kulan Tith stepped past me to greet them, commanding me to follow and be presented.

As I turned toward them it was with difficulty that I controlled my features, for there, listening to Kulan Tith's eulogistic words concerning me, stood my arch-enemies, Matai Shang and Thurid.

"Holy Hekkador of the Holy Therns," the jeddak was saying, "shower thy blessings upon Dotar Sojat, the valorous stranger from distant Hastor, whose wondrous heroism and marvelous ferocity saved the day for Kaol yesterday."

Matai Shang stepped forward and laid his hand upon my shoulder. No slightest indication that he recognized me showed upon his countenance—my disguise was evidently complete.

He spoke kindly to me and then presented me to Thurid. The black, too, was evidently entirely deceived. Then Kulan Tith regaled them, much to my amusement, with details of my achievements upon the field of battle.

The thing that seemed to have impressed him most was my remarkable agility, and time and again he described the wondrous way in which I had leaped completely over an antagonist, cleaving his skull wide open with my long-sword as I passed above him.

I thought that I saw Thurid's eyes widen a bit during the narrative, and several times I surprised him gazing intently into my face through narrowed lids. Was he commencing to suspect? And then Kulan Tith told of the savage calot that fought beside me, and after that I saw suspicion in the eyes of Matai Shang—or did I but imagine it?

At the close of the audience Kulan Tith announced that he would have me accompany him upon the way to meet his royal guest, and as I departed with an officer who was to procure proper trappings and a suitable mount for me, both Matai Shang and Thurid seemed most sincere in professing their pleasure at having had an opportunity to know me. It was with a sigh of relief that I quitted the chamber, convinced that nothing more than a guilty conscience had prompted my belief that either of my enemies suspected my true identity.

A half-hour later I rode out of the city gate with the column that accompanied Kulan Tith upon the way to meet his friend and ally. Though my eyes and ears had been wide open during my audience with the jeddak and my various passages through the palace, I had seen or heard nothing of Dejah Thoris or Thuvia of Ptarth. That they must be somewhere within the great rambling edifice I was positive, and I should have given much to have found a way to remain behind during Kulan Tith's absence, that I might search for them.

Toward noon we came in touch with the head of the column we had set out to meet.

It was a gorgeous train that accompanied the visiting jeddak, and for miles it stretched along the wide, white road to Kaol. Mounted troops, their trappings of jewel and metal-incrusted leather glistening in the sunlight, formed the vanguard of the body, and then came a thousand gorgeous chariots drawn by huge zitidars.

These low, commodious wagons moved two abreast, and on either side of them marched solid ranks of mounted warriors, for in the chariots were the women and children of the royal court. Upon the back of each monster zitidar rode a Martian youth, and the whole scene carried me back to my first days upon Barsoom, now twenty-two years in the past, when I had first beheld the gorgeous spectacle of a caravan of the green horde of Tharks.

Never before today had I seen zitidars in the service of red men. These brutes are huge mastodonian animals that tower to an immense height even beside the giant green men and their giant thoats; but when compared to the relatively small red man and his breed of thoats they assume Brobdingnagian proportions that are truly appalling.

The beasts were hung with jeweled trappings and saddlepads of gay silk, embroidered in fanciful designs with strings of diamonds, pearls, rubies, emeralds, and the countless unnamed jewels of Mars, while from each chariot rose a dozen standards from which streamers, flags, and pennons fluttered in the breeze.

Just in front of the chariots the visiting jeddak rode alone upon a pure white thoat—another unusual sight upon Barsoom—and after them came interminable ranks of mounted spearmen, riflemen, and swordsmen. It was indeed a most imposing sight.

Except for the clanking of accouterments and the occasional squeal of an angry thoat or the low guttural of a zitidar, the passage of the cavalcade was almost noiseless, for neither thoat nor zitidar is a hoofed animal, and the broad tires of the chariots are of an elastic composition, which gives forth no sound.

Now and then the gay laughter of a woman or the chatter of children could be heard, for the red Martians are a social, pleasure-loving people—in direct antithesis to the cold and morbid race of green men.

The forms and ceremonials connected with the meeting of the two jeddaks consumed an hour, and then we turned and retraced our way toward the city of Kaol, which the head of the column reached just before dark, though it must have been nearly morning before the rear guard passed through the gateway.

Fortunately, I was well up toward the head of the column, and after the great banquet, which I attended with the officers of the royal guard, I was free to seek repose. There was so much activity and bustle about the palace all during the night with the constant arrival of the noble officers of the visiting jeddak's retinue that I dared not attempt to prosecute a search for Dejah Thoris, and so, as soon as it was seemly for me to do so, I returned to my quarters.

As I passed along the corridors between the banquet hall and the apartments that had been allotted me, I had a sudden feeling that I was under surveillance, and, turning quickly in my tracks, caught a glimpse of a figure which darted into an open doorway the instant I wheeled about.

Though I ran quickly back to the spot where the shadower had disappeared I could find no trace of him, yet in the brief glimpse that I had caught I could have sworn that I had seen a white face surmounted by a mass of yellow hair.

The incident gave me considerable food for speculation, since if I were right in the conclusion induced by the cursory glimpse I had had of the spy, then Matai Shang and Thurid must suspect my identity, and if that were true not even the service I had rendered Kulan Tith could save me from his religious fanaticism.

But never did vague conjecture or fruitless fears for the future lie with sufficient weight upon my mind to keep me from my rest, and so tonight I threw myself upon my sleeping silks and furs and passed at once into dreamless slumber.

Calots are not permitted within the walls of the palace proper, and so I had had to relegate poor Woola to quarters in the stables where the royal thoats are kept. He had comfortable even luxurious apartments, but I would have given much to have had him with me; and if he had been, the thing which happened that night would not have come to pass.

I could not have slept over a quarter of an hour when I was suddenly awakened by the passing of some cold and clammy thing across my forehead. Instantly I sprang to my feet, clutching in the direction I thought the presence lay. For an instant my hand touched against human flesh, and then, as I lunged headforemost through the darkness to seize my nocturnal visitor, my foot became entangled in my sleeping silks and I fell sprawling to the floor.

By the time I had resumed my feet and found the button which controlled the light my caller had disappeared. Careful search of the room revealed nothing to explain either the identity or business of the person who had thus secretly sought me in the dead of night.

That the purpose might be theft I could not believe, since thieves are practically unknown upon Barsoom. Assassination, however, is rampant, but even this could not have been the motive of my stealthy friend, for he might easily have killed me had he desired.

I had about given up fruitless conjecture and was on the point of returning to sleep when a dozen Kaolian guardsmen entered my apartment. The officer in charge was one of my genial hosts of the morning, but now upon his face was no sign of friendship.

"Kulan Tith commands your presence before him," he said. "Come!"

NEW ALLIES

SURROUNDED BY GUARDSMEN I marched back along the corridors of the palace of Kulan Tith, Jeddak of Kaol, to the great audience chamber in the center of the massive structure.

As I entered the brilliantly lighted apartment, filled with the nobles of Kaol and the officers of the visiting jeddak, all eyes were turned upon me. Upon the great dais at the end of the chamber stood three thrones, upon which sat Kulan Tith and his two guests, Matai Shang, and the visiting jeddak.

Up the broad center aisle we marched beneath deadly silence, and at the foot of the thrones we halted.

"Prefer thy charge," said Kulan Tith, turning to one who stood among the nobles at his right; and then Thurid, the black dator of the First Born, stepped forward and faced me.

"Most noble Jeddak," he said, addressing Kulan Tith, "from the first I suspected this stranger within thy palace. Your description of his fiendish prowess tallied with that of the arch-enemy of truth upon Barsoom.

"But that there might be no mistake I despatched a priest of your own holy cult to make the test that should pierce his disguise and reveal the truth. Behold the result!" and Thurid pointed a rigid finger at my forehead.

All eyes followed the direction of that accusing digit—I alone seemed at a loss to guess what fatal sign rested upon my brow.

The officer beside me guessed my perplexity; and as the brows of Kulan Tith darkened in a menacing scowl as his eyes rested upon me, the noble drew a small mirror from his pocket-pouch and held it before my face.

One glance at the reflection it gave back to me was sufficient.

From my forehead the hand of the sneaking thern had reached out through the concealing darkness of my bedchamber and wiped away a patch of the disguising red pigment as broad as my palm. Beneath showed the tanned texture of my own white skin.

For a moment Thurid ceased speaking, to enhance, I suspect, the dramatic effect of his disclosure. Then he resumed.

"Here, O Kulan Tith," he cried, "is he who has desecrated the temples of the Gods of Mars, who has violated the persons of the Holy Therns themselves and turned a world against its age-old religion. Before you, in your power, Jeddak of Kaol, Defender of the Holies, stands John Carter, Prince of Helium!"

Kulan Tith looked toward Matai Shang as though for corroboration of these charges. The Holy Thern nodded his head.

"It is indeed the arch-blasphemer," he said. "Even now he has followed me to the very heart of thy palace, Kulan Tith, for the sole purpose of assassinating me. He——"

"He lies!" I cried. "Kulan Tith, listen that you may know the truth. Listen while I tell you why John Carter has followed Matai Shang to the heart of thy palace. Listen to me as well as to them, and then judge if my acts be not more in accord with true Barsoomian chivalry and honor than those of these revengeful devotees of the spurious creeds from whose cruel bonds I have freed your planet."

"Silence!" roared the jeddak, leaping to his feet and laying his hand upon the hilt of his sword. "Silence, blasphemer! Kulan Tith need not permit the air of his audience chamber to be defiled by the heresies that issue from your polluted throat to judge you.

"You stand already self-condemned. It but remains to determine the manner of your death. Even the service that you rendered the arms of Kaol shall avail you naught; it was but a base subterfuge whereby you might win your way into my favor and reach the side of this holy man whose life you craved. To the pits with him!" he concluded, addressing the officer of my guard.

Here was a pretty pass, indeed! What chance had I against a whole nation? What hope for me of mercy at the hands of the fanatical Kulan Tith with such advisers as Matai Shang and Thurid. The black grinned malevolently in my face.

"You shall not escape this time, Earth man," he taunted.

The guards closed toward me. A red haze blurred my vision. The fighting blood of my Virginian sires coursed hot through my veins. The lust of battle in all its mad fury was upon me.

With a leap I was beside Thurid, and ere the devilish smirk had faded from his handsome face I had caught him full upon the mouth with my clenched fist; and as the good, old American blow landed, the black dator shot back a dozen feet, to crumple in a broken heap at the foot of Kulan Tith's throne, spitting blood and teeth from his hurt mouth.

Then I drew my sword and swung round, on guard, to face a nation.

In an instant the guardsmen were upon me, but before a blow had been struck a mighty voice rose above the din of shouting warriors, and a giant figure leaped from the dais beside Kulan Tith and, with drawn long-sword, threw himself between me and my adversaries.

It was the visiting jeddak.

"Hold!" he cried. "If you value my friendship, Kulan Tith, and the age-old peace that has existed between our peoples, call off your swordsmen; for wherever or against whomsoever fights John Carter, Prince of Helium, there beside him and to the death fights Thuvan Dihn, Jeddak of Ptarth."

The shouting ceased and the menacing points were lowered as a thousand eyes turned first toward Thuvan Dihn in surprise and then toward Kulan Tith in question. At first the Jeddak of Kaol went white in rage, but before he spoke he had mastered himself, so that his tone was calm and even as befitted intercourse between two great jeddaks.

"Thuvan Dihn," he said slowly, "must have great provocation thus to desecrate the ancient customs which inspire the deportment of a guest within the palace of his host. Lest I, too, should forget myself as has my royal friend, I should prefer to remain silent until the Jeddak of Ptarth has won from me applause for his action by relating the causes which provoked it."

I could see that the Jeddak of Ptarth was of half a mind to throw his metal in Kulan Tith's face, but he controlled himself even as well as had his host.

"None knows better than Thuvan Dihn," he said, "the laws which govern the acts of men in the domains of their neighbors; but Thuvan Dihn owes allegiance to a higher law than these—the law of gratitude. Nor to any man upon Barsoom does he owe a greater debt of gratitude than to John Carter, Prince of Helium.

"Years ago, Kulan Tith," he continued, "upon the occasion of your last visit to me, you were greatly taken with the charms and graces of my only daughter, Thuvia. You saw how I adored her, and later you learned that, inspired by some unfathomable whim, she had taken the last, long, voluntary pilgrimage upon the cold bosom of the mysterious Iss, leaving me desolate.

"Some months ago I first heard of the expedition which John Carter had led against Issus and the Holy Therns. Faint rumors of the atrocities reported to have been committed by the therns upon those who for countless ages have floated down the mighty Iss came to my ears.

"I heard that thousands of prisoners had been released, few of whom dared to return to their own countries owing to the mandate of terrible death which rests against all who return from the Valley Dor.

"For a time I could not believe the heresies which I heard, and I prayed that my daughter Thuvia might have died before she ever committed the sacrilege of returning to the outer world. But then my father's love asserted itself, and I vowed that I would prefer eternal damnation to further separation from her if she could be found.

"So I sent emissaries to Helium, and to the court of Xodar, Jeddak of the First Born, and to him who now rules those of the thern nation that have renounced their religion; and from each and all I heard the same story of unspeakable cruelties and atrocities perpetrated upon the poor defenseless victims of their religion by the Holy Therns.

"Many there were who had seen or known my daughter, and from therns who had been close to Matai Shang I learned of the indignities that he personally heaped upon her; and I was glad when I came here to find that Matai Shang was also your guest, for I should have sought him out had it taken a lifetime.

"More, too, I heard, and that of the chivalrous kindness that John Carter had accorded my daughter. They told me how he fought for her and rescued her, and how he spurned escape from the savage Warhoons of the south, sending her to safety upon his own thoat and remaining upon foot to meet the green warriors.

"Can you wonder, Kulan Tith, that I am willing to jeopardize my life, the peace of my nation, or even your friendship, which I prize more than aught else, to champion the Prince of Helium?"

For a moment Kulan Tith was silent. I could see by the expression of his face that he was sore perplexed. Then he spoke.

"Thuvan Dihn," he said, and his tone was friendly though sad, "who am I to judge my fellow-man? In my eyes the Father of Therns is still holy, and the religion which he teaches the only true religion, but were I faced by the same problem that has vexed you I doubt not that I should feel and act precisely as you have.

"In so far as the Prince of Helium is concerned I may act, but between you and Matai Shang my only office can be one of conciliation. The Prince of Helium shall be escorted in safety to the boundary of my domain ere the sun has set again, where he shall be free to go whither he will; but upon pain of death must he never again enter the land of Kaol.

"If there be a quarrel between you and the Father of Therns, I need not ask that the settlement of it be deferred until both have passed beyond the limits of my power. Are you satisfied, Thuvan Dihn?"

The Jeddak of Ptarth nodded his assent, but the ugly scowl that he bent upon Matai Shang harbored ill for that pasty-faced godling.

"The Prince of Helium is far from satisfied," I cried, breaking rudely in upon the beginnings of peace, for I had no stomach for peace at the price that had been named.

"I have escaped death in a dozen forms to follow Matai Shang and overtake him, and I do not intend to be led, like a decrepit thoat to the slaughter, from the goal that I have won by the prowess of my sword arm and the might of my muscles.

"Nor will Thuvan Dihn, Jeddak of Ptarth, be satisfied when he has heard me through. Do you know why I have followed Matai Shang and Thurid, the black dator, from the forests of the Valley Dor across half a world through almost insurmountable difficulties?

"Think you that John Carter, Prince of Helium, would stoop to assassination? Can Kulan Tith be such a fool as to believe that lie, whispered in his ear by the Holy Thern or Dator Thurid?

"I do not follow Matai Shang to kill him, though the God of mine own planet knows that my hands itch to be at his throat. I follow him, Thuvan Dihn, because with him are two prisoners—my wife, Dejah Thoris, Princess of Helium, and your daughter, Thuvia of Ptarth.

"Now think you that I shall permit myself to be led beyond the walls of Kaol unless the mother of my son accompanies me, and thy daughter be restored?"

Thuvan Dihn turned upon Kulan Tith. Rage flamed in his keen eyes; but by the masterfulness of his self-control he kept his tones level as he spoke.

"Knew you this thing, Kulan Tith?" he asked. "Knew you that my daughter lay a prisoner in your palace?"

"He could not know it," interrupted Matai Shang, white with what I am sure was more fear than rage. "He could not know it, for it is a lie."

I would have had his life for that upon the spot, but even as I sprang toward him Thuvan Dihn laid a heavy hand upon my shoulder.

"Wait," he said to me, and then to Kulan Tith. "It is not a lie. This much have I learned of the Prince of Helium—he does not lie. Answer me, Kulan Tith—I have asked you a question."

"Three women came with the Father of Therns," replied Kulan Tith. "Phaidor, his daughter, and two who were reported to be her slaves. If these be Thuvia of Ptarth and Dejah Thoris of Helium I did not know it—I have seen neither. But if they be, then shall they be returned to you on the morrow."

As he spoke he looked straight at Matai Shang, not as a devotee should look at a high priest, but as a ruler of men looks at one to whom he issues a command.

It must have been plain to the Father of Therns, as it was to me, that the recent disclosures of his true character had done much already to weaken the faith of Kulan Tith, and that it would require but little more to turn the powerful jeddak into an avowed enemy; but so strong are the seeds of superstition that even the great Kaolian still hesitated to cut the final strand that bound him to his ancient religion.

Matai Shang was wise enough to seem to accept the mandate of his follower, and promised to bring the two slave women to the audience chamber on the morrow.

"It is almost morning now," he said, "and I should dislike to break in upon the slumber of my daughter, or I would have them fetched at once that you might see that the Prince of Helium is mistaken," and he emphasized the last word in an effort to affront me so subtilely that I could not take open offence.

I was about to object to any delay, and demand that the Princess of Helium be brought to me forthwith, when Thuvan Dihn made such insistence seem unnecessary.

"I should like to see my daughter at once," he said, "but if Kulan Tith will give me his assurance that none will be permitted to leave the palace this night, and that no harm shall befall either Dejah Thoris or Thuvia of Ptarth between now and the moment that they are brought into our presence in this chamber at daylight I shall not insist."

"None shall leave the palace tonight," replied the Jeddak of Kaol, "and Matai Shang will give us assurance that no harm will come to the two women?"

The thern assented with a nod. A few moments later Kulan Tith indicated that the audience was at an end, and at Thuvan Dihn's invitation I accompanied the Jeddak of Ptarth to his own apartments, where we sat until daylight, while he listened to the account of my experiences upon his planet and to all that had befallen his daughter during the time that we had been together.

I found the father of Thuvia a man after my own heart, and that night saw the beginning of a friendship which has grown until it is second only to that which obtains between Tars Tarkas, the green Jeddak of Thark, and myself.

The first burst of Mars's sudden dawn brought messengers from Kulan Tith, summoning us to the audience chamber where Thuvan Dihn was to receive his daughter after years of separation, and I was to be reunited with the glorious daughter of Helium after an almost unbroken separation of twelve years.

My heart pounded within my bosom until I looked about me in embarrassment, so sure was I that all within the room must hear. My arms ached to enfold once more the divine form of her whose eternal youth and undying beauty were but outward manifestations of a perfect soul.

At last the messenger despatched to fetch Matai Shang returned.

I craned my neck to catch the first glimpse of those who should be following, but the messenger was alone.

Halting before the throne he addressed his jeddak in a voice that was plainly audible to all within the chamber.

"O Kulan Tith, Mightiest of Jeddaks," he cried, after the fashion of the court, "your messenger returns alone, for when he reached the apartments of the Father of Therns he found them empty, as were those occupied by his suite."

Kulan Tith went white.

A low groan burst from the lips of Thuvan Dihn who stood next me, not having ascended the throne which awaited him beside his host. For a moment the silence of death reigned in the great audience chamber of Kulan Tith, Jeddak of Kaol. It was he who broke the spell.

Rising from his throne he stepped down from the dais to the side of Thuvan Dihn. Tears dimmed his eyes as he placed both his hands upon the shoulders of his friend.

"O Thuvan Dihn," he cried, "that this should have happened in the palace of thy best friend! With my own hands would I have wrung the neck of Matai Shang had I guessed what was in his foul heart. Last night my life-long faith was weakened—this morning it has been shattered; but too late, too late.

"To wrest your daughter and the wife of this royal warrior from the clutches of these archfiends you have but to command the resources of a mighty nation, for all Kaol is at your disposal. What may be done? Say the word!"

"First," I suggested, "let us find those of your people who be responsible for the escape of Matai Shang and his followers. Without assistance on the part of the palace guard this thing could not have come to pass. Seek the guilty, and from them force an explanation of the manner of their going and the direction they have taken."

Before Kulan Tith could issue the commands that would initiate the investigation a handsome young officer stepped forward and addressed his jeddak.

"O Kulan Tith, Mightiest of Jeddaks," he said, "I alone be responsible for this grievous error. Last night it was I who commanded the palace guard. I was on duty in other parts of the palace during the audience of the early morning, and knew nothing of what transpired then, so that when the Father of Therns summoned me and explained that it was your wish that his party be hastened from the city because

of the presence here of a deadly enemy who sought the Holy Hekkador's life I did only what a lifetime of training has taught me was
the proper thing to do—I obeyed him whom I believed to be the ruler
of us all, mightier even than thou, mightiest of jeddaks.

"Let the consequences and the punishment fall on me alone, for
I alone am guilty. Those others of the palace guard who assisted in
the flight did so under my instructions."

Kulan Tith looked first at me and then at Thuvan Dihn, as though
to ask our judgment upon the man, but the error was so evidently
excusable that neither of us had any mind to see the young officer suffer
for a mistake that any might readily have made.

"How left they," asked Thuvan Dihn, "and what direction did
they take?"

"They left as they came," replied the officer, "upon their own
flier. For some time after they had departed I watched the vessel's
lights, which vanished finally due north."

"Where north could Matai Shang find an asylum?" asked Thuvan
Dihn of Kulan Tith.

For some moments the Jeddak of Kaol stood with bowed head,
apparently deep in thought. Then a sudden light brightened his
countenance.

"I have it!" he cried. "Only yesterday Matai Shang let drop a hint
of his destination, telling me of a race of people unlike ourselves
who dwell far to the north. They, he said, had always been known to
the Holy Therns and were devout and faithful followers of the ancient
cult. Among them would he find a perpetual haven of refuge, where
no 'lying heretics' might seek him out. It is there that Matai Shang
has gone."

"And in all Kaol there be no flier wherein to follow," I cried.

"Nor nearer than Ptarth," replied Thuvan Dihn.

"Wait!" I exclaimed, "beyond the southern fringe of this great
forest lies the wreck of the thern flier which brought me that far upon
my way. If you will loan me men to fetch it, and artificers to assist
me, I can repair it in two days, Kulan Tith."

I had been more than half suspicious of the seeming sincerity of
the Kaolian jeddak's sudden apostasy, but the alacrity with which he
embraced my suggestion, and the despatch with which a force of
officers and men were placed at my disposal entirely removed the
last vestige of my doubts.

Two days later the flier rested upon the top of the watchtower, ready to depart. Thuvan Dihn and Kulan Tith had offered me the entire resources of two nations—millions of fighting men were at my disposal; but my flier could hold but one other than myself and Woola.

As I stepped aboard her, Thuvan Dihn took his place beside me. I cast a look of questioning surprise upon him. He turned to the highest of his own officers who had accompanied him to Kaol.

"To you I entrust the return of my retinue to Ptarth," he said. "There my son rules ably in my absence. The Prince of Helium shall not go alone into the land of his enemies. I have spoken. Farewell!"

THROUGH THE CARRION CAVES

STRAIGHT TOWARD the north, day and night, our destination compass led us after the fleeing flier upon which it had remained set since I first attuned it after leaving the thern fortress.

Early in the second night we noticed the air becoming perceptibly colder, and from the distance we had come from the equator were assured that we were rapidly approaching the north arctic region.

My knowledge of the efforts that had been made by countless expeditions to explore that unknown land bade me to caution, for never had flier returned who had passed to any considerable distance beyond the mighty ice-barrier that fringes the southern hem of the frigid zone.

What became of them none knew—only that they passed forever out of the sight of man into that grim and mysterious country of the pole.

The distance from the barrier to the pole was no more than a swift flier should cover in a few hours, and so it was assumed that some frightful catastrophe awaited those who reached the "forbidden land," as it had come to be called by the Martians of the outer world.

Thus it was that I went more slowly as we approached the barrier, for it was my intention to move cautiously by day over the ice-pack that I might discover, before I had run into a trap, if there really lay an inhabited country at the north pole, for there only could I imagine a spot where Matai Shang might feel secure from John Carter, Prince of Helium.

We were flying at a snail's pace but a few feet above the ground—literally feeling our way along through the darkness, for both moons had set, and the night was black with the clouds that are to be found only at Mars's two extremities.

Suddenly a towering wall of white rose directly in our path, and though I threw the helm hard over, and reversed our engine, I was too late to avoid collision.

With a sickening crash we struck the high looming obstacle three-quarters on.

The flier reeled half over; the engine stopped; as one, the patched buoyancy tanks burst, and we plunged, headforemost, to the ground twenty feet beneath.

Fortunately none of us was injured, and when we had disentangled ourselves from the wreckage, and the lesser moon had burst again from below the horizon, we found that we were at the foot of a mighty ice-barrier, from which outcropped great patches of the granite hills which hold it from encroaching farther toward the south.

What fate! With the journey all but completed to be thus wrecked upon the wrong side of that precipitous and unscalable wall of rock and ice!

I looked at Thuvan Dihn. He but shook his head dejectedly.

The balance of the night we spent shivering in our inadequate sleeping silks and furs upon the snow that lies at the foot of the ice-barrier.

With daylight my battered spirits regained something of their accustomed hopefulness, though I must admit that there was little enough for them to feed upon.

"What shall we do?" asked Thuvan Dihn. "How may we pass that which is impassable?"

"First we must disprove its impassability," I replied. "Nor shall I admit that it is impassable before I have followed its entire circle and stand again upon this spot, defeated. The sooner we start, the better, for I see no other way, and it will take us more than a month to travel the weary, frigid miles that lie before us."

For five days of cold and suffering and privation we traversed the rough and frozen way which lies at the foot of the ice-barrier. Fierce, fur-bearing creatures attacked us by daylight and by dark. Never for a moment were we safe from the sudden charge of some huge demon of the north.

The apt was our most consistent and dangerous foe.

It is a huge, white-furred creature with six limbs, four of which, short and heavy, carry it swiftly over the snow and ice; while the other two, growing forward from its shoulders on either side of its long, powerful neck, terminate in white, hairless hands, with which it seizes and holds its prey.

Its head and mouth are more similar in appearance to those of a hippopotamus than to any other earthly animal, except that from the sides of the lower jawbone two mighty horns curve slightly downward toward the front.

Its two huge eyes inspired my greatest curiosity. They extend in two vast, oval patches from the center of the top of the cranium down either side of the head to below the roots of the horns, so that these weapons really grow out from the lower part of the eyes, which are composed of several thousand ocelli each.

This eye structure seemed remarkable in a beast whose haunts were upon a glaring field of ice and snow, and though I found upon minute examination of several that we killed that each ocellus is furnished with its own lid, and that the animal can at will close as many of the facets of his huge eyes as he chooses, yet I was positive that nature had thus equipped him because much of his life was to be spent in dark, subterranean recesses.

Shortly after this we came upon the hugest apt that we had seen. The creature stood fully eight feet at the shoulder, and was so sleek and clean and glossy that I could have sworn that he had but recently been groomed.

He stood head-on eyeing us as we approached him, for we had found it a waste of time to attempt to escape the perpetual bestial rage which seems to possess these demon creatures, who rove the dismal north attacking every living thing that comes within the scope of their far-seeing eyes.

Even when their bellies are full and they can eat no more, they kill purely for the pleasure which they derive from taking life, and so when this particular apt failed to charge us, and instead wheeled and trotted away as we neared him, I should have been greatly surprised had I not chanced to glimpse the sheen of a golden collar about its neck.

Thuvan Dihn saw it, too, and it carried the same message of hope to us both. Only man could have placed that collar there, and as no race of Martians of which we knew aught ever had attempted to domesticate the ferocious apt, he must belong to a people of the north of whose very existence we were ignorant—possibly to the fabled yellow men of Barsoom; that once powerful race which was supposed to be extinct, though sometimes, by theorists, thought still to exist in the frozen north.

Simultaneously we started upon the trail of the great beast. Woola was quickly made to understand our desires, so that it was unnecessary to attempt to keep in sight of the animal whose swift flight over the rough ground soon put him beyond our vision.

For the better part of two hours the trail paralleled the barrier, and then suddenly turned toward it through the roughest and seemingly most impassable country I ever had beheld.

Enormous granite boulders blocked the way on every hand; deep rifts in the ice threatened to engulf us at the least misstep; and from the north a slight breeze wafted to our nostrils an unspeakable stench that almost choked us.

For another two hours we were occupied in traversing a few hundred yards to the foot of the barrier.

Then, turning about the corner of a wall-like outcropping of granite, we came upon a smooth area of two or three acres before the base of the towering pile of ice and rock that had baffled us for days, and before us beheld the dark and cavernous mouth of a cave.

From this repelling portal the horrid stench was emanating, and as Thuvan Dihn espied the place he halted with an exclamation of profound astonishment.

"By all my ancestors!" he ejaculated. "That I should have lived to witness the reality of the fabled Carrion Caves! If these indeed be they we have found a way beyond the ice-barrier.

"The ancient chronicles of the first historians of Barsoom—so ancient that we have for ages considered them mythology—record the passing of the yellow men from the ravages of the green hordes that overran Barsoom as the drying up of the great oceans drove the dominant races from their strongholds.

"They tell of the wanderings of the remnants of this once powerful race, harassed at every step, until at last they found a way through the ice-barrier of the north to a fertile valley at the pole.

"At the opening to the subterranean passage that led to their haven of refuge a mighty battle was fought in which the yellow men were victorious, and within the caves that gave ingress to their new home they piled the bodies of the dead, both yellow and green, that the stench might warn away their enemies from further pursuit.

"And ever since that long-gone day have the dead of this fabled land been carried to the Carrion Caves, that in death and decay they might serve their country and warn away invading enemies. Here, too, is brought, so the fable runs, all the waste stuff of the nation— everything that is subject to rot, and that can add to the foul stench that assails our nostrils.

"And death lurks at every step among rotting dead, for here the fierce apts lair, adding to the putrid accumulation with the fragments of their own prey which they cannot devour. It is a horrid avenue to our goal, but it is the only one."

"You are sure, then, that we have found the way to the land of the yellow men?" I cried.

"As sure as may be," he replied; "having only ancient legend to support my belief. But see how closely, so far, each detail tallies with the world-old story of the hegira of the yellow race. Yes, I am sure that we have discovered the way to their ancient hiding place."

"If it be true, and let us pray that such may be the case," I said, "then here may we solve the mystery of the disappearance of Tardos Mors, Jeddak of Helium, and Mors Kajak, his son, for no other spot upon Barsoom has remained unexplored by the many expeditions and the countless spies that have been searching for them for nearly two years. The last word that came from them was that they sought Carthoris, my own brave son, beyond the ice-barrier."

As we talked we had been approaching the entrance to the cave, and as we crossed the threshold I ceased to wonder that the ancient green enemies of the yellow men had been halted by the horrors of that awful way.

The bones of dead men lay man high upon the broad floor of the first cave, and over all was a putrid mush of decaying flesh, through which the apts had beaten a hideous trail toward the entrance to the second cave beyond.

The roof of this first apartment was low, like all that we traversed subsequently, so that the foul odors were confined and condensed to such an extent that they seemed to possess tangible substance. One was almost tempted to draw his short-sword and hew his way through in search of pure air beyond.

"Can man breathe this polluted air and live?" asked Thuvan Dihn, choking.

"Not for long, I imagine," I replied; "so let us make haste. I will go first, and you bring up the rear, with Woola between. Come," and with the words I dashed forward, across the fetid mass of putrefaction.

It was not until we had passed through seven caves of different sizes and varying but little in the power and quality of their stenches that we met with any physical opposition. Then, within the eighth cave, we came upon a lair of apts.

A full score of the mighty beasts were disposed about the chamber. Some were sleeping, while others tore at the fresh-killed carcasses of new-brought prey, or fought among themselves in their love-making.

Here in the dim light of their subterranean home the value of their great eyes was apparent, for these inner caves are shrouded in perpetual gloom that is but little less than utter darkness.

To attempt to pass through the midst of that fierce herd seemed, even to me, the height of folly, and so I proposed to Thuvan Dihn that he return to the outer world with Woola, that the two might find their way to civilization and come again with a sufficient force to overcome not only the apts, but any further obstacles that might lie between us and our goal.

"In the meantime," I continued, "I may discover some means of winning my way alone to the land of the yellow men, but if I am unsuccessful one life only will have been sacrificed. Should we all go on and perish, there will be none to guide a succoring party to Dejah Thoris and your daughter."

"I shall not return and leave you here alone, John Carter," replied Thuvan Dihn. "Whether you go on to victory or death, the Jeddak of Ptarth remains at your side. I have spoken."

I knew from his tone that it were useless to attempt to argue the question, and so I compromised by sending Woola back with a hastily penned note enclosed in a small metal case and fastened about his neck. I commanded the faithful creature to seek Carthoris at Helium, and though half a world and countless dangers lay between I knew that if the thing could be done Woola would do it.

Equipped as he was by nature with marvelous speed and endurance, and with frightful ferocity that made him a match for any single enemy of the way, his keen intelligence and wondrous instinct should easily furnish all else that was needed for the successful accomplishment of his mission.

It was with evident reluctance that the great beast turned to leave me in compliance with my command, and ere he had gone I could not resist the inclination to throw my arms about his great neck in a parting hug. He rubbed his cheek against mine in a final caress, and a moment later was speeding through the Carrion Caves toward the outer world.

In my note to Carthoris I had given explicit directions for locating the Carrion Caves, impressing upon him the necessity for making entrance to the country beyond through this avenue, and not to attempt under any circumstances to cross the ice-barrier with a fleet. I told him that what lay beyond the eighth cave I could not even guess; but I was sure that somewhere upon the other side of the ice-barrier his mother lay in the power of Matai Shang, and that possibly his grandfather and great-grandfather as well, if they lived.

Further, I advised him to call upon Kulan Tith and the son of Thuvan Dihn for warriors and ships that the expedition might be sufficiently strong to insure success at the first blow.

"And," I concluded, "if there be time bring Tars Tarkas with you, for if I live until you reach me I can think of few greater pleasures than to fight once more, shoulder to shoulder, with my old friend."

When Woola had left us Thuvan Dihn and I, hiding in the seventh cave, discussed and discarded many plans for crossing the eighth chamber. From where we stood we saw that the fighting among the apts was growing less, and that many that had been feeding had ceased and lain down to sleep.

Presently it became apparent that in a short time all the ferocious monsters might be peacefully slumbering, and thus a hazardous opportunity be presented to us to cross through their lair.

One by one the remaining brutes stretched themselves upon the bubbling decomposition that covered the mass of bones upon the floor of their den, until but a single apt remained awake. This huge fellow roamed restlessly about, nosing among his companions and the abhorrent litter of the cave.

Occasionally he would stop to peer intently toward first one of the exits from the chamber and then the other. His whole demeanor was as of one who acts as sentry.

We were at last forced to the belief that he would not sleep while the other occupants of the lair slept, and so cast about in our minds for some scheme whereby we might trick him. Finally I suggested a plan to Thuvan Dihn, and as it seemed as good as any that we had discussed we decided to put it to the test.

To this end Thuvan Dihn placed himself close against the cave's wall, beside the entrance to the eighth chamber, while I deliberately showed myself to the guardian apt as he looked toward our retreat.

Then I sprang to the opposite side of the entrance, flattening my body close to the wall.

Without a sound the great beast moved rapidly toward the seventh cave to see what manner of intruder had thus rashly penetrated so far within the precincts of his habitation.

As he poked his head through the narrow aperture that connects the two caves a heavy long-sword was awaiting him upon either hand, and before he had an opportunity to emit even a single growl his severed head rolled at our feet.

Quickly we glanced into the eighth chamber—not an apt had moved. Crawling over the carcass of the huge beast that blocked the doorway Thuvan Dihn and I cautiously entered the forbidding and dangerous den.

Like snails we wound our silent and careful way among the huge, recumbent forms. The only sound above our breathing was the sucking noise of our feet as we lifted them from the ooze of decaying flesh through which we crept.

Halfway across the chamber and one of the mighty beasts directly before me moved restlessly at the very instant that my foot was poised above his head, over which I must step.

Breathlessly I waited, balancing upon one foot, for I did not dare move a muscle. In my right hand was my keen short-sword, the point hovering an inch above the thick fur beneath which beat the savage heart.

Finally the apt relaxed, sighing, as with the passing of a bad dream, and resumed the regular respiration of deep slumber. I planted my raised foot beyond the fierce head and an instant later had stepped over the beast.

Thuvan Dihn followed directly after me, and another moment found us at the further door, undetected.

The Carrion Caves consist of a series of twenty-seven connecting chambers, and present the appearance of having been eroded by running water in some far-gone age when a mighty river found its way to the south through this single breach in the barrier of rock and ice that hems the country of the pole.

Thuvan Dihn and I traversed the remaining nineteen caverns without adventure or mishap.

We were afterward to learn that but once a month is it possible to find all the apts of the Carrion Caves in a single chamber.

At other times they roam singly or in pairs in and out of the caves, so that it would have been practically impossible for two men to have passed through the entire twenty-seven chambers without encountering an apt in nearly every one of them. Once a month they sleep for a full day, and it was our good fortune to stumble by accident upon one of these occasions.

Beyond the last cave we emerged into a desolate country of snow and ice, but found a well-marked trail leading north. The way was boulder-strewn, as had been that south of the barrier, so that we could see but a short distance ahead of us at any time.

After a couple of hours we passed round a huge boulder to come to a steep declivity leading down into a valley.

Directly before us we saw a half dozen men—fierce, black-bearded fellows, with skins the color of a ripe lemon.

"The yellow men of Barsoom!" ejaculated Thuvan Dihn, as though even now that he saw them he found it scarce possible to believe that the very race we expected to find hidden in this remote and inaccessible land did really exist.

We withdrew behind an adjacent boulder to watch the actions of the little party, which stood huddled at the foot of another huge rock, their backs toward us.

One of them was peering round the edge of the granite mass as though watching one who approached from the opposite side.

Presently the object of his scrutiny came within the range of my vision and I saw that it was another yellow man. All were clothed in magnificent furs—the six in the black and yellow striped hide of the orluk, while he who approached alone was resplendent in the pure white skin of an apt.

The yellow men were armed with two swords, and a short javelin was slung across the back of each, while from their left arms hung cuplike shields no larger than a dinner plate, the concave sides of which turned outward toward an antagonist.

They seemed puny and futile implements of safety against an even ordinary swordsman, but I was later to see the purpose of them and with what wondrous dexterity the yellow men manipulate them.

One of the swords which each of the warriors carried caught my immediate attention. I call it a sword, but really it was a sharp-edged blade with a complete hook at the far end.

The other sword was of about the same length as the hooked in-strument, and somewhere between that of my long-sword and my short-sword. It was straight and two-edged. In addition to the weapons I have innumerated each man carried a dagger in his harness.

As the white-furred one approached, the six grasped their swords more firmly—the hooked instrument in the left hand, the straight sword in the right, while above the left wrist the small shield was held rigid upon a metal bracelet.

As the lone warrior came opposite them the six rushed out upon him with fiendish yells that resembled nothing more closely than the savage war cry of the Apaches of the South-west.

Instantly the attacked drew both his swords, and as the six fell upon him I witnessed as pretty fighting as one might care to see.

With their sharp hooks the combatants attempted to take hold of an adversary, but like lightning the cupshaped shield would spring before the darting weapon and into its hollow the hook would plunge.

Once the lone warrior caught an antagonist in the side with his hook, and drawing him close ran his sword through him.

But the odds were too unequal, and, though he who fought alone was by far the best and bravest of them all, I saw that it was but a question of time before the remaining five would find an opening through his marvelous guard and bring him down.

Now my sympathies have ever been with the weaker side of an argument, and though I knew nothing of the cause of the trouble I could not stand idly by and see a brave man butchered by superior numbers.

As a matter of fact I presume I gave little attention to seeking an excuse, for I love a good fight too well to need any other reason for joining in when one is afoot.

So it was that before Thuvan Dihn knew what I was about he saw me standing by the side of the white-clad yellow man, battling like mad with his five adversaries.

WITH THE YELLOW MEN

THUVAN DIHN was not long in joining me; and, though we found the hooked weapon a strange and savage thing with which to deal, the three of us soon despatched the five black-bearded warriors who opposed us.

When the battle was over our new acquaintance turned to me, and removing the shield from his wrist, held it out. I did not know the significance of his act, but judged that it was but a form of expressing his gratitude to me.

I afterward learned that it symbolized the offering of a man's life in return for some great favor done him; and my act of refusing, which I had immediately done, was what was expected of me.

"Then accept from Talu, Prince of Marentina," said the yellow man, "this token of my gratitude," and reaching beneath one of his wide sleeves he withdrew a bracelet and placed it upon my arm. He then went through the same ceremony with Thuvan Dihn.

Next he asked our names, and from what land we hailed. He seemed quite familiar with the geography of the outerworld, and when I said I was from Helium he raised his brows.

"Ah," he said, "you seek your ruler and his company?"

"Know you of them?" I asked.

"But little more than that they were captured by my uncle, Salensus Oll, Jeddak of Jeddaks, Ruler of Okar, land of the yellow men of Barsoom. As to their fate I know nothing, for I am at war with my uncle, who would crush my power in the principality of Marentina.

"These from whom you have just saved me are warriors he has sent out to find and slay me, for they know that often I come alone to hunt and kill the sacred apt which Salensus Oll so much reveres. It is partly because I hate his religion that Salensus Oll hates me; but mostly does he fear my growing power and the great faction which has arisen throughout Okar that would be glad to see me ruler of Okar and Jeddak of Jeddaks in his place.

"He is a cruel and tyrannous master whom all hate, and were it not for the great fear they have of him I could raise an army overnight that would wipe out the few that might remain loyal to him. My own people are faithful to me, and the little valley of Marentina has paid no tribute to the court of Salensus Oll for a year.

"Nor can he force us, for a dozen men may hold the narrow way to Marentina against a million. But now, as to thine own affairs. How may I aid you? My palace is at your disposal, if you wish to honor me by coming to Marentina."

"When our work is done we shall be glad to accept your invitation," I replied. "But now you can assist us most by directing us to the court of Salensus Oll, and suggesting some means by which we may gain admission to the city and the palace, or whatever other place we find our friends to be confined."

Talu gazed ruefully at our smooth faces and at Thuvan Dihn's red skin and my white one.

"First you must come to Marentina," he said, "for a great change must be wrought in your appearance before you can hope to enter any city in Okar. You must have yellow faces and black beards, and your apparel and trappings must be those least likely to arouse suspicion. In my palace is one who can make you appear as truly yellow men as does Salensus Oll himself."

His counsel seemed wise; and as there was apparently no other way to insure a successful entry to Kadabra, the capital city of Okar, we set out with Talu, Prince of Marentina, for his little, rock-bound country.

The way was over some of the worst traveling I have ever seen, and I do not wonder that in this land where there are neither thoats nor fliers that Marentina is in little fear of invasion; but at last we reached our destination, the first view of which I had from a slight elevation a half-mile from the city.

Nestled in a deep valley lay a city of Martian concrete, whose every street and plaza and open space was roofed with glass. All about lay snow and ice, but there was none upon the rounded, domelike, crystal covering that enveloped the whole city.

Then I saw how these people combatted the rigors of the arctic, and lived in luxury and comfort in the midst of a land of perpetual ice. Their cities were veritable hothouses, and when I had come within this one my respect and admiration for the scientific and engineering skill of this buried nation was unbounded.

The moment we entered the city Talu threw off his outer garments of fur, as did we, and I saw that his apparel differed but little from that of the red races of Barsoom. Except for his leathern harness, covered thick with jewels and metal, he was naked, nor could one have comfortably worn apparel in that warm and humid atmosphere.

For three days we remained the guests of Prince Talu, and during that time he showered upon us every attention and courtesy within his power. He showed us all that was of interest in his great city.

The Marentina atmosphere plant will maintain life indefinitely in the cities of the north pole after all life upon the balance of dying Mars is extinct through the failure of the air supply, should the great central plant again cease functioning as it did upon that memorable occasion that gave me the opportunity of restoring life and happiness to the strange world that I had already learned to love so well.

He showed us the heating system that stores the sun's rays in great reservoirs beneath the city, and how little is necessary to maintain the perpetual summer heat of the glorious garden spot within this arctic paradise.

Broad avenues of sod sewn with the seed of the ocher vegetation of the dead sea bottoms carried the noiseless traffic of light and airy ground fliers that are the only form of artificial transportation used north of the gigantic ice-barrier.

The broad tires of these unique fliers are but rubber-like gas bags filled with the eighth Barsoomian ray, or ray of propulsion—that remarkable discovery of the Martians that has made possible the great fleets of mighty airships that render the red man of the outer world supreme. It is this ray which propels the inherent or reflected light of the planet off into space, and when confined gives to the Martian craft their airy buoyancy.

The ground fliers of Marentina contain just sufficient buoyancy in their automobile-like wheels to give the cars traction for steering purposes; and though the hind wheels are geared to the engine, and aid in driving the machine, the bulk of this work is carried by a small propeller at the stern.

I know of no more delightful sensation than that of riding in one of these luxuriously appointed cars which skim, light and airy as feathers, along the soft, mossy avenues of Marentina. They move with absolute noiselessness between borders of crimson sward and beneath arching trees gorgeous with the wondrous blooms that mark so many of the highly cultivated varieties of Barsoomian vegetation.

By the end of the third day the court barber—I can think of no other earthly appellation by which to describe him—had wrought so remarkable a transformation in both Thuvan Dihn and myself that our own wives would never have known us. Our skins were of the same lemon color as his own, and great, black beards and mustaches had been deftly affixed to our smooth faces. The trappings of warriors of Okar aided in the deception; and for wear beyond the hothouse cities we each had suits of the black- and yellow-striped orluk.

Talu gave us careful directions for the journey to Kadabra, the capital city of the Okar nation, which is the racial name of the yellow men. This good friend even accompanied us part way, and then, promising to aid us in any way that he found possible, bade us adieu.

On parting he slipped upon my finger a curiously wrought ring set with a dead-black, lusterless stone, which appeared more like a bit of bituminous coal than the priceless Barsoomian gem which in reality it is.

"There had been but three others cut from the mother stone," he said, "which is in my possession. These three are worn by nobles high in my confidence, all of whom have been sent on secret missions to the court of Salensus Oll.

"Should you come within fifty feet of any of these three you will feel a rapid, pricking sensation in the finger upon which you wear this ring. He who wears one of its mates will experience the same feeling; it is caused by an electrical action that takes place the moment two of these gems cut from the same mother stone come within the radius of each other's power. By it you will know that a friend is at hand upon whom you may depend for assistance in time of need.

"Should another wearer of one of these gems call upon you for aid do not deny him, and should death threaten you swallow the ring rather than let it fall into the hands of enemies. Guard it with your life, John Carter, for some day it may mean more than life to you."

With this parting admonition our good friend turned back toward Marentina, and we set our faces in the direction of the city of Kadabra and the court of Salensus Oll, Jeddak of Jeddaks.

That very evening we came within sight of the walled and glass-roofed city of Kadabra. It lies in a low depression near the pole, surrounded by rocky, snow-clad hills. From the pass through which we entered the valley we had a splendid view of this great city of the north. Its crystal domes sparkled in the brilliant sunlight gleaming above the frost-covered outer wall that circles the entire one hundred miles of its circumference.

At regular intervals great gates give entrance to the city; but even at the distance from which we looked upon the massive pile we could see that all were closed, and, in accordance with Talu's suggestion, we deferred attempting to enter the city until the following morning.

As he had said, we found numerous caves in the hillsides about us, and into one of these we crept for the night. Our warm orluk skins kept us perfectly comfortable, and it was only after a most refreshing sleep that we awoke shortly after daylight on the following morning.

Already the city was astir, and from several of the gates we saw parties of yellow men emerging. Following closely each detail of the instructions given us by our good friend of Marentina, we remained concealed for several hours until one party of some half dozen warriors had passed along the trail below our hiding place and entered the hills by way of the pass along which we had come the previous evening.

After giving them time to get well out of sight of our cave, Thuvan Dihn and I crept out and followed them, overtaking them when they were well into the hills.

When we had come almost to them I called aloud to their leader, when the whole party halted and turned toward us. The crucial test had come. Could we but deceive these men the rest would be comparatively easy.

"Kaor!" I cried as I came closer to them.

"Kaor!" responded the officer in charge of the party.

"We be from Illall," I continued, giving the name of the most remote city of Okar, which has little or no intercourse with Kadabra. "Only yesterday we arrived, and this morning the captain of the gate told us that you were setting out to hunt orluks, which is a sport we do not find in our own neighborhood. We have hastened after you to pray that you allow us to accompany you."

The officer was entirely deceived, and graciously permitted us to go with them for the day. The chance guess that they were bound upon an orluk hunt proved correct, and Talu had said that the chances were ten to one that such would be the mission of any party leaving Kadabra by the pass through which we entered the valley, since that way leads directly to the vast plains frequented by this elephantine beast of prey.

In so far as the hunt was concerned, the day was a failure, for we did not see a single orluk; but this proved more than fortunate for us, since the yellow men were so chagrined by their misfortune that they would not enter the city by the same gate by which they had left it in the morning, as it seemed that they had made great boasts to the captain of that gate about their skill at this dangerous sport.

We, therefore, approached Kadabra at a point several miles from that at which the party had quitted it in the morning, and so were relieved of the danger of embarrassing questions and explanations on the part of the gate captain, whom we had said had directed us to this particular hunting party.

We had come quite close to the city when my attention was attracted toward a tall, black shaft that reared its head several hundred feet into the air from what appeared to be a tangled mass of junk or wreckage, now partially snow-covered.

I did not dare venture an inquiry for fear of arousing suspicion by evident ignorance of something which as a yellow man I should have known; but before we reached the city gate I was to learn the purpose of that grim shaft and the meaning of the mighty accumulation beneath it.

We had come almost to the gate when one of the party called to his fellows, at the same time pointing toward the distant southern horizon. Following the direction he indicated, my eyes descried the hull of a large flier approaching rapidly from above the crest of the encircling hills.

"Still other fools who would solve the mysteries of the forbidden north," said the officer, half to himself. "Will they never cease their fatal curiosity?"

"Let us hope not," answered one of the warriors, "for then what should we do for slaves and sport?"

"True; but what stupid beasts they are to continue to come to a region from whence none of them ever has returned."

"Let us tarry and watch the end of this one," suggested one of the men.

The officer looked toward the city.

"The watch has seen him," he said; "we may remain, for we may be needed."

I looked toward the city and saw several hundred warriors issuing from the nearest gate. They moved leisurely, as though there were no need for haste—nor was there, as I was presently to learn.

Then I turned my eyes once more toward the flier. She was moving rapidly toward the city, and when she had come close enough I was surprised to see that her propellers were idle.

Straight for that grim shaft she bore. At the last minute I saw the great blades move to reverse her, yet on she came as though drawn by some mighty, irresistible power.

Intense excitement prevailed upon her deck, where men were running hither and thither, manning the guns and preparing to launch the small, one-man fliers, a fleet of which is part of the equipment of every Martian war vessel. Closer and closer to the black shaft the ship sped. In another instant she must strike, and then I saw the familiar signal flown that sends the lesser boats in a great flock from the deck of the mother ship.

Instantly a hundred tiny fliers rose from her deck, like a swarm of huge dragon flies; but scarcely were they clear of the battleship than the nose of each turned toward the shaft, and they, too, rushed on at frightful speed toward the same now seemingly inevitable end that menaced the larger vessel.

A moment later the collision came. Men were hurled in every direction from the ship's deck, while she, bent and crumpled, took the last, long plunge to the scrap-heap at the shaft's base.

With her fell a shower of her own tiny fliers, for each of them had come in violent collision with the solid shaft.

I noticed that the wrecked fliers scraped down the shaft's side, and that their fall was not as rapid as might have been expected; and then suddenly the secret of the shaft burst upon me, and with it an explanation of the cause that prevented a flier that passed too far across the ice-barrier ever returning.

The shaft was a mighty magnet, and when once a vessel came within the radius of its powerful attraction for the aluminum steel that enters so largely into the construction of all Barsoomian craft, no power on earth could prevent such an end as we had just witnessed.

I afterward learned that the shaft rests directly over the magnetic pole of Mars, but whether this adds in any way to its incalculable power of attraction I do not know. I am a fighting man, not a scientist.

Here, at last, was an explanation of the long absence of Tardos Mors and Mors Kajak. These valiant and intrepid warriors had dared the mysteries and dangers of the frozen north to search for Carthoris, whose long absence had bowed in grief the head of his beautiful mother, Dejah Thoris, Princess of Helium.

The moment that the last of the fliers came to rest at the base of the shaft the black-bearded, yellow warriors swarmed over the mass of wreckage upon which they lay, making prisoners of those who were uninjured and occasionally despatching with a sword-thrust one of the wounded who seemed prone to resent their taunts and insults.

A few of the uninjured red men battled bravely against their cruel foes, but for the most part they seemed too overwhelmed by the horror of the catastrophe that had befallen them to do more than submit supinely to the golden chains with which they were manacled.

When the last of the prisoners had been confined, the party returned to the city, at the gate of which we met a pack of fierce, gold-collared apts, each of which marched between two warriors, who held them with strong chains of the same metal as their collars.

Just beyond the gate the attendants loosened the whole terrible herd, and as they bounded off toward the grim, black shaft I did not

need to ask to know their mission. Had there not been those within
the cruel city of Kadabra who needed succor far worse than the poor
unfortunate dead and dying out there in the cold upon the bent and
broken carcasses of a thousand fliers I could not have restrained my
desire to hasten back and do battle with those horrid creatures that
had been despatched to rend and devour them.

As it was I could but follow the yellow warriors, with bowed head,
and give thanks for the chance that had given Thuvan Dihn and me
such easy ingress to the capital of Salensus Oll.

Once within the gates, we had no difficulty in eluding our friends
of the morning, and presently found ourselves in a Martian hostelry.

IN DURANCE

THE PUBLIC HOUSES of Barsoom, I have found, vary but little. There
is no privacy for other than married couples.

Men without their wives are escorted to a large chamber, the floor
of which is usually of white marble or heavy glass, kept scrupulously
clean. Here are many small, raised platforms for the guest's sleeping
silks and furs, and if he have none of his own clean, fresh ones are
furnished at a nominal charge.

Once a man's belongings have been deposited upon one of these
platforms he is a guest of the house, and that platform his own until
he leaves. No one will disturb or molest his belongings, as there are no
thieves upon Mars.

As assassination is the one thing to be feared, the proprietors of
the hostelries furnish armed guards, who pace back and forth through
the sleeping-rooms day and night. The number of guards and gor-
geousness of their trappings quite usually denote the status of the
hotel.

No meals are served in these houses, but generally a public eating
place adjoins them. Baths are connected with the sleeping chambers,
and each guest is required to bathe daily or depart from the hotel.

Usually on a second or third floor there is a large sleeping-room
for single women guests, but its appointments do not vary materially
from the chamber occupied by men. The guards who watch the

women remain in the corridor outside the sleeping chamber, while female slaves pace back and forth among the sleepers within, ready to notify the warriors should their presence be required.

I was surprised to note that all the guards with the hotel at which we stopped were red men, and on inquiring of one of them I learned that they were slaves purchased by the proprietors of the hotels from the government. The man whose post was past my sleeping platform had been commander of the navy of a great Martian nation; but fate had carried his flagship across the ice-barrier within the radius of power of the magnetic shaft, and now for many tedious years he had been a slave of the yellow men.

He told me that princes, jeds, and even jeddaks of the outer world, were among the menials who served the yellow race; but when I asked him if he had heard of the fate of Mors Kajak or Tardos Mors he shook his head, saying that he never had heard of their being prisoners here, though he was very familiar with the reputations and fame they bore in the outer world.

Neither had he heard any rumor of the coming of the Father of Therns and the black dator of the First Born, but he hastened to explain that he knew little of what took place within the palace. I could see that he wondered not a little that a yellow man should be so inquisitive about certain red prisoners from beyond the ice-barrier, and that I should be so ignorant of customs and conditions among my own race.

In fact, I had forgotten my disguise upon discovering a red man pacing before my sleeping platform; but his growing expression of surprise warned me in time, for I had no mind to reveal my identity to any unless some good could come of it, and I did not see how this poor fellow could serve me yet, though I had it in my mind that later I might be the means of serving him and all the other thousands of prisoners who do the bidding of their stern masters in Kadabra.

Thuvan Dihn and I discussed our plans as we sat together among our sleeping silks and furs that night in the midst of the hundreds of yellow men who occupied the apartment with us. We spoke in low whispers, but, as that is only what courtesy demands in a public sleeping place, we roused no suspicion.

At last, determining that all must be but idle speculation until after we had had a chance to explore the city and attempt to put into execution the plan Talu had suggested, we bade each other good night and turned to sleep.

After breakfasting the following morning we set out to see Kadabra, and as, through the generosity of the prince of Marentina, we were well supplied with the funds current in Okar we purchased a handsome ground flier. Having learned to drive them while in Marentina, we spent a delightful and profitable day exploring the city, and late in the afternoon at the hour Talu told us we would find government officials in their offices we stopped before a magnificent building on the plaza opposite the royal grounds and the palace.

Here we walked boldly in past the armed guard at the door, to be met by a red slave within who asked our wishes.

"Tell Sorav, your master, that two warriors from Illall wish to take service in the palace guard," I said.

Sorav, Talu had told us, was the commander of the forces of the palace, and as men from the further cities of Okar—and especially Illall—were less likely to be tainted with the germ of intrigue which had for years infected the household of Salensus Oll, he was sure that we would be welcomed and few questions asked us.

He had primed us with such general information as he thought would be necessary for us to pass muster before Sorav, after which we would have to undergo a further examination before Salensus Oll that he might determine our physical fitness and our ability as warriors.

The little experience we had had with the strange hooked sword of the yellow man and his cuplike shield made it seem rather unlikely that either of us could pass this final test, but there was the chance that we might be quartered in the palace of Salensus Oll for several days after being accepted by Sorav before the Jeddak of Jeddaks would find time to put us to the final test.

After a wait of several minutes in an ante-chamber we were summoned into the private office of Sorav, where we were courteously greeted by this ferocious-appearing, black-bearded officer. He asked us our names and stations in our own city, and having received replies that were evidently satisfactory to him, he put certain questions to us that Talu had foreseen and prepared us for.

The interview could not have lasted over ten minutes when Sorav summoned an aid whom he instructed to record us properly, and then escort us to the quarters in the palace which are set aside for aspirants to membership in the palace guard.

The aid took us to his own office first, where he measured and weighed and photographed us simultaneously with a machine ingeniously devised for that purpose, five copies being instantly reproduced in five different offices of the government, two of which are located in other cities miles distant. Then he led us through the palace grounds to the main guardroom of the palace, there turning us over to the officer in charge.

This individual again questioned us briefly, and finally despatched a soldier to guide us to our quarters. These we found located upon the second floor of the palace in a semidetached tower at the rear of the edifice.

When we asked our guide why we were quartered so far from the guardroom he replied that the custom of the older members of the guard of picking quarrels with aspirants to try their metal had resulted in so many deaths that it was found difficult to maintain the guard at its full strength while this custom prevailed. Salensus Oll had, therefore, set apart these quarters for aspirants, and here they were securely locked against the danger of attack by members of the guard.

This unwelcome information put a sudden check to all our well-laid plans, for it meant that we should virtually be prisoners in the palace of Salensus Oll until the time that he should see fit to give us the final examination for efficiency.

As it was this interval upon which we had banked to accomplish so much in our search for Dejah Thoris and Thuvia of Ptarth, our chagrin was unbounded when we heard the great lock click behind our guide as he had quitted us after ushering us into the chambers we were to occupy.

With a wry face I turned to Thuvan Dihn. My companion but shook his head disconsolately and walked to one of the windows upon the far side of the apartment.

Scarcely had he gazed beyond them than he called to me in a tone of suppressed excitement and surprise. In an instant I was by his side.

"Look!" said Thuvan Dihn, pointing toward the courtyard below.

As my eyes followed the direction indicated I saw two women pacing back and forth in an enclosed garden.

At the same moment I recognized them—they were Dejah Thoris and Thuvia of Ptarth!

There were they whom I had trailed from one pole to another, the length of a world. Only ten feet of space and a few metal bars separated me from them.

With a cry I attracted their attention, and as Dejah Thoris looked up full into my eyes I made the sign of love that the men of Barsoom make to their women.

To my astonishment and horror her head went high, and as a look of utter contempt touched her finely chiseled features she turned her back full upon me. My body is covered with the scars of a thousand conflicts, but never in all my long life have I suffered such anguish from a wound, for this time the steel of a woman's look had entered my heart.

With a groan I turned away and buried my face in my arms. I heard Thuvan Dihn call aloud to Thuvia, but an instant later his exclamation of surprise betokened that he, too, had been repulsed by his own daughter.

"They will not even listen," he cried to me. "They have put their hands over their ears and walked to the farther end of the garden. Ever heard you of such mad work, John Carter? The two must be bewitched."

Presently I mustered the courage to return to the window, for even though she spurned me I loved her, and could not keep my eyes from feasting upon her divine face and figure, but when she saw me looking she again turned away.

I was at my wit's end to account for her strange actions, and that Thuvia, too, had turned against her father seemed incredible. Could it be that my incomparable princess still clung to the hideous faith from which I had rescued her world? Could it be that she looked upon me with loathing and contempt because I had returned from the Valley Dor, or because I had desecrated the temples and persons of the Holy Therns?

To naught else could I ascribe her strange deportment, yet it seemed far from possible that such could be the case, for the love of Dejah Thoris for John Carter had been a great and wondrous love—far above racial distinctions, creed, or religion.

As I gazed ruefully at the back of her haughty, royal head a gate at the opposite end of the garden opened and a man entered. As he did so he turned and slipped something into the hand of the yellow guardsman beyond the gate, nor was the distance too great that I might not see that money had passed between them.

Instantly I knew that this newcomer had bribed his way within the garden. Then he turned in the direction of the two women, and I saw that he was none other than Thurid, the black dator of the First Born.

He approached quite close to them before he spoke, and as they turned at the sound of his voice I saw Dejah Thoris shrink from him.

There was a nasty leer upon his face as he stepped close to her and spoke again. I could not hear his words, but her answer came clearly.

"The granddaughter of Tardos Mors can always die," she said, "but she could never live at the price you name."

Then I saw the black scoundrel go upon his knees beside her, fairly groveling in the dirt, pleading with her. Only part of what he said came to me, for though he was evidently laboring under the stress of passion and excitement, it was equally apparent that he did not dare raise his voice for fear of detection.

"I would save you from Matai Shang," I heard him say. "You know the fate that awaits you at his hands. Would you not choose me rather than the other?"

"I would choose neither," replied Dejah Thoris, "even were I free to choose, as you know well I am not."

"You *are* free!" he cried. "John Carter, Prince of Helium, is dead."

"I know better than that; but even were he dead, and I must needs choose another mate, it should be a plant man or a great white ape in preference to either Matai Shang or you, black calot," she answered with a sneer of contempt.

Of a sudden the vicious beast lost all control of himself, as with a vile oath he leaped at the slender woman, gripping her tender throat in his brute clutch. Thuvia screamed and sprang to aid her fellow-prisoner, and at the same instant I, too, went mad, and tearing at the bars that spanned my window I ripped them from their sockets as they had been but copper wire.

Hurling myself through the aperture I reached the garden, but a hundred feet from where the black was choking the life from my Dejah Thoris, and with a single great bound I was upon him. I spoke no word as I tore his defiling fingers from that beautiful throat, nor did I utter a sound as I hurled him twenty feet from me.

Foaming with rage, Thurid regained his feet and charged me like a mad bull.

"Yellow man," he shrieked, "you knew not upon whom you had laid your vile hands, but ere I am done with you, you will know well what it means to offend the person of a First Born."

Then he was upon me, reaching for my throat, and precisely as I had done that day in the courtyard of the Temple of Issus I did here in the garden of the palace of Salensus Oll. I ducked beneath his outstretched arms, and as he lunged past me I planted a terrific right upon the side of his jaw.

Just as he had done upon that other occasion he did now. Like a top he spun round, his knees gave beneath him, and he crumpled to the ground at my feet. Then I heard a voice behind me.

It was the deep voice of authority that marks the ruler of men, and when I turned to face the resplendent figure of a giant yellow man I did not need to ask to know that it was Salensus Oll. At his right stood Matai Shang, and behind them a score of guardsmen.

"Who are you," he cried, "and what means this intrusion within the precincts of the women's garden? I do not recall your face. How came you here?"

But for his last words I should have forgotten my disguise entirely and told him outright that I was John Carter, Prince of Helium; but his question recalled me to myself. I pointed to the dislodged bars of the window above.

"I am an aspirant to membership in the palace guard," I said, "and from yonder window in the tower where I was confined awaiting the final test for fitness I saw this brute attack the—this woman. I could not stand idly by, O Jeddak, and see this thing done within the very palace grounds, and yet feel that I was fit to serve and guard your royal person."

I had evidently made an impression upon the ruler of Okar by my fair words, and when he had turned to Dejah Thoris and Thuvia of Ptarth, and both had corroborated my statements it began to look pretty dark for Thurid.

I saw the ugly gleam in Matai Shang's evil eyes as Dejah Thoris narrated all that had passed between Thurid and herself, and when she came to that part which dealt with my interference with the dator of the First Born her gratitude was quite apparent, though I could see by her eyes that something puzzled her strangely.

I did not wonder at her attitude toward me while others were present; but that she should have denied me while she and Thuvia were the only occupants of the garden still cut me sorely.

As the examination proceeded I cast a glance at Thurid and startled him looking wide-eyed and wonderingly at me, and then of a sudden he laughed full in my face.

A moment later Salensus Oll turned toward the black.

"What have you to say in explanation of these charges?" he asked in a deep and terrible voice. "Dare you aspire to one whom the Father of Therns has chosen—one who might even be a fit mate for the Jeddak of Jeddaks himself?"

And then the black-bearded tyrant turned and cast a sudden greedy look upon Dejah Thoris, as though with the words a new thought and a new desire had sprung up within his mind and breast.

Thurid had been about to reply and, with a malicious grin upon his face, was pointing an accusing finger at me, when Salensus Oll's words and the expression of his face cut him short.

A cunning look crept into his eyes, and I knew from the expression of his face that his next words were not the ones he had intended to speak.

"O Mightiest of Jeddaks," he said, "the man and the women do not speak the truth. The fellow had come into the garden to assist them to escape. I was beyond and overheard their conversation, and when I entered, the woman screamed and the man sprang upon me and would have killed me.

"What know you of this man? He is a stranger to you, and I dare say that you will find him an enemy and a spy. Let him be put on trial, Salensus Oll, rather than your friend and guest, Thurid, Dator of the First Born."

Salensus Oll looked puzzled. He turned again and looked upon Dejah Thoris, and then Thurid stepped quite close to him and whispered something in his ear—what, I know not.

Presently the yellow ruler turned to one of his officers.

"See that this man be securely confined until we have time to go deeper into this affair," he commanded, "and as bars alone seem inadequate to restrain him, let chains be added."

Then he turned and left the garden, taking Dejah Thoris with him—his hand upon her shoulder. Thurid and Matai Shang went also, and as they reached the gateway the black turned and laughed again aloud in my face.

What could be the meaning of his sudden change toward me? Could he suspect my true identity? It must be that, and the thing that had betrayed me was the trick and blow that had laid him low for the second time.

As the guards dragged me away my heart was very sad and bitter indeed, for now to the two relentless enemies that had hounded her

for so long another and a more powerful one had been added, for
I would have been but a fool had I not recognized the sudden love
for Dejah Thoris that had just been born in the terrible breast of
Salensus Oll, Jeddak of Jeddaks, ruler of Okar.

THE PIT OF PLENTY

I DID NOT languish long within the prison of Salensus Oll. During
the short time that I lay there, fettered with chains of gold, I often
wondered as to the fate of Thuvan Dihn, Jeddak of Ptarth.

My brave companion had followed me into the garden as I attacked
Thurid, and when Salensus Oll had left with Dejah Thoris and the
others, leaving Thuvia of Ptarth behind, he, too, had remained in
the garden with his daughter, apparently unnoticed, for he was
appareled similarly to the guards.

The last I had seen of him he stood waiting for the warriors who
escorted me to close the gate behind them, that he might be alone
with Thuvia. Could it be possible that they had escaped? I doubted
it, and yet with all my heart I hoped that it might be true.

The third day of my incarceration brought a dozen warriors to
escort me to the audience chamber, where Salensus Oll himself was
to try me. A great number of nobles crowded the room, and among
them I saw Thurid, but Matai Shang was not there.

Dejah Thoris, as radiantly beautiful as ever, sat upon a small
throne beside Salensus Oll. The expression of sad hopelessness upon
her dear face cut deep into my heart.

Her position beside the Jeddak of Jeddaks boded ill for her and
me, and on the instant that I saw her there, there sprang to my mind
the firm intention never to leave that chamber alive if I must leave
her in the clutches of this powerful tyrant.

I had killed better men than Salensus Oll, and killed them with
my bare hands, and now I swore to myself that I should kill him if
I found that the only way to save the Princess of Helium. That it
would mean almost instant death for me I cared not, except that it
would remove me from further efforts in behalf of Dejah Thoris,
and for this reason alone I would have chosen another way, for even

though I should kill Salensus Oll that act would not restore my beloved wife to her own people. I determined to wait the final outcome
of the trial, that I might learn all that I could of the Okarian ruler's
intentions, and then act accordingly.

Scarcely had I come before him than Salensus Oll summoned
Thurid also.

"Dator Thurid," he said, "you have made a strange request of
me; but, in accordance with your wishes and your promise that it
will result only to my interests, I have decided to accede.

"You tell me that a certain announcement will be the means of
convicting this prisoner and, at the same time, open the way to the
gratification of my dearest wish."

Thurid nodded.

"Then shall I make the announcement here before all my nobles,"
continued Salensus Oll. "For a year no queen has sat upon the throne
beside me, and now it suits me to take to wife one who is reputed
the most beautiful woman upon Barsoom. A statement which none
may truthfully deny.

"Nobles of Okar, unsheath your swords and do homage to Dejah
Thoris, Princess of Helium and future Queen of Okar, for at the
end of the allotted ten days she shall become the wife of Salensus Oll."

As the nobles drew their blades and lifted them on high, in
accordance with the ancient custom of Okar when a jeddak
announces his intention to wed, Dejah Thoris sprang to her feet
and, raising her hand aloft, cried in a loud voice that they desist.

"I may not be the wife of Salensus Oll," she pleaded, "for already
I be a wife and mother. John Carter, Prince of Helium, still lives. I
know it to be true, for I overheard Matai Shang tell his daughter
Phaidor that he had seen him in Kaor, at the court of Kulan Tith,
Jeddak. A jeddak does not wed a married woman, nor will Salensus
Oll thus violate the bonds of matrimony."

Salensus Oll turned upon Thurid with an ugly look.

"Is this the surprise you held in store for me?" he cried. "You
assured me that no obstacle which might not be easily overcome
stood between me and this woman, and now I find that the one in-
superable obstacle intervenes. What mean you, man? What have you
to say?"

"And should I deliver John Carter into your hands, Salensus Oll,
would you not feel that I had more than satisfied the promise that
I made you?" answered Thurid.

"Talk not like a fool," cried the enraged jeddak. "I am no child to be thus played with."

"I am talking only as a man who knows," replied Thurid. "Knows that he can do all that he claims."

"Then turn John Carter over to me within ten days or yourself suffer the end that I should mete out to him were he in my power!" snapped the Jeddak of Jeddaks, with an ugly scowl.

"You need not wait ten days, Salensus Oll," replied Thurid; and then, turning suddenly upon me as he extended a pointing finger, he cried: "There stands John Carter, Prince of Helium!"

"Fool!" shrieked Salensus Oll. "Fool! John Carter is a white man. This fellow be as yellow as myself. John Carter's face is smooth—Matai Shang has described him to me. This prisoner has a beard and mustache as large and black as any in Okar. Quick, guardsmen, to the pits with the black maniac who wishes to throw his life away for a poor joke upon your ruler!"

"Hold!" cried Thurid, and springing forward before I could guess his intention, he had grasped my beard and ripped the whole false fabric from my face and head, revealing my smooth, tanned skin beneath and my close-cropped black hair.

Instantly pandemonium reigned in the audience chamber of Salensus Oll. Warriors pressed forward with drawn blades, thinking that I might be contemplating the assassination of the Jeddak of Jeddaks; while others, out of curiosity to see one whose name was familiar from pole to pole, crowded behind their fellows.

As my identity was revealed I saw Dejah Thoris spring to her feet—amazement writ large upon her face—and then through that jam of armed men she forced her way before any could prevent. A moment only and she was before me with outstretched arms and eyes filled with the light of her great love.

"John Carter! John Carter!" she cried as I folded her to my breast, and then of a sudden I knew why she had denied me in the garden beneath the tower.

What a fool I had been! Expecting that she would penetrate the marvelous disguise that had been wrought for me by the barber of Marentina! She had not known me, that was all; and when she saw the sign of love from a stranger she was offended and righteously indignant. Indeed, but I had been a fool.

"And it was you," she cried, "who spoke to me from the tower!

How could I dream that my beloved Virginian lay behind that fierce beard and that yellow skin?"

She had been wont to call me her Virginian as a term of endearment, for she knew that I loved the sound of that beautiful name, made a thousand times more beautiful and hallowed by her dear lips, and as I heard it again after all those long years my eyes became dimmed with tears and my voice choked with emotion.

But an instant did I crush that dear form to me ere Salensus Oll, trembling with rage and jealousy, shouldered his way to us.

"Seize the man," he cried to his warriors, and a hundred ruthless hands tore us apart.

Well it was for the nobles of the court of Okar that John Carter had been disarmed. As it was, a dozen of them felt the weight of my clenched fists, and I had fought my way half up the steps before the throne to which Salensus Oll had carried Dejah Thoris ere ever they could stop me.

Then I went down, fighting, beneath a half-hundred warriors; but before they had battered me into unconsciousness I heard that from the lips of Dejah Thoris that made all my suffering well worth while.

Standing there beside the great tyrant, who clutched her by the arm, she pointed to where I fought alone against such awful odds.

"Think you, Salensus Oll, that the wife of such as he is," she cried, "would ever dishonor his memory, were he a thousand times dead, by mating with a lesser mortal? Lives there upon any world such another as John Carter, Prince of Helium? Lives there another man who could fight his way back and forth across a warlike planet, facing savage beasts and hordes of savage men, for the love of a woman?

"I, Dejah Thoris, Princess of Helium, am his. He fought for me and won me. If you be a brave man you will honor the bravery that is his, and you will not kill him. Make him a slave if you will, Salensus Oll; but spare his life. I would rather be a slave with such as he than be Queen of Okar."

"Neither slave nor queen dictates to Salensus Oll," replied the Jeddak of Jeddaks. "John Carter shall die a natural death in the Pit of Plenty, and the day he dies Dejah Thoris shall become my queen."

I did not hear her reply, for it was then that a blow upon my head brought unconsciousness, and when I recovered my senses only a handful of guardsmen remained in the audience chamber with me.

*"A dozen of them felt the weight of my clenched fists, and then I
went down, fighting, beneath a half-hundred warriors . . ."*

As I opened my eyes they goaded me with the points of their swords and bade me rise.

Then they led me through long corridors to a court far toward the center of the palace.

In the center of the court was a deep pit, near the edge of which stood half a dozen other guardsmen, awaiting me. One of them carried a long rope in his hands, which he commenced to make ready as we approached.

We had come to within fifty feet of these men when I felt a sudden strange and rapid pricking sensation in one of my fingers.

For a moment I was nonplused by the odd feeling, and then there came to me recollection of that which in the stress of my adventure I had entirely forgotten—the gift ring of Prince Talu of Marentina.

Instantly I looked toward the group we were nearing, and at the same time raising my left hand to my forehead, that the ring might be visible to one who sought it. Simultaneously one of the waiting warriors raised his left hand, ostensibly to brush back his hair, and upon one of his fingers I saw the duplicate of my own ring.

A quick look of intelligence passed between us, after which I kept my eyes turned away from the warrior and did not look at him again, for fear that I might arouse the suspicion of the Okarians.

When we reached the edge of the pit I saw that it was very deep, and presently I realized I was soon to judge just how far it extended below the surface of the court, for he who held the rope passed it about my body in such a way that it could be released from above at any time; and then, as all the warriors grasped it, he pushed me forward, and I fell into the yawning abyss.

After the first jerk as I reached the end of the rope that had been paid out to let me fall below the pit's edge they lowered me quickly but smoothly. The moment before the plunge, while two or three of the men had been assisting in adjusting the rope about me, one of them had brought his mouth close to my cheek, and in the brief interval before I was cast into the forbidding hole he breathed a single word into my ear:

"Courage!"

The pit, which my imagination had pictured as bottomless, proved to be not more than a hundred feet in depth; but as its walls were smoothly polished it might as well have been a thousand feet, for I could never hope to escape without outside assistance.

For a day I was left in darkness; and then, quite suddenly, a brilliant light illumined my strange cell. I was reasonably hungry and thirsty by this time, not having tasted food or drink since the day prior to my incarceration.

To my amazement I found the sides of the pit, that I had thought smooth, lined with shelves, upon which were the most delicious viands and liquid refreshments that Okar afforded.

With an exclamation of delight I sprang forward to partake of some of the welcome food, but ere ever I reached it the light was extinguished, and, though I groped my way about the chamber, my hands came in contact with nothing beside the smooth, hard wall that I had felt on my first examination of my prison.

Immediately the pangs of hunger and thirst began to assail me. Where before I had had but a mild craving for food and drink, I now actually suffered for want of it, and all because of the tantalizing sight that I had had of food almost within my grasp.

Once more darkness and silence enveloped me, a silence that was broken only by a single mocking laugh.

For another day nothing occurred to break the monotony of my imprisonment or relieve the suffering superinduced by hunger and thirst. Slowly the pangs became less keen, as suffering deaded the activity of certain nerves; and then the light flashed on once again, and before me stood an array of new and tempting dishes, with great bottles of clear water and flagons of refreshing wine, upon the outside of which the cold sweat of condensation stood.

Again, with the hunger madness of a wild beast, I sprang forward to seize those tempting dishes; but, as before, the light went out and I came to a sudden stop against a hard wall.

Then the mocking laugh rang out for a second time.

The Pit of Plenty!

Ah, what a cruel mind must have devised this exquisite, hellish torture! Day after day was the thing repeated, until I was on the verge of madness; and then, as I had done in the pits of the Warhoons, I took a new, firm hold upon my reason and forced it back into the channels of sanity.

By sheer will-power I regained control over my tottering mentality, and so successful was I that the next time that the light came I sat quite still and looked indifferently at the fresh and tempting food almost within my reach. Glad I was that I had done so, for it gave me an opportunity to solve the seeming mystery of those vanishing banquets.

As I made no move to reach the food, the torturers left the light turned on in the hope that at last I could refrain no longer from giving them the delicious thrill of enjoyment that my former futile efforts to obtain it had caused.

And as I sat scrutinizing the laden shelves I presently saw how the thing was accomplished, and so simple was it that I wondered I had not guessed it before. The wall of my prison was of clearest glass —behind the glass were the tantalizing viands.

After nearly an hour the light went out, but this time there was no mocking laughter—at least not upon the part of my tormentors; but I, to be at quits with them, gave a low laugh that none might mistake for the cackle of a maniac.

Nine days passed, and I was weak from hunger and thirst, but no longer suffering—I was past that. Then, down through the darkness above, a little parcel fell to the floor at my side.

Indifferently I groped for it, thinking it but some new invention of my jailers to add to my sufferings.

At last I found it—a tiny package wrapped in paper, at the end of a strong and slender cord. As I opened it a few lozenges fell to the floor. As I gathered them up, feeling of them and smelling of them, I discovered that they were tablets of concentrated food such as are quite common in all parts of Barsoom.

Poison! I thought.

Well, what of it? Why not end my misery now rather than drag out a few more wretched days in this dark pit? Slowly I raised one of the little pellets to my lips.

"Good-bye, my Dejah Thoris!" I breathed. "I have lived for you and fought for you, and now my next dearest wish is to be realized, for I shall die for you," and, taking the morsel in my mouth, I devoured it.

One by one I ate them all, nor ever did anything taste better than those tiny bits of nourishment, within which I knew must lie the seeds of death—possibly of some hideous, torturing death.

As I sat quietly upon the floor of my prison, waiting for the end, my fingers by accident came in contact with the bit of paper in which the things had been wrapped; and as I idly played with it, my mind roaming far back into the past, that I might live again for a few brief moments before I died some of the many happy moments of a long and happy life, I became aware of strange protuberances upon the smooth surface of the parchment-like substance in my hands.

For a time they carried no special significance to my mind—I merely was mildly wondrous that they were there; but at last they seemed to take form, and then I realized that there was but a single line of them, like writing.

Now, more interestedly, my fingers traced and retraced them. There were four separate and distinct combinations of raised lines. Could it be that these were four words, and that they were intended to carry a message to me?

The more I thought of it the more excited I became, until my fingers raced madly back and forth over those bewildering little hills and valleys upon that bit of paper.

But I could make nothing of them, and at last I decided that my very haste was preventing me from solving the mystery. Then I took it more slowly. Again and again my forefinger traced the first of those four combinations.

Martian writing is rather difficult to explain to an Earth man—it is something of a cross between shorthand and picture-writing, and is an entirely different language from the spoken language of Mars.

Upon Barsoom there is but a single oral language.

It is spoken today by every race and nation, just as it was at the beginning of human life upon Barsoom. It has grown with the growth of the planet's learning and scientific achievements, but so ingenious a thing it is that new words to express new thoughts or describe new conditions or discoveries form themselves—no other word could explain the thing that a new word is required for other than the word that naturally falls to it, and so, no matter how far removed two nations or races, their spoken languages are identical.

Not so their written languages, however. No two nations have the same written language, and often cities of the same nation have a written language that differs greatly from that of the nation to which they belong.

Thus it was that the signs upon the paper, if in reality they were words, baffled me for some time; but at last I made out the first one.

It was "courage," and it was written in the letters of Marentina.

Courage!

That was the word the yellow guardsman had whispered in my ear as I stood upon the verge of the Pit of Plenty.

The message must be from him, and he I knew was a friend.

With renewed hope I bent my every energy to the deciphering of the balance of the message, and at last success rewarded my endeavor—I had read the four words:

"Courage! Follow the rope."

"FOLLOW THE ROPE!"

WHAT COULD it mean?

"Follow the rope." What rope?

Presently I recalled the cord that had been attached to the parcel when it fell at my side, and after a little groping my hand came in contact with it again. It depended from above, and when I pulled upon it I discovered that it was rigidly fastened, possibly at the pit's mouth.

Upon examination I found that the cord, though small, was amply able to sustain the weight of several men. Then I made another discovery—there was a second message knotted in the rope at about the height of my head. This I deciphered more easily, now that the key was mine.

"Bring the rope with you. Beyond the knots lies danger."

That was all there was to this message. It was evidently hastily formed—an afterthought.

I did not pause longer than to learn the contents of the second message, and, though I was none too sure of the meaning of the final admonition, "Beyond the knots lies danger," yet I was sure that here before me lay an avenue of escape, and that the sooner I took advantage of it the more likely was I to win to liberty.

At least, I could be but little worse off than I had been in the Pit of Plenty.

I was to find, however, ere I was well out of that damnable hole that I might have been very much worse off had I been compelled to remain there another two minutes.

It had taken me about that length of time to ascend some fifty feet above the bottom when a noise above attracted my attention. To my chagrin I saw that the covering of the pit was being removed far above me, and in the light of the courtyard beyond I saw a number of yellow warriors.

Could it be that I was laboriously working my way into some new trap? Were the messages spurious, after all? And then, just as my hope and courage had ebbed to their lowest, I saw two things.

One was the body of a huge, struggling, snarling apt being lowered over the side of the pit toward me, and the other was an aperture in the side of the shaft—an aperture larger than a man's body, into which my rope led.

Just as I scrambled into the dark hole before me the apt passed me, reaching out with his mighty hands to clutch me, and snapping, growling, and roaring in a most frightful manner.

Plainly now I saw the end for which Salensus Oll had destined me. After first torturing me with starvation he had caused this fierce beast to be lowered into my prison to finish the work that the jeddak's hellish imagination had conceived.

And then another truth flashed upon me—I had lived nine days of the allotted ten which must intervene before Salensus Oll could make Dejah Thoris his queen. The purpose of the apt was to insure my death before the tenth day.

I almost laughed aloud as I thought how Salensus Oll's measure of safety was to aid in defeating the very end he sought, for when they discovered that the apt was alone in the Pit of Plenty they could not know but that he had completely devoured me, and so no suspicion of my escape would cause a search to be made for me.

Coiling the rope that had carried me thus far upon my strange journey, I sought for the other end, but found that as I followed it forward it extended always before me. So this was the meaning of the words: "Follow the rope."

The tunnel through which I crawled was low and dark. I had followed it for several hundred yards when I felt a knot beneath my fingers. "Beyond the knots lies danger."

Now I went with the utmost caution, and a moment later a sharp turn in the tunnel brought me to an opening into a large, brilliantly lighted chamber.

The trend of the tunnel I had been traversing had been slightly upward, and from this I judged that the chamber into which I now found myself looking must be either on the first floor of the palace or directly beneath the first floor.

Upon the opposite wall were many strange instruments and devices, and in the center of the room stood a long table, at which two men were seated in earnest conversation.

He who faced me was a yellow man—a little, wizened-up, pasty-faced old fellow with great eyes that showed the white round the entire circumference of the iris.

His companion was a black man, and I did not need to see his face to know that it was Thurid, for there was no other of the First Born north of the ice-barrier.

Thurid was speaking as I came within hearing of the men's voices.

"Solan," he was saying, "there is no risk and the reward is great. You know that you hate Salensus Oll and that nothing would please you more than to thwart him in some cherished plan. There be nothing that he more cherishes today than the idea of wedding the beautiful Princess of Helium; but I, too, want her, and with your help I may win her.

"You need not more than step from this room for an instant when I give you the signal. I will do the rest, and then, when I am gone, you may come and throw the great switch back into its place, and all will be as before. I need but an hour's start to be safe beyond the devilish power that you control in this hidden chamber beneath the palace of your master. See how easy," and with the words the black dator rose from his seat and, crossing the room, laid his hand upon a large, burnished lever that protruded from the opposite wall.

"No! No!" cried the little old man, springing after him, with a wild shriek. "Not that one! Not that one! That controls the sunray tanks, and should you pull it too far down, all Kadabra would be consumed by heat before I could replace it. Come away! Come away! You know not with what mighty powers you play. This is the lever that you seek. Note well the symbol inlaid in white upon its ebon surface."

Thurid approached and examined the handle of the lever.

"Ah, a magnet," he said. "I will remember. It is settled then I take it," he continued.

The old man hesitated. A look of combined greed and apprehension overspread his none too beautiful features.

"Double the figure," he said. "Even that were all too small an amount for the service you ask. Why, I risk my life by even entertaining you here within the forbidden precincts of my station. Should Salensus Oll learn of it he would have me thrown to the apts before the day was done."

"He dare not do that, and you know it full well, Solan," contradicted the black. "Too great a power of life and death you hold over the people of Kadabra for Salensus Oll ever to risk threatening you with death. Before ever his minions could lay their hands upon you, you might seize this very lever from which you have just warned me and wipe out the entire city."

"And myself into the bargain," said Solan, with a shudder.

"But if you were to die, anyway, you would find the nerve to do it," replied Thurid.

"Yes," muttered Solan, "I have often thought upon that very thing. Well, First Born, is your red princess worth the price I ask for my services, or will you go without her and see her in the arms of Salensus Oll tomorrow night?"

"Take your price, yellow man," replied Thurid, with an oath. "Half now and the balance when you have fulfilled your contract."

With that the dator threw a well-filled money-pouch upon the table.

Solan opened the pouch and with trembling fingers counted its contents. His weird eyes assumed a greedy expression, and his unkempt beard and mustache twitched with the muscles of his mouth and chin. It was quite evident from his very mannerism that Thurid had keenly guessed the man's weakness—even the clawlike, clutching movement of the fingers betokened the avariciousness of the miser.

Having satisfied himself that the amount was correct, Solan replaced the money in the pouch and rose from the table.

"Now," he said, "are you quite sure that you know the way to your destination? You must travel quickly to cover the ground to the cave and from thence beyond the Great Power, all within a brief hour, for no more dare I spare you."

"Let me repeat it to you," said Thurid, "that you may see if I be letter-perfect."

"Proceed," replied Solan.

"Through yonder door," he commenced, pointing to a door at the far end of the apartment, "I follow a corridor, passing three diverging corridors upon my right; then into the fourth right-hand corridor straight to where three corridors meet; here again I follow to the right, hugging the left wall closely to avoid the pit.

"At the end of this corridor I shall come to a spiral runway, which I must follow down instead of up; after that the way is along but a single branchless corridor. Am I right?"

"Quite right, Dator," answered Solan; "and now begone. Already have you tempted fate too long within this forbidden place."

"Tonight, or tomorrow, then, you may expect the signal," said Thurid, rising to go.

"Tonight, or tomorrow," repeated Solan, and as the door closed behind his guest the old man continued to mutter as he turned back to the table, where he again dumped the contents of the money-pouch, running his fingers through the heap of shining metal; piling the coins into little towers; counting, recounting, and fondling the wealth the while he muttered on and on in a crooning undertone.

Presently his fingers ceased their play; his eyes popped wider than ever as they fastened upon the door through which Thurid had disappeared. The croon changed to a querulous muttering, and finally to an ugly growl.

Then the old man rose from the table, shaking his fist at the closed door. Now he raised his voice, and his words came distinctly.

"Fool!" he muttered. "Think you that for your happiness Solan will give up his life? If you escaped, Salensus Oll would know that only through my connivance could you have succeeded. Then would he send for me. What would you have me do? Reduce the city and myself to ashes? No, fool, there is a better way—a better way for Solan to keep thy money and be revenged upon Salensus Oll."

He laughed in a nasty, cackling note.

"Poor fool! You may throw the great switch that will give you the freedom of the air of Okar, and then, in fatuous security, go on with thy red princess to the freedom of—death. When you have passed beyond this chamber in your flight, what can prevent Solan replacing the switch as it was before your vile hand touched it? Nothing; and then the Guardian of the North will claim you and your woman, and Salensus Oll, when he sees your dead bodies, will never dream that the hand of Solan had aught to do with the thing."

Then his voice dropped once more into mutterings that I could not translate, but I had heard enough to cause me to guess a great deal more, and I thanked the kind Providence that had led me to this chamber at a time so filled with importance to Dejah Thoris and myself as this.

But how to pass the old man now! The cord, almost invisible upon the floor, stretched straight across the apartment to a door upon the far side.

There was no other way of which I knew, nor could I afford to ignore the advice to "follow the rope." I must cross this room, but however I should accomplish it undetected with that old man in the very center of it baffled me.

Of course I might have sprung in upon him and with my bare hands silenced him forever, but I had heard enough to convince me that with him alive the knowledge that I had gained might serve me at some future moment, while should I kill him and another be stationed in his place Thurid would not come hither with Dejah Thoris, as was quite evidently his intention.

As I stood in the dark shadow of the tunnel's end racking my brain for a feasible plan the while I watched, catlike, the old man's every move, he took up the money-pouch and crossed to one end of the apartment, where, bending to his knees, he fumbled with a panel in the wall.

Instantly I guessed that here was the hiding place in which he hoarded his wealth, and while he bent there, his back toward me, I entered the chamber upon tiptoe, and with the utmost stealth essayed to reach the opposite side before he should complete his task and turn again toward the room's center.

Scarcely thirty steps, all told, must I take, and yet it seemed to my overwrought imagination that that farther wall was miles away; but at last I reached it, nor once had I taken my eyes from the back of the old miser's head.

He did not turn until my hand was upon the button that controlled the door through which my way led, and then he turned away from me as I passed through and gently closed the door.

For an instant I paused, my ear close to the panel, to learn if he had suspected aught, but as no sound of pursuit came from within I wheeled and made my way along the new corridor, following the rope, which I coiled and brought with me as I advanced.

But a short distance farther on I came to the rope's end at a point where five corridors met. What was I to do? Which way should I turn? I was nonplused.

A careful examination of the end of the rope revealed the fact that it had been cleanly cut with some sharp instrument. This fact and the words that had cautioned me that danger lay beyond the *knots* convinced me that the rope had been severed since my friend had placed it as my guide, for I had but passed a single knot, whereas there had evidently been two or more in the entire length of the cord.

Now, indeed, was I in a pretty fix, for neither did I know which avenue to follow nor when danger lay directly in my path; but there was nothing else to be done than follow one of the corridors, for I could gain nothing by remaining where I was.

So I chose the central opening, and passed on into its gloomy depths with a prayer upon my lips.

The floor of the tunnel rose rapidly as I advanced, and a moment later the way came to an abrupt end before a heavy door.

I could hear nothing beyond, and, with my accustomed rashness, pushed the portal wide to step into a room filled with yellow warriors.

The first to see me opened his eyes wide in astonishment, and at the same instant I felt the tingling sensation in my finger that denoted the presence of a friend of the ring.

Then others saw me, and there was a concerted rush to lay hands upon me, for these were all members of the palace guard—men familiar with my face.

The first to reach me was the wearer of the mate to my strange ring, and as he came close he whispered: "Surrender to me!" then in a loud voice shouted: "You are my prisoner, white man," and menaced me with his two weapons.

And so John Carter, Prince of Helium, meekly surrendered to a single antagonist. The others now swarmed about us, asking many questions, but I would not talk to them, and finally my captor announced that he would lead me back to my cell.

An officer ordered several other warriors to accompany him, and a moment later we were retracing the way I had just come. My friend walked close beside me, asking many silly questions about the country from which I had come, until finally his fellows paid no further attention to him or his gabbling.

Gradually, as he spoke, he lowered his voice, so that presently he was able to converse with me in a low tone without attracting attention. His ruse was a clever one, and showed that Talu had not misjudged the man's fitness for the dangerous duty upon which he was detailed.

When he had fully assured himself that the other guardsmen were not listening, he asked me why I had not followed the rope, and when I told him that it had ended at the five corridors he said that it must have been cut by someone in need of a piece of rope, for he was sure that "the stupid Kadabrans would never have guessed its purpose."

Before we had reached the spot from which the five corridors diverge my Marentinian friend had managed to drop to the rear of the little column with me, and when we came in sight of the branching ways he whispered:

"Run up the first upon the right. It leads to the watchtower upon the south wall. I will direct the pursuit up the next corridor," and with that he gave me a great shove into the dark mouth of the tunnel, at the same time crying out in simulated pain and alarm as he threw himself upon the floor as though I had felled him with a blow.

From behind the voices of the excited guardsmen came reverberating along the corridor, suddenly growing fainter as Talu's spy led them up the wrong passageway in fancied pursuit.

As I ran for my life through the dark galleries beneath the palace of Salensus Oll I must indeed have presented a remarkable appearance had there been any to note it, for though death loomed large about me, my face was split by a broad grin as I thought of the resourcefulness of the nameless hero of Marentina to whom I owed my life.

Of such stuff are the men of my beloved Helium, and when I meet another of their kind, of whatever race or color, my heart goes out to him as it did now to my new friend who had risked his life for me simply because I wore the mate to the ring his ruler had put upon his finger.

The corridor along which I ran led almost straight for a considerable distance, terminating at the foot of a spiral runway, up which I proceeded to emerge presently into a circular chamber upon the first floor of a tower.

In this apartment a dozen red slaves were employed polishing or repairing the weapons of the yellow men. The walls of the room were lined with racks in which were hundreds of straight and hooked swords, javelins, and daggers. It was evidently an armory. There were but three warriors guarding the workers.

My eyes took in the entire scene at a glance. Here were weapons in plenty! Here were sinewy red warriors to wield them!

And here now was John Carter, Prince of Helium, in need both of weapons and warriors!

As I stepped into the apartment, guards and prisoners saw me simultaneously.

Close to the entrance where I stood was a rack of straight swords, and as my hand closed upon the hilt of one of them my eyes fell upon the faces of two of the prisoners who worked side by side.

One of the guards started toward me. "Who are you?" he demanded. "What do you here?"

"I come for Tardos Mors, Jeddak of Helium, and his son, Mors Kajak," I cried, pointing to the two red prisoners, who had now sprung to their feet, wide-eyed in astonished recognition.

"Rise, red men! Before we die let us leave a memorial in the palace of Okar's tyrant that will stand forever in the annals of Kadabra to the honor and glory of Helium," for I had seen that all the prisoners there were men of Tardos Mors's navy.

Then the first guardsman was upon me and the fight was on, but scarce did we engage ere, to my horror, I saw that the red slaves were shackled to the floor.

THE MAGNET SWITCH

THE GUARDSMEN paid not the slightest attention to their wards, for the red men could not move over two feet from the great rings to which they were padlocked, though each had seized a weapon upon which he had been engaged when I entered the room, and stood ready to join me could they have but done so.

The yellow men devoted all their attention to me, nor were they long in discovering that the three of them were none too many to defend the armory against John Carter. Would that I had had my own good long-sword in my hand that day; but, as it was, I rendered a satisfactory account of myself with the unfamiliar weapon of the yellow man.

At first I had a time of it dodging their villainous hook-swords, but after a minute or two I had succeeded in wresting a second straight sword from one of the racks along the wall, and thereafter, using it to parry the hooks of my antagonists, I felt more evenly equipped.

The three of them were on me at once, and but for a lucky circumstance my end might have come quickly. The foremost guardsman made a vicious lunge for my side with his hook after the three of them had backed me against the wall, but as I sidestepped and raised my arm his weapon but grazed my side, passing into a rack of javelins, where it became entangled.

Before he could release it I had run him through, and then, falling back upon the tactics that have saved me a hundred times in tight pinches, I rushed the two remaining warriors, forcing them back with a perfect torrent of cuts and thrusts, weaving my sword in and out about their guards until I had the fear of death upon them.

Then one of them commenced calling for help, but it was too late to save them.

They were as putty in my hands now, and I backed them about the armory as I would until I had them where I wanted them—within reach of the swords of the shackled slaves. In an instant both lay dead upon the floor. But their cries had not been entirely fruitless, for now I heard answering shouts and the footfalls of many men running and the clank of accouterments and the commands of officers.

"The door! Quick, John Carter, bar the door!" cried Tardos Mors.

Already the guard was in sight, charging across the open court that was visible through the doorway.

A dozen seconds would bring them into the tower. A single leap carried me to the heavy portal. With a resounding bang I slammed it shut.

"The bar!" shouted Tardos Mors.

I tried to slip the huge fastening into place, but it defied my every attempt.

"Raise it a little to release the catch," cried one of the red men.

I could hear the yellow warriors leaping along the flagging just beyond the door. I raised the bar and shot it to the right just as the foremost of the guardsmen threw himself against the opposite side of the massive panels.

The barrier held—I had been in time, but by the fraction of a second only.

Now I turned my attention to the prisoners. To Tardos Mors I went first, asking where the keys might be which would unfasten their fetters.

"The officer of the guard has them," replied the Jeddak of Helium, "and he is among those without who seek entrance. You will have to force them."

Most of the prisoners were already hacking at their bonds with the swords in their hands. The yellow men were battering at the door with javelins and axes.

I turned my attention to the chains that held Tardos Mors. Again and again I cut deep into the metal with my sharp blade, but ever faster and faster fell the torrent of blows upon the portal.

At last a link parted beneath my efforts, and a moment later Tardos Mors was free, though a few inches of trailing chain still dangled from his ankle.

A splinter of wood falling inward from the door announced the headway that our enemies were making toward us.

The mighty panels trembled and bent beneath the furious on-slaught of the enraged yellow men.

What with the battering upon the door and the hacking of the red men at their chains the din within the armory was appalling. No sooner was Tardos Mors free than he turned his attention to another of the prisoners, while I set to work to liberate Mors Kajak.

We must work fast if we would have all those fetters cut before the door gave way. Now a panel crashed inward upon the floor, and Mors Kajak sprang to the opening to defend the way until we should have time to release the others.

With javelins snatched from the wall he wrought havoc among the foremost of the Okarians while we battled with the insensate metal that stood between our fellows and freedom.

At length all but one of the prisoners were freed, and then the door fell with a mighty crash before a hastily improvised battering-ram, and the yellow horde was upon us.

"To the upper chambers!" shouted the red man who was still fettered to the floor. "To the upper chambers! There you may defend the tower against all Kadabra. Do not delay because of me, who could pray for no better death than in the service of Tardos Mors and the Prince of Helium."

But I would have sacrificed the life of every man of us rather than desert a single red man, much less the lion-hearted hero who begged us to leave him.

"Cut his chains," I cried to two of the red men, "while the balance of us hold off the foe."

There were ten of us now to do battle with the Okarian guard, and I warrant that that ancient watchtower never looked down upon a more hotly contested battle than took place that day within its own grim walls.

The first inrushing wave of yellow warriors recoiled from the slashing blades of ten of Helium's veteran fighting men. A dozen Okarian corpses blocked the doorway, but over the gruesome barrier a score more of their fellows dashed, shouting their hoarse and hideous war-cry.

Upon the bloody mound we met them, hand to hand, stabbing where the quarters were too close to cut, thrusting when we could push a foeman to arm's length; and mingled with the wild cry of the Okarian there rose and fell the glorious words: "For Helium! For Helium!" that for countless ages have spurred on the bravest of the brave to those deeds of valor that have sent the fame of Helium's heroes broadcast throughout the length and breadth of a world.

Now were the fetters struck from the last of the red men, and thirteen strong we met each new charge of the soldiers of Salensus Oll. Scarce one of us but bled from a score of wounds, yet none had fallen.

From without we saw hundreds of guardsmen pouring into the courtyard, and along the lower corridor from which I had found my way to the armory we could hear the clank of metal and the shouting of men.

In a moment we should be attacked from two sides, and with all our prowess we could not hope to withstand the unequal odds which would thus divide our attention and our small numbers.

"To the upper chambers!" cried Tardos Mors, and a moment later we fell back toward the runway that led to the floors above.

Here another bloody battle was waged with the force of yellow men who charged into the armory as we fell back from the doorway. Here we lost our first man, a noble fellow whom we could ill spare; but at length all had backed into the runway except myself, who remained to hold back the Okarians until the others were safe above.

In the mouth of the narrow spiral but a single warrior could attack me at a time, so that I had little difficulty in holding them all back for the brief moment that was necessary. Then, backing slowly before them, I commenced the ascent of the spiral.

All the long way to the tower's top the guardsmen pressed me closely. When one went down before my sword another scrambled over the dead man to take his place; and thus, taking an awful toll with each few feet gained, I came to the spacious glass-walled watch-tower of Kadabra.

Here my companions clustered ready to take my place, and for a moment's respite I stepped to one side while they held the enemy off.

From the lofty perch a view could be had for miles in every direction. Toward the south stretched the rugged, ice-clad waste to the edge of the mighty barrier. Toward the east and west, and dimly toward the north I descried other Okarian cities, while in the immediate foreground, just beyond the walls of Kadabra, the grim guardian shaft reared its somber head.

Then I cast my eyes down into the streets of Kadabra, from which a sudden tumult had arisen, and there I saw a battle raging, and beyond the city's walls I saw armed men marching in great columns toward a near-by gate.

Eagerly I pressed forward against the glass wall of the observatory, scarce daring to credit the testimony of my own eyes. But at last I could doubt no longer, and with a shout of joy that rose strangely in the midst of the cursing and groaning of the battling men at the entrance to the chamber, I called to Tardos Mors.

As he joined me I pointed down into the streets of Kadabra and to the advancing columns beyond, above which floated bravely in the arctic air the flags and banners of Helium.

An instant later every red man in the lofty chamber had seen the inspiring sight, and such a shout of thanksgiving arose as I warrant never before echoed through that age-old pile of stone.

But still we must fight on, for though our troops had entered Kadabra, the city was yet far from capitulation, nor had the palace been even assaulted. Turn and turn about we held the top of the runway while the others feasted their eyes upon the sight of our valiant countrymen battling far beneath us.

Now they have rushed the palace gate! Great battering-rams are dashed against its formidable surface. Now they are repulsed by a deadly shower of javelins from the wall's top!

Once again they charge, but a sortie by a large force of Okarians from an intersecting avenue crumples the head of the column, and the men of Helium go down, fighting, beneath an overwhelming force.

The palace gate flies open and a force of the jeddak's own guard, picked men from the flower of the Okarian army, sallies forth to shatter the broken regiments. For a moment it looks as though nothing could avert defeat, and then I see a noble figure upon a mighty thoat— not the tiny thoat of the red man, but one of his huge cousins of the dead sea bottoms.

The warrior hews his way to the front, and behind him rally the disorganized soldiers of Helium. As he raises his head aloft to fling a challenge at the men upon the palace walls I see his face, and my heart swells in pride and happiness as the red warriors leap to the side of their leader and win back the ground that they had but just lost—the face of him upon the mighty thoat is the face of my son—Carthoris of Helium.

At his side fights a huge Martian war-hound, nor did I need a second look to know that it was Woola—my faithful Woola who had thus well performed his arduous task and brought the succoring legions in the nick of time.

"In the nick of time?"

Who yet might say that they were not too late to save, but surely they could avenge! And such retribution as that unconquered army would deal out to the hateful Okarians! I sighed to think that I might not be alive to witness it.

Again I turned to the windows. The red men had not yet forced the outer palace wall, but they were fighting nobly against the best that Okar afforded—valiant warriors who contested every inch of the way.

Now my attention was caught by a new element without the city wall—a great body of mounted warriors looming large above the red men. They were the huge green allies of Helium—the savage hordes from the dead sea bottoms of the far south.

In grim and terrible silence they sped on toward the gate, the padded hoofs of their frightful mounts giving forth no sound. Into the doomed city they charged, and as they wheeled across the wide plaza before the palace of the Jeddak of Jeddaks I saw, riding at their head, the mighty figure of their mighty leader—Tars Tarkas, Jeddak of Thark.

My wish, then, was to be gratified, for I was to see my old friend battling once again, and though not shoulder to shoulder with him, I, too, would be fighting in the same cause here in the high tower of Okar.

Nor did it seem that our foes would ever cease their stubborn attacks, for still they came, though the way to our chamber was often clogged with the bodies of their dead. At times they would pause long enough to drag back the impeding corpses, and then fresh warriors would forge upward to taste the cup of death.

I had been taking my turn with the others in defending the approach to our lofty retreat when Mors Kajak, who had been watching the battle in the street below, called aloud in sudden excitement. There was a note of apprehension in his voice that brought me to his side the instant that I could turn my place over to another, and as I reached him he pointed far out across the waste of snow and ice toward the southern horizon.

"Alas!" he cried, "that I should be forced to witness cruel fate betray them without power to warn or aid; but they be past either now."

As I looked in the direction he indicated I saw the cause of his perturbation. A mighty fleet of fliers was approaching majestically toward Kadabra from the direction of the ice-barrier. On and on they came with ever increasing velocity.

"The grim shaft that they call the Guardian of the North is beckoning to them," said Mors Kajak sadly, "just as it beckoned to Tardos Mors and his great fleet; see where they lie, crumpled and broken, a grim and terrible monument to the mighty force of destruction which naught can resist."

I, too, saw; but something else I saw that Mors Kajak did not; in my mind's eye I saw a buried chamber whose walls were lined with strange instruments and devices.

In the center of the chamber was a long table, and before it sat a little, pop-eyed old man counting his money; but, plainest of all, I saw upon the wall a great switch with a small magnet inlaid within the surface of its black handle.

Then I glanced out at the fast-approaching fleet. In five minutes that mighty armada of the skies would be bent and worthless scrap, lying at the base of the shaft beyond the city's wall, and yellow hordes would be loosed from another gate to rush out upon the few survivors stumbling blindly down through the mass of wreckage; then the apts would come. I shuddered at the thought, for I could vividly picture the whole horrible scene.

Quick have I always been to decide and act. The impulse that moves me and the doing of the thing seem simultaneous; for if my mind goes through the tedious formality of reasoning, it must be a subconscious act of which I am not objectively aware. Psychologists tell me that, as the subconscious does not reason, too close a scrutiny of my mental activities might prove anything but flattering; but be that as it may, I have often won success while the thinker would have been still at the endless task of comparing various judgments.

And now celerity of action was the prime essential to the success of the thing that I had decided upon.

Grasping my sword more firmly in my hand, I called to the red man at the opening to the runway to stand aside.

"Way for the Prince of Helium!" I shouted; and before the astonished yellow man whose misfortune it was to be at the fighting

end of the line at that particular moment could gather his wits together my sword had decapitated him, and I was rushing like a mad
bull down upon those behind him.

"Way for the Prince of Helium!" I shouted as I cut a path through
the astonished guardsmen of Salensus Oll.

Hewing to right and left, I beat my way down that warrior-choked
spiral until, near the bottom, those below, thinking that an army was
descending upon them, turned and fled.

The armory at the first floor was vacant when I entered it, the last
of the Okarians having fled into the courtyard, so none saw me continue down the spiral toward the corridor beneath.

Here I ran as rapidly as my legs would carry me toward the five
corners, and there plunged into the passageway that led to the station
of the old miser.

Without the formality of a knock, I burst into the room. There
sat the old man at his table; but as he saw me he sprang to his feet,
drawing his sword.

With scarce more than a glance toward him I leaped for the great
switch; but, quick as I was, that wiry old fellow was there before me.

How he did it I shall never know, nor does it seem credible that
any Martian-born creature could approximate the marvelous speed
of my earthly muscles.

Like a tiger he turned upon me, and I was quick to see why Solan
had been chosen for this important duty.

Never in all my life have I seen such wondrous swordsmanship
and such uncanny agility as that ancient bag of bones displayed. He
was in forty places at the same time, and before I had half a chance
to awaken to my danger he was like to have made a monkey of me,
and a dead monkey at that.

It is strange how new and unexpected conditions bring out unguessed ability to meet them.

That day in the buried chamber beneath the palace of Salensus
Oll I learned what swordsmanship meant, and to what heights of
sword mastery I could achieve when pitted against such a wizard of
the blade as Solan.

For a time he liked to have bested me; but presently the latent
possibilities that must have been lying dormant within me for a lifetime came to the fore, and I fought as I had never dreamed a human
being could fight.

That that duel-royal should have taken place in the dark recesses of a cellar, without a single appreciative eye to witness it has always seemed to me almost a world calamity—at least from the viewpoint Barsoomian, where bloody strife is the first and greatest considera- tion of individuals, nations, and races.

I was fighting to reach the switch, Solan to prevent me; and, though we stood not three feet from it, I could not win an inch to- ward it, nor he force me back an inch for the first five minutes of our battle.

I knew that if I were to throw it in time to save the oncoming fleet it must be done in the next few seconds, and so I tried my old rushing tactics; but I might as well have rushed a brick wall for all that Solan gave way.

In fact, I came near to impaling myself upon his point for my pains; but right was on my side, and I think that that must give a man greater confidence than though he knew himself to be battling in a wicked cause.

At least, I did not want in confidence; and when I next rushed Solan it was to one side with implicit confidence that he must turn to meet my new line of attack, and turn he did, so that now we fought with our sides towards the coveted goal—the great switch stood within my reach upon my right hand.

To uncover my breast for an instant would have been to court sudden death, but I saw no other way than to chance it, if by so doing I might rescue that oncoming, succoring fleet; and so, in the face of a wicked sword-thrust, I reached out my point and caught the great switch a sudden blow that released it from its seating.

So surprised and horrified was Solan that he forgot to finish his thrust; instead, he wheeled toward the switch with a loud shriek—a shriek which was his last, for before his hand could touch the lever it sought, my sword's point had passed through his heart.

THE TIDE OF BATTLE

But Solan's last loud cry had not been without effect, for a moment later a dozen guardsmen burst into the chamber, though not before I had so bent and demolished the great switch that it could not be again used to turn the powerful current into the mighty magnet of destruction it controlled.

The result of the sudden coming of the guardsmen had been to compel me to seek seclusion in the first passageway that I could find, and that to my disappointment proved to be not the one with which I was familiar, but another upon its left.

They must have either heard or guessed which way I went, for I had proceeded but a short distance when I heard the sound of pursuit. I had no mind to stop and fight these men here when there was fighting aplenty elsewhere in the city of Kadabra—fighting that could be of much more avail to me and mine than useless life-taking far below the palace.

But the fellows were pressing me; and as I did not know the way at all, I soon saw that they would overtake me unless I found a place to conceal myself until they had passed, which would then give me an opportunity to return the way I had come and regain the tower, or possibly find a way to reach the city streets.

The passageway had risen rapidly since leaving the apartment of the switch, and now ran level and well lighted straight into the distance as far as I could see. The moment that my pursuers reached this straight stretch I would be in plain sight of them, with no chance to escape from the corridor undetected.

Presently I saw a series of doors opening from either side of the corridor, and as they all looked alike to me I tried the first one that I reached. It opened into a small chamber, luxuriously furnished, and was evidently an ante-chamber off some office or audience chamber of the palace.

On the far side was a heavily curtained doorway beyond which I heard the hum of voices. Instantly I crossed the small chamber, and, parting the curtains, looked within the larger apartment.

Before me were a party of perhaps fifty gorgeously clad nobles of the court, standing before a throne upon which sat Salensus Oll. The Jeddak of Jeddaks was addressing them.

"The allotted hour has come," he was saying as I entered the apartment; "and though the enemies of Okar be within her gates, naught may stay the will of Salensus Oll. The great ceremony must be omitted that no single man may be kept from his place in the defenses other than the fifty that custom demands shall witness the creation of a new queen in Okar.

"In a moment the thing shall have been done and we may return to the battle, while she who is now the Princess of Helium looks down from the queen's tower upon the annihilation of her former countrymen and witnesses the greatness which is her husband's."

Then, turning to a courtier, he issued some command in a low voice.

The addressed hastened to a small door at the far end of the chamber and, swinging it wide, cried: "Way for Dejah Thoris, future Queen of Okar!"

Immediately two guardsmen appeared dragging the unwilling bride toward the altar. Her hands were still manacled behind her, evidently to prevent suicide.

Her disheveled hair and panting bosom betokened that, chained though she was, still had she fought against the thing that they would do to her.

At sight of her Salensus Oll rose and drew his sword, and the sword of each of the fifty nobles was raised on high to form an arch, beneath which the poor, beautiful creature was dragged toward her doom.

A grim smile forced itself to my lips as I thought of the rude awakening that lay in store for the ruler of Okar, and my itching fingers fondled the hilt of my bloody sword.

As I watched the procession that moved slowly toward the throne —a procession which consisted of but a handful of priests, who followed Dejah Thoris and the two guardsmen—I caught a fleeting glimpse of a black face peering from behind the draperies that covered the wall back of the dais upon which stood Salensus Oll awaiting his bride.

Now the guardsmen were forcing the Princess of Helium up the few steps to the side of the tyrant of Okar, and I had no eyes and no thoughts for aught else. A priest opened a book and, raising his hand, commenced to drone out a sing-song ritual. Salensus Oll reached for the hand of his bride.

I had intended waiting until some circumstance should give me a reasonable hope of success; for, even though the entire ceremony should be completed, there could be no valid marriage while I lived. What I was most concerned in, of course, was the rescuing of Dejah Thoris—I wished to take her from the palace of Salensus Oll, if such a thing were possible; but whether it were accomplished before or after the mock marriage was a matter of secondary import.

When, however, I saw the vile hand of Salensus Oll reach out for the hand of my beloved princess I could restrain myself no longer, and before the nobles of Okar knew that aught had happened I had leaped through their thin line and was upon the dais beside Dejah Thoris and Salensus Oll.

With the flat of my sword I struck down his polluting hand; and grasping Dejah Thoris round the waist, I swung her behind me as, with my back against the draperies of the dais, I faced the tyrant of the north and his roomful of noble warriors.

The Jeddak of Jeddaks was a great mountain of a man—a coarse, brutal beast of a man—and as he towered above me there, his fierce black whiskers and mustache bristling in rage, I can well imagine that a less seasoned warrior might have trembled before him.

With a snarl he sprang toward me with naked sword, but whether Salensus Oll was a good swordsman or a poor I never learned; for with Dejah Thoris at my back I was no longer human—I was a super-man, and no man could have withstood me then.

With a single, low: "For the Princess of Helium!" I ran my blade straight through the rotten heart of Okar's rotten ruler, and before the white, drawn faces of his nobles Salensus Oll rolled, grinning in horrible death, to the foot of the steps below his marriage throne.

For a moment tense silence reigned in the nuptial-room. Then the fifty nobles rushed upon me. Furiously we fought, but the advantage was mine, for I stood upon a raised platform above them, and I fought for the most glorious woman of a glorious race, and I fought for a great love and for the mother of my boy.

And from behind my shoulder, in the silvery cadence of that dear voice, rose the brave battle anthem of Helium which the nation's women sing as their men march out to victory.

That alone was enough to inspire me to victory over even greater odds, and I verily believe that I should have bested the entire roomful of yellow warriors that day in the nuptial chamber of the palace at Kadabra had not interruption come to my aid.

Fast and furious was the fighting as the nobles of Salensus Oll sprang, time and again, up the steps before the throne only to fall back before a sword hand that seemed to have gained a new wizardry from its experience with the cunning Solan.

Two were pressing me so closely that I could not turn when I heard a movement behind me, and noted that the sound of the battle anthem had ceased. Was Dejah Thoris preparing to take her place beside me?

Heroic daughter of a heroic world! It would not be unlike her to have seized a sword and fought at my side, for, though the women of Mars are not trained in the arts of war, the spirit is theirs, and they have been known to do that very thing upon countless occasions.

But she did not come, and glad I was, for it would have doubled my burden in protecting her before I should have been able to force her back again out of harm's way. She must be contemplating some cunning strategy, I thought, and so I fought on secure in the belief that my divine princess stood close behind me.

For half an hour at least I must have fought there against the nobles of Okar ere ever a one placed a foot upon the dais where I stood, and then of a sudden all that remained of them formed below me for a last, mad, desperate charge; but even as they advanced the door at the far end of the chamber swung wide and a wild-eyed messenger sprang into the room.

"The Jeddak of Jeddaks!" he cried. "Where is the Jeddak of Jeddaks? The city has fallen before the hordes from beyond the barrier, and but now the great gate of the palace itself has been forced and the warriors of the south are pouring into its sacred precincts.

"Where is Salensus Oll? He alone may revive the flagging courage of our warriors. He alone may save the day for Okar. Where is Salensus Oll?"

The nobles stepped back from about the dead body of their ruler, and one of them pointed to the grinning corpse.

The messenger staggered back in horror as though from a blow in the face.

"Then fly, nobles of Okar!" he cried, "for naught can save you. Hark! They come!"

As he spoke we heard the deep roar of angry men from the corridor without, and the clank of metal and the clang of swords.

Without another glance toward me, who had stood a spectator of the tragic scene, the nobles wheeled and fled from the apartment through another exit.

Almost immediately a force of yellow warriors appeared in the doorway through which the messenger had come. They were backing toward the apartment, stubbornly resisting the advance of a handful of red men who faced them and forced them slowly but inevitably back.

Above the heads of the contestants I could see from my elevated station upon the dais the face of my old friend Kantos Kan. He was leading the little party that had won its way into the very heart of the palace of Salensus Oll.

In an instant I saw that by attacking the Okarians from the rear I could so quickly disorganize them that their further resistance would be short-lived, and with this idea in mind I sprang from the dais, casting a word of explanation to Dejah Thoris over my shoulder, though I did not turn to look at her.

With myself ever between her enemies and herself, and with Kantos Kan and his warriors winning to the apartment, there could be no danger to Dejah Thoris standing there alone beside the throne.

I wanted the men of Helium to see me and to know that their beloved princess was here, too, for I knew that this knowledge would inspire them to even greater deeds of valor than they had performed in the past, though great indeed must have been those which won for them a way into the almost impregnable palace of the tyrant of the north.

As I crossed the chamber to attack the Kadabrans from the rear a small doorway at my left opened, and, to my surprise, revealed the figures of Matai Shang, Father of Thern and Phaidor, his daughter, peering into the room.

A quick glance about they took. Their eyes rested for a moment, wide in horror, upon the dead body of Salensus Oll, upon the blood that crimsoned the floor, upon the corpses of the nobles who had fallen thick before the throne, upon me, and upon the battling warriors at the other door.

They did not essay to enter the apartment, but scanned its every corner from where they stood, and then, when their eyes had sought its entire area, a look of fierce rage overspread the features of Matai Shang, and a cold and cunning smile touched the lips of Phaidor.

Then they were gone, but not before a taunting laugh was thrown directly in my face by the woman.

I did not understand then the meaning of Matai Shang's rage or Phaidor's pleasure, but I knew that neither boded good for me.

A moment later I was upon the backs of the yellow men, and as the red men of Helium saw me above the shoulders of their antagonists a great shout rang through the corridor, and for a moment drowned the noise of battle.

"For the Prince of Helium!" they cried. "For the Prince of Helium!" and, like hungry lions upon their prey, they fell once more upon the weakening warriors of the north.

The yellow men, cornered between two enemies, fought with the desperation that utter hopelessness often induces. Fought as I should have fought had I been in their stead, with the determination to take as many of my enemies with me when I died as lay within the power of my sword arm.

It was a glorious battle, but the end seemed inevitable, when presently from down the corridor behind the red men came a great body of reenforcing yellow warriors.

Now were the tables turned, and it was the men of Helium who seemed doomed to be ground between two millstones. All were compelled to turn to meet this new assault by a greatly superior force, so that to me was left the remnants of the yellow men within the throneroom.

They kept me busy, too; so busy that I began to wonder if indeed I should ever be done with them. Slowly they pressed me back into the room, and when they had all passed in after me, one of them closed and bolted the door, effectually barring the way against the men of Kantos Kan.

It was a clever move, for it put me at the mercy of a dozen men within a chamber from which assistance was locked out, and it gave the red men in the corridor beyond no avenue of escape should their new antagonists press them too closely.

But I have faced heavier odds myself than were pitted against me that day, and I knew that Kantos Kan had battled his way from a hundred more dangerous traps than that in which he now was. So it was with no feelings of despair that I turned my attention to the business of the moment.

Constantly my thoughts reverted to Dejah Thoris, and I longed for the moment when, the fighting done, I could fold her in my arms, and hear once more the words of love which had been denied me for so many years.

During the fighting in the chamber I had not even a single chance to so much as steal a glance at her where she stood behind me beside the throne of the dead ruler. I wondered why she no longer urged me on with the strains of the martial hymn of Helium; but I did not need more than the knowledge that I was battling for her to bring out the best that is in me.

It would be wearisome to narrate the details of that bloody struggle; of how we fought from the doorway, the full length of the room to the very foot of the throne before the last of my antagonists fell with my blade piercing his heart.

And then, with a glad cry, I turned with outstretched arms to seize my princess, and as my lips smothered hers to reap the reward that would be thrice ample payment for the bloody encounters through which I had passed for her dear sake from the south pole to the north.

The glad cry died, frozen upon my lips; my arms dropped limp and lifeless to my sides; as one who reels beneath the burden of a mortal wound I staggered up the steps before the throne.

Dejah Thoris was gone.

REWARDS

WITH THE REALIZATION that Dejah Thoris was no longer within the throneroom came the belated recollection of the dark face that I had glimpsed peering from behind the draperies that backed the throne of Salensus Oll at the moment that I had first come so unexpectedly upon the strange scene being enacted within the chamber.

Why had the sight of that evil countenance not warned me to greater caution? Why had I permitted the rapid development of new situations to efface the recollection of that menacing danger? But, alas, vain regret would not erase the calamity that had befallen.

Once again had Dejah Thoris fallen into the clutches of that archfiend, Thurid, the black dator of the First Born. Again was all my arduous labor gone for naught. Now I realized the cause of the rage that had been writ so large upon the features of Matai Shang and the cruel pleasure that I had seen upon the face of Phaidor.

They had known or guessed the truth, and the hekkador of the Holy Therns, who had evidently come to the chamber in the hope of thwarting Salensus Oll in his contemplated perfidy against the high priest who coveted Dejah Thoris for himself, realized that Thurid had stolen the prize from beneath his very nose.

Phaidor's pleasure had been due to her realization of what this last cruel blow would mean to me, as well as to a partial satisfaction of her jealous hatred for the Princess of Helium.

My first thought was to look beyond the draperies at the back of the throne, for there it was that I had seen Thurid. With a single jerk I tore the priceless stuff from its fastenings, and there before me was revealed a narrow doorway behind the throne.

No question entered my mind but that here lay the opening of the avenue of escape which Thurid had followed, and had there been it would have been dissipated by the sight of a tiny, jeweled ornament which lay a few steps within the corridor beyond.

As I snatched up the bauble I saw that it bore the device of the Princess of Helium, and then pressing it to my lips I dashed madly along the winding way that led gently downward toward the lower galleries of the palace.

I had followed but a short distance when I came upon the room in which Solan formerly had held sway. His dead body still lay where I had left it, nor was there any sign that another had passed through the room since I had been there; but I knew that two had done so— Thurid, the black dator, and Dejah Thoris.

For a moment I paused uncertain as to which of the several exits from the apartment would lead me upon the right path. I tried to recollect the directions which I had heard Thurid repeat to Solan, and at last, slowly, as though through a heavy fog, the memory of the words of the First Born came to me:

"Follow a corridor, passing three diverging corridors upon the right; then into the fourth right-hand corridor to where three corridors meet; here again follow to the right, hugging the left wall closely to avoid the pit. At the end of this corridor I shall come to a spiral runway which I must follow down instead of up; after that the way is along but a single branchless corridor."

And I recalled the exit at which he had pointed as he spoke.

It did not take me long to start upon that unknown way, nor did I go with caution, although I knew that there might be grave dangers before me.

Part of the way was black as sin, but for the most it was fairly well lighted. The stretch where I must hug the left wall to avoid the pits was darkest of them all, and I was nearly over the edge of the abyss before I knew that I was near the danger spot.

A narrow ledge, scarce a foot wide, was all that had been left to carry the initiated past that frightful cavity into which the unknowing must surely have toppled at the first step. But at last I had won safely beyond it, and then a feeble light made the balance of the way plain, until, at the end of the last corridor, I came suddenly out into the glare of day upon a field of snow and ice.

Clad for the warm atmosphere of the hothouse city of Kadabra, the sudden change to arctic frigidity was anything but pleasant; but the worst of it was that I knew I could not endure the bitter cold, almost naked as I was, and that I would perish before ever I could overtake Thurid and Dejah Thoris.

To be thus blocked by nature, who had had all the arts and wiles of cunning man pitted against him, seemed a cruel fate, and as I staggered back into the warmth of the tunnel's end I was as near hopelessness as I ever have been.

I had by no means given up my intention of continuing the pursuit, for if needs be I would go ahead though I perished ere ever I reached my goal, but if there were a safer way it were well worth the delay to attempt to discover it, that I might come again to the side of Dejah Thoris in fit condition to do battle for her.

Scarce had I returned to the tunnel than I stumbled over a portion of a fur garment that seemed fastened to the floor of the corridor close to the wall. In the darkness I could not see what held it, but by groping with my hands I discovered that it was wedged beneath the bottom of a closed door.

Pushing the portal aside, I found myself upon the threshold of a small chamber, the walls of which were lined with hooks from which depended suits of the complete outdoor apparel of the yellow men.

Situated as it was at the mouth of a tunnel leading from the palace, it was quite evident that this was the dressingroom used by the nobles leaving and entering the hothouse city, and that Thurid, having knowledge of it, had stopped here to outfit himself and Dejah Thoris before venturing into the bitter cold of the arctic world beyond.

In his haste he had dropped several garments upon the floor, and the telltale fur that had fallen partly within the corridor had proved the means of guiding me to the very spot he would least have wished me to have knowledge of.

It required but the matter of a few seconds to don the necessary orluk-skin clothing, with the heavy, fur-lined boots that are so essential a part of the garmenture of one who would successfully contend with the frozen trails and the icy winds of the bleak northland.

Once more I stepped beyond the tunnel's mouth to find the fresh tracks of Thurid and Dejah Thoris in the new-fallen snow. Now, at last, was my task an easy one, for though the going was rough in the extreme, I was no longer vexed by doubts as to the direction I should follow, or harassed by darkness or hidden dangers.

Through a snow-covered cañon the way led up toward the summit of low hills. Beyond these it dipped again and into another cañon, only to rise a quarter-mile farther on toward a pass which skirted the flank of a rocky hill.

I could see by the signs of those who had gone before that when Dejah Thoris had walked she had been continually holding back, and that the black man had been compelled to drag her. For other stretches only his foot-prints were visible, deep and close together in the heavy snow, and I knew from these signs that then he had been forced to carry her, and I could well imagine that she had fought him fiercely every step of the way.

As I came round the jutting promontory of the hill's shoulder I saw that which quickened my pulses and set my heart to beating high, for within a tiny basin between the crest of this hill and the next stood four people before the mouth of a great cave, and beside them upon the gleaming snow rested a flier which had evidently but just been dragged from its hiding place.

The four were Dejah Thoris, Phaidor, Thurid, and Matai Shang. The two men were engaged in a heated argument—the Father of Therns threatening, while the black scoffed at him as he went about the work at which he was engaged.

As I crept toward them cautiously that I might come as near as possible before being discovered, I saw that finally the men appeared to have reached some sort of a compromise, for with Phaidor's assistance they both set about dragging the resisting Dejah Thoris to the flier's deck.

Here they made her fast, and then both again descended to the ground to complete the preparations for departure. Phaidor entered the small cabin upon the vessel's deck.

I had come to within a quarter of a mile of them when Matai Shang espied me. I saw him seize Thurid by the shoulder, wheeling him around in my direction as he pointed to where I was now plainly visible, for the moment that I knew I had been perceived I cast aside every attempt at stealth and broke into a mad race for the flier.

The two redoubled their efforts at the propeller at which they were working, and which very evidently was being replaced after having been removed for some purpose of repair.

They had the thing completed before I had covered half the distance that lay between me and them, and then both made a rush for the boarding-ladder.

Thurid was the first to reach it, and with the agility of a monkey clambered swiftly to the boat's deck, where a touch of the button controlling the buoyancy tanks sent the craft slowly upward, though not with the speed that marks the well-conditioned flier.

I was still some hundred yards away as I saw them rising from my grasp.

Back by the city of Kadabra lay a great fleet of mighty fliers—the ships of Helium and Ptarth that I had saved from destruction earlier in the day; but before ever I could reach them Thurid could easily make good his escape.

As I ran I saw Matai Shang clambering up the swaying, swinging ladder toward the deck, while above him leaned the evil face of the First Born. A trailing rope from the vessel's stern put new hope in me, for if I could but reach it before it whipped too high above my head there was yet a chance to gain the deck by its slender aid.

That there was something radically wrong with the flier was evident from its lack of buoyancy, and the further fact that though Thurid had turned twice to the starting lever the boat still hung motionless in the air, except for a slight drifting with a low breeze from the north.

Now Matai Shang was close to the gunwale. A long, clawlike hand was reaching up to grasp the metal rail.

Thurid leaned farther down toward his co-conspirator.

Suddenly a raised dagger gleamed in the upflung hand of the black. Down it drove toward the white face of the Father of Therns. With a loud shriek of fear the Holy Hekkador grasped frantically at that menacing arm.

I was almost to the trailing rope by now. The craft was still rising slowly, the while it drifted from me. Then I stumbled on the icy way, striking my head upon a rock as I fell sprawling but an arm's length from the rope, the end of which was now just leaving the ground.

With the blow upon my head came unconsciousness.

It could not have been more than a few seconds that I lay senseless there upon the northern ice, while all that was dearest to me

drifted farther from my reach in the clutches of that black fiend, for
when I opened my eyes Thurid and Matai Shang yet battled at the
ladder's top, and the flier drifted but a hundred yards farther to the
south—but the end of the trailing rope was now a good thirty feet
above the ground.

Goaded to madness by the cruel misfortune that had tripped me
when success was almost within my grasp, I tore frantically across
the intervening space, and just beneath the rope's dangling end I
put my earthly muscles to the supreme test.

With a mighty, catlike bound I sprang upward toward that slender
strand—the only avenue which yet remained that could carry me to
my vanishing love.

A foot above its lowest end my fingers closed. Tightly as I clung
I felt the rope slipping, slipping through my grasp. I tried to raise
my free hand to take a second hold above my first, but the change
of position that resulted caused me to slip more rapidly toward the
end of the rope.

Slowly I felt the tantalizing thing escaping me. In a moment all
that I had gained would be lost—then my fingers reached a knot at
the very end of the rope and slipped no more.

With a prayer of gratitude upon my lips I scrambled upward toward the boat's deck. I could not see Thurid and Matai Shang now,
but I heard the sounds of conflict and thus knew that they still fought
—the thern for his life and the black for the increased buoyancy that
relief from the weight of even a single body would give the craft.

Should Matai Shang die before I reached the deck my chances
of ever reaching it would be slender indeed, for the black dator need
but cut the rope above me to be freed from me forever, for the vessel
had drifted across the brink of a chasm into whose yawning depths
my body would drop to be crushed to a shapeless pulp should Thurid
reach the rope now.

At last my hand closed upon the ship's rail and that very instant a
horrid shriek rang out below me that sent my blood cold and turned
my horrified eyes downward to a shrieking, hurtling, twisting thing
that shot downward into the awful chasm beneath me.

It was Matai Shang, Holy Hekkador, Father of Therns, gone to
his last accounting.

Then my head came above the deck and I saw Thurid, dagger in
hand, leaping toward me. He was opposite the forward end of the

cabin, while I was attempting to clamber aboard near the vessel's stern. But a few paces lay between us. No power on earth could raise me to that deck before the infuriated black would be upon me.

My end had come. I knew it; but had there been a doubt in my mind the nasty leer of triumph upon that wicked face would have convinced me. Beyond Thurid I could see my Dejah Thoris, wide-eyed and horrified, struggling at her bonds. That she should be forced to witness my awful death made my bitter fate seem doubly cruel.

I ceased my efforts to climb across the gunwale. Instead I took a firm grasp upon the rail with my left hand and drew my dagger.

I should at least die as I had lived—fighting.

As Thurid came opposite the cabin's doorway a new element projected itself into the grim tragedy of the air that was being enacted upon the deck of Matai Shang's disabled flier.

It was Phaidor.

With flushed face and disheveled hair, and eyes that betrayed the recent presence of mortal tears—above which this proud goddess had always held herself—she leaped to the deck directly before me.

In her hand was a long, slim dagger. I cast a last look upon my beloved princess, smiling, as men should who are about to die. Then I turned my face up toward Phaidor—waiting for the blow.

Never have I seen that beautiful face more beautiful than it was at that moment. It seemed incredible that one so lovely could yet harbor within her fair bosom a heart so cruel and relentless, and today there was a new expression in her wondrous eyes that I never before had seen there—an unfamiliar softness, and a look of suffering.

Thurid was beside her now—pushing past to reach me first, and then what happened happened so quickly that it was all over before I could realize the truth of it.

Phaidor's slim hand shot out to close upon the black's dagger wrist. Her right hand went high with its gleaming blade.

"That for Matai Shang!" she cried, and she buried her blade deep in the dator's breast. "That for the wrong you would have done Dejah Thoris!" and again the sharp steel sank into the bloody flesh.

"And that, and that, and that!" she shrieked, "for John Carter, Prince of Helium," and with each word her sharp point pierced the vile heart of the great villain. Then, with a vindictive shove she cast the carcass of the First Born from the deck to fall in awful silence after the body of his victim.

I had been so paralyzed by surprise that I had made no move to reach the deck during the awe-inspiring scene which I had just witnessed, and now I was to be still further amazed by her next act, for Phaidor extended her hand to me and assisted me to the deck, where I stood gazing at her in unconcealed and stupefied wonderment.

A wan smile touched her lips—it was not the cruel and haughty smile of the goddess with which I was familiar. "You wonder, John Carter," she said, "what strange thing has wrought this change in me? I will tell you. It is love—love of you," and when I darkened my brows in disapproval of her words she raised an appealing hand.

"Wait," she said. "It is a different love from mine—it is the love of your princess, Dejah Thoris, for you that has taught me what true love may be—what it should be, and how far from real love was my selfish and jealous passion for you.

"Now am I different. Now could I love as Dejah Thoris loves, and so my only happiness can be to know that you and she are once more united, for in her alone can you find true happiness.

"But I am unhappy because of the wickedness that I have wrought. I have many sins to expiate, and though I be deathless, life is all too short for the atonement.

"But there is another way, and if Phaidor, daughter of the Holy Hekkador of the Holy Therns, has sinned she has this day already made partial reparation, and lest you doubt the sincerity of her protestations and her avowal of a new love that embraces Dejah Thoris also, she will prove her sincerity in the only way that lies open—having saved you for another, Phaidor leaves you to her embraces."

With her last word she turned and leaped from the vessel's deck into the abyss below.

With a cry of horror I sprang forward in a vain attempt to save the life that for two years I would so gladly have seen extinguished. I was too late.

With tear-dimmed eyes I turned away that I might not see the awful sight beneath.

A moment later I had struck the bonds from Dejah Thoris, and as her dear arms went about my neck and her perfect lips pressed to mine I forgot the horrors that I had witnessed and the suffering that I had endured in the rapture of my reward.

THE NEW RULER

THE FLIER upon whose deck Dejah Thoris and I found ourselves after twelve long years of separation proved entirely useless. Her buoyancy tanks leaked badly. Her engine would not start. We were helpless there in mid air above the arctic ice.

The craft had drifted across the chasm which held the corpses of Matai Shang, Thurid, and Phaidor, and now hung above a low hill. Opening the buoyancy escape valves I permitted her to come slowly to the ground, and as she touched, Dejah Thoris and I stepped from her deck and, hand in hand, turned back across the frozen waste toward the city of Kadabra.

Through the tunnel that had led me in pursuit of them we passed, walking slowly, for we had much to say to each other.

She told me of that last terrible moment months before when the door of her prison cell within the Temple of the Sun was slowly closing between us. Of how Phaidor had sprung upon her with up-lifted dagger, and of Thuvia's shriek as she had realized the foul intention of the thern goddess.

It had been that cry that had rung in my ears all the long, weary months that I had been left in cruel doubt as to my princess' fate; for I had not known that Thuvia had wrested the blade from the daughter of Matai Shang before it had touched either Dejah Thoris or herself.

She told me, too, of the awful eternity of her imprisonment. Of the cruel hatred of Phaidor, and the tender love of Thuvia, and of how even when despair was the darkest those two red girls had clung to the same hope and belief—that John Carter would find a way to release them.

Presently we came to the chamber of Solan. I had been proceeding without thought of caution, for I was sure that the city and the palace were both in the hands of my friends by this time.

And so it was that I bolted into the chamber full into the midst of a dozen nobles of the court of Salensus Oll. They were passing through on their way to the outside world along the corridors we had just traversed.

At sight of us they halted in their tracks, and then an ugly smile overspread the features of their leader.

"The author of all our misfortunes!" he cried, pointing at me. "We shall have the satisfaction of a partial vengeance at least when we leave behind us here the dead and mutilated corpses of the Prince and Princess of Helium.

"When they find them," he went on, jerking his thumb upward toward the palace above, "they will realize that the vengeance of the yellow man costs his enemies dear. Prepare to die, John Carter, but that your end may be the more bitter, know that I may change my intention as to meting a merciful death to your princess—possibly she shall be preserved as a plaything for my nobles."

I stood close to the instrument-covered wall—Dejah Thoris at my side. She looked up at me wonderingly as the warriors advanced upon us with drawn swords, for mine still hung within its scabbard at my side, and there was a smile upon my lips.

The yellow nobles, too, looked in surprise, and then as I made no move to draw they hesitated, fearing a ruse; but their leader urged them on. When they had come almost within sword's reach of me I raised my hand and laid it upon the polished surface of a great lever, and then, still smiling grimly, I looked my enemies full in the face.

As one they came to a sudden stop, casting affrighted glances at me and at one another.

"Stop!" shrieked their leader. "You dream not what you do!"

"Right you are," I replied. "John Carter does not dream. He knows —knows that should one of you take another step toward Dejah Thoris, Princess of Helium, I pull this lever wide, and she and I shall die together; but we shall not die alone."

The nobles shrank back, whispering together for a few moments. At last their leader turned to me.

"Go your way, John Carter," he said, "and we shall go ours."

"Prisoners do not go their own way," I answered, "and you are prisoners—prisoners of the Prince of Helium."

Before they could make answer a door upon the opposite side of the apartment opened and a score of yellow men poured into the apartment. For an instant the nobles looked relieved, and then as their eyes fell upon the leader of the new party their faces fell, for he was Talu, rebel Prince of Marentina, and they knew that they could look for neither aid nor mercy at his hands.

Talu took in the situation at a glance, smiling.

"Well done, John Carter," he cried. "You turn their own mighty power against them. Fortunate for Okar is it that you were here to prevent their escape, for these be the greatest villains north of the ice-barrier, and this one"—pointing to the leader of the party—"would have made himself Jeddak of Jeddaks in the place of the dead Salensus Oll. Then indeed would we have had a more villainous ruler than the hated tyrant who fell before your sword."

The Okarian nobles now submitted to arrest, since nothing but death faced them should they resist, and, escorted by the warriors of Talu, we made our way to the great audience chamber that had been Salensus Oll's. Here was a vast concourse of warriors.

Red men from Helium and Ptarth, yellow men of the north, rubbing elbows with the blacks of the First Born who had come under my friend Xodar to help in the search for me and my princess. There were savage, green warriors from the dead sea bottoms of the south, and a handful of white-skinned therns who had renounced their religion and sworn allegiance to Xodar.

There was Tardos Mors and Mors Kajak, and tall and mighty in his gorgeous warrior trappings, Carthoris, my son. These three fell upon Dejah Thoris as we entered the apartment, and though the lives and training of royal Martians tend not toward vulgar demonstration, I thought that they would suffocate her with their embraces.

And there were Tars Tarkas, Jeddak of Thark, and Kantos Kan, my old-time friends, and leaping and tearing at my harness in the exuberance of his great love was dear old Woola—frantic mad with happiness.

Long and loud was the cheering that burst forth at sight of us; deafening was the din of ringing metal as the veteran warriors of every Martian clime clashed their blades together on high in token of success and victory, but as I passed among the throng of saluting nobles and warriors, jeds and jeddaks, my heart still was heavy, for there were two faces missing that I would have given much to have seen there—Thuvan Dihn and Thuvia of Ptarth were not to be found in the great chamber.

I made inquiries concerning them among men of every nation, and at last from one of the yellow prisoners of war I learned that they had been apprehended by an officer of the palace as they sought to reach the Pit of Plenty while I lay imprisoned there.

I did not need to ask to know what had sent them thither—the courageous jeddak and his loyal daughter. My informer said that they lay now in one of the many buried dungeons of the palace where they had been placed pending a decision as to their fate by the tyrant of the north.

A moment later searching parties were scouring the ancient pile in search of them, and my cup of happiness was full when I saw them being escorted into the room by a cheering guard of honor.

Thuvia's first act was to rush to the side of Dejah Thoris, and I needed no better proof of the love these two bore for each other than the sincerity with which they embraced.

Looking down upon that crowded chamber stood the silent and empty throne of Okar.

Of all the strange scenes it must have witnessed since that long-dead age that had first seen a Jeddak of Jeddaks take his seat upon it, none might compare with that upon which it now looked down, and as I pondered the past and future of that long-buried race of black-bearded yellow men I thought that I saw a brighter and more useful existence for them among the great family of friendly nations that now stretched from the south pole almost to their very doors.

Twenty-two years before I had been cast, naked and a stranger, into this strange and savage world. The hand of every race and nation was raised in continual strife and warring against the men of every other land and color. Today, by the might of my sword and the loyalty of the friends my sword had made for me, black man and white, red man and green, rubbed shoulders in peace and good-fellowship. All the nations of Barsoom were not yet as one, but a great stride forward toward that goal had been taken, and now if I could but cement the fierce yellow race into this sodality of nations I should feel that I had rounded out a great lifework, and repaid to Mars at least a portion of the immense debt of gratitude I owed her for having given me my Dejah Thoris.

And as I thought, I saw but one way, and a single man who could insure the success of my hopes. As is ever the way with me, I acted then as I always act—without deliberation and without consultation.

Those who do not like my plans and my ways of promoting them have always their swords at their sides wherewith to back up their disapproval; but now there seemed to be no dissenting voice, as, grasping Talu by the arm, I sprang to the throne that had once been Salensus Oll's.

"Warriors of Barsoom," I cried, "Kadabra has fallen, and with her the hateful tyrant of the north; but the integrity of Okar must be preserved. The red men are ruled by red jeddaks, the green warriors of the ancient seas acknowledge none but a green ruler, the First Born of the south pole take their law from black Xodar; nor would it be to the interests of either yellow or red man were a red jeddak to sit upon the throne of Okar.

"There be but one warrior best fitted for the ancient and mighty title of Jeddak of Jeddaks of the North. Men of Okar, raise your swords to your new ruler—Talu, the rebel Prince of Marentina!"

And then a great cry of rejoicing rose among the free men of Marentina and the Kadabran prisoners, for all had thought that the red men would retain that which they had taken by force of arms, for such had been the way upon Barsoom, and that they should be ruled henceforth by an alien Jeddak.

The victorious warriors who had followed Carthoris joined in the mad demonstration, and amidst the wild confusion and the tumult and the cheering, Dejah Thoris and I passed out into the gorgeous garden of the jeddaks that graces the inner courtyard of the palace of Kadabra.

At our heels walked Woola, and upon a carved seat of wondrous beauty beneath a bower of purple blooms we saw two who had preceded us—Thuvia of Ptarth and Carthoris of Helium.

The handsome head of the handsome youth was bent low above the beautiful face of his companion. I looked at Dejah Thoris, smiling, and as I drew her close to me I whispered: "Why not?"

Indeed, why not? What matter ages in this world of perpetual youth?

We remained at Kadabra, the guests of Talu, until after his formal induction into office, and then, upon the great fleet which I had been so fortunate to preserve from destruction, we sailed south across the ice-barrier; but not before we had witnessed the total demolition of the grim Guardian of the North under orders of the new Jeddak of Jeddaks.

"Henceforth," he said, as the work was completed, "the fleets of the red men and the black are free to come and go across the ice-barrier as over their own lands.

"The Carrion Caves shall be cleansed, that the green men may find an easy way to the land of the yellow, and the hunting of the sacred apt shall be the sport of my nobles until no single specimen of that hideous creature roams the frozen north."

We bade our yellow friends farewell with real regret, as we set sail for Ptarth. There we remained, the guest of Thuvan Dihn, for a month; and I could see that Carthoris would have remained forever had he not been a Prince of Helium.

Above the mighty forests of Kaol we hovered until word from Kulan Tith brought us to his single landing-tower, where all day and half a night the vessels disembarked their crews. At the city of Kaol we visited, cementing the new ties that had been formed between Kaol and Helium, and then one long-to-be-remembered day we sighted the tall, thin towers of the twin cities of Helium.

The people had long been preparing for our coming. The sky was gorgeous with gaily trimmed fliers. Every roof within both cities was spread with costly silks and tapestries.

Gold and jewels were scattered over roof and street and plaza, so that the two cities seemed ablaze with the fires of the hearts of the magnificent stones and burnished metal that reflected the brilliant sunlight, changing it into countless glorious hues.

At last, after twelve years, the royal family of Helium was reunited in their own mighty city, surrounded by joy-mad millions before the palace gates. Women and children and mighty warriors wept in gratitude for the fate that had restored their beloved Tardos Mors and the divine princess whom the whole nation idolized. Nor did any of us who had been upon that expedition of indescribable danger and glory lack for plaudits.

That night a messenger came to me as I sat with Dejah Thoris and Carthoris upon the roof of my city palace, where we had long since caused a lovely garden to be made that we three might find seclusion and quiet happiness among ourselves, far from the pomp and ceremony of court, to summon us to the Temple of Reward— "where one is to be judged this night," the summons concluded.

I racked my brain to try and determine what important case there might be pending which could call the royal family from their palaces on the eve of their return to Helium after years of absence; but when the jeddak summons no man delays.

As our flier touched the landing stage at the temple's top we saw countless other craft arriving and departing. In the streets below a great multitude surged toward the great gates of the temple.

Slowly there came to me the recollection of the deferred doom that awaited me since that time I had been tried here in the Temple by Zat Arrras for the sin of returning from the Valley Dor and the Lost Sea of Korus.

Could it be possible that the strict sense of justice which dominates the men of Mars had caused them to overlook the great good that had come out of my heresy? Had they so soon forgotten the debt they owed me in releasing them from the bondage of their horrid belief? Could they ignore the fact that to me, and me alone, was due the rescue of Carthoris, of Dejah Thoris, of Mors Kajak, of Tardos Mors?

I could not believe it, and yet for what other purpose could I have been summoned to the Temple of Reward immediately upon the return of Tardos Mors to his throne?

My first surprise as I entered the temple and approached the Throne of Righteousness was to note the men who sat there as judges. There was Kulan Tith, Jeddak of Kaol, whom we had but just left within his own palace a few days since; there was Thuvan Dihn, Jeddak of Ptarth—how came he to Helium as soon as we?

There was Tars Tarkas, Jeddak of Thark, and Xodar, Jeddak of the First Born; there was Talu, Jeddak of Jeddaks of the North, whom I could have sworn was still in his icebound hothouse city beyond the northern barrier, and among them sat Tardos Mors and Mors Kajak, with enough lesser jeds and jeddaks to make up the thirty-one who must sit in judgment upon their fellow-man.

A right royal tribunal indeed, and such a one, I warrant, as never before sat together during all the history of ancient Mars.

As I entered, silence fell upon the great concourse of people that packed the auditorium. Then Tardos Mors arose.

"John Carter," he said in his deep, martial voice, "take your place upon the Pedestal of Truth, for you are to be tried by a fair and impartial tribunal of your fellow-men."

With level eye and high-held head I did as he bade, and as I glanced about that circle of faces that a moment before I could have sworn contained the best friends I had upon Barsoom, I saw no single friendly glance—only stern, uncompromising judges, there to do their duty.

A clerk rose and from a great book read a long list of the more notable deeds that I had thought to my credit, covering a long period of twenty-two years since first I had stepped the ocher sea bottom beside the incubator of the Tharks. With the others he read of all that I had done within the circle of the Otz Mountains where the Holy Therns and the First Born had held sway.

It is the way upon Barsoom to recite a man's virtues with his sins when he is come to trial, and so I was not surprised that all that was to my credit should be read there to my judges—who knew it all by heart—even down to the present moment. When the reading had ceased Tardos Mors arose.

"Most righteous judges," he exclaimed, "you have heard recited all that is known of John Carter, Prince of Helium—the good with the bad. What is your judgment?"

Then Tars Tarkas came slowly to his feet, unfolding all his mighty, towering height until he loomed, a green-bronze statue, far above us all. He turned a baleful eye upon me—he, Tars Tarkas, with whom I had fought through countless battles; whom I loved as a brother.

I could have wept had I not been so mad with rage that I almost whipped my sword out and had at them all upon the spot.

"Judges," he said, "there can be but one verdict. No longer may John Carter be Prince of Helium"—he paused—"but instead let him be Jeddak of Jeddaks, Warlord of Barsoom!"

As the thirty-one judges sprang to their feet with drawn and upraised swords in unanimous concurrence in the verdict, the storm broke throughout the length and breadth and height of that mighty building until I thought the roof would fall from the thunder of the mad shouting.

Now, at last, I saw the grim humor of the method they had adopted to do me this great honor, but that there was any hoax in the reality of the title they had conferred upon me was readily disproved by the sincerity of the congratulations that were heaped upon me by the judges first and then the nobles.

Presently fifty of the mightiest nobles of the greatest courts of Mars marched down the broad Aisle of Hope bearing a splendid car upon their shoulders, and as the people saw who sat within, the cheers that had rung out for me paled into insignificance beside those which thundered through the vast edifice now, for she whom the nobles carried was Dejah Thoris, beloved Princess of Helium.

Straight to the Throne of Righteousness they bore her, and there Tardos Mors assisted her from the car, leading her forward to my side.

"Let a world's most beautiful woman share the honor of her husband," he said.

Before them all I drew my wife close to me and kissed her upon the lips.